THE BRIDES OF NORTH BARROWS

CLAIRE DELACROIX

DEBORAH A. COOKE

THE BRIDES OF NORTH BARROWS

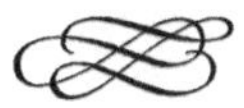

SOMETHING WICKED THIS WAY COMES

THE BRIDES OF NORTH BARROWS #1

Seven years ago, Sophia Brisbane lost everything—her father, her brother, her family fortune—but worse, was rejected by the man she loved. She's determined not to yearn for the past and its pleasures—until she encounters Lucien de Roye again. Although he knew Sophia could never be his own, Lucien vowed to retrieve her squandered inheritance—even wagering his very soul to a demon. When Sophia learns what he has done, no force on heaven or earth will convince her to let him pay the demon's due, no matter what the cost to herself.

A solitary park in London—October 1811

I t was the kind of wager Lucien had come to like best.

A dangerous one.

With very long odds against him.

Which was precisely why he had proposed it.

On this misty morning, he stood not a dozen paces away from Eugene Tremblay, Marquess of Lyndenhurst, the man he despised most in all the world. It was just dawn, and the first touch of the red sun could be seen on the horizon. Lyndenhurst lifted his dueling pistol, one of a fine pair brought by Lucien, and took his aim. Lucien let his weapon hang at his side and waited. Lyndenhurst squinted down the barrel. Lucien took a breath, and his opponent fired.

A flock of ducks quacked with indignation at the sound and noisily took flight from the river.

The blow struck Lucien so hard that he thought his luck had turned, at the worst possible moment.

He was thrown back onto the turf from the force of impact, and the breath was hammered out of him. His chest burned long enough for him to fear terror, then he felt the ball shift and slide through his body.

It emerged from his back like a bubble piercing the surface of a pond, and as a warm glow replaced the pain.

His luck *hadn't* turned. Lucien fought his smile of satisfaction.

He'd won.

Lyndenhurst swore and his footsteps could be heard trudging closer.

Lucien couldn't resist the temptation. He waited, lying utterly still, until he felt Lyndenhurst leaning over him. The older man was breathing heavily, though whether it was fear that he had killed a man or the exertion of haste was unclear. Lucien enjoyed the notion that his enemy might be having second thoughts—or fears of retribution. Lucien felt a shadow as Lyndenhurst reached over him to touch the front of his dark tailcoat. He smelled the brandy on Lyndenhurst's breath. He held his breath and waited.

"Fool!" the older man declared with disgust. "His life sacrificed in exchange for a piece of property so worthless that no one in London will purchase." Lucien felt the cloth of his tailcoat reweaving itself to close the hole, a soft whisper of threads pulling against each other. Lyndenhurst's tone turned scornful. "I pray I do not die as foolish as you did, Lucien de Roye. The dogs will find you here."

Lucien chose that moment to open his eyes. "I think that unlikely," he said. "Although I am glad to learn that you would not have summoned any to my aid."

Lyndenhurst turned as white as a ghost and stepped back in astonishment. Lucien had never seen his opponent reveal his emotions so clearly, and he was sufficiently wicked to savor the view.

"Upon my word!" Lyndenhurst declared. He was quick to recover from his surprise, though, and his eyes narrowed in speculation. He looked left and right, but there were no witnesses of their endeavor, by Lucien's design.

Then Lyndenhurst bent closer, peering through his quizzing glass, seeking a flaw or a trick. "The hole is gone," he whispered. His eyes glinted as he watched the blood disappear from Lucien's tailcoat, vanishing as if it had never been. That familiar cool smile, the one that made Lucien think of hungry wolves, curved Lyndenhurst's lips, his usual assurance restored. "By all rights, you should be dead."

"Yet I am not, exactly as I foretold." Lucien sat up and brushed off his sleeves before rising to his feet.

"How did you do it?" The interest in Lyndenhurst's tone could not be mistaken. "How did you cheat death?" He walked around Lucien, shaking his head. "It must be a trick, an illusion…"

Lucien bent leisurely and plucked the ball from the ground where he had fallen. It had passed directly through him and now rested in the turf. He held it between gloved finger and thumb to display it to Lyndenhurst. "Yours, I believe?"

Lyndenhurst blinked, surprised again for the barest of moments. "And yours," he said, offering the pistol. He then seized the ball and pinched it tightly. "Is this genuine? Or is it a substitution?"

"You loaded the pistol with your own shot."

"But still, it defies belief." Lyndenhurst lifted his glass to examine the ball, shaking his head as he marveled. "I must have this ability. What price?"

"My winnings first, if you please."

Lyndenhurst reached into his pocket and removed a document, then impatiently thrust it at Lucien. Lucien unfolded the deed and read it with care, ensuring that all of the properties were included that they had wagered upon.

"Well?" Lyndenhurst demanded. "What price?"

Lucien smiled. "Another game, of course, with stakes we agree upon."

"What stakes?"

"You have only one thing I desire enough to wager such a secret."

"St. Maurice!" Lyndenhurst exhaled and surveyed the river. It was clear that he was calculating. He nodded quickly when his decision was made. "Done. When and where?"

Lucien disguised his delight. The bait was taken. Seven years of vengeance would come to its culmination very soon, and Sophia—and Charles, and Mr. Brisbane—would be avenged.

"It will have to be in Bocka Morrow in Cornwall, on the night of the 31st."

"So far away?"

"I have business in the region."

Lyndenhurst's eyes darkened with suspicion. "How many players?"

"You and I. No others."

Lyndenhurst's expression turned shrewd. "I shall be there."

"At the Mermaid's Kiss. I will secure a private room."

Lyndenhurst folded his arms across his chest. "*Vingt-et-un*, winner take all?"

"A long journey for a short game," Lucien replied easily. "Why not best of three games?"

"Why not?" Lyndenhurst shrugged, but his anticipation was palpable. "Why not sooner? Why not here in town?"

"I find appeal in the notion of playing for immortality on the night of Samhain in a village believed to be haunted." That wasn't half of the truth. Lucien met the man's cold gaze. "Let alone one where there can be no witnesses of what passes between us."

Lyndenhurst nodded agreement. "It does seem fitting. Ten?"

"Ten for dinner, and then the game," Lucien agreed and offered his hand. "We shall be done by midnight."

He would win easily.

Lyndenhurst shook Lucien's hand and gripped it hard. His gaze lingered on the spot on Lucien's tailcoat where the bullet hole had been. "How can it be so?" he mused, but Lucien didn't want him to follow the course of his thoughts.

"Does it matter, if you can cheat death forever?"

Lyndenhurst's lips set in a hard line. "No. It doesn't matter." There was satisfaction in his stride as he marched back to his horse, and Lucien surveyed the park once more to confirm that it was still empty. Victory was finally within reach.

He'd gambled and won, and this time, it would be worth it.

Taking vengeance from Lyndenhurst would be his last living deed.

The only disappointment was that Sophia would never know that he'd kept his word to her. Lucien would die on November 1, his soul forfeit in exchange for seven years of service from the demon who had ensured he could never lose.

He wouldn't even see his beloved in the afterlife, for he was surely bound for Hell and Sophia had to be in Heaven.

Lucien knew theirs had always been a star-crossed match, but he didn't have to take pleasure in yet one more reminder of that.

Justice done and a promise kept would have to suffice.

MEANWHILE, at North Barrows Dower House, Cumbria

A DISTINCT RAP upon the polished floor of the foyer alerted the disguised Sophia Brisbane to the fact that her employer would likely soon join the lesson in the drawing room.

Seven years before, at the insistence of her beloved governess, Sophia had taken Amelia Findlay's place. Amelia had been ill with pneumonia, and when she died, she was buried under the name Sophia Brisbane. Sophia had exchanged her clothes for those of Amelia, and had begun to powder her hair to make it appear more silver, like that of an older woman. She had donned the spectacles of her former governess—although she had mystified the maker by having the lenses exchanged for plain glass—then taken a post as far away from London and any chance of recognition as possible.

Seven years later, she still feared discovery.

Eugene Tremblay, Marquess of Lyndenhurst had taken everything from her, everything except her life, and Sophia didn't trust him to have abandoned the hunt for that.

Who interrupted their lessons and why? She couldn't dismiss her sense of doom. Her heart in her throat, Sophia stood up.

The girls were too engrossed in their lessons for once to notice the tap on the door. They were competing again, Eurydice writing fluidly, while Daphne frowned at her younger sister's rapid progress. The envy would be reversed when it was time for a dance lesson.

Daphne was the taller of the two, as well as the older. She was exquisitely lovely and even at sixteen, possessed of the kind of rare beauty that made people turn to stare. Her hair was as golden as sunlight and her skin was as fair as ivory. She was as slender and supple as a willow, and the joy of every dressmaker who had ever fitted her.

Eurydice was smaller and more stocky, although that might yet change as she was just fourteen. Her hair was closer to the hue of wild-flower honey and nowhere near as fastidiously arranged for she was impatient with such fussing. There was a solemnity about her that her sister did not share, and no one was ever surprised to learn that she was an avid reader who wished to become a writer herself. Sophia hoped the girl married a man who was tolerant of her aspirations, for Eurydice had talent. She had a mole upon her cheek, which Amelia thought quite attractive but which Eurydice called the bane of her existence.

"I *hate* German!" Daphne declared, pushing her page of exercises to the floor just as her grandmother entered the room.

Octavia Goodenham, Viscountess of North Barrows, halted in her steps and arched a silver brow. "And how do you imagine that you will secure a husband of merit if you have no education?" that lady demanded crisply. "Only peasants prefer stupid women, no matter how pretty they are."

The girls leaped to their feet and curtsied. "Good afternoon, *Grand-maman*," said Eurydice and Daphne in unison.

"Your ladyship, how delightful," Sophia said, offering a much deeper curtsy.

Lady North Barrows ignored these greetings. She was an older lady of considerable poise and some eccentricity. The stark black she favored made her look more slender than she was, although she was as lean as a whip. She carried a black umbrella by habit, one with an ebony handle shaped like a bird's head, and used it both as a cane and a weapon. Her lady's maid, Nelson, had shared her mistress's conviction that only elderly women required canes, while an umbrella, they both agreed, was always a prudent accessory in the north of England. The viscountess' features were angular, her gaze sufficiently sharp to draw blood. She fixed a look upon her oldest granddaughter that might have struck terror into one less accustomed to her manner.

Or one unfamiliar with the softness of her heart, particularly with regard to these two orphaned girls. Sophia had come to recognize that

Lady North Barrows would fight lions for her granddaughters. Fortunately, the need for such heroics was unlikely at the dower house in North Barrows.

Daphne lifted her chin proudly. "I will captivate a duke with my beauty, *Grandmaman*," she said, with no small measure of confidence. "You need not fear for my future. It is Eurydice who will be a spinster."

Sophia noticed the poisonous glance the younger sister spared the elder.

Lady North Barrows looked Daphne up and down. "It is true that you are more than pretty, Daphne, but that is a fleeting virtue. You have an increment of charm, but are utterly lacking in decorum. *This* is a serious liability."

"I shall have to steal the duke's heart then, and persuade him to propose quickly."

Lady North Barrows looked skeptical. "And when you have had four children, your blossom has faded and he has no interest in your charms? What then?"

"Then I will be rich, for I will have married a duke and provided him with at least one heir. I will have hats and gowns and gloves and parasols, at least one fine carriage and a pair of footmen to carry my parcels. I will have parties at his country manor, or at his London townhouse, and I will drink champagne whenever I desire." She shrugged. "He might be bald and fat by then, and of no interest to me. Let him have a mistress and leave me to amuse myself."

Lady North Barrows removed her spectacles and gave them a determined polish before donning them once again. Apparently, the view of her defiant granddaughter was not much improved, for her grim expression didn't change. "The question of decorum remains." She rapped her umbrella tip on the floor and turned her attention to Sophia. "Miss Findlay, I come to inform you that we will depart on the morrow, immediately after breakfast."

Sophia bowed her head, assuming this departure did not include her.

But she was mistaken.

"You will ensure that sufficient material is taken with us for the girls' lessons to continue in Cornwall, where we shall linger for about a week."

"Cornwall?" Daphne declared with some horror.

"Cornwall?" Eurydice echoed with delight of equal magnitude.

I will have you and your inheritance, at any price.

Sophia's head snapped up, Lyndenhurst's long-ago threat echoing in her thoughts. "It will be an arduous journey for a week's stay, my lady."

"And so it must be." Lady North Barrows braced her hands upon her umbrella and surveyed her granddaughters. "We must consider that Daphne will need a season soon."

"A season!" Daphne squealed in delight and seized her sister's hands. Eurydice permitted herself to be spun around but she was trying desperately to attend her grandmother's words.

"And it is most clear that she has learned nothing at all of how to conduct herself in society. I propose this journey that she might have some practice before we descend upon London and she makes a mockery of all of us."

"London!" Daphne flung herself at her grandmother. "Balls and parties every night. Dressmakers and milliners and darling little kid gloves."

"Museums," Eurydice said with awe. "Galleries and concerts."

"Decorum," Lady North Barrows concluded. "And with any luck, the son of a man with a respectable title."

"A duke!"

"We shall see. Miss Findlay, I shall need every possible measure of your assistance."

"It is yours, my lady." A quiver began deep within Sophia, for she had no desire to abandon her safe haven, even for Cornwall. She had sought out this employment deliberately and couldn't conceive of a better place to keep her disguise intact.

But she could not defy her employer and risk losing her place.

She tried not to think about the fact that she had deceived that employer, who had only been good to her thus far.

I will have you and your inheritance, at any price.

She clasped her hands together and tried to appear more calm than she felt. Surely having no inheritance meant that she was safe from his avarice?

But Sophia did not wish to risk discovering otherwise.

Daphne showed no such restraint. She hugged herself with delight at the prospect of both a journey and a London season, then spun in place. Sophia bit back a smile at her charge's pleasure, for it made her recall her own anticipation of her first arrival in London. Daphne's was unlikely to end as poorly.

Lady North Barrows sighed with apparent exasperation. Her indulgence was evident in the twinkle in her eyes, though, which even she could not quell. Sophia met her gaze and smiled, for it was true that Daphne's delight with life and its pleasures had a way of winning favor from even those most reluctant to admire her.

"And so, to details." Lady North Barrows seated herself upon a settee with a swish of dark taffeta. Her hands remained braced upon the umbrella handle, and Sophia knew she would issue detailed instructions. "I have had a letter this morning, Miss Findlay, from the solicitor Mr. Timothy Hunt to inform me of the passing of my brother, Jonathan Hambly, the Earl of Banfield."

"My condolences, my lady." This death must have somehow influenced Lady North Barrows' decision to see Daphne come out.

"I thank you, Miss Findlay." Lady North Barrows cleared her throat. "Mr. Hunt also noted that the reading of Jonathan's last will and testament will occur on November 1. It will be done at Jonathan's estate, Castle Keyvnor, in Cornwall, where I lived as a girl, and undoubtedly the lion's share of his wealth will pass to our second cousin, Allan."

"Cornwall," Eurydice said again with no less wonder than before. She perched on a stool before her grandmother. "There must be pirates and ghosts."

"Of course, there are," her grandmother agreed with a dismissive gesture. "The castle has been haunted for at least two hundred years." She rapped her umbrella on the floor when Eurydice might have asked for more detail. "The point is that much of the extended family will gather for this ceremony. While it is true that any token Jonathan might have bequeathed to me—and truly, I expect little—can be managed by solicitors." She paused and raised a hand to her throat.

"Although my mother possessed a very fine cameo..." She shook her head and continued in her usual crisp tones. "It has occurred to me that this event offers an opportunity for the practice of decorum, and the cultivation of manners within society." She nodded once with satisfaction at her own plan. "And that within the confines of family, any serious faux pas might be overlooked."

Eurydice laughed and Daphne looked daggers at her.

Lady North Barrows nodded. "We shall visit Cornwall first, then perhaps—if a *certain* miss shows improvement—London next year for the season."

Surely no one would recognize Sophia in Cornwall. She had never been there. And even the inns between North Barrows and Castle Keyvnor were unlikely to play host to anyone she had met seven years before.

And perhaps by the time Lady North Barrows went to London, Sophia could find another post in an equally remote location. The girls would have less need for her by then.

"Oh, *Grandmaman*, I shall be a marvel, just for you," Daphne declared, flinging herself down beside her grandmother and kissing the jet ring on that lady's hand.

"You need not be a marvel, child, simply more like a lady."

"I will!"

"Until you forget," Eurydice noted, with some truth.

Lady North Barrows stood. "We shall depart in the morning. We shall take the large carriage, for there will be ourselves, plus Nelson and Sara, and we shall hope for good roads that we arrive in time." She inclined her head. "We will have many long days in the carriage. I trust you will be prepared, Miss Findlay."

"You may be certain of that, my lady."

The older woman surveyed the girls with a slight smile. "I expect there will be little German mastered in what remains of this afternoon. I have sent Sara to pack for the girls. Perhaps they might assist her with their choices." Lady North Barrows strode to the door. "They will join the party for one dinner, two if their manners are sufficiently improved." Daphne squealed at this. "They will take lunch with the ladies, undoubtedly will walk into the village of Bocka Morrow at least once, and may be invited to ride. Please remind Sara that they will need sturdy cloaks and boots. The weather can be most foul in that corner of the world."

"And what shall we pack to fend against the ghosts?" Eurydice demanded.

Her grandmother paused on the threshold and turned back. "Your wits, of course. You have need of nothing more when it comes to ghosts." With a final rap of her umbrella upon the floor, Lady North Barrows departed.

Leaving Sophia with much to plan and more than a little trepidation.

It was almost midnight when Philip removed Lucien's tailcoat and Lucien checked the fabric over his heart. There was no sign of the hole that had briefly graced the tailcoat, and none of the one that must have been in the tailcoat's back. His shirt was perfect, unmarred by blood or gunshot, if a little wrinkled from the day. Even after all this time, he still had to check. The bullet should have pierced his heart and killed him.

But it hadn't, because of the baron.

"So, he did shoot you," Philip said, his manner grim. "And you let him. You rely too much on that demon."

"The baron will be gone soon enough," Lucien said and his friend shuddered that he named the demon aloud. "Seven years is almost over, Philip."

The other man gave him a look that spoke volumes. "You're a fool to trust him. He's a trickster and a cheat. He won't go easily."

"He'll take what he was promised."

"He'll take more. It's his way."

"We have an agreement."

"He's never satisfied with the terms, not at the end."

"He will be this time." Philip's eyes narrowed but Lucien didn't elaborate. He'd dragged his old friend through enough trouble these past seven years. It was time for all of it to end—but he knew that if he confided in Philip, Philip would try to save him. It couldn't be done. The baron's tithe had to be paid.

In a strange way, Lucien was ready to pay it.

"And then what?" Philip demanded.

"And then you will take the money I give you and go home, find a beautiful woman to marry and live out your life in prosperity and joy."

Philip sniffed. "I won't leave you," he insisted and hung up Lucien's clothes. "I suppose you will spend the night in the drawing room."

"I've never shirked from paying the baron's due, and I won't start now." Lucien smiled. "That's why we get along so well."

"I would never have imagined he could corrupt you so completely." Philip eyed Lucien. "What did you promise him? It must have been a lot for a seven year run of luck."

Lucien only smiled. He changed to his dressing robe, retrieved the token from the pocket of his tailcoat—to Philip's visible disgust—and left the bed chamber. He carried a candle in one hand as he descended to the drawing room, the charm in the other.

He could feel his companion waiting for him.

Expectant.

Hungry. The baron was becoming stronger as they neared the end of their seven-year agreement. More watchful, as if he suspected a trick.

But Lucien wouldn't flinch from what had to be done.

He had nothing to live for once Sophia's inheritance was regained, after all.

The room was chilly, colder than it should have been, and the candle flame danced wildly in a wind Lucien couldn't detect.

To think Lucien hadn't truly believed that a wager with this demon would make him invincible. Yet he had tested the baron repeatedly, and the baron had saved him every time. Lucien had ridden into seven battles, he had set foot on no less than five ships said to be doomed, he had bedded the wives of nineteen peers of the realm rumored to be jealous beyond all expectation, and then the mistresses of seven of them just for good measure, and he had fought—and won—thirty-two duels. Thirty-three. He had been shot through the heart repeatedly and stood up to duel again moments later, not suffering so much as a scratch.

Every time.

His run of luck was unquestionable.

It was unholy, and it was unshakable. The baron couldn't be beaten, and Lucien couldn't die because he was in the baron's care. He couldn't lose at cards or any other game of chance. He couldn't stop gambling, and he couldn't keep from winning.

There had been a time when he would have called such a situation paradise.

Now Lucien knew better. He had lived enough in seven years to exhaust him.

But he was almost done. There was just St. Maurice, the gem in the crown, the last property to fulfill the oath he'd sworn. By November 1, it would be done.

On November 1, the baron would demand payment.

And Lucien would be at peace.

In the drawing room, he strode to the mirror over the hearth to examine his own reflection. He put the candle down on the mantel, where the flame continued to flicker. He heard a chuckle and wasn't surprised to see the familiar specter take the place of his reflection. The baron was an old black man, with white at his temples and merriment in his bloodshot eyes. He was both ancient and ageless, a familiar and not always welcome companion. He was impeccably dressed, as always, his cravat perfectly tied and a blood red rose in his buttonhole. He posed as if he were Lucien's reflection, straightened his cravat and bowed a little.

He winked and Lucien looked away.

"Seven years," the baron said, speaking as always in the French patois of Saint Domingue. "The debt comes due soon, *mon petit*."

"I know. I will pay it."

"I know, *mon petit*."

Lucien lit the larger candle on the mantelpiece and placed the shade around it so the flame couldn't blow out. He filled a glass almost to the rim with dark rum and placed it beside the candle. The small vivid painting of Saint Martin de Porres kept on the mantelpiece was moved closer to the candle. Lucien added the strange little tied bundle that he'd carried for almost seven years between picture and candle.

He bowed and retreated, feeling the baron's satisfaction with the offering.

By the morning, the candle would have burned itself out. The rum would be gone. The picture would be face down, and the cloth bundle would be warm, as if it had been held tightly all the night long.

Lucien locked the door to the drawing room, so none of the servants would discover the makeshift altar, and stretched out on the settee to sleep. Music emitted from his grandmother's pianoforte as soon as his eyes closed, and he knew the servants would assume—as always—that he was the restless musician. Philip could have told them otherwise, but he never would.

Not even when it was over.

Philip would have preferred that the baron didn't exist, or at least that he hadn't been invoked—much less welcomed. On November 1, Philip would get his wish.

The music rapidly grew in volume. It was feverish, wild, chaotic, both thrilling and disturbing. If Lucien squinted, he could almost make out the silhouette of the baron, his fingers dancing over the keys. The candle flame flickered, as if it would dance to the music. Some of the rum was already gone.

Lucien closed his eyes, knowing the baron would be amused all the night long, and that he would not sleep until dawn. He was enough of his father's son to recognize that when you make a deal with a devil, it's clever to keep the demon close at hand.

CHAPTER 1

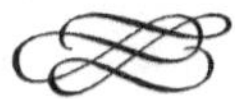

London—September 1804

After weeks at sea, Sophia Brisbane was more than ready to have her feet on dry ground again. She had become progressively more chilled the farther they sailed from St. Maurice, home and haven, and she began to fear she would never be truly warm again. The ship had to be towed into the port, given the density of the fog. She stood at the rail in her thick cloak and shivered within it, watching. The prison hulks loomed out of the mist on one side, the raucous sounds of the prisoners secured there reminding her of crows.

"Will Mr. Brisbane greet us?" Miss Findlay asked, her manner a little less resolute than usual. Sophia's governess and companion had felt the cold particularly.

"I would expect as much."

"Or perhaps that Mr. Lucien he always writes about. He does seem to be entrusting that young friend of Master Charles with a good deal of responsibility."

Sophia nodded. "I think Father likes him, but I wouldn't know him to see. I hope Charles comes."

Miss Findlay nodded but didn't respond.

It took an eternity to be hauled into port, but the fog was thinner there. Sophia was relieved to see her father, hands braced on his hips as he surveyed

17

the mooring of his ship with satisfaction. Charles was behind their father, more richly dressed than she could have expected. He had become quite dashing since she had last seen him. As she watched, her older brother fastidiously took a pinch of snuff.

Sophia laughed that he should pretend to be a dandy for her entertainment. Perhaps Charles did not notice her reaction, for he didn't smile.

There was another young man with her father, one with ebony hair and an intent gaze. He was tall and broad, of an age with Charles but not as stocky. He was dressed more simply, in black and white, his garb so plain as to be austere. He scanned the ship, then her father pointed to her, and his gaze locked upon her. Even at a distance, Sophia felt a strange heat at his steady perusal. She dropped her gaze and felt herself flush.

He had to be Lucien de Roye, and Sophia felt new interest in her brother's friend.

The gangplank was lowered and the captain escorted Sophia to her father himself. Many compliments were exchanged, then her trunks were retrieved as her father made introductions. "You've read about Lucien in my letters, of course," he said, gesturing to the younger man.

"At your service, Miss Brisbane," Lucien said and bowed for Sophia. He was more handsome than she had realized, and his attention flustered her. Sophia was accustomed to the company of women and older male servants, her father's bluster, but not the charm of a handsome man almost of an age with herself. She felt very much out of her element when she offered her gloved hand.

"I thank you," she said and he smiled, the gleam in his eyes making her heart leap.

"You'll not make a conquest here," Charles complained, catching Sophia in a tight hug and giving her a buss on each cheek. "Sophia is doomed to make a brilliant marriage."

Sophia saw a shadow appear in Lucien's eyes before he turned away.

"I say, Father, must we linger about this hideous place?"

"Hideous? This is where money is made, Charles." Their father's voice boomed in his enthusiasm. "As I've told you a hundred times, a man must greet his shipment at the docks, even when it arrives on his own ships, tally it and count it and ensure he isn't cheated."

"But I want to show Sophia my new gelding. And she needs to be driven

around the park, so everyone can see her." Charles granted her an engaging smile.

"Can I not possibly go to the house first?"

"Pshaw!" Charles dismissed the notion. "She can't possibly want to remain here."

"I'll help with the tallying, Mr. Brisbane," Lucien offered.

"Of course, you will, boy. I can always rely upon you." Sophia's father slanted a glance at Charles. "You will have to learn one day, Charles, particularly if you continue to show such a taste for spending."

"But it will not be today, Father!" Charles offered Sophia his elbow. "Come along, Sophia, and Miss Findlay, as well. I will take you to the new house."

"A new house?"

Her father's chest puffed with pride. "I am to be knighted, Sophia. We could scarce remain in Kensington."

"Dear God, how much has he spent?" Sophia asked Charles in an undertone.

"Not nearly enough," her brother replied tartly. "There was a fine townhouse to be had in Mayfair, but he would not dispense the coin." Charles grimaced. "Instead, we are to make due with Chelsea." He shook his head. "Chelsea! Even Lucien has a house in Cavendish Square."

"He does?" Sophia found herself glancing back at her brother's friend from Eton and Oxford, only to find Lucien still watching her. "I thought he had no fortune."

"Well, he hasn't a fortune and he hasn't a title, not anymore, but he has his grandmother's house. I thought he should sell it to Father but he wouldn't. I don't know why he keeps it, for it is in need of much repair."

"Does he have other family?"

Charles shook his head, and Sophia found herself liking that Lucien kept his grandmother's house, though he didn't need it. "Perhaps it has fine memories for him," she said warmly.

"Memories, Sophia, are worthless. What you want are connections with the right people."

"I thought you were learning Father's trade."

Charles scoffed. "Father has social ambitions. I am pursuing them. Let Lucien inventory the stock. I have better things to do."

And so it proved he did, for no sooner had Charles deposited Sophia and

Miss Findlay at the new house—which proved to be sumptuously furnished—than he abandoned them.

Presumably for better social connections.

It was Lucien who called later to ensure that they were settled, Lucien who instructed the housekeeper to build up the fires as the new arrivals would feel the dampness particularly, and Lucien who offered to show the two women the charms of London.

It was Lucien who, one month later, gave Sophia her first kiss. An awakening kiss. A kiss that had been tentative, then had heated and become a force of its own.

A kiss that had been both an end and a beginning.

Castle Keyvnor—Tuesday, October 29, 1811

Sophia awakened, her lips burning in memory of the kiss that had set her soul afire.

She sat up abruptly, heart thumping, halfway convinced that it had been more than a dream. But she was in the small room under the eaves at Castle Keyvnor, and she was alone. Her dream of Lucien had been so vivid that it was difficult to dismiss.

It was even more difficult to dismiss the yearning she felt for his touch.

What she should remember was his rejection.

Seven years and Lucien still haunted her.

It was more than long enough. The past was over and done, and the present was all that mattered. Sophia swung her legs out of bed, determined to banish him from her memory. Lucien had been her brother's best friend, the first man who had looked at her with appreciation, the first man who had kissed her.

And he had rejected her. Who knew what had become of him? Sophia did not care.

Well, she cared very little.

It would be clever not to care at all.

Why would she dream of him now? That music must have been responsible for her unsettling dreams. What kind of guest was so rude as to play the harpsichord in the middle of the night? Even if he or she were unable to sleep, it was scarcely fitting to awaken the entire house.

Or maybe it was guilt that had given her a restless night. Sophia had been sick at heart for the entire journey south, convinced that some maid or chance traveler would call her by name and her ruse would be revealed.

She'd even planned a dozen responses, each an improvement on the last, all of which professed her ignorance of Sophia Brisbane.

The fact remained that she had lied to Lady North Barrows. She had deceived people who had been good to her, and the fact that she had done so out of fear seemed a paltry excuse.

I will have you and your inheritance, at any price.

Sophia shivered and got out of bed. It had been pouring rain when they arrived the day before, and even Lady North Barrows had appeared to be exhausted. She'd waved them all to their rooms and commanded that their dinners be served there, and Sophia had been grateful.

This day, though, she would be subject to greater scrutiny.

Her disguise would have to suffice. Sophia pulled her hair back tighter than ever. She powdered it a little more liberally to make it look more gray. She donned her spectacles and her plainest dress, hoping she could disappear into the woodwork of the castle.

No one really looked at governesses, did they?

No one here could possibly recognize her or realize who she really was.

No one.

Everyone she truly knew in England other than Lucien and Lyndenhurst was dead, after all. Neither of them could possibly be here in Cornwall.

Amelia would have told her that she was foolish to be agitated, and looking for trouble where there could be none.

～

MORNING ALWAYS CAME TOO EARLY when there were guests in the house. That was Mrs. Bray's thinking and each day since the earl's death only reaffirmed it. She would sleep for a week when this ruckus was through.

She had been through the house, ensuring that every maid was quick about her tasks and that every fire was lit when she found Morris in his pantry, frowning at the inventory. His stillness caught her eye and prompted her impatience. If the butler had nothing to do or oversee on a morning such as this, she could be of help in that!

"Are they more fond of the wine than you anticipated?" she asked.

He waved off the very suggestion. "There's more than sufficient in the cellar." He lifted a bottle. "It's the rum. No one favors it, but the earl believed we should have some, in case there was a guest desiring it."

"And so last night there was," Mrs. Bray said, nodding at the half-empty bottle.

He spared her a glance. "But none of the gentlemen indulged in it last night. The bottle was yet sealed when I retired." He swirled its contents. "It is a veritable antique, this one. I don't even recall when we acquired it."

"And someone drank of it in the night? Just helped himself?" Mrs. Bray's lips thinned. "That smacks of theft. One of the visiting valets, then? As if a good room and hearty fare aren't enough generosity!"

"Did you hear anyone about the house?"

"After the day I had? I slept like the dead last night, to be sure—or I would have if that M. de Roye hadn't arrived at all hours. Time was that a young gentleman like that would remember his manners and arrive in the afternoon, like decent people, instead of rousing the house after midnight." She took a deep breath of indignation. "And bringing that Negro valet besides. Black as the bottoms of Cook's pots, he is, and in this house! The earl would have been dismayed, to be sure."

"I suspect not," Morris said. "That valet's manners are impeccable, and that is all that would have mattered to the earl."

Mrs. Bray sniffed with sufficient indignation to communicate her thoughts on that matter.

"Perhaps it *was* M. de Roye," Morris mused.

"Perhaps it was his fine valet."

"*Someone* was playing the harpsichord last night, and it was after M. de Roye's late arrival."

"The harpsichord? Is it still in tune?" Mrs. Bray couldn't recall the last time anyone had shown an interest in the instrument. If a guest were inclined to play, she should call old Fitzwilliam up from the village to ensure the notes were true.

Even if it was played in the middle of the night.

"I didn't get back to sleep quickly after M. de Roye was settled in his room and I heard the music. I didn't recognize the melody, but it was played very fast. I found this empty glass there this morning." Morris sniffed it. "Rum. Fortunately, the glass didn't leave a ring on the veneer."

"I suppose it is better if it was M. de Roye helping himself than any of the visiting valets."

"And far better than one of the maids doing so," Morris agreed. He squinted at the bottle, as if to remember the level of the rum within it. "I shall keep an eye on it, just the same."

"AND THEN THE GOVERNESS DIES."

Sophia halted at the emphatic comment that carried clearly from the castle's library. Of course, it was Daphne.

Although ordering an execution did seem to be an excessive means of avoiding a German lesson.

It was five minutes to nine, and they were scheduled to continue their regular lessons at the stroke of the hour, per Lady North Barrows' instruction.

"No!" Eurydice replied, her outrage clear. "She's the princess of a distant realm, hidden for her own safety, who claims the heart of the duke. There's no happy ending if she *dies*." Her tone turned disparaging. "Have you failed to note anything about stories in your life?"

Ah. Eurydice was writing her story again, and had made the mistake of asking her sister for advice. Sophia fought against her smile.

"I know what I like." Daphne was pouting.

"How can you like it if the princess dies?" Eurydice was exasperated.

"I could if she spoke perfect German."

"Of course, she does. She couldn't be a princess otherwise."

Daphne snorted in a very unladylike fashion.

"And flawless French, and Spanish," Eurydice taunted. "I think she might excel at mathematics, too."

"That's the best kind of person to die in a book. No one likes heroines like that."

"I'm a heroine like that!"

"You're not in a book."

"I mean to see that repaired."

"Then no one will read the book, because everyone will think the heroine should die!"

Their voices rose in dispute as Sophia stepped briskly into the library to intervene.

They didn't even notice her arrival.

Sophia dropped the German grammar book on a desk. It was a volume of considerable heft and made a satisfying thump on impact.

It also loosed a cloud of fine dust.

Both girls fell silent and pivoted at the sound, their eyes wide.

"Good morning," Sophia said. "*Guten morgen.*"

Eurydice tucked her work away, her face alight with anticipation. Daphne pouted—she even did that prettily—and took her seat. There was boredom in every line of her figure and mutiny in her eyes.

"*Guten morgen,*" the girls repeated in unison but in vastly different tones.

"*Fräulein Findlay,*" Eurydice added.

"The past perfect of 'to read,' if you please, Daphne. *I had been reading Eurydice's book...*"

"We should learn French," that student declared. "It sounds nicer."

"We did learn French," Eurydice corrected. "Except that you didn't like it either."

Daphne stuck out her tongue at her sister.

Sophia cleared her throat.

"*Ich hatte gelesen; du hattest gelesen; er/sie/es hatte gelesen,*" Eurydice said. "*Wir hatten gelesen; ihr hattet gelesen; sie/Sie hatten gelesen.*"

"Very good. How about the future, Daphne? As in *I will read Eurydice's book when it's finished.*"

Daphne blinked.

"*Ich werde lesen,*" Eurydice hissed.

"*Du wirst lesen,*" Daphne added, then fell silent.

"*Er/sie/es wird lesen; wir werden lesen, ihr werdet lesen; sie/Sie werden lesen,*" Eurydice continued.

"Very good. Did you study last night?"

"I did some of the exercises." Eurydice took a superior tone. "Daphne was too busy deciding what to wear today and looking out the window."

"I suppose you have a fine view of the sea." Sophia gave Eurydice a look.

The younger girl narrowed her eyes for a moment, then smiled with triumph. "*Ich nehme an, Sie haben einen schönen Blick auf das Meer.*"

"Very good. But if you were speaking to Daphne..."

"I'd say *du hast* instead of *Sie haben* because she's just my sister."

Daphne ignored this jibe and sighed. "Our room has a view of the gates."

"*Unser Zimmer hat einen Blick auf die Tore,*" provided Eurydice. "But it wasn't the gates you were looking at last night."

A sparkle lit in Daphne's eyes. "No, I saw something *much* better."

"You might as well tell us," Sophia said, pretending to be less curious than she was.

"A carriage arrived at midnight."

Eurydice leaned forward. "It raced through the gates, at reckless speed. It was black, and pulled by a perfectly matched team of four blacks..."

"At midnight, you could see this?" Sophia had to ask.

"The moon is almost full," Eurydice said. "They halted at the portal, the horses stamping and breathing fire."

Sophia arched a brow. "I thought Daphne was telling us."

Eurydice grimaced. "I would tell it better."

"And the most handsome man in the world leaped out of the

carriage," Daphne added. "He was dressed all in black, except for his white cravat."

"Which was adorned with a gem of uncommon brilliance," Eurydice said. "It glittered in the moonlight and had to have been worth a king's ransom. It was probably stolen, or an heirloom, or won in a gaming hell in London."

Daphne sighed with rapture. "He must be a duke or the son of a duke. He's wealthy beyond compare, I'm sure, and gallant..."

"I would stop short of gallant," a rich male voice contributed from behind Sophia. Her heart stopped cold, so certain was she that she recognized that voice. She felt a shiver run from her scalp to her toes.

No. It couldn't be Lucien de Roye. Not after all this time. It would be against every conceivable possibility.

He was in her thoughts because of her dream.

She probably wouldn't even recognize his voice. It *had* been seven years, after all.

But it was suddenly cold in the library, the air turning frigid just as it had the last time she'd seen him.

Sophia pivoted, her expression properly prim, and caught her breath at the sight of the man leaning in the doorway.

It *was* Lucien de Roye.

And he was every bit as handsome as he had been seven years before.

But terrifying. Once he had been serious but with humor in his smile, with a manner that invited her trust. Now, his eyes glittered, like faceted gems. The line of his mouth was harsher, almost cruel. He looked even colder than he had when he had rejected her. She had the sense that he was reckless, assessing, dangerous, heartless.

And as unlike the man she had loved as was possible. Lucien might have had a wicked twin. Sophia barely kept herself from taking a step back.

She should have been relieved that he barely noted her presence. Her disappointment had to be because his gaze lingered on Daphne, a girl he would have found predictable seven years before. What more proof did she need that the man she loved was gone?

If he had ever existed.

Had Lucien changed or had his hidden truth simply been revealed? Sophia could not say.

"You interrupt our lesson, sir," she said with authority. "Is there good cause for this?"

"Curiosity is always good cause," he said with a cool smile. He sauntered into the library with that lithe grace she remembered so well. "It has been a long time since I've been accused of gallantry," he said to Daphne, who stared at him with awe. "Much less chivalry. In league with the Devil is a more common attribute, or wicked to my very marrow."

Daphne blinked. Sophia was quite certain that the girl had never had a man like this speak to her before. She took advantage of Lucien's diverted attention to survey him, seeking some hint of his past self.

He was dressed in black, from his trim jacket to his breeches to his polished boots. That was consistent. His taste in clothing had always been austere. The cloth was fine, and the tailoring, exquisite. His cravat was starkly white in contrast, his waistcoat made of a brocade that only revealed a hint of blue because of the splendor of that sapphire. His hair and brows were as black as ever, his eyes as vivid a blue, his chiseled features as handsome as that of any Greek god.

If anything, he was more confident. He still emanated an impression of power just barely contained. He was intense and watchful in a way that was utterly different from the man she remembered. She was put in mind of a predator, and stifled a shudder.

Once he had won her heart: now he frightened her.

It was a poor moment to recall that Lucien had always been particularly perceptive.

Sophia dropped her gaze to the floor. She reminded herself that they would only be at Castle Keyvnor until the end of the week and that she could surely evade the attention of a man like this for that long.

"Lucien de Roye, at your service," he said to Daphne.

"Miss Goodenham," Sophia supplied and her charge recovered herself well enough to curtsy.

"Delighted to meet you, sir." Daphne smiled and fluttered her lashes, dipping her chin to show her charms to best advantage. Sophia realized that the girl had probably chosen her new sprigged muslin specifically because she had seen Lucien arrive.

Lucien granted her an appraising survey. Daphne, for her part, had a good look at him through her lashes. "This is my sister, Miss Eurydice Goodenham," she said, but only after Sophia cleared her throat.

"Delighted, sir." Eurydice bobbed a quick curtsy.

"Delighted," he replied. "But I regret that I must disappoint you both yet again. I am not, regrettably, the son of a duke either." Lucien turned a smile upon Eurydice that made the girl blink. "Thus no inherited gem." He fingered the sapphire in his cravat. It was as big as Eurydice's thumb and glittered deep blue.

"Stolen or won, then, sir?" the girl had the audacity to ask.

Lucien chuckled and the dark sound awakened a flutter in Sophia's stomach. "Won, of course. And might well be lost before the moon is full again." He bowed to the girls, then paused beside Sophia. She kept her gaze fixed on her boots, fighting to ignore the blush that rose from her breasts. "I do apologize for the interruption, Miss...?"

"Miss Findlay," she replied firmly, summoning the spirit of her former tutor. "If you would excuse us, sir, we have a great many lessons to complete this morning."

"Of course. I would not hope to compete with the pleasures of conjugating German verbs." There was something in his tone that made Sophia think he was teasing her and her gaze flew to his. He held her gaze without blinking and her heart clenched that she had been recognized. Then he arched a brow. "German has never been my strength."

Daphne was delighted by this confession and smiled at him radiantly.

He bowed again then strolled to the door. Sophia was almost ready to take a breath of relief but he halted on the threshold to glance back. "*Je serais ravi de vous aider dans vos leçons dans cette langue.*"

Daphne looked confused.

"He says he'll tutor you," Eurydice whispered.

Daphne's eyes lit. "Oh! *Merci, M. de Roye.*"

Lucien inclined his head, his gaze flicking to Sophia.

No. He was baiting her.

"That will not be necessary, sir," Sophia interjected crisply. "Although your offer is most generous."

"I doubt you believe that, Miss Findlay," he purred, punctuated the address with a piercing look that made Sophia quiver to her marrow. He made to leave the library then hesitated again. "And Miss Eurydice, you are right. They are *perfectly* matched blacks. If you come to the stables after luncheon, I will prove it to you."

Sophia kept her irritation from her voice with an effort. Why was he so determined to tempt the girls to folly? "I regret that she will be occupied with her studies," she said with force. "If you will excuse us. Good day, M. de Roye."

Lucien's smile flashed. "Such a taskmaster you have, ladies," he drawled, his gaze lingering on Sophia. She thought he might say more, but he was gone as suddenly as he had appeared.

He couldn't know.

Could he?

Even if he had recognized her, why would he care? Sophia took a steadying breath, glad the library was their own again. Her hands were shaking, to her dismay. Eurydice was peering at her, her curiosity evident, but Sophia straightened and returned the girl's gaze sternly. The library warmed to its former temperature.

Five days. A veritable eternity.

"Lady North Barrows!" Lucien's words floated back to the library. Daphne was immediately as alert as a hound that had caught a scent. "What an unanticipated delight."

"Is it? Then you've forgotten your relations, too," Lady North Barrows said with an acidity that gave Sophia great pleasure. "I thought it was the Devil himself arrived last night, but I see it was only you, Lucien. Is it true what they whisper, that you are in league with the dark fiend?"

In league with the Devil? Sophia had not heard that rumor.

Daphne abandoned her lessons and hastened to the door, unable to disguise her curiosity. Eurydice hesitated only a moment before following to do the same. Sophia could have commanded them back to their seats, but truth be told, she was curious as well.

The more she knew of Lucien's activities over the past seven years, the better she could avoid him. It was an excuse and Sophia knew it, but she listened all the same.

~

Sophia Brisbane wasn't dead.

And Lucien had almost said too much in his relief.

Her survival was a marvel. It meant that keeping his word wasn't just a quixotic quest, but that he would actually set matters to rights.

Sophia was alive!

And he was not quite as sanguine about dying in three days.

Lucien had been devastated when he found the notation of her death in the register of that woe-be-gone parish church. All the same, he'd been surprised that he hadn't known of it sooner. It seemed he should have felt a stabbing pain when she breathed her last, or felt an ache that couldn't be dismissed because she was no longer in the world.

He'd blamed the baron for that. He didn't feel much of anything anymore, not since the charm had been created and tied, binding demon and mortal together for seven years. He felt much of the time as if he was dead already and the world around him was a dream.

But Sophia hadn't died.

Lucien felt a flicker of warmth where his heart used to be, a glow that could only be joy, that it was so.

To be sure, she was paler than he recalled and thinner. She looked taut, as her governess often had, and that she was in service told him all he needed to know about her financial situation. Did she pretend to be Amelia Findlay solely for that reason, or did she hide from someone?

He wouldn't blame her for hiding from him, not after the way they had parted.

But Sophia was alive!

The rap of an umbrella on the floor made Lucien look up. Lady North Barrows stood before him, her hair a little whiter than he recalled, but no less sharp and shrewd than she'd been the last time they crossed paths. He'd been wary of her before the baron, and even now recognized a formidable will.

He admired fearless and outspoken women. The baron hadn't changed that.

He bowed even as she sniffed with disapproval. "Lady North Barrows! What an unanticipated delight."

"Is it? Then you've forgotten your relations, too," she replied, looking him up and down. "I thought it was the Devil himself arrived last night, but I see it was only you, Lucien. Is it true what they whisper, that you are in league with the dark fiend?"

Blunt, as well. Lucien had always appreciated the honesty of direct speech. Sophia had charmed him from the first with her inability to keep from expressing her thoughts aloud. He'd believed once that she was the only woman in London who would tell him the truth—although now he didn't want to hear her view of him. He smiled. "You can't believe every rumor you hear, Lady North Barrows."

She glared at him. "Yet you are surprised to encounter me here, at the reception to read my own brother's will. You thought I wouldn't attend."

"The journey is long from North Barrows." Which made North Barrows a perfect place for Sophia to hide. Lucien realized the wisdom of her scheme. She had always been clever. "I didn't expect you to undertake it."

Lady North Barrows' gaze lingered on the sapphire in his cravat and Lucien would have wagered that she assessed its value within a shilling.

He could have won that wager without the baron's assistance.

"Then you thought wrongly." Her eyes narrowed. "I suppose this is an excellent opportunity to confess my disappointment in you, Lucien. I had thought that you might evade your father's inclination to dissipation and ruin. I regret that you have not been able to avoid temptation."

"But my father always lost when he gambled, Lady North Barrows," he said smoothly. "In contrast, I always win."

She smiled tightly. "No one always wins, unless he is being tricked."

It was unfortunate that Charles Brisbane had never believed that fact.

"Then I have been tricked for seven years." It was true, but not in the way she meant it. No dealer lured him in by ensuring he won the hand and bet more in the next. The baron, though, was definitely a trick of the most unholy kind. "And how would you know of my habits, Lady North Barrows? I thought you didn't go to London anymore."

"I do not need to be in London to hear news of it, and I have heard a great deal of unwelcome news about you." She rapped her umbrella on the floor. "I suppose you still have that Negro valet."

"You suppose rightly." Lucien hid the way her reference to Philip Larousse made him bristle.

But her objection surprised him. "It is outrageous for you to employ such a man simply to disconcert others. You use him poorly and most immorally."

"On the contrary, I owe Larousse a debt and I always pay my debts," Lucien countered. "He shall have employ with me for as long as he desires it."

"You pay your father's debt," Lady North Barrows accused softly.

"The matter could be viewed that way."

Her gaze turned assessing then. "And do you anticipate a legacy here?"

"I learned long ago to expect nothing from my family save their censure." Lucien brushed his coat sleeve. "I come for a meeting in the village, no more and no less."

"You come to gamble," she muttered, then sighed. "I suppose we shall have to endure your presence at luncheon."

"Alas, I must make arrangements in Bocka Morrow for my meeting. I will take refreshment there."

Lady North Barrows' gaze darkened in understanding. "In the tavern, with the whores and the witches, instead of at table with your betters. I should have expected no less. You have been many things, Lucien de Roye, but I am saddened to see you become a coward."

"Not a coward, Lady North Barrows, but a man previously engaged."

She pointed her umbrella at him and he refrained from taking a step back. "Be warned, Lucien, that if you mean to despoil either of my granddaughters or link their names with yours in some scandalous nonsense, I shall ensure that you regret it through eternity."

Lucien had regrets enough to occupy him for that duration. "I have no desire to rob the nursery, my lady."

"No? Then why were you in the library at all?"

"I sought a book, of course."

"I doubt that." She glared at him, so intent upon having an answer that Lucien chose to give her one.

He glanced back to the doorway to that room, not doubting that their conversation was being attended by at least two young women. He took a step closer to the older woman and lowered his voice. "Because I find myself intrigued by Miss Findlay."

"How cruel you are to make such a jest," Lady North Barrows said with vigor. "Truly, Lucien, you are no more than a shadow of your former self. I am appalled!"

"And so you should be," he agreed, surprised that she should inadvertently speak the truth. He *was* a shadow of his former self.

And in three days, he wouldn't even be that.

"Do not feign remorse." Lady North Barrows' eyes snapped. "Your mother was a fool and your father was a wastrel, but *you* have taken your family name to uncharted depths of depravity. That is no cause for pride."

"But it has always been my objective to live my life with distinction."

"You promised Margaret never to gamble!"

"And she is long dead."

"So you would keep no vows to the dead."

"On the contrary, I keep whatever vows I must to achieve the ends I desire."

The umbrella beat a staccato on the floor. "Reprehensible, Lucien!"

"I do have a reputation to protect, Lady North Barrows." Lucien bowed deeply once again before he took his leave. He felt the weight of her furious gaze follow him, but he didn't care what she thought of him.

Sophia was alive!

CHAPTER 2

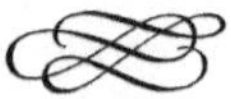

"Utterly scandalous," Lady North Barrows declared to no one in particular at luncheon. She gestured to the clear soup before her, as yet untasted, and a footman promptly removed it. Sophia knew that Lady North Barrows had strong feelings about the merit— or the lack—of a clear soup. The older woman was nothing if not consistent. "But that line of the family was not always so, to be sure.

As the fish course was served, Sophia watched the girls, ensuring that they chose the proper utensils. It was only to ensure their tutelage that she had been permitted to join the other guests at the meal, and that of Lady North Barrows' insistence. Sophia had been seated below the girls but close enough that they could glance her way for confirmation on their choices. Eurydice did so, showing her usual care with protocol, but Daphne was too interested in the conversation to bother. She had already used her dessert spoon for the soup, and the only mercy was that Lady North Barrows was seated too far away to have noticed her granddaughter surreptitiously lick it and return it to its place. They would have to review table settings in their lessons before the girls were invited to a dinner.

At least Lucien wasn't present. Sophia was glad of small mercies.

Even if she was curious about whatever meeting he planned.

"It was considered a decent match at the time, not brilliant, of

34

course, but better than expected for poor Eloise," Lady North Barrows continued. "She was always rather plain." This last was confided in the lady seated beside her with a shake of her head. The lady made a sound of commiseration and shot a glance at the other lady seated across the table. They were friends, then, and perhaps allied in their tolerance of Lady North Barrows. One of them was Lady Widcombe.

"And my cousin, Margaret, Eloise's mother, was absurdly convinced that only a duke would suffice for her sole child." Lady North Barrows sighed and attacked her salmon with the enthusiasm of a woman starved for a month. "Eloise was twenty-two by the time they settled her, and truly I think they would have taken anyone at that point. Michel de Roye appeared most appealing. He was handsome and charming. Wealthy, to be sure."

"I believe I have been told that the de Roye lands were abroad," one lady suggested.

"Indeed!" Lady North Barrows agreed. "Michel's father owned a large sugar plantation in Saint Domingue. *Very* affluent. He had been raised there, for they had lost their French title during the terror, you know." The ladies made sympathetic noises. "They perhaps did not have quite the polish of English gentry, but it seemed as if Eloise had done rather well for herself." Lady North Barrows nodded. "They said it was a love match."

"How providential!"

"Until she died in the bearing of his son, less than a year after the wedding," Lady North Barrows said grimly. "Then Michel took the boy back to Saint Domingue, abandoning all decent society in his grief."

"The boy was Lucien de Roye?"

"Of course. I believe the shock of it all contributed to the demise the following year of my cousin's husband, then dear Margaret was left all alone, not just a widow but denied any chance to see her only grandson. She was not so hale as to take to the high seas!" Lady North Barrows shook her head. "A wretched business, to be sure."

The ladies might have changed the subject, but Lady North Barrows finished her fish and continued her tale with enthusiasm. "And *then*, if that were not sufficient, there was a revolt in Saint Domingue and the de Roye family lost their sugar plantation. Michel brought the boy back to England—he must have been about ten years of age—and began to gamble heavily. Michel died destitute, as such men often do, in such debt that Lucien's future seemed to be doomed. Margaret, of course, could not simply stand aside. She took the boy under her wing and paid for his education on the condition that he never gamble. He was learning the trade of a successful merchant, the one who had established Brisbane's Emporium, when she died."

Sophia's heart jumped at the mention of her father.

"Brisbane's Emporium! *Maman* always insists they have the best offering of ribbons, but I find their selection disappointing," said the one lady.

"Never mind the cottons and muslins. They are priced so high there!"

"*Maman* says Brisbane's Emporium is not what it used to be, not since Mr. Brisbane died."

"Was he the one who died within one day of being elevated to the knighthood?"

"Oh, yes! And his son promptly lost his entire inheritance in the gaming hells."

The ladies clicked their tongues as Sophia felt that old mortification again at Charles' folly. Fury heated her blood, as well, for she knew that Lyndenhurst had baited her brother and tempted him to risk more, perhaps even cheating to ensure Charles lost. She would not recall the Marquess' insistence that he would make her regret breaking their betrothal. She couldn't think of it and retain her composure.

Eurydice was already watching her keenly.

Lady North Barrows cleared her throat. "But when *Margaret* died, Lucien *did* take up gambling, abandoning his promise to her. He has been a rake and a wastrel ever since."

"I hear he has won and cast away fortunes," said one of the ladies, clearly finding favor with this activity.

"And that he fights duels with some regularity," contributed the other with enthusiasm.

Daphne's approval was more than clear.

"Scandalous," Lady North Barrows concluded, her eyes lighting at the pork roast that was carried into the room next. "You should *all* ensure the defense of your reputations with such a man in the house."

Daphne gave a little shiver of delight, and Lady North Barrows fired one of her fearsome glares down the length of the table. Sophia wondered whether Lady North Barrows regretted having increased Lucien's appeal by sharing his tragic story.

At least the ladies declined to savor the misfortunes of the Brisbane family. Sophia could not have borne to have heard her father and brother discussed by strangers.

Both men were dead and she had loved them dearly, despite their weaknesses.

ARRANGEMENTS MADE FOR THE GAME, Lucien ordered another tankard of ale.

To see Sophia one last time was a hope he had not dared to have, but it begged the question: why now? Was it coincidence that he'd found her on the veritable eve of his own demise? He'd lived with the baron long enough to recognize that fiend's influence. Was Philip right that the baron would trick and cheat him in the end?

How did Sophia fit into the baron's scheme?

A fire lit within Lucien, a need to ensure that he protected Sophia this time as he had failed to do before, and he thought he heard the baron chuckle.

Her presence changed everything. Lucien had often been in the presence of greed, but had never felt it himself. As he drank his ale, he felt it fire within him. He wanted to see Sophia alone. He wanted to talk to her. He wanted to brush a fingertip over her freckles. He wanted to make her smile. He wanted to hear her laughter—no, to provoke it. He wanted to confide in her. He wanted one last kiss.

No, he wanted more than a kiss from Sophia.

Mere hours before, there had been no chance of any of these temptations, thus he had no desire for them. Now, he yearned to seek Sophia out and claim as many as possible before his time on earth was done. He wanted to see her expression when she realized what he had done.

He wanted to redeem himself in her eyes.

Could he? Or would doing so put Sophia at risk from the baron? Lucien didn't know and he didn't imagine the baron would give him a straight answer.

Best to avoid temptation.

Even if Sophia was the only one that truly tempted him.

If the baron meant to trick him, he had baited his hook well.

Lucien supposed Miss Findlay must have been the one who had died, which was regrettable, although Sophia disguising herself as her governess explained perfectly why he hadn't been able to find her.

He could still see Sophia on her father's ship, bonnet clutched in her hand, chestnut curls escaping their bonds, eyes alight with excitement. One look and Lucien had been lost. Her attire was attractive without being at the height of fashion, made of good quality by an excellent dressmaker. It was her attitude that snared his attention. She looked about herself with curiosity, unafraid to show her emotions. She had freckles and her face was tanned, an uncommon attribute and one that would have been vigorously battled with lemon juice by any young women of his acquaintance. She'd been like a breath of air in a crowded room, for her arrival in London gave him a clarity about his own future that had been lacking.

He'd known immediately that he could love her.

He wondered whether he could win her, and build a future with her father's trade. It was clear to any observer that Charles had no interest in the emporium. Though Mr. Brisbane yearned for aristocratic connections, Lucien had believed Charles would be the one to make the good match.

Unlike his friend, Lucien had enjoyed being under the tutelage of Mr. Brisbane. Charles' father was open and generous, a patient man who answered every question. He was clever and practical, and his conviction that hard work would be rewarded was a welcome notion to Lucien. He had assured Lucien that a man could become whatever he desired, if he were prepared to work for it.

Lucien had been prepared to work, as Charles had not. His friend routinely abandoned his father's lessons for more material pleasures, while Lucien remained to attend them. He'd been intrigued by the older man's ability to anticipate changes in fashion and to ensure that his goods were of the best quality, available at the best price at the right time.

Then Sophia had arrived. She'd greeted her father with affection, then met Lucien's gaze steadily, like an equal, when introduced. She spoke her mind. She laughed openly. She was as honest and practical as her father, as generous and charming as her brother.

Lucien had been glad to be assigned to escort her to her father's house. He'd expected to be given the task of making an inventory of the newly arrived stores, but Mr. Brisbane had, for once, been disinclined to indulge his only son. Charles had taken poorly to his father's insistence that he begin learning more about the business on this very day.

Despite the presence of Miss Findlay, Lucien and Sophia had talked, of all things, about sugar plantations. Once Sophia had learned that he had spent his boyhood in Saint Domingue, she had peppered him with questions. Their discussion was so lively that they reached the townhouse more quickly than he might have believed, and he found himself offering to show her the sights of London.

It had been the first of many excursions. He wondered that Mr. Brisbane allowed it, then dared to hope Sophia's father had discerned his dream. He couldn't have been more wrong.

Lucien supposed he shouldn't have been surprised when Mr. Brisbane announced that he had arranged a match for Sophia with Eugene Tremblay, Marquess of Lyndenhurst.

Sophia, in contrast, had been devastated.

No. He wouldn't remember that day. Lucien drained his ale and set the tankard aside. It didn't matter, not now. He would be dead within days.

His destiny was with the baron.

～

A BRISK WALK was the best solution to any trouble. That had been Amelia Findlay's conviction, and her former pupil agreed. It had rained earlier and was still drizzling, but Sophia didn't care. With the girls summoned to attend their grandmother, she had a few hours to herself, which was the last thing she desired. Anything had to be better than lingering in the castle, expecting to be revealed at any moment, thinking about Lucien.

She donned her thickest stockings and her sturdy boots, buttoned up a long jacket and wrapped a scarf around her throat. Her dark bonnet was warm and she had brought a thick pair of gloves. It wouldn't be enough to keep the damp wind from chilling her, but if she walked with purpose, she should be warm enough.

She walked toward the village, then was enticed by the glitter of the sea. It was a thousand hues of silver on this day, and stretched flawlessly to the horizon. Beyond it, far to the west, was the island of St. Maurice that held the place of honor in her heart.

She would never see it again, but she had her memories.

On impulse, Sophia climbed a rising path, hoping it would take her to a cliff and a view. Her heart was racing when she reached the summit, but it was well worth the effort. She stood, letting the wind snap at her skirts, and drank in the sight.

Six weeks at sea, perhaps four. That was all it would take to be home and barefoot in the sunshine again. To be warm again. To be free of social constraints. To be able to speak her mind once more. Sophia stood and yearned, knowing it was impossible, but wanting to be in the Caribbean again all the same.

A futile wish, like wishing Lucien had been tempted to take what she'd offered.

She frowned and turned to leave. Amelia Findlay would have disapproved of such whimsy. What was done was done.

"Your freckles have faded." A man's familiar voice carried from somewhere behind her. Sophia's heart jumped and she pivoted to find Lucien leaning against a tree, in the shade beyond the path. He looked just as dangerous as he had earlier. She shivered, but couldn't look away from his steady gaze.

"But I suppose they disappeared with your tan." He paused, watching her, eyes glinting, and spoke with deliberation. "Sophia."

Her name on his lips made her heart thunder.

It was tempting to lie, to deny that she was herself, but that was even more foolish than longing for home—or imagining that the man she had known was still within this stranger.

Sophia exhaled and turned her back upon Lucien, trying to stop the race of her pulse. "I suppose you want a boon to refrain from revealing me," she said, as if annoyed with him, realizing too late as if she sounded like a woman desiring a kiss. She felt unsettled and uneasy, both wishing he would leave and yearning for him to stay.

He came to stand behind her and she closed her eyes, knowing it was smarter not to want anything from Lucien.

"Once you invited me to ruin you," he murmured, his voice low and close, and she winced at the reminder.

"It turned out to be unnecessary, didn't it?" she said curtly. "What a relief to both of us that you weren't tempted."

"Not tempted?" His surprise was clear in his tone. "Surely you never thought that?"

She couldn't help herself then, but turned to look at him. His eyes were vivid blue, his gaze boring into hers with familiar intensity. For a heartbeat, she saw the man who had looked at her as if she were a marvel. She smelled the ale upon his breath, though, and turned her back upon him once more.

She was a fool six times over.

His fingertip landed on her shoulder, the weight of it creating a line of fire even through the layers of cloth. She swallowed, closing her eyes against his unholy allure.

"You always tempted me, Sophia," he said softly and she wished it were true. "From that very first day."

"Yet you managed to resist that temptation rather well," she said, hearing the sharpness of her tone.

"Sophia," he murmured and her heart skipped.

"There's no need to pretend now, sir," she said, sounding more like Amelia than she realized. "We know enough of each other that there's no need for pretense."

He was silent for a moment, then his next words were harsh. "Of course, you are right. I apologize for any offense."

Sophia grimaced, knowing he couldn't see her. She'd provoked the answer she expected, but she felt no triumph in it. No, she felt raw and vulnerable, as she hadn't in years.

Just because she was alone with Lucien.

"You've fared well, evidently," she said. "Is it true that you're in league with the Devil?" She repeated Lady North Barrows' words to provoke him, but in truth, she could not imagine how he had come to be dressed as a wealthy rake, much less have such a reputation as a gambler. The Lucien she had known had refused to gamble, and had been unlucky at cards.

Her heart clenched in recollection of his jest that he might be lucky in love instead.

"You've been listening to Lady North Barrows," he said, his tone unruffled by the accusation. A weight dropped over her shoulders and Sophia realized he'd placed his greatcoat over her jacket. It smelled of his skin, a scent she thought she'd forgotten. She hadn't. It made her toes curl and her lips burn all over again, as well as that welcome heat unfurl in her belly. She gripped the lapels without intending to do as much.

"Still cold?" He sounded close and seductive.

She swallowed and stared resolutely at the view. "Always."

"Me, too." His hands closed over her shoulders, his grip resolute, and she wanted to lean back against him. Once she had trusted him. Once she had believed she knew him as well as herself. Once she had thought their minds were as one. She savored even this touch, greedy for more of him even though she knew it was foolish.

He had changed.

She had changed, as well.

"Why not go home?" he whispered, and she thought of the serpent tempting Eve in the garden.

Sophia laughed despite herself. "Where is home now?"

"St. Maurice, of course. Where it always was."

"It can be home no longer," she said with bitterness. "Charles saw to that. Even if I could pay the passage, why would I cast myself into the marquess' power?" She shook her head, fighting tears. "He has probably planted it all in sugar, destroyed its beauty for his own financial gain." Lucien said nothing though his grip tightened a little on her shoulders. Sophia straightened. "No, this is my destiny now. I am not discontent."

It sounded like a lie, or at least like wishful thinking. She bit her lip as the silence stretched long between them.

"I thought you were dead," Lucien said finally.

"That was Amelia's idea." Sophia shivered in recollection of her companion's last days, and blinked back tears in memory of the finality of her last breath. The grief she had denied rose within her, tightening her throat and chilling her anew.

They were all gone.

She was all alone.

"But your being in service was hardly your father's aspiration for your future."

"His dream came at too high of a price."

"So, Miss Findlay found a solution. Was it her intent to save you from Lyndenhurst or from me?"

That he could jest about Sophia's situation meant there was no point in varnishing the truth. "Both," she snapped.

"Ever direct." Sophia stole a glance to find him frowning toward the town. He looked forbidding and remote, utterly unlike the Lucien she had loved. He might have been a stranger, which only made his next words more startling. "At least, my Sophia has not become circumspect."

His Sophia?

Sophia tugged off the coat and offered it to him. "I am *not* your Sophia!"

But Lucien did not take the garment. He put his hands into his pockets and faced her, his eyes glittering. "Look in my pocket, Sophia, before you cast away my coat," he said, his tone challenging. "A wise man taught me to use caution with what I would discard, lest something of value be lost."

Annoyed beyond belief with Lucien for provoking her to forget her father's advice, Sophia felt her cheeks heat. She found a document in the breast pocket of the garment. The seal was broken already.

Only once she held the document did he pluck his greatcoat from her grasp. "Leave service, Sophia," he said. "You are not so penniless as you imagine." His eyes blazed, then he pivoted to march away. He strode down the hill as he shrugged into his coat, never sparing a glance back at her. Did Lucien flee from her? It was a remarkable notion, one so strange that Sophia could only dismiss it as absurd.

This Lucien had no heart. He certainly could have no fear of her.

She unfolded the document, and her curiosity was replaced with astonishment. It was the title for Brisbane's Emporium.

Was this a joke? Her brother Charles had lost everything to Lyndenhurst. She would never forget such a detail—much less how drunk Charles had been when he'd admitted the truth.

Or the fact that Lucien had brought him home.

Sophia read the document three times, unable to dispel her impression that the title was genuine. It included the warehouses and the inventories, such as they were, the building that held the emporium and the living quarters above. She stared at it, amazed that she had a choice.

Because Lucien had given it to her.

Why?

Suddenly, she could see again a younger version of Lucien, determination burning in his sapphire gaze after he had brought Charles home that fateful morning.

"I will retrieve every shilling for you, Miss Brisbane, no matter what the cost."

Sophia fingered the deed with new wonder. She had never expected him to even try such a feat. That he had retrieved this much of her father's legacy and simply given it to her meant that the Lucien she had known was not gone. Her heart fluttered and her tears rose.

But how could he have done such a thing? She knew Lyndenhurst well enough to know that he would not surrender any of her father's fortune willingly. He had vowed to do as much. Lyndenhurst was a gambler, and Lucien had never been fortunate at cards. Lady North

Barrows was right that he had promised his grandmother that he would never enter the gaming hells.

What had changed? Lady North Barrows thought him dissolute, but Sophia wondered.

Had Lucien broken the promise to his grandmother to keep his vow to her?

~

LUCIEN KNEW he shouldn't have been surprised that he and Sophia had ended up at the same place, absorbing the same view. It had been a jest, all those years ago, how their impulses ran in the same direction. They'd frequently encountered each other in the same corner of the park or in town, and quite by accident.

There had been a time when it had seemed to be a sign that they were meant to be together.

Lucien rode hard back to the castle, fighting against the desire that seemed to have redoubled in their years apart. He could see Sophia softening before his very eyes, slipping from her guise of Miss Findlay and becoming herself again. He felt her thaw. He sensed that she reawakened, and he caught her old audacity in her words. He wanted to heal her, to hold her close, to console her as he had no right to do.

He had no right to even think of her.

Worse, he felt his own resolve softening. If it were not for the baron, he could offer for her. He had more than sufficient fortune. But he had only three days until the baron claimed his due, and Lucien knew all too well the price he would pay.

He couldn't lose his resolve now. He couldn't falter now. He had to give Sophia what he could—and that didn't include a future he didn't have.

He had to make sure she was safe from the baron, too.

One last game. One last victory.

Then his labor on this earth would be done.

Funny how it no longer felt like a triumph.

. . .

It was remarkable to Lucien that Mr. Brisbane, a man of such splendid good sense, could not see how his decision to betroth his only daughter to the Marquess of Lyndenhurst would only make her miserable. He had ignored Lyndenhurst's reputation and Sophia's fear of that man, seeing only the splendor of his title.

"Your son will be a marquess!" he exclaimed in the office of the emporium when Sophia protested her lack of affection for Lyndenhurst. "Think of it, Sophia! Aristocrats! Your mother would be so proud." He patted her hand, as if she were a pet, and only Lucien had glimpsed the fullness of Sophia's dismay. "It is not uncommon for a maiden to be shy, but you will come to care for him and be glad I saw you so advantageously married. You will thank me, Sophia, when your first son is born." Then he had hastened back to his warehouses, giddy to share the good news with all and sundry.

Sophia turned and saw Lucien, frozen in his steps, in the act of returning from an errand when he overheard the news.

"You heard," she whispered.

Lucien nodded.

"What am I to do?"

He had retreated to the office, sickened by his lack of prospects, knowing he would have to watch her be married to a man they both disliked. "Prepare your wedding clothes," he said gruffly, ignoring how she stared at him.

Sophia entered the office in a rustle of skirts and a cloud of the scent that was hers alone. She shut the door and his heart leaped. The weight of her hand landed on his shoulder, and he turned to see the resolve in her gaze. "I cannot do it, Lucien. I cannot marry that man."

"You have no choice. Your father has made the arrangements."

Her lips set and a determined glitter had dawned in her eyes. "I'll change his mind."

"I doubt you can..." Lucien began, then was silenced by her finger landing upon his lips.

"I will and I know how."

"Sophia..."

"Ruin me, Lucien. Lyndenhurst will not take me then."

Lucien feared the other man would. He wanted the fortune, not the bride, but Sophia gave him no chance to argue.

She replaced her fingertip with her lips and he was lost. Sophia was soft and willing, her kiss enough to set his blood on fire. Lucien turned, like a man in a dream, and gathered her into his embrace. He savored the sweet weight of her in his arms, the press of her against him, the feeling of completion when he held her close.

The surety that he betrayed his employer's trust.

He set her aside, abandoned her there, her glorious eyes filling with tears at what she saw as his rejection. He'd walked away. He hadn't said a word in his own defense, hadn't dared to utter one with his heart so full of yearning.

LUCIEN DISMOUNTED BEFORE THE STABLES, restless with his newfound desire. Was it so wrong for a condemned man to desire one last kiss from his beloved?

SOPHIA PASSED Larousse on the stairs when all were hastening to dress their lords and ladies for dinner and halted in delight. She was going down to the kitchens, for she had no one to assist, and their gazes clung for a moment.

He was still with Lucien. Sophia was relieved.

Whatever Lucien had done, his oldest and best friend hadn't despaired of him.

Larousse would know the truth, too, whatever it was.

But Larousse averted his gaze and continued up the stairs without speaking to her. Did he spurn her on purpose, or did he maintain the ruse that she was Amelia Findlay?

Despite herself, Sophia turned to watch him depart, but Larousse didn't glance back.

It was only when she continued her course that Sophia realized that Mrs. Bray had noticed her reaction. "M. de Roye's valet, that's who he is. Never thought I'd see the day to have his like in the castle, to be sure."

"He looks like a most elegant man," Sophia said.

Morris, who was ahead of her on the stairs, made a sound suspiciously like a chuckle. His eyes twinkled when he turned to confront Sophia. "I suppose you are wanting a cup of tea, Miss Findlay?"

"It would be most welcome. I walked to the village and am a bit chilled."

"As if there is not enough to manage before the dinner," Mrs. Bray complained, but Morris indicated the chamber that the servants used.

"Tea," Mr. Morris said firmly. "Is seldom any trouble to prepare and is often quite welcome." He gave Mrs. Bray a look that sent her scurrying and Sophia couldn't completely suppress her smile.

CHAPTER 3

She's here," Philip said as he laid out a freshly pressed shirt.

"She is," Lucien agreed, having no doubt who his friend and valet meant. He was seated at the small writing desk in his bedroom and composing a letter. He felt Philip study him but offered no more detail.

"You told me she was dead."

"I thought she was, on account of her death having been recorded in the parish register." Lucien signed the missive and folded it.

"So, they traded places."

"Evidently." Lucien sealed the letter and rose to his feet.

"And what do you mean to do now?"

Lucien offered the letter to a wary Philip. "The same as I planned before. You will depart here on the second, with or without me, and deliver this to my solicitor in London."

Philip regarded the letter with suspicion, as if it might bite. "What does it say?"

"I gave her the title to the Emporium. This authorizes its transfer to her."

The valet took the letter then, and fingered it before he tucked it into his jacket.

"Escort her to London, if she intends to go. It will be safer for her in my carriage than to travel alone."

"You could go with her."

Lucien did not reply. He concentrated upon his cravat, because it allowed him to avoid Philip's gaze.

"She looks sad. Lonely."

"I expect that is the plight of all those who are alone in the world."

"Like you?"

"I'm not alone. I have you."

Philip snorted. "She doesn't need to be alone. Neither do you."

Lucien met his old friend's gaze steadily. "No one needs to be alone, but there are those who choose comparative solitude because it is safer for everyone else."

"Or because they are afraid."

Lucien's fingers froze, then he completed the knot.

Philip exhaled. "She might be able to help you."

"I don't need any assistance." Lucien was dismissive of the very notion. "Take her to London and let the past be forgotten."

Let him be forgotten.

"If only it were so easy to forget," Philip muttered, then brushed the shoulders of Lucien's coat. He looked at Lucien in the mirror. "You're wrong. You're wrong to trust the baron to keep to your wager, whatever it is. The fact that she's here at this moment is proof of that. Only love can defeat him and his tricks. She *can* help you."

"No." Lucien turned away from the mirror and met Philip's gaze. "She will *not* become involved. I forbid it."

Philip's lips set. "And I remind you that my service as your valet is a convenient ruse. I am a free man, Lucien."

"She must remain safe."

"But..."

"I need to know that she's safe," Lucien insisted. "I can endure anything if that's the case."

Philip exhaled. "What did you offer in exchange for your seven years of luck?"

"That is not for you to know."

"You're protecting me, just as you're protecting her."

"Whether I am or not is irrelevant." Lucien couldn't quell his concern, but he hid it from Philip. "I will not need you again tonight," he said, then pivoted to cross the room.

Two more days and the deception would be done.

Sophia believed he had never been tempted by her.

Maybe there was one more legacy he could leave her.

It might have been a lesson that Sophia's father died the very night after his much-anticipated elevation to the knighthood. He'd had no opportunity to enjoy what he had earned. He broke his own rule and imbibed a little too much, tripped when alighting from the carriage and hit his head on the cobblestones before the new house. He had only lived in it for a month. He was dead by the time the doctor arrived.

His passing sent new resolve through his daughter. She would not accept a match she could not endure. She would not accept a half-measure. She would pursue her desires and her dreams, and not care what any person in London thought of her choices. She broke her engagement with the Marquess of Lyndenhurst.

The marquess did not accept the news well.

Charles, meanwhile, descended into madness.

Sophia knew her brother was gambling. She knew he was unchecked without their father to control the purse strings. She knew he was deaf to her entreaties. Lucien had vanished, so she could not appeal to him and his influence over her brother. She feared the result of Charles' recklessness.

When she heard the commotion in the foyer that October morning, Sophia expected little good. The bell had rung and Fawcett had answered, but clearly something unusual transpired. There were murmurs and the scuffle of boots, then a moan that was evocative of Charles' voice.

Sophia abandoned her tea and stood. Miss Findlay had gone to visit a cousin in Northumberland, so Sophia was alone.

The front door was open, offering a view of the rain falling steadily beyond. A damp breeze wafted into the house. Lucien carried Charles into the foyer and she was fiercely glad to see that he was yet loyal to her brother. Charles was unconscious, but not apparently injured. Sophia could smell the brandy upon him. He was drunk but not otherwise injured, much to her relief.

She took a moment to savor the sight of her beloved. Lucien's boots were wet and raindrops glistened in his dark hair. His cravat was yet perfectly tied and his expression was slightly impatient. Her brother, taller and broader than most, was cast over his shoulder, limp as a sack of flour. Lucien was so handsome—black hair and blue eyes, chiseled features and a perfect aquiline nose—that Sophia's heart clenched with the awareness that their single kiss would be their last.

His gaze swept over her coolly, as if she were no more interesting than a shop girl, then returned to Fawcett, the butler. He arched a brow, his impatience growing.

And no wonder. Fawcett was fluttering, as he was wont to do when things went deeply awry. Fawcett called for Charles' valet and tried, unsuccessfully to take the burden of his lord and master.

Lucien, to his credit, didn't facilitate this transfer. He eyed the stairs, looking for all the world ready to carry Charles wherever he needed to be.

Sophia knew she should retreat into the dining room. She knew she should pretend not to have seen her brother so indisposed.

She also knew that she was even less inclined to do as she should than ever.

"You had best put him in the drawing room," she said, her voice crisp with command.

Fawcett jumped and his mouth worked in silence that she should witness this unfortunate incident. "But Miss Sophia, surely his lordship should be taken to his bedchamber."

"I doubt you will get him up those stairs," Sophia replied. "The drawing room will be infinitely easier."

"Thank God for practical women," Lucien muttered and their gazes met for a moment that sent heat surging through Sophia. She felt again that seductive sense that they could be as one.

If Lucien had wanted her.

Before Fawcett could protest, Sophia opened the door to the drawing room, and Lucien carried Charles there. Fawcett sputtered until Sophia directed him to fetch a tonic for Charles, then he disappeared. At her gesture, Lucien settled Charles on a settee. Sophia unfastened her brother's cravat and loosed his jacket, keenly aware that this was the first time she had been with Lucien since he had rejected her.

"What has happened?" she asked him.

His eyes flashed and his lips tightened. "The tale is his to tell."

Sophia might have been irritated that he wouldn't even speak to her any more, but his grim tone sent terror through her. "Charles?" She patted his cheek. "Charles, what have you done?"

Her brother groaned and his ginger lashes fluttered. "Oh, Soph," he murmured when he saw her, his words sluggish. "I lost."

Her heart clenched, but she forced a smile for him. "Papa always advised you to choose your vice. Drink or gamble, but not both together."

"To be fair, he began drinking only after he had gambled," Lucien contributed.

"Because he lost?" Sophia guessed.

"Lost." Charles winced. "Lost all of it," he murmured, shaking his head.

"All of it?" Sophia echoed, feeling a little dizzy.

"It took him a fortnight."

Sophia stood up, her legs unsteady. "Since our father's death," she whispered then gave Charles a shake.

"No," Lucien said, his voice hard. "Since you broke your engagement with Lyndenhurst."

She turned to face him, not understanding. "What has one to do with the other? He only wished to wed me for Father's fortune. Charles' choice is not my fault!"

"But now Lyndenhurst has claimed your father's fortune in another way."

Sophia caught her breath. "Charles lost it all to Lyndenhurst?"

Lucien nodded, his eyes narrowed. "Every shilling."

Sophia could not believe it. "But how could one man be so lucky as to win it all?"

"No," Lucien corrected, his voice harsh. "The question is how one man could be unlucky enough to lose it all."

She met his gaze, seeing her own dislike for Lyndenhurst mirrored there. "Lyndenhurst cheated?"

Lucien shrugged. "It cannot be proven, and to be sure, Charles could have halted the game at any moment. Instead, he was seduced by his victories and wagered more each time."

"Until it all hung in the balance."

Lucien nodded grimly.

Sophia sat down hard. "He lost it all to Lyndenhurst." She poked Charles, more than a little frustrated with his irresponsibility. "Were you so determined to be rid of your legacy as that?"

"I wanted more, more for you and for Elizabeth." Charles closed his eyes then, as if there was no reason why he shouldn't indulge in sleep.

But Father was not alive to set Charles' errors to rights.

Sophia clenched her fists. She would have no dowry. They would have no home. Charles had no fortune and he would not be able to wed his beloved. And St. Maurice, her sanctuary, was lost to a man who would plant it in sugar and ruin it utterly.

Lyndenhurst had won.

And the Brisbanes were ruined.

What would she do?

To her surprise, Lucien dropped to one knee before her and took her hand in his. When he met her gaze, his own eyes blazed sapphire. "He was cheated, and I will see justice done. I will retrieve every shilling for you, Sophia, no matter what the cost."

He gave Sophia no opportunity to ask what he would do, much less to remind him of his promise to his grandmother.

He was gone, and she was alone as she had never been before.

THE MUSIC AWAKENED SOPHIA AGAIN.

Her room was illuminated by the moonlight that slanted through the window. It was a harpsichord she heard, for the sound of the instrument was unmistakable. Although the tune was being played very quickly, it was vaguely familiar.

Who was the inconsiderate—if talented—guest?

The music had first echoed through the castle after Lucien's arrival the night before. She remembered the pianoforte in the house he had inherited from his grandmother. Did he play? She had never heard him do so, but something about the music reminded her of the strange glitter that was now in his eyes.

It made her shiver.

She wouldn't sleep again, not with the recollection of Charles' loss so fresh in her thoughts. She fingered the deed again, still amazed that Lucien had given it to her. She fought a persistent sense that there was more to the tale than he had confessed to her.

As well as a dawning conviction that he had not changed, much less that she had misjudged him. He had kept his word, which meant that the Lucien she had loved was alive and well.

If disguised.

Sophia could have no quibble with that, given her own disguise.

The music grew in volume and tempo. Who played with such abandon? She rose on impulse and donned a robe, then left her room. The servants' quarters were quiet. She passed like a wraith along the empty corridor and down the stairs, following the sound of the music. It grew steadily louder until she stood outside a door near the library where she taught the girls. Even this corridor was in darkness, though there was a glow within the room from which the music emanated.

She touched the door with her fingertips and it swung open to reveal a lit candle on the mantel. Its golden light only partly illuminated the room and Sophia entered cautiously. The room was as cold as midwinter.

There was no one seated at the harpsichord, although there was an empty glass on top of it. She smelled rum. There was something else beside the glass, a cloth bundle bound with cord. Sophia stared in astonishment when she came around the instrument. The keys moved with no fingers upon them.

The music grew impossibly louder. Sophia leaned closer and reached for the cloth bundle.

As soon as her fingers closed around it, the music stopped.

The candle burned out.

The cold faded and she was left, standing in darkness beside the silent instrument, a bundle of cloth in her hand. It was warm.

As if she had taken it from another.

Sophia shivered involuntarily and straightened. Then she felt it in the darkness, confirming her suspicions of what she held. She knew the charm for what it, as much from the cord wrapped around it as the heat it shouldn't have had. She hadn't seen such a charm since leaving the islands, and had only glimpsed one there once, but the cold dread it awakened in her told her all she needed to know.

In that moment, she knew what Lucien had done.

To keep his word to her.

"C. P. E. Bach," Lucien murmured and she spun to find him leaning in the doorway. He had shed his jacket and his cravat was loosened. His dark hair was tousled, as if he had shoved his fingers through it, and he looked less forbidding than he had before. His eyes didn't seem as icy and there was a familiar curve to his wry smile. "His favorite." He shrugged and cast his jacket over a chair. "I'm sure he's delighted to have found a harpsichord here. The pianoforte is always a compromise."

"Who is your *loa*?" Sophia asked bluntly. She saw that Lucien meant to pretend he didn't understand, but she deliberately placed the charm on the instrument. Lucien's gaze lingered on it and his lips tightened. She didn't know all the spirits the slaves invoked, but she knew enough of Vodou to recognize its presence.

And its tools. Charms like this one bound the spirit to the man, and were made during the ritual of invocation. Its presence told her much of what she needed to know.

That Lucien had made such a wager to keep his word to her was something she'd have to think about later.

When his presence wasn't making her heart flutter.

He heaved a sigh and looked suddenly very tired. "Baron Samedi, of course."

Sophia looked to the seat then back to Lucien as she fought her horror. Even she knew that Baron Samedi was one of the most powerful *loas*. "Not him," she whispered.

"Who else?" Lucien raised his brows. "The *loa* of death and resurrection, lover of rum and debauchery. No one else could have given me such luck at gambling." He pushed a hand through his hair again. "I quickly learned that I was my father's son."

He had done this for her.

And he had known what he was doing. This was the man she

remembered, the man whose honor was unshakable, the man who protected those he loved.

Sophia gripped the edge of the harpsichord, feeling Lucien's survey as surely as a touch. "Did you see him?"

She shook her head. "Just the keys moving."

Lucien sauntered closer. "He means to intrigue you, Sophia," he murmured, apparently unaware that he was the one who succeeded in that endeavor. His voice was so low and seductive, the sound of her name like an incantation. "He means to fascinate you and draw you close, so that he might take a toll from you, as well." He paused in front of her, his gaze searching. "Do not be deceived, my Sophia."

She was keenly aware that she wore only a chemise and a robe, and that Lucien was so close, so potent, so male. His gaze was fixed upon her and she had to drop her own, even as she felt herself flush in awareness. Her lips burned in recollection of that kiss and she thought she heard him catch his breath. The moonlight fell through the window, making the room look silvery.

She could have been in a dream.

Her dream.

"Were you deceived by him?" she asked.

His tone turned harsh. "I knew what I was doing."

"What did you offer him?"

Lucien's eyes narrowed and he was forbidding once more. "Go to bed, Sophia."

Sophia knew that he was trying to protect her. She picked up the charm again, sensing how he disliked her touching it. She didn't like touching it either, but she knew that her doing so diminished its power.

She held it before him. "You're bound together," she whispered, knowing there would be items inside the charm to secure the bond. Earthy tokens to bind soul to spirit. Some of Lucien's hair might be included, or even his blood, soil from the place the ritual had been performed, feathers from the chicken, maybe the blood of the chicken or some of the rum spilled on the ground. "I want to break the bond."

"Don't try."

"I owe you thanks for the Emporium. This would be my gratitude."

"No!" His eyes glimmered. "Put it down, Sophia."

She played with it more deliberately instead, understanding why he had changed. "It wasn't your responsibility to undo Charles' folly..."

Lucien's lips set. "I made a promise and I will keep it."

"What was the wager? Good luck until you won it all back?"

"Seven years good luck and invincibility."

Sophia caught her breath. Charles had lost his inheritance at the end of October, seven years before. "What did you offer the baron in exchange?"

"The only possession I could call my own." Lucien's gaze was locked with hers, as if he would dare her to believe his words. "My soul."

"Lucien! No!"

He plucked the charm from her hand and put it back on the harpsichord. "It was the only way I could win." Lucien held her gaze, as if challenging her to ask.

"And then what?" she asked.

"Then the wager is over," he said, his manner so evasive that she knew the truth was dire. He turned away, but she seized his sleeve to halt him.

"Then what, Lucien?"

"The deal is done, Sophia," he said with resolve. "It cannot be undone, so I must accept its repercussions."

"Even if the fault is partly mine?"

He met her gaze then, his surprise clear.

"If I hadn't spurned Lyndenhurst, he wouldn't have cheated Charles of his inheritance."

"This isn't about Lyndenhurst..."

"No, it's about your promise to me. How did you even win back the emporium? I cannot believe Lyndenhurst risked it willingly."

"I convinced him."

"How?"

"He couldn't manage it. He couldn't hire anyone to do as much. He couldn't sell it." Lucien smiled. "I did him a favor by accepting it as a wager."

"What about St. Maurice? Has he destroyed it?"

"He hasn't had the funds to so much as visit it."

Sophia caught her breath, almost overwhelmed by her relief. "Lucien!" she whispered and would have flung herself at him, but he turned away, putting distance between them. "You can't just do this," she said, her words falling in a rush. "You can't have defended St. Maurice and given me the emporium for nothing."

"Can't I?"

"What can I do, Lucien? What can I do for you?"

Lucien's gaze clung to hers for a moment, then he turned away. He strolled around the instrument, and she feared that he would evade her question. "I remember that you always yearned to travel, Sophia."

"I did," she agreed, wondering what he intended to tell her. She couldn't begin to guess his thoughts.

"And yet you have spent these years disguised as Amelia Findlay, tutoring young girls at distant North Barrows." He flicked a glance at her. "It must be cold there."

"It most certainly is."

"Penance, then?"

Sophia shrugged. "Maybe just safety."

He nodded understanding. "In contrast, I have spent these years winning every bet I take." Lucien halted before her. She still had to tip her head back to meet his gaze. He was serious, watchful, just as she remembered him. "It causes some complications."

"Too many funds?"

He took her hand in his and Sophia welcomed his touch. "One cannot win all the time at the same establishment. I have been compelled to journey in Europe." He laced their fingers together, watching his own motions with curious intensity. Sophia was enthralled. "You ask what you can do," he murmured, then touched his lips to her fingertips. His gaze lifted to hers. "Indulge me, Sophia, one last time."

"Of course."

He smiled as if she were a marvel. "You agree without hesitation."

"I trust you." The second sweeter confession caught in her throat, but Lucien didn't seem to notice.

"In Vienna, they dance a most beguiling dance," he continued, then his eyes filled with challenge. "You might like it."

"Then teach me," she said on impulse, the moonlight and his presence making it impossible for her to do otherwise.

Lucien's voice dropped low. "I warn you, Miss Findlay, it is scandalous."

Sophia smiled because she knew he was teasing her. "Miss Findlay is asleep, M. de Roye."

His smile flashed and Sophia's heart skipped. "I am glad to hear it. A chaperone of any merit would most thoroughly disapprove of what we are about to do."

Sophia smiled in return, and felt her anticipation rise. Her heart leaped when Lucien pulled her close. His arm locked around her waist so tightly that her breasts were close to his chest. She was keenly aware that there was only thin fabric between them, and the intensity of Lucien's expression revealed that he knew it too.

She thought of her father's sudden demise, and the surety she'd once had that no opportunity should be wasted.

Sophia wouldn't waste this one.

She took a step closer, ensuring that her breasts were crushed against Lucien's strength. He inhaled sharply, his gaze brightening, and she feared that he might push her away. But then his fingers spread out to span the back of her waist.

"How could you believe that you didn't tempt me, my Sophia?" he asked quietly. "How could you have imagined that I didn't want everything you offered and more?"

"But..."

He silenced her with the barest brush of his lips across hers. "But I knew what was mine to take and what was not. Your father had spoken often of his plans for your future."

Sophia's heart soared. Lucien did desire her.

He had been tempted.

But he had done what was right.

Sophia smiled up at him in delight. Lucien held her other hand fast and turned her in place, murmuring the steps to the dance in her ear. His face was close enough that she could turn and kiss him, and she swore she could feel the beat of his heart so near her own. It was hard to concentrate on his instructions, but she didn't want this moment to end.

Ever.

The music began again and the candle flickered to life. It made no sense, but Sophia didn't care. They danced, their speed increasing as Sophia learned the steps. In no time, they were whirling around the floor of the room.

The music sped faster and faster, and Lucien's sapphire gaze bored into her own, his satisfaction more than clear. She smiled up at him, loving him anew, trusting him, wanting him as she had once before.

There was only Lucien, only Lucien and the spellbinding dance, only Lucien and the future that had been stolen from them both.

When the music came to an end with a flourish, he halted but didn't release her from his embrace. Sophia whispered his name, hearing the entreaty in her voice.

And her heart soared when he bent and captured her lips beneath his own.

~

SOPHIA'S KISS was a taste of Heaven, when Lucien was consigned to Hell.

Yet she was so irresistible that he couldn't end it, even knowing he should.

It was just a kiss, just unbearably sweet and hot, just a reminder of everything that would never be his. It warmed him to his marrow, compelled him to draw her closer, to partake of the feast she offered, to imagine what might have been. He might have taken more from her and surrendered to temptation, but the baron whispered in his ear.

"I like women with daring," he said in that familiar patois, and Lucien's blood turned to ice. "You can bring her with you."

Lucien tore his lips from Sophia's and held her at arm's length, appalled by the suggestion. The sight of her surprise made his heart clench. Her lips were swollen, her cheeks were flushed and her nipples were pert beneath her shift. Her gaze was filled with a confusion that was too familiar to be borne.

He shouldn't have confessed so much to her.

He shouldn't have confided in her.

He shouldn't have let her touch the charm.

He felt the baron's interest and knew he had put her at risk.

"Go to bed, Miss Findlay," he snapped, speaking so harshly that her eyes flashed a beguiling fire.

The baron chuckled as Lucien marched to the harpsichord and snatched up the charm. He strode to the door, snatching his coat on the way, and jamming the charm into the pocket.

"Then go to London," he ordered. "Take Larousse with you."

He saw Sophia part her lips to argue, but pivoted and left the room.

Distance was the only way to ensure he didn't take more from her than he had any right to claim.

He had to keep away from her for just two more days.

Even if his heart yearned to spend every moment with his beloved.

SOPHIA DID NOT SLEEP.

Not after Lucien's kiss had made her blood simmer. She was restless, her thoughts churning, her fears multiplying in the moonlight. There had to be a solution, even if Lucien wouldn't share it or didn't know it.

She dressed with haste in the morning and went in search of Larousse.

She found him on the stairs, carrying a pair of black boots polished to a gleam. "Were you there when the baron was invoked?" she demanded, knowing they wouldn't have much time.

Larousse, to his credit, didn't pretend ignorance. "Are you mad? I would never have let him do it."

"When he loses his soul to—"

Larousse held up a finger to keep her from saying the name aloud.

Sophia corrected herself. "To the wager, he must also lose his life."

"I cannot imagine it would be otherwise." Larousse shook his head, then made to continue.

"And the seven years ends when?"

"Tomorrow night."

Sophia was horrified. "He shouldn't have done it."

"He gave his word to you."

"I never expected him to keep it, certainly not at such a price."

"But it is done. A *loa* does not negotiate once the deal is made"

"What can I do?" Sophia made a sound of frustration when Larousse didn't answer. "What do you know of his plans? What does he mean to do?"

Larousse sighed, glanced up the stairs, then leaned closer to whisper. "He almost has all of your father's legacy. There is one last piece. There will be one last game."

"St. Maurice," Sophia whispered.

Larousse nodded. "He kept his word on principle, but now that he knows you're alive, it will all be left to you. I already have one letter to his solicitor. You will have the freedom to do as you desire, Miss Brisbane. He has bought you this."

Sophia's heart clenched. "The price is too high if it means losing Lucien forever. You have to tell me when and where the game is. I have to stop him!"

"They meet at ten tomorrow night," Larousse replied. "At the tavern in Bocka Morrow, the Mermaid's Kiss. He's booked a private room, dinner first, the game later."

"So late?" Sophia asked and Larousse nodded.

"On November 1, all the baron's debts come due. The game must be done by midnight."

Less than two days away. Sophia seized Larousse's sleeve when he would have turned away. "I want to be there. I need your assistance!"

Larousse shook his head. "He will never allow it."

"I beg of you!"

"You know that only one thing heals all wounds." When she shook her head because she didn't understand, Larousse leaned down and whispered something in French. His accent was such that Sophia couldn't understand him clearly.

"What do you mean?" she demanded.

Nelson came into view at the foot of the stairs, carrying the breakfast tray for Lady North Barrows, and surveyed them both. "Well, well," she said, her tone knowing.

Sophia realized she had her hand upon Larousse's sleeve and that they were bent together like lovers.

Or conspirators.

Larousse inclined his head to the lady's maid and continued up the stairs with purpose.

"Strange place to find affection, Miss Findlay," Nelson said on her way past. "But I always thought there was more to you than met the eye."

Sophia felt her cheeks burn as she descended to the kitchens, hearing the whispers begin to follow her. She had more important matters to consider, though. How could she save Lucien?

What had Larousse said?

THERE WAS something distinctly odd about Miss Findlay's manner.

Eurydice had noticed the change as soon as *Grandmaman* had announced their journey to Castle Keyvnor. She had assumed at first that their governess didn't like to travel, but that woman's manner had become progressively more unusual with each passing day.

Eurydice was certain that Miss Findlay had blushed when Lucien de Roye had invaded the library the day before. *Blushed.* At her age. She must be over forty!

And why had Lucien de Roye come into the library at all? Eurydice had not been fooled by his survey of Daphne. No, he wasn't intrigued by her older sister—which was to his credit in Eurydice's view. She had heard him simply listen to *Grandmaman's* comments in the corridor, as if such scathing conclusions about his character were irrelevant.

Did he truly not care?

Or was he in disguise? Eurydice liked that notion. He could be a spy, on a mission for the crown. He was French, after all. Maybe he spied upon Napoleon. She was sure that would suit his daring nature. Her cousins said he was an excellent shot, always dueling and winning.

Always gambling and winning. He was a rogue, to be sure, but Eurydice decided it would be much better if he had a heart of gold.

Miss Findlay was late this morning, and looked flustered when she arrived. She even appeared to be younger, as if her hair had turned less gray overnight. She seemed to be distracted, too, as if she considered a problem beyond awakening a fascination with German grammar in Daphne. Eurydice noted those inconsistencies and wondered at them.

It was a mystery, and she was going to solve it.

THERE HAD NEVER BEEN a day when Sophia had less patience with her charges. They had met various cousins and second cousins the afternoon before and were filled with new information and excitement.

"There's a ghost in this castle," Daphne pronounced as soon as Sophia entered the library.

She was late, and to her amazement, the girls were already seated with their German textbooks open.

"There are *two* ghosts," Eurydice corrected. "One in the attic and one under the stairs." She nodded with the surety of someone who had done her research. "The woman is in the attic and the man is under the stairs. There may be even more."

Daphne waved off this clarification as irrelevant.

"The woman is the one who screamed last night," Eurydice said, but Sophia hadn't heard a scream. Just the music. She felt hot in recollection of her dance with Lucien and irritated anew that she had no scheme to save him.

Daphne continued. "There are witches in the village, who sell love spells."

"What do you care about love spells?"

"I will buy one to make Lucien de Roye fall in love with me!"

Sophia cleared her throat, noticing how keenly Eurydice was watching her. "Your grandmother would scarcely approve of that course," she said crisply.

"I'll bet he is a man who knows how to kiss," Daphne said, propping her chin upon her hand. Sophia felt her cheeks heat. "I've decided that I will only marry a man who knows how to kiss."

"Who is the son of a duke, and handsome, and rich," Eurydice said with scorn. "I'm sure there are thousands of them to be had."

Daphne grimaced at her sister. "All I need is one."

"Then why do you care about Lucien de Roye?" Eurydice asked. "He isn't a duke and will never be one."

"He will be my lover," Daphne said smoothly. "I will marry the duke who knows how to kiss, bear him sons, then take M. de Roye as my lover."

"I doubt he will wait that long for you."

"You are just jealous, because he looked longest at me!"

"I thought he was most interested in Miss Findlay."

Sophia glanced up in shock, only to find both girls staring at her. She opened her grammar book with purpose. "We will walk to the village this afternoon to see the witches," she said, making no effort to simplify the phrase.

There was silence for a long moment. Daphne folded her arms across her chest and glared at Sophia.

"*Wir werden zu Fuß das Dorf an diesem Nachmittag zu sehen, die Hexen,*" Eurydice finally said with triumph in her tone.

"*Je vais prendre un amant français après j'épouser un duc,*" Daphne said smoothly and with conviction.

Sophia blinked in surprise.

"I thought you hated French," Eurydice said.

Daphne smiled. "I just needed the right incentive." Her smile broadened. "Perhaps I need a better tutor."

Sophia raised her hand to her brow. The last thing she needed was Daphne seeking out Lucien when the baron was preparing to take his toll. Then she blinked, realizing that Larousse had spoken in French.

L'amour vainc toutes choses.

That was what Larousse had said. *Love conquers all.*

What if *she* seduced Lucien?

Would that expression of her love save him from the baron?

He had refused to ruin her before, but Sophia wasn't inclined to take a refusal from him this time. Even if her choice failed to save him, didn't she want to be with him one time before he was lost forever? Even if his soul was sacrificed, Sophia realized she couldn't lose Lucien without one last kiss.

Or more.

SOPHIA'S PULSE was fluttering when the harpsichord music began to echo through the halls once more. The moon was almost full, its light shining brightly through her window.

She hadn't even made a pretense of retiring. She'd been sitting on the side of her bed, in the dark, for hours. She would have loved to have had a bath, but there was no question of her requesting such a luxury as a governess. She'd fetched her own hot water and made do. She wore her shift, her dress without stays, and her shoes without stockings. She had no notion of whether she might be able to seduce Lucien, much less whether it would matter to his fate.

The one thing she knew was that the man she loved was doomed, and she would do whatever she could to save him.

She doubted Lucien would make it easy for her.

She didn't intend to be turned aside.

Not this time. She'd start with a kiss. Maybe another dance. Maybe she'd touch him. When his life was at risk, she didn't think she could go too far. Sophia swallowed at her own audacity and resolve.

The first bar hadn't even finished when she rose to her feet. Her hair was brushed out, and there was no powder in it to disguise its color. Miss Findlay's glasses were abandoned on the small night table.

Sophia Brisbane meant to claim her one desire this very night.

LUCIEN TRIED to hide his impatience with the baron's restless fingers. He supposed this would be the last night he would have to be troubled by the wild music. There was no instrument at the tavern—maybe the baron would hum his favored melodies. Lucien knew he would have little opportunity to miss the sound of it. He paced the length of the music room and back, ignoring how the candle flames danced in time to the baron's raucous playing.

Just after the stroke of midnight on Samhain, he'd be dead.

Before that, he reminded himself, he would have won back Sophia's inheritance, written to the solicitor to make it hers, and ensured that her life was as filled with opportunity as could be. Before he died, Lucien would have kept his promise to her, and no matter what else he had done in his life, that would be his measure.

The music made him feel the power of the baron surging within him. Would he miss that?

No, he would miss Sophia.

He would regret the pleasure they hadn't shared.

He'd avoided her all day long and into the evening, and missed her already. Would she come when she heard the baron's music on this night? The baron grinned and did a little trill with his fingers, then attacked the keyboard again.

It gave Lucien a bad feeling.

Then there was a light tap at the door.

Lucien spun to look across the room, wondering whether he had imagined the sound. Certainly, he had imagined his conviction that it had to be Sophia. The baron shook his head and winked, even as his fingers fell on the keys with new enthusiasm.

It must be Philip, come to chastise him about the music.

If that man meant to lecture him again, Lucien wouldn't listen. He crossed the floor and flung open the door, a stern word dying on his lips when he found Sophia there.

Sophia, as she filled his dreams.

There was no pretense of her being Miss Findlay, not this time. Her hair was brushed out in gleaming waves that fell over her shoulders to her elbows. The lantern light picked out its golden glints and made her eyes look wide and dark. She appeared to be both uncertain but resolute, a combination he remembered so well that his heart clenched.

His Sophia would face dragons when she believed herself to be right.

She was even facing him.

"You shouldn't be here," Lucien said, trying to sound stern, but her fingertips landed upon his mouth. She studied him, leaning closer, and he took a step back. Too late, he realized that she would only follow him into the room. She kept her hand upon his lips, doing just as anticipated, then shut the door behind them. She studied him so long that he thought his heart would burst, then stretched to her toes to replace her fingers with her lips.

Lucien should have retreated. He should have turned away. But once her mouth was upon his, her breasts against his chest, her hands in his hair, Lucien was lost.

He didn't want to be found.

It was his last chance to taste Sophia, and he wasn't nearly strong enough to deny temptation this time. Their kiss was feverish, hungry, filled with a desperation that told him she understood his fate. Once again, their thoughts were as one. Once again, they sought the same goal. His fingers were in her hair, her hands framed his face, her kiss demanded more. He smelled her scent and caught her closer as he deepened his kiss.

When he broke their kiss, she smiled at him.

"Ruin me," she invited in a whisper, just as she had once before.

The ardor shining in her eyes undid him completely. She loved him, despite what he had done, and this time, Lucien wouldn't refuse her invitation.

He captured her mouth beneath his own once more, and swept Sophia into his arms. He carried her to a settee in triumph, barely noticing the baron's departure as he began a long-overdue seduction.

CHAPTER 4

Sophia awakened to the distinctive sound of an umbrella rapped upon a hardwood floor. She tried to sit up but it was too late. Her shift was untied, her hair in disarray. She was yet on the settee in the music room. The candles had guttered themselves and Lucien dozed beside her, his hand locked possessively over her bare breast.

Lady North Barrows, dressed in full black splendor, stood in the doorway of the music room. Her expression was more than disapproving, her sharp gaze unlikely to have missed a single detail.

Even Sophia's nipple caught between Lucien's nimble fingers.

"Well, well," Lady North Barrows said. "I now see, Miss Findlay, that you are a poor choice to teach my granddaughters about decorum." She scowled. "I had disregarded Nelson's tidings of your conduct, but clearly, in granting you the benefit of the doubt, I erred."

Sophia could not find it within herself to apologize, much less to ask forgiveness. She was sorry that Lady North Barrows was disappointed in her, and couldn't blame that lady since she regretted the deception herself, but she was also filled with a burgeoning sense of relief.

No more lies.

Her life could be her own again.

Lady North Barrows sniffed. "Consider yourself dismissed from my service. I will give you no letters. If you send word to the dower house of your address, I will have your belongings forwarded, otherwise, they will be burned." She rapped the umbrella twice on the floor for emphasis, then marched away.

"A complication," Lucien drawled from beside Sophia, but the twinkle in his eyes prompted her smile. He looked like his former self, and his hand was warm upon her skin. Sophia dared to hope that she might be saving him.

"You *are* wicked."

"*Au contraire.* You are the one who engineered this seduction, Miss Findlay. I profess myself shocked by your disregard for social convention." He stretched, yawned, and drew her back into his arms. He traced a lazy circle around her nipple with a fingertip and kissed her neck. Sophia thought she felt him purr. She felt like purring herself. "Even if I was powerless to resist your charms."

The harpsichord began to play abruptly, a little trill that might have been celebratory if not for the change that came over Lucien. He got to his feet in one fluid movement and that glitter reclaimed his eyes. The room chilled. His eyes narrowed as he stared at the instrument, and he paled so that Sophia wondered what his *loa* looked like.

"Go," he said, his tone so dismissive that he might have slapped her. "We have done what you wished to see done."

"What I wished to see done?" Sophia echoed. She got to her feet and pointed at the settee. "I was not alone last night, Lucien de Roye, and you were not seduced against your will."

He stood back, so wary that her hope faded. "Yet you are ruined, just the same, and I have a wager to keep. Farewell." He paused at the threshold and glanced back, as if he couldn't keep himself from doing so.

As if he didn't trust himself to leave. "Be happy, Sophia." His words were softer, heartfelt.

"Not without you."

"You must be."

Sophia watched him go, her frustration rising. The harpsichord played with wild abandon, as if the player were triumphant. Surely she hadn't risked everything to gain nothing in return?

Why hadn't her love saved Lucien?

She marched back across the room and swept a hand across the keys of the instrument, as if to push away those ghostly fingers. It fell silent. "I won't let you have him," she declared to the room, which appeared to be empty.

"You don't have a choice, *ma chère*," a man said, his shadowy figure visible on the far side of the harpsichord. He spoke in French, in a patois that Sophia hadn't heard for a long time. "The wager must be paid."

"In blood?"

"As the best ones always are." There was another trill of notes, and Sophia stepped back, shivering as a new chill swept through the room.

"There has to be a way," she murmured, almost to herself.

"*Absolument, ma chère.* You and I could come to an agreement, to be sure," a man whispered in her ear. Out of the corner of her eye, she could see him with sudden clarity, an older black man attired as if for a ball, a red rose in his buttonhole. There was laughter in his eyes and hunger in his smile. He blew her a kiss, then disappeared into nothing at all.

Sophia shuddered, revulsion feeding her determination.

She had to save Lucien. Somehow.

LUCIEN COULD HAVE REMAINED in his bedchamber on his last day of life, but he wasn't one to hide from confrontation. He could have gone to the tavern and met with Lyndenhurst, but that pleasure could wait. He could have gone for a ride, or joined the other men to hunt, but his thoughts were locked upon the sweet passion he had shared with Sophia.

She was ruined and without a position. He knew she would be wealthy, but she didn't, not as yet.

And he knew she was fond of her charges.

He had an unassailable urge to defend her.

The two girls were in the library, enduring a lecture from their grandmother. "And so, in the face of considerable impropriety, Miss Findlay has left our service."

"What kind of impropriety?" demanded the younger and certainly more clever of the pair.

"I don't care," the older declared. "I hate German lessons."

"Your German lessons will continue, with or without Miss Findlay's instruction," Lady North Barrows said firmly, rapping her umbrella once on the floor for emphasis. "However, that will have to wait until I find a new tutor for you."

"Then we can abandon our lessons today," the older one said with evident delight. "The others are going to the village, and..."

"And we shall review proper etiquette for dining," Lady North Barrows interrupted. "I would wish for you to take at least one meal with the other guests on this visit, but your conduct at luncheon yesterday was utterly unacceptable."

"Spoons and forks," the younger one complained. "I much prefer German."

"Perhaps an instructor could be found," Lucien said, revealing his presence by stepping into the doorway. The older girl's features lit with pleasure, Lady North Barrows looked grim and the younger girl smiled at him in welcome. He nodded to her. "*Fräulein Findlay ist ein Betrüger,*" he said in a whisper, confessing that their governess had been in disguise.

"I knew it!" that girl said. "And she's an heiress in hiding."

"*Sie ist in der Tat eine Erbin in der Verkleidung,*" he confirmed.

"What are you talking about?" the older girl cried, rising to her feet in exasperation. "What is he saying?"

Lady North Barrows tapped her umbrella, gesturing for her granddaughter to be silent. "What heiress?" Her eyes gleamed. "And how much of a fortune?"

"*Sie ist die Tochter von Sir William Brisbane.*"

"The daughter of Sir William Brisbane!" Lady North Barrows repeated. "Not *that* Brisbane, of Brisbane's Emporium?"

"The very one," Lucien confirmed.

"Well, then." Lady North Barrows took only a moment to absorb these tidings. "How much?"

"Am Morgen geht es dreißig tausend Pfund, sowie einige Eigenschaften."

"Thirty thousand pounds!" the younger girl exclaimed. *"And property?"*

When Lucien nodded, Lady North Barrows sat down heavily.

"Why will it change by morning?" the younger girl demanded.

"Because I have yet to win the rest of it. It was lost by her brother in a gaming hell, and I have recovered almost every shilling."

"Why would you undertake such a thing?" Lady North Barrows demanded. It was clear she expected him to confess at least admiration for Sophia, but Lucien would not give Sophia any reason to mourn his loss.

Lucien held the older woman's gaze steadily. "Because I promised her I would do so, no matter what the cost to myself." He smiled. "And so, it shall be done." He bowed to the trio, taking advantage of Lady North Barrows' rare silence. *"Au revoir, mes petites,"* he said, then left them with much to consider.

He had only taken a few steps before the younger girl exclaimed. "I *knew* she was an heiress in disguise, and now she'll be rescued by the prince who everyone thinks to be a scoundrel!"

"I never thought he was a scoundrel," insisted the older girl.

The distinct rap of an umbrella silenced both girls, and Lady North Barrows' declaration was the last thing Lucien heard. "Thirty thousand pounds. I think we shall have to ensure that Miss Brisbane is safely escorted to London."

"London!" the older girl cried with abandon.

But Sophia, he knew, would not be in need of such an escort. Philip could take her wherever she desired in Lucien's own carriage.

It would all be hers by morning.

For he would be dead.

Not, alas, a scoundrel revealed to be a prince intent upon marrying her.

He returned to his chamber and ensured that his belongings were packed. He took the stuffed charm that he had carried for seven years and put it into his pocket, for it was bound to his destiny as well.

THE LAST PERSON Sophia ever wanted to see again was Eugene Tremblay, the Marquess of Lyndenhurst. The sight of him, dismounting from a carriage outside the tavern in Bocka Morrow, sent fear surging through her and brought her steps to an abrupt halt.

She stepped into the shadow of a tree to verify that it was him. Oh yes. It couldn't be anyone else. Lyndenhurst was still tall and lean, his nose was still hooked like a beak. He looked like the predator she knew he was.

I will have it all, Miss Brisbane, without regards to your ambitions. You will soon realize that it would have been much more comfortable for you to have become my wife.

Sophia caught her breath, pushing the memory of that exchange from her mind.

Truth be told, she shouldn't have been surprised by the sight of Lyndenhurst. Lucien meant to gamble for St. Maurice, and she knew that Lyndenhurst had taken every crumb of her father's estate from Charles.

Charles. Dear impetuous Charles. It was too easy to recall her brother's despair at the loss of his inheritance and his subsequent flight north with his beloved Elizabeth. Her parents had never been enamored of the match, but once Charles had lost his fortune, they had forbidden it. Charles and Elizabeth had taken matters into their own hands and fled for Gretna Green, but they had never reached their destination. Dead in a carriage accident, both of them lost.

Sophia swallowed, reminding herself that they were together forever.

The loss of their lives was even more horrific if Lucien was right and Lyndenhurst had cheated to seduce Charles into risking everything he owned.

Sophia took a steadying breath and looked again. The carriage had no insignia, though she doubted Lyndenhurst had given up either of his teams. She supposed he hadn't wanted anyone to know his destination. He shook out his coat, sparing a disapproving glance to the village as he donned his hat. He paid the driver and made a sharp comment, then strode toward the Mermaid's Kiss before the driver had urged the horses onward again.

What had Lucien offered to tempt Lyndenhurst to wager St. Maurice?

Sophia clenched her fists and watched Lyndenhurst enter the tavern. It was wrong beyond all belief that this man should survive and Lucien should die. Larousse wouldn't contrive her entry into the game room, so Sophia had to find a solution. She burrowed in her satchel and retrieved Miss Findlay's spectacles, which she had declined to wear this day. Fortunately, her warmest bonnet had a wide brim, so her face would be disguised. She doubted that Lyndenhurst would grant her a second glance even if she ran right into him. He had admired her fortune, not her person, after all.

She had to enter the tavern, though, because she had to find the keeper.

Then she had to convince him to accept a barter with her. Sophia knew exactly what she wanted.

It was better that Lucien didn't see Sophia again.

He told himself that repeatedly throughout the day, although he didn't believe it for a moment. He wished he could have said one last farewell, even though he knew he would have been tempted to never leave her again. The baron was close behind him all day long, his cold presence a reminder that the grave awaited Lucien this very night.

The skies were clear when he rode to Bocka Morrow in the evening, and the moon was full. He met Lyndenhurst for dinner at the tavern, as arranged, and had the meal served in the private room upstairs that would be the site of the game. Lyndenhurst complained about the rustic nature of the accommodation and the trials of his journey, but Lucien knew the other man would have followed him to Hell and back for the prize of immortality.

His eyes were shining in anticipation of his win.

Lucien also guessed that Lyndenhurst would try to cheat.

The meal was indifferent, but neither of them cared about the fare.

The serving maid was old and slow, but that didn't matter either. She might have listened to their conversation, but they spoke of the weather and little else. The wine was musty, but neither of them would drink much until the game was over. Lucien had brought rum for the baron and offered some to Lyndenhurst who declined.

A clock somewhere in the tavern struck eleven.

Lucien nodded to Philip, who stepped out of the shadows to deal.

Lyndenhurst leaned forward. "I brought cards," he said, offering a sealed deck.

"We will use mine or none at all," Lucien said, and Lyndenhurst's lips tightened. "You are welcome to examine them before we play."

Philip laid out the cards on the table for examination before the game. They were new and unblemished, every one accounted for and no extras in the deck. Lyndenhurst checked them with care. He wanted the secret, though, and wanted it badly enough to abandon the protest. He nodded once and sat back.

The cold filled Lucien's mind, the sense of pending death growing ever stronger. He tugged on his gloves, wondering whether his fingers would be too cold to hold the cards. The room seemed to fill with a fog, and he focused his attention on the cards.

This game would be his last living feat.

The letter was written to his solicitor and Philip had instructions to take the deed and ride to London. All would be set to rights.

Lucien thought he felt a draft, as if a door opened. He heard the music of a familiar tune played upon a harpsichord, although that was impossible. Neither of his companions seemed to hear it and he knew that the baron arrived for his due.

Not long now.

Philip acted as dealer, disapproval emanating from him in waves, but Lucien ignored his old friend. He fought the urge to shiver and struggled to draw breath into his lungs. His heart slowed and he felt that he walked in a dream.

He won the first game with a queen and a ten. Lyndenhurst had a jack and a nine.

That man's expression grew more grim as the cards were dealt again. The baron gripped Lucien's shoulder then, his bony fingers digging into the flesh as a wave of pure ice coursed through Lucien's veins.

"I have dug your grave," the baron whispered in that familiar patois. "Everything is ready, *mon petit*. The time is near."

Lucien looked down and could see the baron's hand on his shoulder. He could feel the cold emanating from that grip to fill his body. He saw a red rose in his buttonhole that hadn't been there before.

The music was louder, rising and falling in a mad cacophony of sound. The moonlight slanted through the window, making the scene look unreal.

Two more games. Lucien nodded to Philip.

Lyndenhurst was dealt a nine, face up on the table.

Lucien was dealt a king, face up on the table.

Lucien watched Lyndenhurst as he looked at his second card and couldn't guess what he had been dealt. Lyndenhurst was impassive, as usual. Lucien was dealt a nine. The baron chuckled. Lucien knew that if he took another card, it would be a deuce.

Lyndenhurst took another card.

The baron prodded, but Lucien held. The baron pushed, but Lucien held.

Lyndenhurst held. He then turned over his cards to reveal a nine, a seven and a four. Twenty. Lucien congratulated him and turned over his cards. The baron crowed a protest, his fingers like icicles stabbed into Lucien's flesh.

"Nineteen!" Lyndenhurst declared with a cold smile. "Then the rumors are false. You can lose!"

"Everyone can lose," Lucien said mildly. He spoke aloud to remind the baron. "But it's best of three." The baron chuckled with glee and Lyndenhurst drummed his fingers on the table in a rare show of impatience.

"My luck has turned just in time," Lyndenhurst said, eyes shining. His voice could have come from a thousand miles away. Everything glittered to Lucien's view, like it was coated in frost. His heart slowed and he had a hard time drawing a breath.

The clock struck the half hour, and the chiming made Lucien's bones rattle.

The tension in the room rose palpably even as the cold increased. Lucien couldn't feel his feet anymore. They were frigid. He knew he was shivering. Philip stirred up the fire in the grate before he shuffled the cards and Lyndenhurst exhaled in vexation.

"Don't take all night at it," he snapped, and Philip returned to the table to deal.

First card to Lucien, face up. It was an eight.

Lyndenhurst's first card was an ace.

Lucien's second card was a nine.

Lyndenhurst was pleased with his second card, and Lucien expected it was a ten or a face card.

He indicated that he would have another, his finger shaking with the cold.

A three. He had twenty.

Lyndenhurst took another card, his features implacable. The second card hadn't been a ten, then.

Philip gave Lucien an expectant look.

The baron's breath was on Lucien's ear, his grip tight on Lucien's shoulders. Lucien could smell the roses in their buttonholes, and the stench of death the blooms failed to disguise. He felt a cold wind in his hair and it took an eternity for his heart to beat again.

Lucien beckoned for another card.

Of course, it was an ace.

Lyndenhurst held.

Lucien held.

Lyndenhurst turned over his cards. The seven was joined by an eight and a five.

Twenty.

He eyed Lucien with expectation and hope.

Lucien turned over his cards, smearing them across the table. "Twenty-one," he said, his voice no more than a whisper of frost. "St. Maurice is mine."

Lyndenhurst sat back, his displeasure more than clear. He frowned and seized a satchel, opening it to reveal the documents inside. They were surrendered to Lucien, who gave them to Philip.

His word was kept.

Sophia would have her father's estate returned to her. It was only a measure of what she had lost, but he had kept his word.

It was over and he should have felt triumphant. Instead, he was so cold that he could feel little at all. He might as well have been dead already. He was shaking to his very marrow.

Lyndenhurst shoved the cards across the table in frustration. "What else do you want?" he demanded. "I haven't come all this way to go home with an empty purse. I want your secret!"

Lucien parted his lips but couldn't make a sound. The baron's arms were closing around him as if he were no more than a child and he didn't have the strength to fight.

Why should he fight? The price was due.

"How badly do you want it?" a woman demanded.

Lucien looked up to see Sophia by the chamber door. When she remained in the shadows, she might have been no more substantial than a dream. Was he dreaming of her presence? No. He belatedly realized that she wore the dress of the old serving maid, the one they had ignored during their meal. Now that she stood straight and had cast off her cap, he recognized the truth.

When she stepped forward, she seemed to be surrounded by golden light, like an angel come to save him. Lucien knew it couldn't be so, but his heart skipped at the sight of her, sending heat through his veins.

"Too late, *ma chère*," the baron murmured, but Lucien was glad that his dying glance would be of Sophia, resolve shining in her eyes. He drank in the sight of her, then the music rose to a deafening crescendo, the baron's embrace tightened, and there was only cold and emptiness.

Lucien looked terrible.

He was pale and Sophia could see that he was shaking like an old man. His lips looked slightly blue and she guessed that he was cold.

As cold as the grave.

His eyes were the eyes of a stranger, the blue as frosty as a winter morning.

She could almost see the baron behind him. There was a man's shadowy silhouette there, and when she averted her gaze, she could see the old black man in his fine dinner jacket from the corner of her eye. As she watched, the baron's arms closed around Lucien, and Lucien sagged against him, as if he had gone to sleep.

Why did Lucien have a red rose in his buttonhole, just like that of his *loa*?

He could not be lost, not yet!

The clock chimed the third quarter of the hour.

She strode to Lucien's side and reached into his pocket. She found the charm there and claimed it, even as the *loa's* chuckle filled the chamber.

"He is mine, *ma chère*," came a whisper that was everywhere and nowhere, but Sophia held fast to the charm.

"No," she declared. "He is mine."

"I am owed a soul, *ma chère*."

And he would have it.

"What business is it of yours, woman? Get back to your labor and leave us in peace!" Lyndenhurst said, then seized Sophia's arm, perhaps to hurl her from the room. He caught his breath when Sophia looked up at him and paled. "Sophia Brisbane! I thought you were dead."

"I am not, sir, and I am once again in possession of my father's emporium."

Lyndenhurst's eyes glittered as he glanced at Lucien. "He *gave* it to you? He gave it away?"

"And the island," Larousse contributed. "I have the letter to the solicitor."

Lyndenhurst looked between Sophia and Lucien, his disdain clear. "He won to restore it all to a woman?"

"This one," Sophia thought with vigor. *"I will win this soul for you instead."*

The baron chuckled and she heard the harpsichord music once more. Lucien was pale and still but she could see that he was still breathing.

She had to risk it all to save his life. Sophia leaned closer to Lyndenhurst, her resolve to save Lucien giving her strength. "And I will wager it all, the entire fortune and St. Maurice."

Lyndenhurst's eyes lit. "In exchange for what?"

"You don't seem to have much left," Sophia observed. "Lucien told me you had lost your fortune."

Lyndenhurst's nostrils pinched. "There is no reason to discuss such details, though I suppose the daughter of a tradesman is accustomed to such vulgarity."

"Even I have heard the extent of your debts," Larousse said.

Sophia pulled up a chair and sat at the table. "Why not wager your soul, sir? Assuming you have one."

"Such audacity!" Lyndenhurst laughed. "How would you claim it? What would you do with it?" He shook his head, evidently thinking he risked little. "I will take your wager, Miss Brisbane, though do not blame me when you regret it."

"I will not regret it," Sophia said and nodded to Larousse. "I will see my brother avenged."

"Charles Brisbane was a fool, who did not understand his own incompetence at cards."

"Is it incompetent to be cheated?"

Lyndenhurst inhaled sharply. "Do you accuse me?"

"You seduced him at the gaming table. You let him win until he wagered it all. Then you won and he lost his entire inheritance."

"The follies of indulged young men are not my responsibility."

"Even though he died, along with his betrothed, as a result of losing his fortune?"

"Every carriage accident is not my concern." Lyndenhurst glared at Sophia. "I warned you not to break our betrothal, Miss Brisbane. I warned you that I would have it all, with or without you."

"So you did, but now I have it all once more." Sophia smiled.

Lyndenhurst's eyes flashed with annoyance. "Do we play or do we not, Miss Brisbane?"

"We play." Sophia heard a gleeful chuckle and the faint sound of harpsichord music. Larousse crossed himself and dealt the cards.

Lyndenhurst's first card was a queen.

Sophia's first card was a ten.

Lyndenhurst looked at his second card and almost smiled.

Sophia looked at her second card and laid her hand over it on the table.

Lyndenhurst beckoned for a third card.

Sophia held.

Lyndenhurst held.

Sophia turned over her cards. She had an ace with her ten. Twenty-one.

Lyndenhurst turned over his cards, his manner wary. He had a queen, a four and a six.

Twenty.

"So you have a beginner's good fortune." Lyndenhurst pushed to his feet, scorn curling his lip. "I should like to see you collect your due."

"Oh, I will," Sophia said with such conviction that Lyndenhurst paused to study her.

"Not everything can be bought and sold, Miss Brisbane."

"Not in this world, to be sure." Sophia flung the charm into the fire and it loosed a cloud of black smoke.

The clock struck midnight.

Sophia heard the baron howl with delight even as an unholy wind rushed through the chamber, like a winter wind bringing a storm. The lanterns were suddenly extinguished and the fire blazed high before it was snuffed out. The curtains whipped, the table was overset, and she closed her eyes against the wind's chilly fingers. She smelled roses and heard music at a deafening volume.

Lyndenhurst screamed.

The door slammed and the wind stilled as abruptly as it had started.

She opened her eyes to see that Lyndenhurst was gone. There was frost on the inside of the window, on what was left of the glass. Larousse ran a hand over his head as he looked about himself in wonder. The moonlight slanted through the broken window to touch Lucien's face.

Which had lost its pallor.

The rose was gone from his buttonhole and when he opened his eyes, they were the same clear honest blue that Sophia remembered from the first day they had met on the docks. He smiled and opened his arms to her, and she almost fell into his embrace.

"Is he gone?" she whispered, welcoming the warmth of him.

"Both of them are gone," he replied, his smile as open and admiring as it had ever been. "Because you did what had to be done."

"Because you gave me a hint."

"Because we defeated him together." And Lucien sealed his words with a thorough and most welcome kiss.

Sophia was vaguely aware that Larousse cleared his throat. "I shall see you in the morning, my lord, but not too early."

"No, not too early," Lucien said, breaking their kiss. He stared down at Sophia. "As much as I would like to make an early start back to London, I was invited to attend the reading of the will."

"Do you think the earl left you a legacy?" Sophia asked.

Lucien winced. "I can only hope it is not a harpsichord."

Sophia laughed at his rueful expression.

"So, Philip, we will stay through the second, then depart for London the following morning. It would be best to have legal matters arranged quickly so that we can sail home before the winter seas."

Home. Sophia smiled up at him. Home with Lucien. It was all she had ever wanted and more.

"Very good, sir."

"We shall have to restore the inventory of the emporium," she said.

"Of course. It would be best to oversee it personally." Lucien held her tightly. "Do you have any objection, Miss Brisbane, with dividing your time between London and St. Maurice?"

Sophia laughed again, more than pleased with the suggestion. "Not the least objection, sir. Our children will have need of English schools and St. Maurice summers."

Larousse cleared his throat again. "I will fetch Miss Brisbane's belongings for the morning," he said. "I trust there is nothing else you need this evening?"

"Not one thing. Thank you, Philp."

Larousse retreated, closing the door behind himself. Sophia smiled at the sound of his happy whistle as he left them together.

"A night alone with you in a tavern? I am truly ruined, M. de Roye," she teased.

Lucien slid a fingertip along her cheek. "I don't think you are totally ruined yet, Miss Brisbane," he murmured in reply, his eyes glowing. "But we have several nights to remedy that situation." He brushed his lips across hers. "I mean to leave you no choice but to marry me by special license as soon as we reach London."

Sophia laughed, unable to resist the opportunity to tease him. "I regret to inform you, sir, that I have no argument with that."

It was the last thing she said for quite some time, although she did continue to tease him, for that night and many more to come.

A DUKE BY ANY OTHER NAME

THE BRIDES OF NORTH BARROWS #2

Daphne Goodenham has always been determined to wed a duke—not just because she loves fine dresses and parties, but because she wants to guarantee that she and her sister are never destitute again. When she meets the Duke of Inverfyre, a notorious fop, she immediately notices intriguing inconsistencies. Is there more to the duke than meets the eye? Why would he hide the truth if he were handsome, young, rich and a duke?

Alexander, the Duke of Inverfyre, is bent on catching a notorious thief who injured his sister, no matter what the cost. But confronted by the lovely Miss Goodenham, Alexander's disguise proves to be no defense against her curiosity—and he has no resistance to her kiss. Will Daphne inadvertently foil Alexander's plan? Will he have to sacrifice her interest to avenge his sister? Or can Daphne ensure Alexander's triumph and make her own Christmas wish come true?

PROLOGUE

Airdfinnan Castle, Scotland—December 1811

Alexander Magnus Armstrong, Duke of Inverfyre, read his aunt's letter again and frowned. It was after dinner and he was alone in his library, the darkness of the night pressing against the windows and a robust fire blazing on the grate. He had been looking forward to an entire winter of savoring the pleasures of home.

The letter meant his desire was not to be.

He poured himself a port in consolation, took his favorite seat by the fire and sipped as he read the letter again. The last thing Alexander wanted to do was to abandon his sanctuary and ride for Cornwall, but it appeared that he had little choice.

He had baited a trap and his prey was poised to seize the cheese. It would be irresponsible to surrender the chase now.

Even if his sister Anthea would be disappointed.

Alexander frowned. His aunt, a baroness who had worked her way into every ballroom in London, was also his primary source of information. Penelope sent him chatty letters at regular intervals, cleverly managing to include all of the intelligence he needed amidst the drivel of who had cut whom and who had pawned their silver, substituting sterling for plate. No other soul could have read this missive and noticed the one gem of valuable information amidst the gossip.

In the employ of the crown, Alexander hunted criminals who preyed upon high society. He had been in pursuit of a jewel thief for a year. He had guessed long ago that the villain was the same man who had seen Anthea blamed for his crimes during her first season, but soon Alexander might be able to prove it. He had to catch the scoundrel in the act. A gentleman and gem collector who had experienced losses due to this very thief was aiding in the hunt. Mr. Timothy Cushing had shown the Eye of India to many in London and was dispatching it to the perfect recipient.

Alexander's aunt shared the news that her good friend, Mr. Cushing, would be giving the fabulous brooch as a surprise to Lady Tamsyn Hambly, who was being married at Castle Keyvnor in Cornwall at Christmas. Aunt Penelope speculated on the bride's delight at this surprise, for truly, who would not be thrilled?

Clearly, Alexander would also be spending Christmas in Cornwall, although not at Castle Keyvnor. The local village and its tavern would have to do.

He considered the calendar. Since it was only the beginning of December, he could arrive in time by carriage if he set out immediately.

He grimaced, for he was not yet ready to don his foppish disguise again.

Findlay entered with a tray and inhaled sharply, probably because his master had already poured his own port and was simultaneously making a face. "I apologize for the delay, Your Grace," he said quickly. "Or is it the quality of the port that causes disfavor?"

"Neither, Findlay. You were neither late nor remiss. I was bored with my aunt's tattle and too impatient to wait. Any blame is entirely mine."

The older man stole a glance at Alexander as he wiped the decanter and ensured that all was as it should be. "Is there any detail that I can repair, Your Grace?"

"No, Findlay. You will never change my aunt." Alexander smiled, then folded the letter and tucked it into his pocket. He surveyed the cozy library and sighed. "I will be departing at first light with the coach and six. I'll want the black team again, though Rodney will not be pleased to have them run again so soon."

"If he knows now, Your Grace, he will ensure that they are pampered tonight."

"Yes. The big coach, please. It gives me more room to stretch my legs."

"Oh, Alexander!" Anthea said from the doorway. "You can't be leaving. You've only just returned home." She looked to be on the verge of tears and Alexander hastily finished his port. At a telling glance, Findlay filled his glass again.

It was well established at Airdfinnan that the Duke of Inverfyre could not bear the sight of his sister's tears.

"I fear I must, Anthea, but will return as quickly as possible." Alexander nodded to Findlay. "Perhaps you could see to the details."

"Of course, Your Grace."

Alexander could see that Findlay was itching to know where he was going and why, but the older man didn't ask. "Could you send Haskell to me to discuss the packing of my portmanteau, as well, please?"

"Your portmanteau, sir?"

"Yes, I will be gone for at least a month, probably longer."

"Alexander!" Anthea protested. "What about Christmas?"

"You will enjoy the festivities without me." When she might have protested, he lifted a hand. "I am somewhat irked to be leaving again so quickly, but there is nothing to be done about it. Dr. MacEwan insists that I take the sea air in Cornwall in December."

To Alexander's dismay, a tear not only slid down Anthea's cheek but she came into the library to sit opposite him and make her appeal. "Dr. MacEwan," she muttered under her breath and dashed at her tears with her fingertips. "Is the air in January truly so different in Cornwall?"

"So he insists."

"I think him a fool. You are more hale than any seven men I know."

Findlay bowed and departed, so obviously wanting to linger and eavesdrop that Alexander smiled.

The change in his expression evidently encouraged his sister to speak her mind. "Of course, you would not have to worry so much about your health if you had an heir," she reminded him yet again. "High time it is, Alexander, for you to take a bride."

"Anthea!"

"It is fearsome quiet at Airdfinnan, Alexander, especially at Christmas. It would be much merrier with little ones underfoot." She smiled. "I wouldn't miss you so much if there were half a dozen children here."

"Then you should accept a suitor and have children of your own," Alexander suggested gently.

His sister blushed and dropped her gaze, her expression like a dagger to his heart. "Not I," she said softly, then forced a smile. "And it is you who must have a son to ensure the succession, after all. Is there a woman behind this speedy departure, or a damsel in distress?"

As much as he liked the bright gleam of curiosity in her eyes, Alexander could not lie to Anthea. "There is no damsel, in distress or otherwise."

Anthea made a face, then stole his glass, taking a tiny sip of the port. "I do not believe your health is compromised. I suspect you simply want away from here."

Alexander laughed. "Away from Airdfinnan is the last thing I desire." He could not keep himself from casting a longing glance over the library and its comforts.

"Then you should wed. You'd have every excuse to remain home then and it could only improve your health."

"Perhaps I will wed after you do," he teased.

"Perhaps I should wed after *you*," Anthea countered. "In fact, I will make you a wager, Alexander."

"Ladies do not wager, Anthea. Surely Mama taught you that."

"Surely she did, but I would like to, all the same." Anthea had her stubborn look, which was all too rare these days. It seemed she seldom cared sufficiently about any matter to be stubborn, and just the sight was enough to make Alexander take her wager, whatever it might be. "You always wish for me to return to London and society, at least for a season. I will go with you and your bride, once you choose to wed."

"Anthea!"

Anthea sat back, looking pleased with herself. "So, the sooner you wed, brother, the sooner I will follow go to London and find a husband."

"You mean to make a wager you will not be required to fulfill," he jested. "For each of us are as set against marriage as the other."

To his surprise, Anthea shook her head. "No, that is not true, Alexander. I would love to marry and to have children." Her tone was so wistful that he was prepared to find her a spouse this very night. "But it must be the right man, for I would have the same kind of love as Mama and Papa shared."

"Theirs was a rare bond."

"So, I must dream of what is mundane, instead of what is rare and precious?" she replied, her tone light. "Alexander, are you the brother I believe I know so well?"

He laughed. "A man has more time to linger over such a choice than a woman."

"Indeed, and I am already twenty-five, Alexander. You had best hurry to find your lady wife."

"It is not so simple as that..."

"No, it is not," Anthea agreed, interrupting him. She leaned forward, her skirts rustling as she removed something from her pocket. "Mama warned me of that. She told me to find a partner who was honest, and one with no secrets, one whose nature I could admire and whose appearance gave me pleasure. She told me the rest would follow."

"Did she?"

"And for you, I would add that your bride should be young, so she will have had less time to have cultivated secrets. You will be the one to teach her of many worldly matters, and she will adore you for it."

Alexander was amused. "Is that how a good marriage is contrived?"

"It will be so for you, I am certain of it. Here, I have a token for you."

Alexander extended his hand. Anthea dropped something small and round into it. It was black and about the size of a pea. He held the small dark sphere to the light, suspecting that he knew what it was. "A seed?"

Anthea laughed. "Not a seed, Alexander, *the* seed. The seed from the vine of Airdfinnan, from the last time it grew and flowered."

"That is a fairy tale!" Alexander had heard the fanciful stories about the thorned vine that covered the walls of his castle and home, that it was from a seed brought back from the crusades by a knight, that after its arrival at Airdfinnan it grew only when the laird of Airdfinnan met his bride-to-be. He certainly did not believe that its perfume abetted the laird's courtship and conquest.

But Anthea clearly did. "It is not! Mama told me that it grew when Papa courted her, and that she had never seen the like of it. She told me that its perfume was like an enchantment. Papa's mother advised her upon your birth to save the seeds for your courtship."

"Mama gave me several herself, before she died. They never grew, Anthea, which is proof that the tale is nonsense."

"It is proof only that you had not met the lady who could claim your heart. Certainly, Miranda Delaney, no matter how fine her lineage and how lovely her countenance, would never have held your affections for long. What a viper!" Anthea's disdain was clear, though the very mention of Miranda's name reminded Alexander what a fool he had been. "Her memory should not be of sufficient merit to keep you from happiness. That is why the seed did not grow."

Alexander tossed the seed into the air and caught it. "And what would you have me do? Plant a seed each time I meet a pretty woman?"

"I would have you seek a suitable woman, one who is honest and true, and pretty enough to tempt you, just as Mama advised."

"And young."

"And young," Anthea agreed. "And if she is amenable to your attentions, I would have you plant the seed, so that the vine might aid your suit."

Alexander drained his glass and set it aside, rising to his feet with purpose. "I suppose this errand cannot wait?"

Anthea laughed. "I should not delay in your place, Alexander, not if I wished my only sister off the shelf next season."

"You are relying upon my taking this wager."

Anthea took a deep breath. "I am seeking inspiration, Alexander. I know I should wed. I know I should leave Airdfinnan." He watched her pleat her dress with nervous fingers. She swallowed and he ached at the sight of her unhappiness. "I know I should return to London and put all the rumors to rest." Her gaze met his. "But I am afraid, Alexander."

He dropped to his knee before her. "You know I would go with you, and defend you..."

She silenced him with a touch. "I know, but it would be so much easier to go with you and your wife, if she is your beloved. Your happiness would give me strength, and she would be able to accompany me where you cannot go."

She was so lovely in her appeal that Alexander felt her will becoming his own. He had always been damnably susceptible to feminine beauty, and the malady had become more acute while he hunted the thief. The fire caught the red-gold of Anthea's curls as if to toy with it, and her blue eyes were wide. She looked fragile and vulnerable and he wanted nothing more than to see her hand placed in that of a deserving and honorable man. Even her conviction in the truth of the tale of the vine was compelling to him on this night.

He bent and touched his lips to her fingers. "I will try, Anthea."

She smiled. "That is all a person of sense can expect, Alexander."

Alexander had no sooner put the seed into the pocket of his waistcoat than his valet tapped once upon the door, then entered the library.

Rupert Haskell was of an age with Alexander, the youngest son of a baron who had lost his father's favor. He had chosen to earn his way and Alexander had been glad to give the other man a position. Haskell had a keen affection for travel and a similar loyalty to the crown. He had dark hair and a ready smile, but his wits were quick and his blade was quicker. He was a good man to have at one's back, particularly in Alexander's chosen profession. He was completely in Alexander's confidence and when alone, they spoke as friends, not as master and servant, for they had been such at school.

Haskell spared a quick glance at Anthea, as if surprised to find her there, and color rose on the back of his neck.

"I will leave you to your arrangements, Alexander," Anthea said, rising to her feet. "Godspeed to you, for I'm certain you'll be gone before I rise in the morning." She kissed Alexander's cheeks then left, barely sparing Rupert a glance.

Rupert looked after her with an unmistakable yearning in his gaze, at least until Alexander cleared his throat. The other man then closed the door. "Where?" he asked, mouthing the word more than saying it aloud.

"Cornwall," Alexander said, replying in kind.

Rupert crossed the room and noted the letter on Alexander's desk. He smiled. "Your aunt?"

"Just as planned."

"The full rig?" Rupert asked, referring to Alexander's disguise.

Alexander sighed and nodded, then sat at his desk to respond to his aunt.

"Thank goodness those salmon and lemon striped trousers were delivered before we left London," Rupert said more loudly. "You'll be quite the sight, Your Grace."

Alexander gave Rupert a poisonous glance, knowing that his valet enjoyed his flamboyant clothing a little too much. "There will be stealthy work to be done, as well," he said in an undertone. "Bring the black, and my favorite boots, too."

"You could just stay home, or leave it to another."

Alexander impaled him with a look for the very suggestion. "My chase. My kill."

"I know." Rupert smiled then bowed. He raised his voice. "I shall see the portmanteau packed immediately, Your Grace, and be prepared to leave at dawn."

"Excellent, Haskell."

The other man left the library, admitting a cool draft that made Alexander think of cold carriages, draughty taverns and stone castles in Cornwall cold enough to freeze a man's marrow. If he had a wife, he'd have warmth in his bed, to be sure.

But if he had a wife, he'd have a wealth of other problems.

Like having a wife. It was one thing to be less than completely honest with Anthea, but he doubted he could hide the truth of his profession from a wife.

And that meant he would have to completely trust the woman he married. Given his experience with feminine deception, Alexander thought that unlikely to occur soon.

Still, Anthea's proposed wager was her first sign of interest in marriage in years. He removed the seed and rolled it between his finger and thumb, considering.

It could not hurt to try again. He didn't imagine for a moment that the old stories were true, but Anthea would expect him to make a report upon his return. Perhaps if he tried, even if the seed failed, that would be sufficient to coax her back to London for the season.

It was more than worth a try.

That prospect put a smile on his lips. He lifted his quill and dipped it into the ink, thinking of how best to use their established code.

My dear Aunt Penelope—
What a delight to arrive home and find your letter already awaiting me here.
It appears the post does not dally as I do! And such news! You make me yearn
again for London. I regret that I will not be back in Town soon, for my doctor,
the excellent Dr. MacEwan, has insisted that I take the sea air in Cornwall
this month. He recommends ten thousand deep breaths a day—ten thousand!—
and I heartily doubt that will leave me sufficient time to pen you a single
line...

CHAPTER 1

I wish we could go faster," Daphne complained, looking out the carriage window yet again. "Why are the horses so slow? We should have reached the next tavern by now!"

Her younger sister, Eurydice, who was so oblivious to the marvels of the fashionable world that Daphne sometimes doubted they were truly siblings, looked up from her book. "Getting to Castle Keyvnor sooner won't get us to London sooner. May is *months* away."

"But we'll be in London for the new year," Daphne replied, impatient to begin the adventure of her coming-out season. Her sister didn't know that Daphne had made a wish on Stir-Up Sunday, a wish that by Christmas a year from now, she would be married to a rich duke. The further they rode from North Barrows, the greater the likelihood of there being a duke in the vicinity.

London would be thick with them.

"I can happily delay the expense of our upcoming venture," her grandmother said with some acidity. Octavia Goodenham, the dowager Viscountess of North Barrows, raised a hand when Daphne's alarm must have shown. "You'll have your season, my dear, then Eurydice will have hers as well. A promise made is a promise kept."

Nelson, their grandmother's maid, nodded and smiled primly at the supreme good sense of her employer. Jenny, the maid for the girls, watched and listened as always she did. The five women were packed into the carriage, for the weather was a foul mix of rain and wet snow, and *Grandmaman* refused to let Nelson or Jenny ride outside. Daphne sat beside her grandmother on the bench that faced forward, while Eurydice was opposite her. Nelson had the window opposite Daphne's grandmother, and Jenny was wedged between Eurydice and Nelson. The young maid was sniffling and shivered at intervals, which was why she'd been given the warmer place in the middle.

"I would rather go to the Continent and save you the expense of a season, *Grandmaman*," Eurydice said. "For there are fine museums there, and I would prefer to visit them than find a husband."

"A husband will do you more good in the end than a glimpse of a statue," their grandmother retorted. "If he is chosen well."

"I will have a duke, *Grandmaman*," Daphne said. To wed well, preferably to a wealthy duke, had been her ambition since the death of their parents. She ignored how Eurydice snorted. Her sister thought it was a vain and silly goal, but Daphne had sound reasons for her scheme. Eurydice didn't remember very much of events after they had news of their parents' death, but Daphne still had nightmares about those days of uncertainty. "You need not fear for *my* future."

Nor would she have to worry about Eurydice's future. Daphne would take care of her sister forever.

"You might be right," the dowager replied. "You are pretty enough to tempt a man's eye, that is for certain."

"If Daphne becomes that rich, then I won't have to marry at all," Eurydice said, as if she had guessed Daphne's secret scheme. "I could become a governess, like Sophia." She referred to Sophia Brisbane who had left their service after winning the affections of Lucien de Roye at Castle Keyvnor just months before.

Their grandmother straightened and fixed Eurydice with a glare. "You. Will. Do. No. Such. Thing."

"But, surely it matters what *I* desire..."

Daphne looked out the window to hide her smile, for she knew that Eurydice could not win this argument, at least not while *Grandmaman* drew breath. After that, if Daphne succeeded, her very clever sister would be able to make her own choices, however unconventional they might be.

She had to wed a duke.

A rich duke.

Surely her wish on the Christmas pudding could only help?

"Surely not!" *Grandmaman* said to Eurydice. "You will desire what you are told to desire, which can only be an affluent husband. After that, you may appeal to him to decide what you are permitted to desire. The matter will be out of my hands."

Eurydice looked as if she might argue that, but Daphne kicked her, hiding the move beneath her skirts. She couldn't bear if they argued all the way to Cornwall. Eurydice's lips tightened but she fell silent.

Grandmaman shook her head. "Though all this racing about may end my days." She appealed to Nelson. "We only just returned to North Barrows and caught our breath, and now it's back to Castle Keyvnor again."

"Indeed, my lady," agreed the maid.

Jenny nodded, though she had not been with them on the last journey.

"And not to celebrate Christmas at home." *Grandmaman* sighed. "It does test one's patience."

"But it might be quite lovely and festive, my lady," Nelson dared to suggest.

"A Christmas wedding is *so* romantic, never mind a double wedding," Daphne agreed. "What do you think the brides will wear?"

"Does it matter?" Eurydice asked.

"Of course, it matters! When I marry my duke, I will wear a dress the color of champagne," Daphne said. She closed her eyes, perfectly able to see herself in the dress in question. It greatly resembled one she had seen amongst the fashion plates at her grandmother's dressmaker, a confection of silk and lace that had haunted her imagination ever since.

"You'll be all yellow then with your blonde hair," Eurydice said. "I will wear red when I marry."

"You will not!" *Grandmaman* declared. "If it's not the rushing about that finishes me, it will be the pair of you!"

"You will survive us all, *Grandmaman*," Daphne said soothingly.

Her grandmother harrumphed and rapped her umbrella on the floor of the carriage. "I will see you both married at the very least, though it may be the last deed I do."

"Let us not hope for that, my lady," Nelson said with vigor. "I'm certain you would like to see each of the girls deliver their first son."

"You are right, of course, Nelson." *Grandmaman* nodded with resolve. "Clearly, I shall have to live a good deal longer." Her eyes flashed. "But I will faint with hunger if we don't reach the next tavern soon." She tapped her umbrella on the roof and roared with a vigor that indicated her demise could not be imminent. "Thompson! Why do we proceed so slowly?"

Daphne wondered whether the driver would pretend that he hadn't heard her grandmother. He would have to have been deaf to have missed that shout. She wiped the condensation from the inside of the window and peered out into the rain. The carriage leaned as they took a corner, and she caught a glimpse of the road ahead.

She gasped, then polished the window a little more to get a better look. "There's a coach and four ahead of us, with an insignia on the door." All of the occupants of the carriage straightened a little at the prospect of a diversion. Even Eurydice looked up from her book. Unfortunately, the road had straightened and they had completed the turn, so one glimpse was all Daphne would have.

"Who is it?" Eurydice asked.

"I don't know, but there are six black horses pulling the carriage!"

"Six. And the coach?" *Grandmaman* demanded.

"Very large. Black, as well, with gold trim. It seemed to have flourishes of gold upon the doors."

Her grandmother inhaled. "How many footmen?"

"Two on the back, *Grandmaman*, plus the driver and one other."

The dowager nodded and narrowed her eyes as she peered through the glass. "I know that coach. There cannot be another so fine as far north as this."

"Whose is it?" Daphne demanded.

"It was made in France for the Duke of Inverfyre when I was a young bride."

There was a duke in close proximity?

Daphne was delighted.

Her grandmother continued. "I remember the old duke bringing it home. Oh, he made certain every soul saw it between Portsmouth and Airdfinnan, including your grandfather and me." She nodded. "It was quite marvelous. I wonder how well it has been maintained."

Daphne sat back in defeat. A duke her grandmother considered to be old must be ancient indeed. Eurydice grinned, for she had undoubtedly guessed her sister's dashed hopes, and Daphne longed to jab her. She had to ask. "The duke is old, then?"

"Old?" her grandmother echoed. "He's dead. His grandson inherited the title, for the old duke's son died before him."

"How long has the new duke been married?" Eurydice asked.

"He isn't," *Grandmaman* admitted and Daphne smiled, her hopes restored. "He's quite eligible, at least on paper, but he's not married."

On paper?

"I don't understand," Daphne said when no one else spoke.

Grandmaman smiled and patted Daphne on the knee. "It means, my dear, that I don't recall his name being linked romantically with that of any woman."

Daphne sensed that her grandmother meant more than she was saying, but she couldn't imagine what it might be. "Then he hasn't found true love yet?"

Grandmaman laughed. "If he has, it won't be with a woman."

This made no sense to Daphne at all.

To her relief, Eurydice seemed to be similarly mystified, so for once, she wasn't the last one to figure something out.

"And a great shame it is, to be sure. The family are most affluent. There is a decided aversion to gambling in the Armstrong line, matched with a good fortune with investments that is almost unholy." *Grandmaman* twirled her cane. "It is said that this duke's fortune is one of the greatest in all of England. Pity about his preferences. If his sister does not marry, that great lineage might come to an end."

Preferences? Daphne and Eurydice exchanged a glance of confusion.

The carriage slowed and turned, and they heard Thompson whistle.

"Ah, here we are," *Grandmaman* declared with a decisive tap of her umbrella. "And not a moment too soon, for I am ravenous." The door was opened and one of the footmen put down the stool for the dowager viscountess. Another held an umbrella high so she wouldn't have to use her own for the short walk to the tavern. "Ah!" she declared as she alighted. "You will soon see what I mean, my dears. The duke is also taking refreshment here. I shall remind him of our family's acquaintance."

Daphne squeezed Eurydice's fingers with delight, then emerged from the carriage herself, her heart thundering.

She should have made a wish sooner.

She stared in shock at the man speaking to her grandmother near the doorway to the tavern. He smiled and bowed over Lady North Barrow's hand, his manners impeccable and his clothing so garish that Daphne didn't know what to say or do.

Eurydice gave her a hard nudge from behind. "Move, you goose," she muttered. "We can't get out because of you and it's freezing cold."

Daphne took a few steps, still startled to silence.

A moment later, Eurydice halted beside her. "Oh!" she said, apparently similarly astonished.

Grandmaman raised a hand to beckon to them, and the duke turned to survey them with polite curiosity. His waistcoat was a splendid and hideous garment, made of a vivid blue cloth thick with gold embroidery. Eurydice said something through her teeth, but Daphne ignored her. The duke raised his quizzing glance and peered at them, blinking as if he had trouble with his vision. There was no difficulty with his appetite, for he had a considerable paunch. His cheeks were fat, but his legs were surprisingly trim.

And he was a duke.

"Oh," Daphne agreed, then tried to be gracious. "I don't believe I've ever seen that shade of apricot used with such enthusiasm in a man's garments before."

"It's orange," said Eurydice.

"No, I'm certain he calls it *abricot*."

"You don't have to say it French!"

"I think I do," Daphne mused.

"And with green." Eurydice grimaced.

"*Chartreuse*," Daphne corrected, for she saw definite possibilities in her near future.

"The blue is a horrifying addition."

"*Azure*," Daphne said, then smiled at the duke. He took a closer look. She was glad to be wearing a new dress in the shade of pink that flattered her coloring so well.

"He's wearing more rouge than *Grandmaman*," Eurydice whispered wickedly, but Daphne ignored her. Her sister surveyed her and her eyes widened in horror. "You wouldn't."

"He's a duke," Daphne said mildly, then met her sister's gaze. "Me first."

Eurydice laughed. "You needn't fear any competition from me in pursuit of that silly fop. Look at him! He's a joke from head to toe!"

Daphne smiled. There were no other unwed aristocrats in the vicinity, nor were there likely to be any. She had no competition at all and might very well save her grandmother the expense of a season in London.

For a duke.

Daphne couldn't have cared less how he dressed. His finery was expensive, which meant her grandmother was right about his finances.

He did have fine legs and he was tall.

This was her chance. She crossed the yard with her chin high and her skirts gathered in one hand. Her steps were quick and delicate, as if she joined a dance, and in a way, she did. A thrill of anticipation coursed through her as she wondered just how well—and how quickly —she could charm him. Oh, there was no deceit in Daphne. She meant to make whatever duke she won a most delightful and attentive wife.

The duke lifted his glass a little higher to watch her approach.

Daphne wasn't so innocent that she didn't notice the glimmer of interest in his very blue eyes as she curtseyed before him.

WHAT A BEAUTY!

Alexander savored the sight of Lady North Barrow's granddaughter as she came tripping toward him, her lifted skirt hem granting him a glance of her neat ankles, and her cheeks a little flushed. Her hair was like spun gold and her eyes shone with what appeared to be good nature. Her dark green cloak parted as she walked, giving him a glimpse of her figure. She was slim through the waist and hips but curved sufficiently to invite a man's caress. That deep green of her cloak made her eyes appear to be a deeper hue than they were. The pink of her dress became her very well and she put him in mind of apple blossoms in the spring. Though she was fair, her lashes and brows were dark, and her lips were both sweetly full and ruddy.

Alexander was certain that he hadn't seen such a splendid beauty in years.

When she smiled at him, he was reminded of exactly how long he had been celibate.

And he completely forgot why.

Indeed, he found himself recalling Anthea's challenge and almost fingered the small seed in his pocket.

Lady North Barrows made curt introductions, as was her way. He hadn't seen her since Anthea's season, but she hadn't changed much. Miss Goodenham's lashes fluttered as she curtseyed before him. He caught a glimpse of creamy cleavage, then she met his gaze and blushed prettily.

Alexander's heart gave a leap, though he fussed over her hand, bending to kiss it with flair. He caught a whiff of her scent then, roses mingled with the perfume of her own skin, and that sent an unwelcome stab of desire through him.

There was a second girl, Miss Eurydice, who was younger, stockier, slightly darker in coloring and who eyed him with suspicion. Lady North Barrows then ushered her granddaughters into the tavern ahead of her, as if they were wayward chicks. Alexander watched them go, telling himself he should be pleased that the dowager viscountess was not intent upon flinging her eligible granddaughters at him, like every other ambitious mama in the *ton*, but in truth he was disappointed to have enjoyed their company for so short an interval.

Even though it was undoubtedly for the best.

To his surprise, Miss Goodenham turned to glance back at him, her remarkable eyes filled with appeal. "But *Grandmaman*," she whispered, loudly enough for him to overhear. "Surely we cannot let His Grace eat luncheon alone. It would be unforgivable."

Lady North Barrows paused in the midst of giving instruction for their meal to her maid, which she wished to have served in a private room. She eyed him, her misgivings more than clear. "We would not wish to intrude on His Grace's meal," she said, her tone chiding, and Miss Goodenham appeared to be so disappointed that Alexander almost spoke out.

Instead, he took out his snuffbox and fussed over a pinch, ensuring that he looked a perfect fool. The working men regarded him with disdain, but that was part of the plan. His disguise kept anyone from looking closer.

No sooner had Alexander savored his snuff and stepped into the tavern, then Rupert appeared and bowed. "Your Grace, all has been made ready for your luncheon."

"Thank you, Haskell. Is there a fire? I cannot bear the cold in this place! And is the soup very hot?" He shuddered elaborately, then ran a finger across the top of a table. He eyed his glove with distaste. "I hope it is *clean*, Haskell."

"Of course, Your Grace." Rupert bowed once more and smiled. "I have ensured that all will meet with your approval."

"And dessert?" Alexander whined. "I must have a choice of *two* desserts."

"There is only one pudding, Your Grace, but I will fetch some oranges from the carriage."

Alexander sighed. "I suppose that will suffice. One must endure so many hardships while travelling." He waved to the ladies with his lace-trimmed handkerchief and followed Haskell, ensuring that his steps were mincing. He then held that handkerchief to his nose, as if the smell of the tavern was too much for him to endure, and heartily regretted losing sight of Miss Goodenham.

He couldn't help but overhear the discussion Lady North Barrows had with the proprietor.

"I apologize, my lady, but there is only one private chamber," that man informed her with a bow. Alexander paused to listen. "We seldom have such noble guests. If you would like to take your meal in the far corner, there, I will have that fire set..."

"In the *tavern?*" the dowager protested. "It is unthinkable! Surely you have some chamber available."

"I am sorry, my lady, but..."

Alexander cleared his throat. "How large is the chamber where I shall dine?" he asked Rupert.

His man bit back a smile. "It is a fair size, Your Grace. I am certain you will have every comfort there."

"Is it of sufficient size that the ladies might join us?"

Miss Goodenham turned to him, her eyes alight with pleasure and her lips parted. Zounds, but she was an alluring creature!

Was she as conniving as that beauty, Lady Miranda Delaney, had been? Alexander wished very much to know, although already he doubted as much. There was something open about her expression, something that hinted at an honest heart.

He couldn't help but recall his sister's list of attributes in a potential wife. *A suitable woman, one who is honest and true, pretty enough to tempt you—and young.*

Miss Goodenham appeared to have every quality on that list.

The seed seemed heavily in his pocket.

"There is no need, Your Grace," Lady North Barrows began to protest, for undoubtedly she did not wish to be in his debt.

"There is every need when the comfort of three ladies is at stake," Alexander said with a bow. "I insist that you accept my hospitality and dine with me this day. Our conversation will pass the time pleasantly until we continue on our separate ways."

"Oh, *Grandmaman,* what a wonderful invitation!" Miss Goodenham enthused. "Surely we cannot decline such generosity?"

"Surely we cannot," Lady North Barrows said grimly. She gave a stiff curtsey. "I thank you, Your Grace. Your kindness is most welcome."

"The pleasure will be all mine," Alexander replied, then offered his arm to the elderly viscountess. Lady North Barrows hesitated only a moment before placing her hand upon his elbow. He was keenly aware of Miss Goodenham trailing behind him and could not quell his own sense of triumph.

~

THE ROOM *WAS* of a goodly size, both comfortable and warm. The fire had been stoked up and the table had been set with hearty fare, both hot and cold. There was wine, because Alexander ordered it, and he fussed over the vintage as well as the cushion on his seat. Of course, the viscountess seated them in order of precedence and he was ridiculously pleased to have Miss Goodenham at his left hand.

He wished with all his heart that he might not have been in disguise.

Perhaps he might encounter her again, after this quest was completed, and appear to her as a reformed man.

Perhaps he would ensure that eventuality.

The meal was served and various pleasantries exchanged. Alexander ensured that he slurped his soup loudly and took great satisfaction in the way Lady North Barrows winced at the sound. The viscountess turned and began a conversation with Eurydice, enquiring after that girl's choice of reading.

Miss Goodenham, however, regarded Alexander with shining eyes, apparently oblivious to his bad manners. Was she stupid? He supposed it was possible, though it would be disappointing.

"Your Grace, would you indulge me by telling me of Airdfinnan?" she asked.

"Faith! Why? What would you know about it?"

"What does it look like? Where is it? I have only been to Scotland once, and that was to visit Edinburgh. I did love that city and always wished to see more."

"Airdfinnan is in the Highlands," he said. "Filthy weather there. Cold and snow and rain, then heat and sun and rain." He shivered again. "I endeavor to be there as little as possible." In truth, of course, Alexander would have been glad to retreat to Airdfinnan and never leave his estate again.

Miss Goodenham was not daunted. "I love the rain in Scotland, and the lush green of the hills. I think it may be the most beautiful place in all the world."

Alexander spared her a glance, distrusting that they were in such agreement. "Have you seen much of the world?"

She laughed, a delightful sound. "Almost none of it, but what I have seen of Scotland is so pretty that it seems unlikely any place could be finer."

"Filthy weather," he repeated.

"But you must have a fine house to provide shelter from the elements."

Did she mean to assess his wealth? Alexander saw no reason to hide the truth, for Lady North Barrows could tell her all she desired to know and more. "A castle," he confided. "Built on an island in the river Finnan."

"How romantic!"

"Damp," he said flatly, then lied. "I am never warm when I am there."

"Perhaps you need a wife to keep you warm, Your Grace," she said, blushing at her own daring comment. Her eyes danced though, as if she invited him to smile with her, and Alexander was sorely tempted to do just that.

If not to kiss her. Her lips were enticing.

"Daphne!" Lady North Barrows snapped. "Such impertinence is unnecessary."

"I meant only to make a jest. I do apologize, Your Grace, if you thought me rude."

"Of course not," he said and was rewarded by her smile. "You cannot have had your first season yet."

"No, not yet!" Her eyes shone, reminding him of Anthea's long-ago enthusiasm. "We are going from Castle Keyvnor to London to prepare for it." She reached out and fleetingly touched his cuff. "Could you perhaps give me some advice as to the best shops and dressmakers, Your Grace? A man of your sartorial flair must know where the most talented needles are to be found."

Was she flirting with him? It was unthinkable. Eligible women, no matter how ardently their mothers cast them into his path, invariably fled from Alexander in this guise.

"I know little of women's clothing, to be sure," he said, laughing loudly so that the food in his mouth was displayed.

"But I love this color," Daphne said, touching his cuff again and letting her fingers stray to the back of his hand. She flicked a glance at her grandmother who had not noticed her gesture and her eyes were filled with beguiling mischief when she met his gaze again. He did like a little audacity in a woman. "What would you call it, Your Grace?"

"*Abricot*, of course," he said, using the French pronunciation.

"*Abricot*," she echoed perfectly. "I think I shall have a dress made in this hue, with the green, too."

"*Chartreuse*," he supplied.

"That is what I thought it should be called!" she confessed with delight. "It reminds me of spring, which is a welcome thought at this dreary time of year." She bit her lip. "I do not think I could carry the *azure* at the same time, though."

"Perhaps a Spencer?"

"That is a wonderful notion!" Daphne cleared her throat. "That is, if you would not be insulted to be my inspiration, Your Grace." She lifted her gaze to his, an invitation in those eyes that fairly stole his breath away.

It had been a long time since a woman had given him such a welcoming look, and none had ever granted him one while he was in disguise.

Alexander swallowed. "Of course not!" he cried, gesturing with his fork. "One must take inspiration where it can be found. I saw a gentleman in Town in these very colors and knew I had to have a suit of similar gaiety."

"In Town! Oh, I envy you such travels, Your Grace."

She would not be dissuaded. Alexander was in peril of being enchanted by this damsel. "It is the food that I love best there," he confided, then patted his padded belly. "I could eat all the day long there, and invariably, I need to have my waistcoats let out after a sojourn in London."

She laughed lightly. "Perhaps I would have to loosen my stays."

Alexander nearly offered to help with that task, but he recalled himself. He giggled in a frivolous fashion. "Oh, I have to loosen mine!" he confided in a girlish voice.

She faltered only briefly, then fixed her attention upon him again. "But you must find some appeal at Airdfinnan. Surely the hunting is excellent there."

"I am told that it is, and I suppose we do eat game there with some frequency." Alexander made a moue of distaste. "But I could never hunt. To kill something? Never! The blood! The horror!" He waved his hands helplessly, then seized upon his fork and gobbled his roast duck and gravy.

"I love to hunt," Miss Goodenham admitted, much to his surprise. "I've only been once, though. My cousin, the viscount, invited us this autumn after he returned to North Barrows with his new wife. I found it thrilling."

'Thrilling' was exactly how Alexander felt about the hunt.

Indeed, the quest he undertook was a hunt and he savored every moment of it.

His mouth went dry. It was easy to imagine riding to hunt at Airdfinnan with this alluring beauty by his side.

"I suppose the weather was fine," he said.

She laughed and he'd never heard a more wondrous sound. "It was horrible, Your Grace! It rained and rained. We were filthy with muck, but my cousin took a deer. It was so exciting!" Her eyes shone at the memory, and Alexander found himself shifting on his chair.

This was madness. He could not have any matter in common with this beautiful girl. He should not be tempted. He had no time for distraction.

Not until this mission was completed and the villain brought to justice.

Despite Anthea's challenge.

In the back of his mind, Alexander was already considering the merit of opening the London house early, and journeying there from Cornwall himself. If his mission was successful, he would have to return the gem to Cushing and make his report to the crown, after all.

What harm would it be to take the delightful Miss Goodenham shopping?

"Perhaps you are a better man than me, Miss Goodenham," he said with a giggle.

She smiled at him. "Perhaps opposites truly do attract, Your Grace."

Oh, she was bold, and he was charmed.

"Dessert!" he cried, putting down his cup so sloppily that he might have been drunk. His wine spilled. Miss Goodenham had taken only the barest sip of her wine. Rupert filled his cup again, then brought him a pudding.

"Is it apple?" Miss Goodenham asked. She watched as he tasted it.

"I suppose it might be. It needs a rum sauce to be edible," Alexander declared, although it was delicious, and Rupert left in pursuit of that very thing.

"May I be so bold as to ask your destination, Your Grace?"

"Cornwall. My doctor believes that the sea air will be restorative, though I will not bore you with a full list of my maladies..."

"Cornwall!" Miss Goodenham said, interrupting him with delight. He nodded warily. "Well, that is where we are going," she confessed. "To Castle Keyvnor. There will be a double wedding there on Christmas Eve. I think it is so romantic!"

They had the same destination.

Praise be that he had remained consistent with his disguise.

And he would see her again. His heart lurched at the prospect.

Miss Goodenham continued. "We were there at All Hallows, and now we return for the weddings. Where in Cornwall are you destined, Your Grace?"

"My man has booked a room in some place called Bowkum..." He waved to the returning Haskell as if he'd forgotten their destination.

"Bocka Morrow, Your Grace," Haskell supplied. "The inn is called The Mermaid's Kiss. It is most reputable."

Miss Goodenham was clearly pleased. "Bocka Morrow! Why, that is the village near Castle Keyvnor! Will we see you at the castle itself, Your Grace? We attend the weddings of the two daughters of the Earl of Banfield."

"Regrettably, I am not acquainted with the current earl."

"But you must come and walk with me," she insisted, her hand stealing to his cuff again. "I should so like to see you again, Your Grace."

Their gazes met and clung, and Alexander's heart clenched.

"Daphne!" Lady North Barrows barked. "You have scarcely eaten a bite and we must carry on." She inclined her head. "Although the duke has been most gracious in his hospitality, I am certain he desires a little time to himself. Regrettably, we have no leisure for dessert."

The pudding was set before him again, fairly submerged in a rum sauce, and Alexander hoped the ladies did leave him shortly. There was no way he could eat the entire massive serving, but his disguise meant that he would have to do as much if he were witnessed.

"Regrettably," Miss Goodenham echoed under her breath.

"That is a shame," Alexander said, rising to his feet. He acted as if he were unsteady and gripped the table, wondering if he could tip the entire thing without injuring any of the ladies. It was a sturdy table, unfortunately, for the feat would have made a fine display of his apparent shortcomings. The ladies rose and each came to express their thanks, as well as to say farewell, and he would not have been a man if Miss Goodenham's sweet smile had not sent heat surging through him again.

What would he give for a single kiss?

He bowed and fussed, and they finally left, the beautiful Miss Goodenham last to depart.

Alexander pushed away his dessert with impatience once they were gone, more than ready to have this final victory behind him. He found himself thinking about the allure of watching a lovely girl being introduced to the pleasures of London.

The seed seemed to wriggle in his pocket. He pulled it out and looked at it, halfway thinking it had changed shape.

As if it grew a root.

He would put it in water when they reached The Mermaid's Kiss. Alexander didn't believe in it, but it couldn't hurt.

And when it came to Miss Goodenham, he was inclined to take a chance.

~

"You are shameless," Eurydice muttered beneath her breath.

Daphne cast her sister a smile. "In the end, you will call me duchess."

"He's awful!"

"He's sweet."

"He ate with his mouth open!"

"He's unaccustomed to the company of women."

Eurydice gave Daphne a skeptical glance. "I suppose you think you'll be able to charm him into changing his ways."

"I don't care if he changes actually." Daphne paused and looked back at the tavern, hearing the truth in her own words. There was a face in one upper window, watching. She couldn't make out the person's features, but there was an unmistakable area of peach-toned fabric. She waved, a little surprised to realize how little the details mattered. She liked talking to him, and the rest was irrelevant. People changed over their lives after all, becoming thinner or heavier, balder or more grey. It was their essence that mattered most and she liked the duke. "He'll suit me well, just as he is."

Eurydice climbed into the carriage, her disgust clear. "He hates the country."

"He hasn't seen it at its best. The viscount never favored North Barrows until he took a wife."

"He drank too much."

"He did not. I watched. He gave the appearance of being besotted but he drank very little." Daphne bit her lip. "I wonder why he would do that?"

"Perhaps he drinks so seldom that wine affects him more powerfully."

"Perhaps. But then, how would he have known so much about the vintages?"

Eurydice shrugged, having no ready answer for that.

Grandmaman took her place in the carriage then, and began to dictate orders to Nelson about their stop that night. The girls ceased their conversation, Daphne looking out the window and Eurydice returning to her book. Jenny's sniffle was louder and the girl blew her nose with increasing frequency.

Daphne was thinking furiously. The fact was that her impressions of the duke did not fit together. On the one hand, he appeared to be a frivolous fop, concerned only with his own comfort and desires. On the other, she felt a strange thrill when his gaze met hers, and those blue eyes carried an intensity that did not match his words. His belly was large as if he were fat, but his legs were most fine, and his face—when she ignored the rouge—was both masculine and handsome.

It made no sense.

Perhaps she was wrong. Eurydice was the clever one and she thought the duke was precisely as he appeared.

In the end, it mattered little, though. He was interested in her and she did not care why. Daphne was more than delighted that she would have the opportunity to see the Duke of Inverfyre again, and very soon.

*I*t's a remarkable piece," Rupert said, his admiration a perfect echo of Alexander's own. "But then, you've seen the original."

"The resemblance is uncanny." Alexander turned the replica in his hand, letting the candlelight catch the facets of the cut stones. They shone brilliantly, and he was impressed by the workmanship. "I've never seen so fine a fraud. I could only tell them apart when I had the genuine Eye of India in one hand and this counterfeit one in the other, and then only with close examination." He didn't tell even Rupert about the small mark on the back of the forgery, made so that they could be reliably distinguished. Cushing was nothing if not diligent.

The two men were in Alexander's rented quarters at the Mermaid's Kiss. The hour was so late that the tavern had quieted below and they kept their voices very soft as they conferred. Alexander had shed his disguise with relief and sat at the table before the fire in his shirt, boots and breeches. Rupert had drawn the drape and locked the door before Alexander removed the pin from its hiding place.

The pin, which was a duplicate of the one being sent to Lady Tamsyn, was oblong in shape and filled Alexander's palm. In its middle was a large cut oval sapphire of deep blue color, as large as the nail of

Alexander's thumb. It was surrounded by cut diamonds in glittering ribbons, the whole set in platinum.

At least, the original was a sapphire with diamonds set in platinum. The one Alexander held was glass and paste set in tin. He tilted it toward the light and smiled. "Look. Even the eye portrait has been faithfully reproduced."

"Eye portrait?" Rupert leaned closer.

"It's a piece that was originally exchanged between lovers. That's why it's called the Lover's Eye. The original recipient was given the gem by a lover, and this is a portrait of his eye."

"Who was he?"

"No one knows, but Cushing has contrived a tale that Jonathan Hambly had it made for Emily Hawkins but never gave it to her due to her early and sudden death. That's why he's sending it to the bride, who is the oldest daughter of the current earl."

"Quite a generous gift."

"Remarkably so."

"Won't she be suspicious?"

"Cushing is believed to be eccentric and, in my experience, people are most willing to accept rich gifts, even with meager explanations. Cushing *is* a distant relation." Alexander slipped the gem back into its velvet sack, knotted the drawstring, then placed it into a second velvet bag. Even the bags containing the real gem and the copy were perfect replicas, which made his task much simpler. "You confirmed that it was delivered today?"

"By Cushing's great-nephew, as anticipated. Nathaniel Cushing."

Alexander nodded. "Then the exchange must be made tonight."

"Are you certain you should go alone?" Rupert asked, peeking around the window shade. The evening was clear, the moon nearly full. Alexander might have wished for a few clouds to better hide his activities, but he would make do.

He donned his dark jacket, a large soft hat and his hooded cloak. He tugged on his boots and shoved his gloves into his belt. "Absolutely. You may have to pretend to be me in my absence." Alexander smiled at the very thought.

"Good Lord!" Rupert exclaimed, imitating Alexander's foppish tone very well. "Is there no decent flame to be had in this hovel?" He raised his voice, sounding shrill. "This chimney smokes beyond belief and the bed is as cold as ice. Go and fetch more wood for the fire, Haskell. I don't care what these barbarians have to say of it!"

The men exchanged a glance and a nod, then Alexander unbolted the door. "Aye, Your Grace," he said gruffly, knowing he was not as good a mimic as his friend. "Immediately, Your Grace."

"Well, don't stand there, letting in the draft," Rupert whined. "I already have a sniffle and you know I can't tolerate a chill. Hurry, man!"

Alexander strode from the chamber, but he fetched only one load of wood for the fire. He descended as if to gather a second load, but left the tavern instead. It would take him a good half hour to walk to Castle Keyvnor by a circuitous route, and he could only hope that there were few souls abroad at this hour to notice his passage.

DAPHNE AWAKENED when Castle Keyvnor was dark and quiet, her heart pounding and her palms slick. It had been her familiar nightmare again, the one in which *Grandmaman* passed and they were left close to penniless.

Again.

Eurydice did not recall that fortnight between the news of their parents' death and *Grandmaman*'s return from Bath, when uncertainty had filled young Daphne's every moment. She was determined to never be so vulnerable again.

But *Grandmaman* grew older and still Daphne wasn't married.

Everything could change in a moment. She clutched the linens and wished again that her Christmas wish would come true.

It had been a long time since Daphne had vowed to take care of Eurydice forever, and perhaps her sister had forgotten the pledge. Daphne never would.

She had to marry well and soon.

Her wish had seemed to show promise when they'd unexpectedly encountered the Duke of Inverfyre—even more so when he watched her so intently—but his carriage had passed theirs that afternoon and they hadn't seen him again.

Daphne had liked him, too. Surely the opportunity wasn't lost forever?

Jenny's cold had grown steadily worse as they journeyed south and Eurydice had a slight sniffle by the time they arrived. She'd gone to bed early and was still sleeping deeply in the room when Daphne's dream awakened her.

Daphne stared at the ceiling and feared for the future.

She wished she was the clever one.

The one kind of tutelage to which Daphne took naturally was her grandmother's instruction about the management of finances. She had expressed curiosity and her grandmother had explained, apparently thinking that a taste would suffice. But Daphne had been curious and more interested in following the path of money than conjugating German verbs. Their lessons had continued ever since, and it was Daphne who was summoned to help her grandmother with the accounts. She knew the sum of the inheritance left to herself and her sister, and recognized that it was a pittance.

Their grandfather had stipulated in his will that if he pre-deceased his wife, she might remain in the smaller house now known as the dower house for her lifetime. Of course, he had passed away before Daphne had been born, before even her father and heir to the estate had taken a wife. Once *Grandmaman* passed, Daphne and Eurydice would have no home, unless their cousin, the viscount, chose to be charitable in Lady North Barrows' absence.

Daphne would rather be reliant upon a husband than a cousin, and thus she was resolved to marry for both money and title. Her sister thought this was a foolish whim, but it was an utterly practical choice.

Eurydice was right on one account: the title *was* a whim. Daphne didn't truly need to be a duchess. People were more accepting of an ambition to marry a duke than one to wed a wealthy man—and she knew that her grandmother would never permit her to marry an untitled man, independent of his financial situation.

A duke with a fortune it would have to be.

Like the Duke of Inverfyre.

Who had ridden onward, as if he'd forgotten her.

In the night, with uncertainty lingering from her dream, all horrors seemed possible.

Daphne tossed and turned but could not go back to sleep.

At home, she often went to the kitchen after her nightmare.

Her belly growled, as if to encourage the idea.

Daphne rose and donned a robe. She debated the merit of ringing the bell, but knew that Jenny needed her sleep to battle that fearsome cold. She didn't want to awaken Nelson or Eurydice either.

Surely no one would mind if she went to the kitchen here?

Surely it would ease her fears to *do* something, rather than lie abed and fret?

Feeling very bold, she slipped out of their chamber and into the darkened hall. Castle Keyvnor was quiet and cool, filled with shadows. Daphne struck the flint when she was in the corridor and lit the candle she'd brought from the chamber.

The flame blew a little in a draft. Daphne put the flint in her pocket and cupped her hand around the flame, then hurried quietly down the hall.

It seemed the only sound was the rumbling of her stomach. She had a strange sense that she was being watched, which was ridiculous.

Daphne paused at the summit of the stairs, listened and felt her heart skip. Had that been a swishing sound behind her, like the swirling skirt of a taffeta dress?

Of course not. She continued a little more quickly.

A clock chimed somewhere far below her. If it was right, the hour was three in the morning. She retraced their path of earlier in the evening to the foyer, then tried to guess the location of the kitchens. At the end of the corridor on the main floor, there was a smaller door tucked into the corner. It looked as if it led to the servants' quarters, as it was too plain and small to lead anywhere else.

Daphne opened the door with care and discovered another staircase. This one was less ornate, a very functional staircase that led both up and down.

The servants' stairs. The kitchen would be down.

She held her candle high and hurried down the stairs. She could smell roast meat then, soap, herbs, and baking. Her nose led her to the darkened kitchen, which was clean and empty. Banked coals glowed on the hearth and a dog was curled up, sleeping there. Its tail thumped at the sight of her but it didn't abandon its cozy spot.

On one long table, there was a basket with a cloth over it. That was just as Cook left extra baking at home. Daphne lifted the cloth and smiled at the sight of the scones.

Triumph! There were a dozen. She would eat just one. She wouldn't leave a mess.

Daphne reached in just as someone spoke.

"Who are you and what are you doing here?"

The words were uttered softly, but Daphne was still surprised. She jumped, dropped both candle and scone, then spun to face the person who spoke. The candle extinguished itself, then fell out of the holder and rolled. "I am Daphne Goodenham," she confessed, a little breathless. "I was hungry."

A young girl stepped out of the shadows. She was a few years older than Daphne and clearly a maid. "Didn't you ring for your maid?"

"Jenny is sick. I couldn't think to trouble her at this hour."

Her companion seemed to be surprised.

Or suspicious.

"I often go to the kitchen at home. I didn't think it would be any trouble here."

"It's not." The maid nodded toward the basket. "There are plenty left from today, and they'll be making new ones in a few hours." She picked up the candle then set it into the holder again. Daphne used the flint to light it again, and had a better look at her companion. She had curly brown hair and looked to be just as wide awake as Daphne.

She was glad to not be alone.

"I'm Mary," the maid said with a quick smile and a curtsey.

"How pleasant to meet you," Daphne said, thinking it would be rude to eat in front of the other woman. Maybe she'd take the scone back to her room.

"You might as well eat here. I won't tell, and there won't be crumbs in your room, then."

"Thank you."

"Let me get the butter." Mary also poured Daphne a glass of milk. She then stood on the other side of the heavy table.

"It's the middle of the night," Daphne chided, making a gesture of invitation. "You need not stand as if we are at dinner."

Mary smiled and bobbed a curtsey, then took a seat. Daphne pushed the basket of scones toward her and the girl glanced over her shoulder as if fearful of being caught.

"Tell them I had two," Daphne said and Mary took one. The girl ate quietly and Daphne chose to take advantage of the opportunity to learn more. "Can you tell me who has come for the wedding?"

"Certainly. The castle is full of guests and so is Hollybrook Park." Mary ticked off on her fingers. "There's...."

In the long list, she made no mention of the Duke of Inverfyre, much to Daphne's disappointment. Daphne smiled. "What a large and merry wedding it will be, with so many guests come to wish them well."

"And there are more in the village, too."

"Truly? Is there a tavern there, then?"

"Two of them. The Mermaid's Kiss is where the gentry will stay, to be sure. The Crown and Anchor is more for sailors."

Daphne finished her scone, thinking furiously. She was sure the duke had mentioned the Mermaid's Kiss. Could she find a way to see him again? "I'm curious about Bocka Morrow. We didn't have time to visit during Samhain. Isn't there an apothecary's shop I might visit?"

Mary laughed. "There is, and the witches are there."

"Witches?"

"Aye, they make love spells." Mary finished her scone. "But you didn't even ask about the ghosts."

Daphne didn't much care for ghost stories—her recurring night-mare provided sufficient fear—but she knew those at Castle Keyvnor were much taken with their ghosts. "When we were here before, they said there was a young boy, named Paul, who cries in the night."

Mary nodded. "The earl's young son."

"And Baron Tyrell, who killed himself when his beloved Lady Helena wed another. Isn't her portrait in the gallery?" Daphne said, remembering.

Mary's eyes shone. "But now Lord Snow has arrived wearing a ring, called the Grimstone, which banishes the ghosts."

"That I do not believe," Daphne said firmly.

"That's only because you weren't here when he arrived. There was a sound like a crack of lightning and ghosts were cast into the sky."

"Did you see it?"

"I heard about it. My uncle is the groom, and he said there was such a commotion in the stables as you have never seen." Mary's eyes shone. "He told me about the Grimstone, which he never thought was real until he saw it this day." She sobered and sighed. "I can only hope that it doesn't banish Benedict."

She must have been referring to yet another ghost. "Why not?"

"Because I love him, and I could not bear it if we were parted forever."

Although the other woman appeared to be convinced of her tale, Daphne remained skeptical. Ghosts thrown into the sky? If they were banished and thrown anywhere, it would be into the great beyond. She thought it would not be prudent to note that this Benedict was dead and Mary was not, thus they were already parted.

The girl had been kind, after all.

Daphne stood and picked up her candle. "It will be morning soon enough. Thank you for the butter and the conversation. Perhaps I will see you tomorrow."

"Perhaps you will. Have a care on your way back upstairs, my lady," Mary said. "The ghosts are not always friendly at Castle Keyvnor, and after today, they may be very angry indeed."

"I thank you for the warning." Daphne retraced her steps, climbing the servant's stairs to the main floor, thinking that worldly concerns were more worrisome than ghosts.

She peeked around the door at the summit and realized she'd already taken a wrong turn. This wasn't the foyer she recognized. There was a staircase in the shadows ahead, but it was smaller than the one she'd descended.

She looked back down the stairs but it was silent and dark below. Surely she could find her way once she was in the main house? The servant's corridors would be like a maze—that she'd already gone the wrong way meant that she was likely to become even more lost.

She stepped into the corridor and closed the door behind herself. The sole illumination was a shaft of moonlight. A clock chimed the half hour. It sounded like the same clock she'd heard before, but it was more distant. She hurried up the stairs to find that the hall above was lined with closed doors, all of which looked the same.

Was that the little alcove near the room she shared with Eurydice? It was too far away to be certain, but Daphne thought it might be. She hurried toward it, her heart beginning to pound. Instead of being silent, the house also sounded to be full of whispers. She was certain that she heard the swish of taffeta again, the scuttle of mice, the stealthy step of someone following her. She remembered the story of an old wing of the castle being out of use and the whispers that ghosts and madwomen lived there. She thought about ghosts and walked a little more quickly. She glanced over her shoulder but saw no one.

Daphne was sure she heard someone else breathing.

Was it a ghost?

Nonsense! Still, she hastened on.

The alcove wasn't the one she recalled. The corridor bent ahead and Daphne hurried toward the corner. Sanctuary must be just ahead. As she approached the corner, she felt a chill and heard a moan that made the hair stand on the back of her neck. Ghosts! There was a gust of air and her candle was extinguished.

Rather than stopping to light it again, Daphne ran.

She rounded the corner in terror and collided with something too solid to be a ghost. She gasped. A man's hands locked around her shoulders to steady her.

He swore and she had the barest glimpse of his blazing blue eyes before he spun her around so that her back was turned to him. "And a good morning to you, my fair damsel," he said in a low whisper that made Daphne's toes curl.

Her heart raced in shock but he didn't release her. She should have run but she didn't want to be alone again just yet. His grip was strong and the warmth of his hands reassuring.

Who was he? Daphne swallowed, recalling that he had been dressed all in black, a shadow against the darkness. He was taller and broader than her, and she couldn't forget the brilliance of his eyes. She tried to turn to face him again but his grip tightened slightly.

"Haven't you heard that curiosity killed the cat?" he murmured, his breath fanning her ear. Daphne could feel the hard heat of him close behind her and her knees weakened.

"Are you a ghost?" she managed to say and he chuckled.

"Not yet. Are you?"

She shook her head and felt his hand slide over her shoulder in a caress. She glanced down and watched his fingers. Even with his black leather glove, she could see that his hands were long and elegant, strong hands. To her astonishment, he lifted a tendril of her hair and let it slide through his gloved fingers, the blond curl gleaming against the black leather.

"Maybe you're just a dream," he whispered. "Sadly, there is only one way to be certain."

Daphne didn't know who he was or why he was there, but she didn't care. This was the stuff of the novels she and Eurydice devoured! "How will you discover the truth?" she asked lightly.

"With a kiss, of course," he replied without hesitation. Perhaps he read those same stories. "Every disreputable vision or ghost is dispelled by a kiss."

"Sirens dissolve with a kiss," Daphne agreed.

"Indeed." His voice rumbled low, awakening a yearning within Daphne. He still held her shoulders, his thumbs caressing her through her robe. She thought of those eyes, that barest glimpse of a square jaw, and swallowed.

"A fine suggestion," she said boldly, keeping her voice low. "For I should like to be certain that you are no apparition, sir." She heard him catch his breath in surprise, then his lips were against her ear.

"Close your eyes, my temptress," he murmured.

Daphne did as he requested and without delay. "Done." She was immediately spun in place, and the weight of one gloved hand slid around her nape. His other hand was on the back of her waist, drawing her close. She felt him lean closer and her breasts collided with his hard chest. She could have run. She could have twisted out of his embrace. She could have opened her eyes. He granted her the time to be certain.

But it was far too perfect to be kissed by a handsome stranger in the dark, when no one else would ever know. It was a delicious secret, one to be held between herself and this man of mystery, and Daphne couldn't resist the invitation to know more.

"You promised me a kiss, sir," she dared to whisper. She rose to her toes and put her hands on his shoulders, keeping her eyes closed as she parted her lips in invitation.

She didn't have to wait long for him to accept.

WHAT WAS the delightful Miss Goodenham doing, wandering the corridors of Castle Keyvnor in the early hours of the morning? Alexander didn't know and as soon as she collided with him, he didn't care. She smelled seductively feminine. She wore only a chemise and a robe, and when his hands closed over her shoulders to steady her, he felt an overwhelming urge to draw her into his embrace. That she smelled so sweet, that she wore so little, that her hair was in a loose braid, that it was dark and they were alone, made the encounter enticingly intimate.

As if he had come to her in her bedchamber.

Alexander couldn't dismiss that notion, not once he had touched her.

Had she seen his features? He couldn't imagine that she had had time to recognize him, especially as she'd only seen him before in his disguise. It was a mercy that he had used his foolish voice at the tavern, for he had spoken in his own usual tones when he addressed her in the night, too surprised to disguise his voice.

He should have released her. He should have frightened her. He should have let her flee. He gave her the opportunity, despite his desires, because he was a gentleman—even if on this particular night, he played the role of a thief.

But she welcomed his kiss. It was a invitation he couldn't deny.

One kiss.

Alexander knew it couldn't be a chaste kiss, not when Miss Goodenham's lips softened beneath his and she leaned against him. He caught her closer and deepened his kiss before he could think twice about the wisdom of that, and when she melted against him in surrender, he locked his arms around her, crushing her against his chest. She wasn't afraid, though, but seemed to welcome his tutelage. She mimicked his movements, sliding one hand around his neck and one around his waist, just as he held her, meeting him touch for touch. The kiss heated his blood and made him yearn for more.

More than was his right to take, even if she was impulsive enough to give it.

A clock chimed the quarter hour, recalling Alexander to his senses. He broke the kiss with reluctance, gazed upon her flushed cheeks, then drew his hood over his head to shadow his features. He stepped back when her lashes fluttered, then touched his finger to the tip of her nose.

"A siren after all," he murmured, his voice husky. He watched her smile. "But you must not see me. I was no more than a shadow in the night."

"But..."

He dropped his finger to her lips and couldn't resist the urge to slide it across them. She shivered, so responsive that he felt a fool for stepping away from her. "Not a word, my siren. You did not see me. We did not meet. You will return to your chamber and have sweet dreams, your reputation intact."

"I will dream of a specter in the night," she agreed. "Whose kiss is a dangerous temptation."

Alexander smiled. "Keep your eyes closed," he whispered. "I will fetch your candle."

"I have a flint in my pocket," she said.

"Then you can relight it once I am gone." He retrieved the candle and restored it to the candlestick she'd dropped, then placed the candlestick in her hand. He leaned closer, unable to resist touching his lips to her cheek once more. "Count to twenty before you open your eyes," he murmured.

"Aye, sir," she agreed, her lips curving in a smile that invited his touch.

Alexander surveyed her once more, knowing he would recall this vision often. "Sleep well, my siren."

"And you, sir," she whispered, then began to count.

Alexander did not delay. He fled on silent feet, ensuring there was no sign of him before she finished her count.

Before he had even left Castle Keyvnor—slipping out the unlocked window in the library, just as he had entered the castle—his decision was made. He would definitely go to London for the season, journeying there directly from Cornwall. He could not tolerate the notion of his innocent seductress being claimed by another man.

Back in his room at the inn, his arrival unobserved, Alexander removed the seed that Anthea had given him and once again rolled it between his finger and thumb. He could not deny that it had swollen a bit, a young root pushing against the shell from the inside.

The story was whimsy.

It was nonsense.

It was time to know for certain. He put water in the glass from his wine then dropped the seed into it, watching it sink to the bottom and roll to one side. He set the glass before the fire, having no expectations, and finally got himself to bed.

"Where were you?" Eurydice said the next morning as Daphne was getting dressed. Eurydice was lacing Daphne's stays since Jenny was staying downstairs for the day. Her cold had gotten much worse and *Grandmaman* had insisted. Nelson was with *Grandmaman* and Daphne was too impatient to wait.

But without her stays laced, Daphne couldn't escape her sister's questions.

She was sure Eurydice had planned it that way.

Daphne felt as if the entire world would know at a glimpse that she'd kissed a stranger in the night—or that she'd thought about him incessantly ever since—but was determined to keep her promise to that man. "Whatever do you mean?"

"I woke up in the middle of the night and you were gone. A clock was striking three."

"I was hungry. I went down to the kitchen."

"You should have rung for Jenny."

"I didn't want to wake her up for the sake of a scone."

"You were gone a long time," Eurydice said, showing the annoying persistence that was typical of her. Sometimes Daphne thought her sister could smell a secret and then she was like their grandmother's terrier, reluctant to leave the matter until she'd unearthed the prize.

Daphne gave her sister an exasperated look. "I got lost. This castle is enormous." It wasn't precisely a lie.

Eurydice rolled her eyes. "It's not that complicated."

"Well, maybe I'm not that clever," Daphne replied.

"Did you find the kitchen? Or did you just give up and come back here?"

"I found it. And there were some leftover scones from tea. I met Mary who told me a story about a magical ring."

Eurydice perched on the bed to listen. "Here?"

"Of course, here! One of the gentlemen, Lord Snow, wears it and it's supposed to banish ghosts."

Eurydice smiled. "If it's true, the ring will have plenty of chances to do that here."

"I thought it foolish, but Mary said ghosts were thrown into the sky on his arrival yesterday." Daphne put on her shoes and considered her reflection in the mirror. "You made these curls very nicely," she said, admiring her sister's handwork.

"You did mine better."

"But I enjoy it. You hate doing it, though you are improving."

"I took especial care as doubtless you intend to talk to the duke again."

To be sure, the duke offered a little less temptation on this day than he had at the tavern. Was it conceivable that such a man, however rich he might be, would be able to kiss her as the stranger in the night had done? Daphne had tingled in a most pleasurable way. Indeed, just thinking about that kiss—and the intensity of his blue eyes—made her flush all over again.

But then, the duke had blue eyes and an intense gaze as well.

How curious.

Daphne smiled because her sister was watching her. "And here I thought you were considering a post as a lady's maid, since *Grandmaman* has forbidden you to become a governess."

They laughed together.

"And perhaps you don't really wish to meet this particular duke again. Goodness, Daphne, but he reminds me of Falstaff."

Daphne frowned as they left their chamber together. "In that play *Grandmaman* took us to see in London?"

Eurydice nodded. "*Henry IV*. Falstaff was so fat. I couldn't believe that any man could be that large and still manage to walk, but your duke proves it can be so."

"I can't remember that actor's name," Daphne said, recalling another detail. "We scarce recognized him when we saw him in town."

Eurydice laughed. "The power of disguise. Come along. I'm famished, probably because I didn't have a scone in the middle of the night. Let us have something to eat before we walk to Bocka Morrow for church."

Daphne slanted a glance at her sister. "You just want to tease me about the duke."

"I just want to see you realize your mistake. I don't think you will like him nearly as well on second acquaintance. He is a fool, Daphne, and not a man who will ever hold your heart."

Daphne didn't reply. She was thinking about the handsome stranger and wondering what she would say to him if they met again at breakfast. Her heart skipped at the prospect. Would he look as dashing in the daylight as at night? Would she recognize him?

And what was he doing, abroad in the middle of the night? She'd never asked and only wondered in the morning if his kiss had been a way to keep her from doing as much.

He might well be a scoundrel or a rake.

Then she thought of the duke, his fine legs and the intense glitter of his eyes. Could it be that he and the actor who had played Falstaff had a disguise in common?

Or had she become as whimsical as the maid Mary after her midnight adventure?

CHAPTER 3

*A*lexander awakened to find that a lush plant growing from his wine glass. Surely, his eyes deceived him. That small seed couldn't have grown so much in a few hours!

He rubbed his eyes and rose to examine the plant, but it was no illusion. He could see its roots coiled inside the cup, and it had grown a vine of at least a foot long, one adorned with fleshy dark leaves. There was even a bud tucked beneath one leaf.

Rupert was suitably astonished by the sight of it, but Alexander didn't explain. He didn't think the truth would sound plausible.

He halfway didn't believe it himself. Could Anthea have been right about the old tale and the vine's habit of growing when the laird courted a wife?

If so, he knew which lady he would court. Miss Goodenham was the most captivating girl he'd met in years.

As he dressed, he considered that he scarcely knew her.

He recalled how he relied upon his instincts in all other matters and wondered whether to trust them in this one.

When the bells rang for church at St. David's, the bud burst into a blossom. Alexander could almost hear the petals unfurling. They were as red as blood and the flower was as wide as his palm. Rupert swore and took a step away from the vine. Alexander could only take its blooming as a sign. He plucked the deep red flower and tucked it into his buttonhole.

It had a most enchanting perfume, and one deep breath of it reminded him of the fire in a certain damsel's kiss.

◠

THERE WAS no man at breakfast who might have been the mysterious stranger Daphne had met in the night. The gentlemen were fine, but not a one was the right height and breadth, had the right hands or the same wondrous blue eyes. None of them gave her more than a passing glance.

Who was he?

Where was he? Daphne supposed he could have been a servant or another guest who had not yet come down for breakfast. What had he been doing in the corridor at such an hour? The more she considered it, the more details she recalled. He had been dressed all in black, but he hadn't worn a nightshirt. No, he had been dressed in breeches and boots, with a great cloak.

Had he been an intruder?

No one mentioned a theft or other villainous deed, which puzzled Daphne even more.

Why had her mysterious man been within Castle Keyvnor?

The conversation in the dining room was interrupted by a man's hearty laugh in the foyer. All the women at the table looked up, particularly when he was greeted by the Earl of Bansfield. "Young Nathaniel! I hope you slept well!"

"I did, thank you, cousin. I trust that Lady Tamsyn is pleased?"

The earl laughed. "She is delighted."

"Then my mission is complete. I shall ride for home this morning."

"But you cannot reach London before Christmas, Nathaniel," the earl said. "Surely you will stay for the wedding?"

"I would not be so presumptuous. I know I am not expected to linger..."

"But I have ensured there is a chamber for you all the same," the earl said heartily. "We cannot send you from the doors at Christmas!"

"I thank you kindly, sir."

The earl entered the dining room with a young man who smiled at the gathered company.

"My wife's second cousin, Nathaniel Cushing, for those of you who did not meet him yesterday," the earl said. "Surely you know everyone here, Nathaniel?"

"Those I do not I will meet soon enough." Mr. Cushing bowed to the earl. "Thank you again for your generosity, sir." The earl nodded and departed, and the new arrival helped himself to breakfast.

Daphne took the opportunity to study him. Nathaniel Cushing was about a decade older than herself. He had dark hair and was both fiercely handsome and elegantly dressed. He appeared to be a most genial individual. He heaped a plate from the sideboard then took a place beside Daphne, introducing himself before he sat down.

He could have been the man she had encountered the night before. He looked suitably dashing, to be sure, and bold enough to have demanded a kiss in the night. But when he bestowed a warm smile upon her, his gaze lingering with appreciation, she noticed that his eyes were brown, not blue.

He had not been the one to kiss her, of that she was certain.

"What a marvel this place is," he said with enthusiasm. "Have you been here before?"

"Once. This autumn we visited briefly."

"How fortunate for you, Miss Goodenham. Perhaps I might prevail upon you to give me a short tour?"

"I mean to attend church this morning, Mr. Cushing. It would have to wait until after lunch."

"That would be marvelous. What better than a walk on a Sunday afternoon?"

"Cushing, do you know what Great Uncle Timothy sent to Lady Tamsyn?" asked another guest from down the table. It was one of the gentlemen.

"I would wager it is a gem," Mr. Cushing said. "Though I could not imagine which one. When I make a delivery for my great uncle, the box is sealed and locked before it is given to me. The key is dispatched separately to the recipient."

"But surely someone could steal the box?" Daphne asked.

Mr. Cushing's manner turned grim. "They would have to kill me first," he vowed.

"Indeed?"

"Indeed. My uncle entrusts me with these tasks and I would never fail him." He winked at Daphne and tucked into his eggs. "Beggars cannot be choosers and poor relations must earn their own way. I do quite like being Uncle Timothy's runner, though."

"Why is that?"

"I see the most wondrous places." He gestured with his fork. "I should never be invited to such a place as Castle Keyvnor at Christmas, much less have the opportunity to meet so many people throughout the year. His gifts give me purpose and adventure. I hope he never runs out of gems to give away."

"Does he often give gems away?"

"He is a collector of some renown, and has neither wife nor children. As he ages, he seems more inclined to bestow fine gifts on others. It is a mark of his splendid character."

"He might honor you with such a gift, surely?" Daphne suggested.

Mr. Cushing laughed easily, as if he had never given the notion any consideration. "But why? If he made me rich, he might lose me as a servant. Indeed, I might decline such a gift if it meant surrendering the opportunity to meet ladies like you, Miss Goodenham." He smiled at her, his eyes twinkling merrily, and Daphne could not help but be flattered by his attentions.

He had admitted he was penniless. He certainly had no title. Encouraging his attentions would do naught in the achievement of her goal to ensure the future of herself and Eurydice.

Daphne smiled, then excused herself. She did not want to be late for church, lest she miss a glimpse of the duke, and she did not want to walk to Bocka Morrow with Nathaniel Cushing, lest his presence keep the duke from speaking to her.

Her grandmother had taught her much of choosing practicality over romance.

~

MISS GOODENHAM CAME TO CHURCH.

Alexander hid his smile behind the gesture of taking a pinch of snuff, for he was absurdly glad to see her. He watched as she surveyed the congregation and noted that her gaze lingered upon him. His smile broadened that it was admiration lighting her gaze and not revulsion.

Yet he had chosen this hideous outfit of mauve and silver to appall one and all. Even the red flower clashed.

Perhaps the lady had bad taste.

Or perhaps she was sufficiently perceptive to see beyond illusion to the truth. As if to reinforce that notion, she smiled prettily when their gazes met, then seated herself with her cousins.

How could he determine how trustworthy she was? Anthea had hit the mark when she suggested he wed an honest woman. The trick was to find one.

Perhaps he could charm a dinner invitation from the family. It would give him both the opportunity to observe Nathaniel Cushing and to learn more about Miss Goodenham.

Before the bells of St. David's had finished their merry pealing after the service, Alexander was expected at eight at Castle Keyvnor for dinner. Miss Goodenham's pleasure in the news was unmistakable.

"What a marvelous buttonhole you have today, Your Grace," she said, then leaned closer to sniff the flower. Her eyes widened and he wondered if its perfume sent the same surge of desire through her.

Her gaze dropped to his lips and parted slightly, even as she flushed.

He recalled the sweetness of her kiss and wanted another.

"Wherever did you find it?"

"Ah, I could never tell!" he said with a giggle. "A man must keep some secrets to himself."

"As must a lady," she agreed. "Secrets, do you not think, add a wondrous spice to any exchange?"

"Secrets," he agreed, "sift the observant from those less so."

Her smile was radiant. "I see we are of one mind in this. Do you ever attend the theater, Your Grace?"

Her cousins were heading for the castle and her sister gave her a glare, but Miss Goodenham lingered. Alexander offered his elbow to her to escort her a bit of the way, and she accepted with a smile. She leaned against him a little so he could feel the curve of her breast against his arm.

"The theater?" he echoed, raising his quizzing glass to examine her. She was utterly perfect. "I do. And you?"

"Oh, not very often, but I did see a Shakespearean play the last time we were in London." Her smile was impish. "*Grandmaman* took us to see *Henry IV*."

"Perhaps she thought it a good way for you to learn more of border politics."

"Perhaps, though it would have been a more compelling lesson if she had not fallen asleep herself."

Alexander chuckled.

"I should have preferred to have seen something more amusing."

"Which of the plays would you have favored?"

She cast him a knowing glance. "*Twelfth Night* is my favorite, Your Grace."

"Because love conquers all?"

"You sound like my sister!"

"And mine, to be sure. But that is not your reasoning?"

She frowned. "I should like to think love would be triumphant, Your Grace, but find it easier to believe that justice will prevail." She met his gaze. "It is a more reassuring notion, do you not think?"

"I do."

"Plus I find characters in disguise most beguiling."

Alexander's heart stopped, then leaped. "But surely it is implausible for people to so readily err in identification?"

"I do not think so. Few people truly look or pay attention. And people pretend to be other than they are all the time. Some simply do it better than others."

"Does that make them dishonest?"

"Not if they have good cause. I am certain, for example, Your Grace, that if you or I ever donned a disguise, it would be for only the very best reasons."

"And how might you be so certain of that?"

She smiled sunnily. "My heart tells me so, and I trust it implicitly."

She continued, not giving him a chance to reply, "But what I most remember from that play was Falstaff."

"A rogue and a scoundrel."

"To be sure, and a very fat one, at least upon the stage." Her gaze dropped to his belly and he had the sudden suspicion that she had seen through his ruse. "Your waistcoat is most splendid today, Your Grace," she said lightly. "I have never seen such lavish embroidery."

"For church, you know. Lord knows one must wear one's best."

"Indeed. This silvery shade of mauve is most attractive. What do you call it?"

"*Lavande*, of course."

"Of course. Lavendar. And the grey?"

"*Argent*."

"Oh, no, sir, it cannot be *argent*. *Argent* is darker, like the spots on a dappled horse." She bit her lip and surveyed his waistcoat, which was filled with such bulk that it had required a considerable measure of cloth. Then she smiled. "It is the color of a dove. *Gris tourterelle*."

He simpered, to disguise how thoroughly he was charmed. "Everything sounds so much better in French, don't you think?"

"I do!" She laughed up at him. "While it sounds worse in German."

"More earthy, to be sure."

"I also think that your inspiration will cost *Grandmaman* a fortune once we reach London. Why, each suit you wear makes me wish for a dress in the same combination, Your Grace. Imagine a dress in this *lavande*, embellished with silver beads. It would be like moonlight."

He could imagine her in just such a dress, with his mother's amethysts. Daphne Goodenham would look like a goddess who had set foot on the earth. "It would be magnificent," he agreed. "With slippers of silver silk to match."

She laughed. "You would be perilous to a dressmaker's budget, Your Grace."

"So my sister has often said."

"You mentioned before that you had a sister. Will you tell me of her?"

"She is younger than me by a few years. Anthea is her name."

Daphne looked up at him, her expression sober. "You are very fond of her. I hear it in your words."

"Indeed. She is the sweetest of ladies."

"Has she had her debut?"

Alexander frowned despite himself. "It did not proceed well, despite my best efforts. Her heart was broken, and now she remains at Airdfinnan. No amount of cajoling will convince her to leave."

"How sad! Since you have said you frequent Town, it must be lonely there."

"She insists she prefers solitude."

"But she will never find a man of merit or fall in love so long as she remains secluded."

"You think I should compel her to leave her sanctuary?"

"No, no, Your Grace. I think it is a fine and noble thing that you offer her a haven, and that you defend her desire." Miss Goodenham frowned a little. "But it is so much easier when a beloved sister desires something that will make her happy in the end."

"Might I assume that you refer to Miss Eurydice?"

"I do. She thinks she does not need to wed, or that she can marry for love independent of fortune." The lady shook her head so that her blond curls danced. "It is whimsy, Your Grace. Women like us must be practical."

He was intrigued. "Women like you?"

"My sister and I were orphaned nine years ago, when our parents both died in an accident. We were very fortunate that *Grandmaman* saw fit not only to take us into her home, but to see us educated. She even intends to give us each a season."

"But surely you are her only granddaughters."

"We are, but her fortune is not infinite and she is of an age that I rather imagine she would prefer to be left to her letters and her gardens. The fact remains that she grows older." She lifted her chin, looking valiant and wise. "When our parents died, *Grandmaman* was in Bath. It took a fortnight for her to hear the news and come for us. I will never forget feeling responsible for Eurydice, that we two had only each other in the world. I vowed then that I would ensure our futures myself with a good marriage."

She must have been very young. It clearly had been a frightening experience.

"Eurydice thinks I wish to wed a duke because I am a frivolous fool," she said with a little smile.

"Perhaps you are not so frivolous as that."

"I do like clothes and I like parties and I suspect I could love a man simply because he granted me the security I desire most. Does that mean I am frivolous?"

"Not entirely so."

"I also like to balance the accounts with *Grandmaman* and ensure that every penny ends up where it belongs."

Alexander was impressed. "That is not frivolous!"

She smiled fleetingly. "Eurydice will wed for passion or not at all, so I must be the one to see that she always has a sanctuary." She glanced up at him. "I suppose that might sound conniving."

"It sounds sensible to me," Alexander acknowledged, forgetting to use his foppish voice. "And it is most admirable that your love for your sister takes such expression." He smiled. "I do not doubt that if you bent your will upon it, you could make any man happy indeed."

"I hope so, Your Grace. I am not as clever as Eurydice, that much is certain."

"But neither are you a fool, my dear."

"No," she agreed, casting him a glance of such mischief that the sight fairly stole Alexander's breath away. "If I may be so bold as to say so, Your Grace, you have the bluest eyes I have ever seen."

"I favor my mother in that, to be sure."

Her gaze dropped to his lips and lingered there, a flush staining her cheeks. Alexander halted and made a show of being out of breath, then doffed his glove to take a pinch of snuff. She watched his hands avidly, a conviction dawning in her eyes.

"Are you ever restless at night, Your Grace?" she asked and Alexander's heart stopped cold.

"Nay, never!" he lied, taking a hearty tone. "My valet says I snore fit to wake the dead!" He giggled again, but her gaze did not waver.

"How fortunate you are." Her cousins called and she glanced toward them, then curtseyed before him. "I shall look forward to seeing you at dinner tonight, Your Grace." Her eyes danced. "I cannot wait to see what you will wear!"

Alexander laughed, trying to turn the sound into a chortle.

"Miss Goodenham!" a man cried and Alexander sobered at the sight of his prey. Nathaniel Cushing swept in beside the girl and took her arm with such confidence that Alexander longed to challenge him. "The finest prize in the company will be left behind and I cannot permit it to be so."

Daphne's gaze clung to Alexander's for a moment and he wondered what she saw. "I do not mean to be left behind," she said lightly, putting a bit of distance between herself and Nathaniel. "It is a beautiful day and there is yet some time before luncheon."

"But I desire every moment with you," Cushing insisted. "For there is no greater beauty at Castle Keyvnor this Christmas."

Alexander did not hear Miss Goodenham's reply but he watched her depart, wondering all the while at the perils of her guessing his secret. She had guessed. He was certain of it and the notion was terrifying.

Surely she could not cost him the prize?

THE DUKE *WAS* THE INTRUDER. His eyes were just as blue. His lips were just as firm. Despite his paunch, his face was lean. His hands were long and strong, just like those of the intruder, and his legs were muscled. The duke used a similar disguise as the actor playing Falstaff, though apparently only Daphne had pierced the veil of his illusion.

The realization only redoubled her determination to win him. She was certain he had good reason for his disguise. He defended his sister, which was ample measure of his noble character, and his kiss nearly melted her bones. That he was a duke was as icing on the cake.

The Duke of Inverfyre was perfect.

She fancied that she was not the sole one who felt the attraction. The hungry blue glance he gave her at intervals was utterly out of character with his foppish guise, and reminded her all too well of his kiss.

The look he had given Mr. Cushing for interrupting had been pure fire.

The sight had sent heat through her, as well.

Daphne could not wait to see him again. She managed to separate herself from Mr. Cushing upon arrival at the castle as there was word that *Grandmaman* was coming down with Jenny's cold. She had remained in her rooms and resented the lack of news. She demanded to know who had gone to the village.

"Nathaniel Cushing," she said with disdain, then punctuated the words with a sneeze. "A ne'er-do-well if ever there was."

"Anyone with sense can see with a glance that he's a rake and a scoundrel," Eurydice agreed and her grandmother beamed at her.

"Anyone," Daphne agreed.

"I'm surprised you don't like him," Eurydice said. "He's handsome and charming, after all."

Daphne shrugged. "I don't."

"Because he's not rich," Eurydice said.

"How could you know such a thing?"

"When you were walking with the duke, our cousins were gossiping. They said he has nothing to his name but debt. He's something of a black sheep."

"But the earl expected him. Mr. Cushing must have had some reason for coming," Daphne said. "In fact, I believe he acted as a courier for his uncle, Mr. Timothy Cushing."

"Maybe he means to steal the Eye of India!" Eurydice declared.

Grandmaman snorted, then sneezed again. "From what I hear, he must have come to ask for money. Or a rich wife." She peered at Daphne. "Don't let him lead you astray, my dear, tempting you under the mistletoe or kissing you in the moonlight."

"Daphne has no money," Eurydice contributed. "Perhaps she won't tempt him."

"Any man might be tempted by Daphne, even if he couldn't do anything honorable about it," her grandmother corrected sternly. "I will not have scandal over a man like Nathaniel Cushing. Am I understood?"

"Yes, *Grandmaman*," Daphne and Eurydice agreed in unison.

What about a scandal over a man like the Duke of Inverfyre? Daphne didn't ask, but counted the moments until dinner.

"Now tell me," their grandmother demanded. "Just how richly was the church decorated for the holidays? I hope there was holly and a fine Advent wreath..."

~

"I'M NOT certain you would be wise to sleep in this chamber," Rupert said with some aggravation. "That wretched vine might completely engulf you during the night."

Alexander stared at the plant in question. While he had been at church, the plant had grown with astonishing speed. It was the size of a small shrub, both growing upright and trailing over the table. It was covered in deep red blooms and the scent of it was dizzying. Rupert had opened the window, admitting a damp chill, but the plant did not wilt.

Alexander thought of Daphne, the suspicion that she had pierced his disguise, and let admiration fill his heart.

The plant grew before his very eyes.

Rupert swore with enthusiasm. "I should chuck it out!"

"Not until my quest is complete."

"I fail to see what this infestation has to do with springing the trap."

Alexander knotted his cravat with care, declining to tell Rupert that he referred to another quest altogether. He liked the scent of the red flowers. The perfume seemed to lighten his heart, and optimism was a fine asset.

Miss Goodenham *had* admired his buttonhole. He took a fresh flower and a bud, twining them with several leaves to make a more elaborate buttonhole for dinner. He then turned and flaunted his splendor for Rupert, who shuddered.

"You are a vision that will be impossible to forget, Your Grace."

"Indeed."

Rupert brushed the shoulders of Alexander's silk brocade coat. "Are you certain Lady Tamsyn has received the gem?"

"Yes. I hope she will wear it at dinner, as Mr. Timothy Cushing requested."

"Surely the villain will not attempt anything more than admiration before the household?"

"Surely not." Alexander met Rupert's gaze in the mirror. "The sooner it has been admired, the sooner he will steal it. And then we shall finally discover how he removes his prize from the house."

"He has never been caught with the stolen gems on his person, no matter how thoroughly house and guests are searched."

"Never. But mark my words, the Eye of India will be his undoing."

*D*aphne was doomed to disappointment when she reached the dining room, due to the order of precedence and the vast size of the party at dinner. The duke might as well have dined in Bocka Morrow, for all her opportunity to speak with him. He was at the head of the table, which at least meant she could observe him from her place near the other end, but she couldn't even hear his words.

Mr. Cushing paused beside her and granted her an engaging grin. Daphne returned his smile politely. "What good fortune is mine," he said gallantly, sweeping into the seat beside her.

"I could argue that it is mine," Daphne replied in kind, though her heart was not in the words. She might have said something else, but Mr. Cushing suddenly leaned forward.

"I say! Is that the legendary Eye of India, Tamsyn?" he fairly shouted, peering down the table at one of the brides-to-be.

"It is, Nathaniel." Lady Tamsyn's hand rose to touch the brooch. "Great uncle Timothy sent it to me as a wedding gift. He said it belonged in the coffers of the Earl of Banfield and since I'm oldest, it should be mine."

"Is he truly our uncle?" asked Lady Morgan.

"Technically, he's probably a cousin," said Lady Rose.

"Or a great uncle," Lady Morgan suggested.

"I thought he was dead," confided Lady Gwyn, raising a horrified hand to her lips.

"We should have heard if he was," jested Lady Marjorie. "There would have been a ruckus when his gem collection was sold or given in bequests."

Daphne couldn't help but stare at the brooch. She'd never seen such a splendid piece of jewelry. In its center was an enormous sapphire of clear deep blue. The stone was surrounded by swirls of silver, each jammed with sparkling clear gems. It caught the light and glittered.

Surely those stones couldn't all be diamonds?

It would be worth a fortune, then.

"What a handsome gift," Daphne said.

"It is!" Lady Tamsyn said. "I was so surprised."

"I'm glad he sent it to you instead of me," Lady Morgan said. "I should be terrified that it would be stolen."

"Oh, it won't be," Lady Tamsyn said lightly. "Not here at Castle Keyvnor." She smiled at her betrothed. "And after the holidays, Gryffyn will take it to Lancarrow to be locked up for safekeeping."

"You won't be wearing it daily, after all," he replied with a teasing smile.

"Only until the wedding. Uncle Timothy asked me to wear it for luck until then. It seemed the least I could do."

"Although we have no need of luck," her beloved agreed.

The pair beamed at each other, so happy that they evidently had forgotten every other soul in the room. Daphne knew that she herself had too many expectations of a suitor to hope for love, as well.

She might hope for desire, perhaps.

Respect.

She spared a glance down the table to the duke, flushing when she realized he was watching her. His expression was serious and his eyes vehemently blue.

Then he lifted his quizzing glance and spoke in that falsely high voice. "Upon my word, *there* is a gem!" Evidently not satisfied with the view, he rose from his seat and trotted down the side of the table to Lady Tamsyn's side. He peered at it. "What a marvel! Do you know that the Prince Regent himself has a brooch similar to this, but admittedly somewhat smaller, that he often wears in his cravat?"

"I didn't know that," Lady Tamsyn said. "Although I wouldn't be surprised."

The duke gazed at the gem, nodding to himself. "A prize, to be sure." He flicked a glance across the table. "Do you not agree, Miss Goodenham?"

She colored more deeply to be so singled out. "I have never seen the like, Your Grace, although my experience of gems is limited."

"Marry well, my dear, and that may change," he replied jovially, then winked at her. Daphne blushed as Mr. Cushing chuckled.

"There is sound advice," he murmured.

Meanwhile, the duke took another look. "A magnificent sapphire," he pronounced, then returned to his seat, his heels clicking as he walked.

"But why is it called the Eye of India?" Daphne asked.

"Oh, it has a painting beneath the sapphire, of a man's eye," Mr. Cushing said.

Lady Tamsyn leaned across the table and Daphne could just barely glimpse the eye. "Great Uncle Timothy wrote that it was a gift from a gentleman to his lady love, as a token of his undying affection."

"But we don't know who he was," Lady Morgan added.

"Or the lady, for that matter," Lady Tamsyn agreed. "It is a lovely romantic story, but one that leaves as many questions as answers."

"Such as how Great Uncle Timothy came by it in the first place," Lady Morgan agreed.

Mr. Cushing cleared his throat. "I expect he bought it," he said. "My uncle buys a great many gems, and not always at public auctions. There are many jewelers who know of his collection."

"There you are, Tamsyn," Gryffyn said. "Lord Timothy has ensured your future, for you could always sell the brooch if need be."

Lady Tamsyn laughed prettily, for her future was clearly in no doubt given her betrothed's wealth.

Mr. Cushing cleared his throat. "I would venture to suggest that the man in question might be suspected to have been a Hambly for Uncle Timothy to believe the Eye of India belonged in your possession."

"How perfectly scandalous!" Lady Tamsyn said. "Who do you think it might have been?"

They laughed lightly and began to speculate as the soup was brought in.

After the soup had been served, Mr. Cushing leaned toward her. "I'm not surprised that the duke had a good look at the Eye of India."

"Indeed? Is he reputed to have a taste for gems, like your uncle?"

"More than a taste, to be sure. There is said to be an avarice for them in his family."

"Truly?"

"Truly. His sister Anthea was accused of being a thief and banished from polite society as a result."

"Oh! How horrible."

"It was horrible." Mr. Cushing shook his head. "In her debut season, as well."

"What a ghastly thing. Was she guilty?"

"What do you mean?"

"Well, you said she was accused, not discovered to be guilty. It's not quite the same thing."

He smiled at her indulgently, as if she were a child. "You take the side of a stranger?"

"If it was her debut, I can't imagine she would be scheming to steal gems. She would be too busy thinking about dance cards and eligible beaus and dresses."

Mr. Cushing seemed to find this a foolish view. "Nonetheless, she was accused and fled London for Scotland. Surely no one innocent would have done as much? That she would hurry home and never leave again indicates her guilt."

Daphne could well imagine that the duke's sister might have left the city out of mortification, even at being so accused, not necessarily of guilt. "And was the gem found?"

"No, but then they didn't look at Airdfinnan." Mr. Cushing nodded down the table. "The duke would not let anyone through the gates to search. Perhaps he knows where it is."

"I think it admirable that he defended his sister against rumor and innuendo," Daphne said primly. She rather imagined that the duke might fight dragons for his sister and admired him for that.

"It was not admirable if she was guilty. To harbor a thief is reprehensible." Mr. Cushing shook his head. "And one does wonder how he comes by such wealth. It is said that he doesn't owe so much as a shilling to any man."

Daphne straightened, finding much to admire in fiscal responsibility and knowing that it did not necessarily mean the duke funded his purchases with theft. She chose not to share her grandmother's comment about the family declining to gamble.

"Is that so uncommon, then?" she asked, feigning ignorance of such matters.

Mr. Cushing gave a bark of a laugh. "To me, it seems a miracle."

Yes, he might be the sort of man to live far beyond his own means. She smiled and ended the conversation, then turned to the cousin on her other side to ask about the wedding preparations.

Daphne was not certain what awakened her.

For once, it wasn't her nightmare.

It was the middle of the night, the room still dark. Eurydice snored, her breath rattling as if she too would take Jenny's cold. That clock chimed in the distance.

Three in the morning again, but this time, Daphne was not hungry.

She felt rather than saw that there was another presence in the room. She couldn't have named what alerted her to the intruder, a faint scent of cologne, perhaps, or a rustle of cloth. She kept her eyes closed, rolled over with a sigh and breathed as if she were asleep.

She heard a footfall. Was it the duke? Even if he was the intruder, surely he was too honorable to assault a girl in her own room? Daphne was prepared to scream if a finger was laid upon her, even as she doubted her duke would act in such a way.

She heard a click, like the closing of her trunk. She opened her eyes slightly and saw a wedge of moonlight as the door to the corridor was opened. She had the barest glimpse of a shadow passing through the door, then the door was closed and there was only the sound of Eurydice's breathing.

Who had been in their room?

Why?

Daphne waited until first light because she didn't want to light a candle and risk awakening Eurydice. She slipped from her bed as quietly as possible and went to her trunk. It looked just as it had the night before and she wondered if she had dreamed of the intruder. She quietly opened her trunk and surveyed the contents in the dim light, then patted the folded chemises and petticoats.

Her hand stilled over a hard shape that hadn't been there before.

It was an unfamiliar drawstring bag, made of deep blue velvet. Daphne's mouth went dry. She cast a glance at Eurydice, then opened the bag, tipping its contents into her hand.

It was the Eye of India.

Panic rose hot in her chest as she stared at the gem.

What should she do?

Daphne recalled Mr. Cushing's tale of the night before and knew that she could not let herself be named as a thief. Who would believe her if she said someone had placed it in her room? Would she be falsely accused and banished from polite society, like the duke's sister? Daphne could not bear it.

She could not risk it.

Not if she was to guarantee Eurydice's future.

Daphne returned the brooch in its velvet bag and knotted the cord, just as it had been, then replaced it in her trunk. She went back to bed, her thoughts spinning. The others would be awakening. The loss would be discovered. What should she do? If there was a search for the gem, she didn't want to have it with her. Neither did she want it to be found in her possessions.

She wished she could talk to the duke and seek his advice, but it was impossible for her to get to Bocka Morrow without being observed.

Or was it?

No one had seen Jenny since their arrival.

It was not even dawn.

Did she dare? Daphne rang for her maid before she could question her impulse.

One thing was certain: the duke would know what to do.

It was Alexander's custom to rise early in the morning, and travel did not change his routine. It was before dawn but he had risen and washed. He remained in his chamber in his plain breeches, boots and open shirt. The tavern was still quiet, and he knew Rupert stood guard outside the door. He sat with his tea and reviewed his recent correspondence, hoping against hope that he was right about this scheme. He seldom had doubts about his course, but in the final hours before a plan came to its conclusion, it seemed that all the other possibilities became infinitely more plausible.

What if he was wrong about Nathaniel Cushing being the thief?

No, he could not be.

What if he could not prove that Nathaniel Cushing was the thief?

There was a distinct possibility. If Cushing did not take the bait, if he did not try to steal the Eye of India, if he was not caught with it in his possession...Alexander rose to pace his humble chamber, restless with uncertainty.

What if Cushing changed the pattern of his behavior? It would have been ideal to have been at Castle Keyvnor the night before, but Alexander dared not take a second chance when the house was full of guests.

There would be severe repercussions if the true Eye of India was lost in the attempt. Alexander checked upon it again. He had retrieved it from the castle that first night and only Daphne Goodenham knew he had been there. It remained safely in his belongings at the tavern.

And what of Miss Goodenham? How had she guessed that he wore a disguise? Who had she told? He should have demanded her secrecy instead of assuming it. She might tell her sister, and who could tell where that girl would place her confidence?

Alexander gave a low growl of frustration and wished he had something stronger than tea. It was all too easy to think of his other source of frustration, that tantalizing kiss in the night, and the sweetness of Miss Goodenham's lips. He disliked that Cushing talked to her so much. Surely she could not be Cushing's ally? Surely she could not reveal Alexander?

How could he be certain?

When would he see her again?

How would he know she was trustworthy?

There was a commotion in the tavern below and Alexander frowned at the door. A woman raised her voice, her Scottish brogue thick and her voice high. "I must see His Grace!" she cried, which was remarkable given the early hour.

"His Grace is not receiving guests," Rupert said firmly.

There was the sound of a scuffle and feet racing up the wooden stairs. Rupert swore and heavier footfalls echoed after the lighter ones. Alexander spun to seize his cloak but he was too late. He only had his hand upon it when the door to his chamber was thrown open and a woman in a hooded cloak flung herself toward him.

"Your Grace!" Rupert exclaimed, his annoyance more than clear. "I do apologize. She is as slippery as a fish!"

"Your Grace," the maid cried as she fell prostate at his feet. "I beg you to aid my mistress!"

Alexander was astonished. He might have asked a question, but the maid stretched out her hand, offering a very familiar blue velvet bag.

It was not empty. He could see the shape of the gem through the cloth.

Why had she brought the counterfeit Eye of India to him?

He gestured to the door with an imperious fingertip, knowing it was too late to don his disguise. He would have to hope that the girl did not dare to look into his face. "Remain with us, Haskell, and stand witness to this business."

"Of course, Your Grace." The door was secured and Rupert leaned back against it, his expression one of complete distrust. The maid remained on the floor before Alexander and he could see that she was out of breath.

"Who is your mistress?" he demanded.

"I dare not utter her name, Your Grace," she said and something in her voice was achingly familiar. Alexander took a step closer as the maid lifted her head, letting him see her face for the first time.

It was Miss Goodenham herself.

Who showed considerable promise in mimicry.

"Oh!" she whispered, her eyes lighting and a smile curving her lips as she looked upon him.

"Oh," he replied, then arched a brow. He was both vexed and intrigued, and uncertain which reaction to show her. He indicated the velvet sack. "Where did you get it?"

She lowered her voice to a whisper. "Someone was in my room last night. Eurydice was asleep. I thought it might have been you, sir," she confessed, blushing prettily.

Rupert cleared his throat.

She lifted the bag with a shaking hand. "But I found this in my trunk this morning. I don't know what to do, but I knew you would give me good advice."

So, this was how the gems left the house after they were stolen. Cushing selected a guest with an excess of luggage, relied upon the gem not being discovered before that guest's departure, then retrieved it at some later point. Perhaps he chose someone who openly admired the prize, as Miss Goodenham had.

He recalled Anthea mentioning that they'd encountered Nathaniel Cushing at a tavern on the way home to Inverfyre after the accusations were made against her. He had reportedly been sympathetic about the accusations against her and had shared a meal with Anthea and her companion.

Alexander could imagine that the other man had also retrieved the stolen gem from Anthea's luggage.

But there had been a search. How had the gem not been found in the house where Anthea had stayed? He was missing yet a piece of the puzzle.

His decision made, he turned to Daphne. "Put it back."

She paled. "But it will be missed. There must be a search for such a treasure..."

"There should be, and if there is not, I would ask you to encourage there to be one. A word to the butler should see it done."

Her lips parted in astonishment and she rose unsteadily to her feet. She looked very young and uncertain. "But I should be accused when it is found."

"I wonder if it will be found," Alexander said. "For if it were, there would be no point to the theft."

She frowned and looked down at the velvet sack. "I do not understand."

"Tell me who is given the task of searching your chamber," Alexander advised.

Her eyes lit. "You think the thief will volunteer to assist, that he or she will search my chamber but fail to find the gem!" She bit her lip. "But why?

"So you would take the gem from the castle, unwittingly."

"And the thief would waylay us somewhere and reclaim it."

"I see no other solution. Do you?"

"It is bold and clever." She stroked the velvet and looked so fearful that he wished to ease away every one of her concerns. "But what if you are wrong, Your Grace?" she asked quietly.

"Then I will defend you to my dying breath, Miss Goodenham," he murmured, holding her gaze so that she could see his conviction.

She shook her head. "I thank you for the sentiment, but your word might not matter, not with something of such value as this prize."

Alexander smiled. "But the value is exactly the key." Her lack of comprehension was clear. "The gem you hold is a fake, Miss Goodenham, created solely to trap the villain."

"Oh!" Her pleasure made her cheeks flush and her eyes sparkle. She lowered her voice to an enticing whisper. "I knew, sir, that if you donned a disguise, it would be for a good reason."

"It is."

"It was this same villain who ensured that your sister's name was tainted," she guessed.

"Indeed it was, and I have vowed to avenge her."

"So, justice will prevail," she said with complete satisfaction.

"Only with your assistance."

"I shall do as you instruct, Your Grace."

The heat of his own pleasure must have shown in his expression, for she modestly dropped her gaze and glanced across the room.

She did not leave, however, which was all the encouragement he needed.

"Might I confide in my sister to see your quest accomplished?" she asked.

"Do you trust her?"

"Utterly," she said without hesitation. "Eurydice would never betray me, nor I her."

Because they had been reliant upon each other when they were orphaned.

"And she is clever," Miss Goodenham admitted. "I think the prospect of success much higher with her aid."

Alexander nodded understanding, moved more by her trust in Miss Eurydice than her confidence in her sister's wits. "Then by all means, confide in her, but not others, I beg of you."

"It shall be as you say, Your Grace." Still she did not meet his gaze and it seemed to him that her breath came quickly. He guessed that she wished for further reassurance but knew not how to ask for it.

The situation was damnably unconventional.

His gaze rose to Rupert, who evidently was fascinated with the ceiling. Should he send the other man away? His desire for Miss Goodenham was acute, but he would not ruin her and leave her with doubts of his intent. He did not know precisely what he might say to feed her confidence in his honor.

Inspiration came from the fact that Daphne was staring at the vine, which now spilled to the very floor and reached for the ceiling.

Alexander knew its tale might be of aid. "The seed was a gift from my sister," he confessed. "And a legacy of Airdfinnan. I dropped it into water but one night ago."

"But that cannot be! It is of such a size."

"It is said to grow and bloom only when the Laird of Airdfinnan courts a bride."

"Am I wrong that you would be that laird, Your Grace?" she whispered.

"You are not, and before you ask, I do mean to court a bride once this matter is concluded," he admitted. "To be sure, I had no plan of doing as much, but I met a most beguiling girl, in a tavern, no less."

She flushed and began to smile. "Beguiling, sir?"

"And marvelously perceptive, as well," he agreed and smiled. "I like people who look beyond appearances."

Her gaze clung to his. "As do I, Your Grace."

"It would please me greatly if she granted me some small sign of encouragement."

Alexander barely had time to utter the words before Miss Goodenham cast herself at him with pleasure. He caught her in his arms, savoring the sweet press of her against his chest.

She framed his face in her small hands and studied him intently. "'Twas your eyes that gave you away, sir," she murmured. "You must promise not to look at any other girl so intently before your quest is complete or you might be revealed."

"The quest to name the thief or the quest to have your hand in mine?"

"Both!" she said with a smile.

Alexander chuckled and held her closer. "I vow that I will not," he agreed, then bent to taste her lips again.

Daphne could not believe her good fortune.

The duke was not a fop! No, he was the most handsome man she had ever seen. And he had no ungainly paunch. She had pierced his disguise and even better, he had trusted her with the truth and vowed to defend her. She was convinced that she was the most fortunate woman in all of England, and that was before he kissed her.

It was even better than the first time.

She was the most fortunate woman in all the world.

He broke his kiss and looked down at her, his gaze filled with a lazy satisfaction that thrilled her beyond all else. "My true appearance must remain a secret."

"I will never betray you, Your Grace."

"You cannot even confide this in Eurydice."

"I will not. I pledge it to you." She swallowed. "I vow to be the best wife, Your Grace, and to bear you a dozen sons..."

He smiled. "You will call me Alexander, when we are alone, and I think three sons will do nicely."

"As you wish." Daphne licked her lips. "Alexander."

It felt both sinful and right to say his name, much as kissing him felt both wicked and heavenly.

She smiled at him. "You should call me Daphne, then."

"Indeed, I should." His eyes fairly glowed and the intensity of his look made her shiver. With obvious reluctance, he released her. He seized a dark jacket and a cloak, as well as a large hat. "And now I will see you safely back to the castle."

"But..."

He raised his voice and interrupted her protest before it began. "Upon my word, Haskell, must you bring your wenches and conquests into my own chambers? For all I know, she may have *fleas!*"

"I am sorry, Your Grace," his manservant said, also speaking loudly enough to be overheard.

"Take her away and see her home again, and make haste about it." Then Alexander changed the tone of his voice, sounding for all the world like the manservant. "Of course, Your Grace."

Daphne might have stepped into a play herself.

The manservant spoke shrilly then, mimicking Alexander's foppish voice perfectly. "I would have my chocolate upon your return, Haskell! Hurry, man! I will not be kept waiting for the sake of your wench, no matter how comely she might be!"

"Immediately, Your Grace," Alexander said.

The two men exchanged a wink before Alexander opened the door. He pulled up his hood, then Daphne's as well, then hastened her down the stairs and out of the tavern.

They were barely spared a glance by those arriving to work in the kitchen, and she was spirited toward Castle Keyvnor with impressive speed. He took her through the forests and by paths where they would not be observed, tucking her beneath his cloak when he heard a sound and sweeping her into his arms when he found her pace too slow. The journey was thrilling and all too soon, they approached the castle from behind.

"You are so clever," she said with awe. "You could be upon the stage."

He laughed, a lovely rich sound that made Daphne heat to her toes. "I will give up the disguise once this villain is caught, Daphne, and spend my days beguiling you instead."

"I cannot wait, Your Grace," she whispered and he raised a finger, his eyes gleaming. "Alexander," she corrected. "Though you shall have to convince Grandmaman. She said that you would never wed."

"Fear not, my Daphne. I will win her consent," he growled and Daphne's heart skipped a beat before he kissed her again.

The third time was the best kiss yet.

THE THIEF WAS AWAKE, for the game came rapidly to its conclusion. He seldom slept until his quarry was securely within his grasp and this time, he sensed that something went awry.

What had that small mark been on the back of the gem? It was new, but not a scratch. A maker's mark and not one he recognized.

It troubled him, deeply.

Something was afoot, though the villain could not name what it was.

He was standing at the window of the chamber he had been given—a small room with a view of the working side of the castle, rather than the sea or the village or even the gates—at the moment that two cloaked figures made a dash from the edge of the woods to the back wall.

Their manner was so furtive that he pressed against the glass, watching.

Were they servants? He could not imagine as much. Every servant was hard at work at this hour of the morning. A noble couple returning from an assignation? There was no doubt that he watched a woman and a man. Did their actions have any relevance to his own plan?

The woman glanced up at the castle walls, just before the couple parted. It was Miss Goodenham, in humble garb. The villain recognized her immediately.

The man's face was not revealed but he left Miss Goodenham at the door and strode back by the same route they had arrived. The villain watched until he disappeared into the shadows of the forest, noting his height and breadth, and his manner of walking. He did not recognize the man, but he was clearly not staying at the keep.

Had Miss Goodenham sought him out? The villain could think of no other way she could have returned in the other man's company.

Could he be the Duke of Inverfyre's man? He had kissed Miss Goodenham before they parted. Would she be so fool as to accept the attentions of a valet? It was difficult to believe she would be so unambitious, but she might be one to put much credit in love.

The greater concern was for the prize that the villain had thought safely hidden in Miss Goodenham's trunk. Had she discovered and removed it, perhaps granting it to her paramour for safekeeping?

The villain did not know.

And what of that mark? What if the gem was a forgery? He could not fathom how it had been replaced in the single night between its delivery and his theft of it, but what if it had been switched?

What if he had stolen a fake?

How much did Miss Goodenham know?

The villain did not like surprises or uncertainty.

He certainly did not intend to be caught.

Which meant that he had to speak to Miss Goodenham alone and learn the truth of whatever she had done.

No matter what the cost.

CHAPTER 5

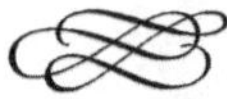

*E*urydice awakened to find that Daphne was gone. Jenny was inexplicably huddled in the corner of the room, still sniffling from her cold. She was wrapped in a blanket from Daphne's bed and looked to be miserable.

Eurydice sat up and felt so chilled that she shivered. How she hated to fall ill! "Where is Daphne?" she asked and the maid lifted a finger to her lips.

"She told me to wait here and be utterly silent," Jenny confessed in a whisper.

"But why?"

The maid shrugged, proving once again that she was possessed of less curiosity than Eurydice. Even if Daphne had been stern and mysterious, Eurydice would have been more interested in the truth than Jenny appeared to be. She made to get out of bed and sneezed again.

"My lady, it seems you had better stay in bed today," Jenny said, still keeping her voice low. "I'll fetch you water to wash, for a change of nightrail will be welcome, as soon as Miss Goodenham returns."

"But where has she gone?" Eurydice asked in exasperation. She could hear the house beginning to stir and she was hungry.

Jenny shrugged again, and then Daphne herself came quickly through the door. She was out of breath from running and dressed in

Jenny's clothes. Her hair was only braided but her eyes shone with audacity and satisfaction. She was flushed and delighted in a way that Eurydice did not trust.

Surely her sister had not been so foolish as to meet a man?

Daphne quickly shed the clothes she wore and helped Jenny to don them, then sent the maid for hot water. Once the maid was gone, she hurried to her trunk and tucked something into it before facing Eurydice.

"What are you doing?" Eurydice demanded, sensing a scheme and wanting all the details. "Tell me that you did not have an assignation!"

"Shhhh!" Daphne said, practically flying across the chamber to lay her finger across Eurydice's lips. "Do not speak of it, and keep your voice low no matter what you say."

"Where did you go?"

Daphne glanced to the door and leaned close, her lips practically against Eurydice's ear. Even so, Eurydice had to concentrate to hear her. "There is a thief in the house and the duke is intent upon catching him," she confided. "I heard someone in our room and found the Eye of India in my trunk this morning. I knew the duke would best advise me what to do."

"You went to him?"

Daphne nodded.

"I imagine you had a shock if you saw him before he was dressed. Is he bald, too?"

Daphne shook her head, impatient with such details. "He bade me put it back and said there would be a search called this morning. If not, I'm to encourage one."

Eurydice sat back in horror. "But then you'll be named..."

"No," Daphne said. "He said he'd defend me if so, but he thinks it will not be so. I am to observe who searches our chamber and report to him."

"Why would the thief hide it here?"

"The duke has a notion that he would see proven." Daphne glanced about herself again then whispered even more quietly, "He thinks the thief uses an unwitting guest as his accomplice to remove his prize from the house, then pilfers that person's luggage later."

"What a devious fiend."

"Indeed."

"And he is here, perhaps a guest at the castle." Already Eurydice was reviewing the list of guests and considering which was most likely to be a jewel thief.

"So it appears." Daphne frowned. "I believe the duke's sister's reputation was soiled by this man and his schemes."

"Then he must be caught."

"Agreed."

Eurydice reflected upon the matter. "If I were to organize a search to find such a missing treasure, I would wait until all the gentlemen were in the dining room, as well as whatever ladies were coming down. I would then search the gentlemen's rooms quietly, without their awareness, and search the ladies' rooms after they had made their way downstairs for the activities of the day. It could all be accomplished with great discretion, save the searching of individual persons."

"Do you think the earl will allow that?"

"Not if he wishes to keep the theft and the search secret. It will be up to the butler, Morris, to orchestrate the details. You should dress and go down for breakfast as soon as possible, to learn as much as you can of their scheme."

"And you?"

Eurydice smiled. "I fear I am too sick to leave our chamber." She sneezed with gusto and pretended to sniffle. "Jenny has already told me to remain in bed. I will do as much and feign sleep. Then I will see who searches our chamber and where he or she looks."

"Jenny should remain with you."

"If I were the thief, I would not search the chamber until she was gone."

"Do you think it quite safe for you to be alone here?"

"Perhaps not, but it is devilishly exciting." Eurydice smiled. "Like something from a novel. Return before luncheon and I will tell you what I have seen. After all, I would not have you be without tidings for your duke."

Daphne gripped her hand. "Thank you, Eurydice."

"I still cannot fathom what you find appealing about the man."

Her sister's smile was quick and triumphant. "Perhaps love works in mysterious ways."

"Love?!" Despite her protestation, not another word about the duke could Eurydice pry from Daphne's lips.

❧

DAPHNE LISTENED with care as she descended the main staircase. She could hear the murmur of men's voices, and thought she detected a thread of urgency. The earl was conferring quietly with the butler, Morris, the pair of them very solemn.

"And are you not a fine sight with which to greet the day, Miss Goodenham?" Mr. Cushing demanded cheerfully, his voice behind Daphne enough to make her jump. "I daresay you are the prettiest girl in Cornwall."

"I thank you, sir," she said, taking his elbow to continue into the dining room. "Do you mean to ride today?"

"Oh, I think not," he said easily, then wagged a finger at her. "You neglected to give me a tour yesterday."

"Indeed, I did. I am sorry but my grandmother required our attendance."

"And I am heartbroken," he said lightly. "Would you do the honors this morning instead?"

Daphne frowned as Gryffyn Cardew joined the other two men and their murmuring continued.

The theft had been discovered then, and they were deciding what to do.

She continued to chatter, as if oblivious, though her heart was skipping. "I had thought of taking a walk in the garden," Daphne said.

"Oh, but that would suit me perfectly!" Mr. Cushing said. "Is it true that there is a maze?"

"A very fine one, sir."

"Then I would entreat you to show it to me this very morning." He made a pout, although his eyes were twinkling. "Otherwise, Miss Goodenham, my heart may never recover from the blow you have dealt it."

Daphne laughed, as she was certain she was meant to. She truly didn't care about showing Mr. Cushing any detail of the house or garden, but she supposed she should behave as if all were normal. The duke could act brilliantly, so she would try to do the same. The gentlemen in the foyer clearly came to some agreement with Morris. The butler then conferred with Mrs. Bray before the pair set off together.

There was purpose in their strides.

But if only Morris and Mrs. Bray did the searches, did that mean one of them was the thief?

Or had Alexander been mistaken?

Daphne's throat tightened with the prospect of the Eye of India being found in her trunk. What would her grandmother say? What could she do? She had promised the duke to do as instructed, and this was but the first test of her obedience.

She would not fail him.

It was the housekeeper, Mrs. Bray, who knocked on the door.

"Whatever are *you* doing here?" she demanded when Jenny opened the door.

"Lady Eurydice is ill, Mrs. Bray, and thought I should attend to her..."

Eurydice managed to summon an impressive sneeze. She sniffled and dabbed at her eyes as the housekeeper surveyed her with disapproval. "Good morning, Mrs. Bray," she said, ensuring that she sounded as if her nose was blocked.

"If I may say so, it does not appear to be a good day for you, Miss Eurydice," the older woman said sourly, then turned to Jenny again. "What you should do is tell Nelson of your mistress' illness so that Lady North Barrows is fully aware of the situation."

"Yes, Mrs. Bray."

"I suggest you do so immediately."

Jenny cast a glance at Eurydice.

"It would be very sensible, Jenny," Eurydice said. "Please go."

No sooner had the door closed behind the maid, then Mrs. Bray fixed Eurydice with a look. "I do apologize for the inconvenience, miss, but there has been a theft. Morris has instructed me to search the baggage of lady guests in the remote chance that the Eye of India has been...misplaced."

Eurydice strove to appear both surprised and alarmed. "The Eye of India? Isn't that the gem that was given to Lady Tamsyn?"

"The very same."

"I cannot imagine how it might be in our luggage."

The housekeeper gave her a quelling look. "Surely you do not wish to obstruct the course of justice, Miss Eurydice?"

"Surely not, Mrs. Bray," Eurydice said, clenching her hands together beneath the sheets. Was Mrs. Bray the thief? It did seem unlikely.

But if the housekeeper wasn't the thief, then the duke had given Daphne bad advice. The gem would be found and Daphne would be accused of taking it. Had her sister granted her trust in the wrong place?

Eurydice could scarcely breathe in her terror, but she did her best to continue the ruse of being ill. To be sure, she did not have to do it long.

Within moments, Mrs. Bray had found the gem. She froze in the act of searching Daphne's trunk, then straightened slowly with the velvet sack in her hand. She opened it and Eurydice saw a flash of the stones, then Mrs. Bray turned to face her with it on her palm. "I suppose you know nothing of how this came to be here?"

Eurydice didn't have to pretend to be shocked. "Nothing!" she squeaked. "Daphne would never have taken it. She doesn't even take my hair ribbons!"

The grim housekeeper did not reply. She simply left the room, inclining her head briefly to Eurydice, then called for Morris.

Eurydice felt truly ill then.

Daphne was doomed.

She flung herself from the bed and began to dress with haste.

～

ALEXANDER PACED in his chamber at the tavern. He had to leave time for the trap to be sprung, but he did not like that Daphne was alone and undefended. He was tense. Uncertain. Fearful of the outcome.

"You are going to the castle for luncheon," Rupert murmured, his tone reassuring. He was polishing Alexander's boots. "She cannot find much trouble in the span of several hours."

"I would argue that a girl could find boundless trouble in so much time as that," Alexander replied grimly. "I, for example, could have ruined her in thirty minutes."

"Given your recent chastity and her beauty, it might have only taken ten."

Alexander glared at his friend, not so much because he was annoyed but because he felt it was expected.

Rupert grinned. He then sobered. "Are you certain you should have trusted her?"

"Why would I not have done so?"

"She could be part of the scheme. The villain might mean to draw you out. You did, after all, walk with her after church yesterday."

"And so?"

"And so, if the thief guesses your role, he might have chosen her as an ally in exposing you. She might be in his trust and sent to draw you out."

Alexander shook his head, trusting his instinctive sense of her honesty. "Daphne has no guile."

"She might be a pawn, used without her awareness that she is being so manipulated."

There was a prospect that Alexander could not readily refute.

Before he could summon a reply, there was a sound from the table before the fire. He spun to see that the vine had dropped a large bud, which had made a noise when striking the floor. He might have expected that the blooms would eventually fade, but another fell with a thud as he was watching. In fact, there were no open flowers left at all. They were all either closed or closing, their hue turning as dark as midnight, and more of them fell before his eyes.

The vine even seemed to wilt, drooping with no hint of its former vigor.

"Finally, that wretched thing reaches its limit. I had wondered what we were to do with it on our departure," Rupert began but Alexander held up a hand.

"It thrives when the laird's courtship finds favor," he said with resolve. "That is the tale. Either she has turned against me, or she is in peril." His voice rose to a roar. "My boots! My jacket! A horse, for the love of God!"

"Aye, go," Rupert replied, taking the foppish tone of Alexander's disguise. "Leave me with this mess of a cravat while you pursue your paramour!"

Alexander realized that his friend was thinking more clearly than he was. It would be much quicker for him to leave if he pretended to be Haskell.

That man continued as he gave Alexander the dark jacket and cloak, helping him dress with all haste. "I tell you, Haskell, one more *billet-doux* and we are finished. Finished! If I cannot rely upon your undivided attention, then I have no need of your services at all!" He dropped his voice. "Take the bay. She is more than ready to run."

Alexander nodded and left the chamber as Haskell complained mightily about his supposed shortcomings, hoping with every step that he reached Daphne in time.

Daphne did not manage to eat much more than a morsel at breakfast, although the food was delicious. She smiled and nodded, but had little idea what was said to her.

Morris came into the dining room, his expression stern, and bent to whisper something to Mr. Cushing. That man excused himself and left the room, and Daphne swallowed in her fear.

She excused herself and left the dining room, heading back to the chamber she shared with Eurydice. She wanted desperately to know what had happened in her absence.

She only made it to the base of the stairs before Mr. Cushing came striding out of the library. He seized her elbow and fairly shoved her into a parlor. "Quickly!" he said in a whisper. "We must hurry!"

His manner was so imperious that Daphne obeyed. It was only when he closed and locked the door behind them that she wondered at his scheme. "But why? What is amiss?"

Someone called her name from the corridor. Daphne thought it was the earl, but Mr. Cushing shoved her toward the doors that opened to the gardens. "They mean to hunt the duke and his man," he whispered. "It is a terrible mistake. We have to warn him!"

Alarm surged through Daphne. "Of course! I will just fetch my cloak."

Mr. Cushing's grip tightened on her arm. "There is no time! You can wear my jacket," he said, shedding it and wrapping it around her. "Quickly!"

Daphne did as instructed, terrified for Alexander. "What did you hear? What is this about?"

"The Eye of India," Mr. Cushing said, urging her across the lawn. "It was stolen."

"No!" Daphne protested because she thought she should.

She had expected they would either go to the stables to fetch horses or walk toward the village. Mr. Cushing, though, was leading her toward the maze.

What was he doing?

"Yes," he said with conviction and she noticed a hardness in his eyes that she had not seen before. "And worse, the one they recovered is a forgery." He flung her forward, casting her into the maze so savagely that she stumbled. She realized belatedly that no one would be able to see them.

He seized his coat, hauling it from her shoulders and leaving her shivering as he glared down at her. "Where is it, Miss Goodenham?"

"Where is what?" she asked, retreating carefully.

"The real Eye of India," Mr. Cushing said, taking measured steps in pursuit. She could not believe she had ever thought him charming and good-natured. "What have you done with it?"

"Nothing!" Daphne backed away, rounding a corner. Could she get a confession from him for Alexander? Could she be of assistance to her duke in disguise?

"But you met someone this morning."

"How do you know that?" With every question, Daphne retreated further into the maze. She had no choice. She could not pass Mr. Cushing and she didn't want him to touch her.

"I saw from the window," he said with a sneer. "And that kiss, as well. Who was it? Did you give it to him?"

"I gave nothing to anyone," she declared, which was true. He raised a hand, but she spoke first. "Were you the one who put the gem in my trunk?"

Mr. Cushing laughed. "So you did find it."

"It was there when I went to breakfast. Did you put it there?"

"Of course, I did. Who else has the wits to steal such gems with perfect success?"

"It is not so perfect a success if there is only a forgery remaining," she could not help but say.

He struck her then, slapping her across the face. His blow stung and revealed his true nature. "Where is the real gem now?"

"I don't know. Perhaps you took it back."

"Liar!" He lunged after her with fury in his eyes and Daphne fled. "I will have the gem!" he snarled and she ran as quickly as she could.

She knew she was going deeper into the maze. She knew she hadn't paid nearly enough attention to find her way back out. But with such a villain in hot pursuit, she feared she had little chance of escape.

"Alexander!" she screamed with all her might, hoping against hope that her duke was close enough to hear her.

ALEXANDER GALLOPED the bay toward Castle Keyvnor. He heard Daphne scream his name and the sound was enough to make his blood run cold.

Sadly, he could not tell where she was. The gardens were enormous and seemingly empty. She could be on the parapet walk or at a window. He pulled the horse up short and turned it in place, uncertain where to look.

"You there!" a girl cried and he spied a young woman racing toward him.

It was Miss Eurydice.

"Please, sir, you must help my sister!" she said. "He dragged her into the maze..."

She managed to say no more before Alexander gave the mare his heels. He leaped from the saddle at the entrance to the maze and strode inside. He paused to listen and heard a woman catch her breath.

"You lying vermin," she said. "*You* stole the Eye of India."

"I never suggested otherwise."

"But you lied to the earl and to your uncle," Daphne said. "They both trusted you, Mr. Cushing, but you deceived them."

"Great Uncle Timothy thought I was stupid," Cushing said, a sneer in his tone. "He liked keeping me poor, passing expensive gems through my hands, rubbing my nose in the fact that I'd never be able to afford even the smallest stone in his collection. He could have given the Eye of India to me! I would have sold it for a fortune! It would have changed my life. But no, he had to give it to some niece who barely remembered that he existed."

On stealthy feet, Alexander proceeded further into the maze. Could it be that Daphne knew he was there? Was she aiding him to get a confession of guilt? If so, she was a marvel worth every luxury he could shower upon her.

"But this can't be the first gem you've stolen?" she taunted. "You can't call yourself a brilliant thief if you've stolen only once and then been left with a forgery."

Cushing swore and Alexander moved more quickly in pursuit.

"Of course it's not the first. I'm notorious."

"But still you're said to be penniless." Daphne sighed. "I think perhaps you're not so clever after all."

"I lose at cards because they cheat me!" Cushing roared. Alexander heard Daphne make a little gasp and then her running footfalls. Cushing crashed after her, Alexander following. Deeper into the maze they went until there was suddenly the sound of a fall.

Followed by silence. Alexander eased around a shrub to find Cushing creeping toward a corner ahead. The toe of a familiar slipper could be seen beyond the turn of the maze.

The crash had been the sound of her falling.

She must be unconscious.

She must be injured.

Cushing leaped around the corner, and Alexander saw the astonishment on his face just before he saw Daphne's small fist. She tried to strike him, but Cushing recovered quickly enough to seize her wrist.

He didn't manage to twist it behind her back, because Alexander grabbed Cushing by the collar, spun him around and punched him in the nose. He struck the other man in the gut, then in the chin, so that he fell moaning to the ground.

Daphne smiled at Alexander with pleasure. "I knew you would come," she said, then her lips worked. "Did you hear his confession, Haskell?"

Alexander smiled that she understood the ruse instinctively. "All of it, my lady. You have ensured his condemnation."

Daphne had also proven that she was utterly trustworthy and that his instincts about her had been right.

"Good," she said, surveying the fallen man with disapproval. "I despise dishonesty in a man."

Alexander heard Eurydice arrive behind him, her breath coming quickly, and doubtless some measure of the household following behind, given the noise.

"Miss Goodenham," he said, bowing to her even as he seethed that there was a bruise rising on her cheek. "His Grace, the Duke of Inverfyre, sent me to enquire as to whether you and your grandmother, Lady North Barrows, might accept a call from him this afternoon."

Daphne's smile was radiant. "I should be delighted, Haskell. I am certain that my grandmother will also be amenable. Please do take my every encouragement to His Grace."

"I will and I am glad that the timing of my arrival was so fortuitous."

"As am I, Haskell. You have my thanks."

Alexander glanced at the earl. "But first, I will see this ruffian taken into the custody of the magistrate." He pulled a velvet sack from his pocket, for this was his chance to put the real gem in the earl's possession. "And this prize returned to where it rightfully belongs."

"An excellent plan, Haskell," Daphne said and it took everything within Alexander to keep from bestowing a triumphant kiss upon her lips.

That would have to wait until the afternoon, assuming that Lady North Barrows accepted his offer for Daphne's hand.

∾

"I FIND IT MOST CURIOUS," Eurydice said that night when the sisters were alone in their chamber together dressing for dinner.

"That the duke should want to marry me?" Daphne teased, certain that nothing could be better in her world. All had been explained to the earl and the true gem exchanged for the replica, Nathaniel Cushing had been taken into custody and through it all, Alexander had pretended to be his own man, Haskell.

He had arrived in his full splendor in the afternoon to ask for Daphne's hand in marriage. *Grandmaman* had been surprised and had only agreed when Daphne entreated her to do as much. The match was a brilliant one for Daphne, to be sure. If *Grandmaman* cast a more shrewd glance over Alexander after that, it could not be that much of a surprise.

Alexander had brought a salve for Daphne and insisted upon applying it to her cheek with his own fingers, the blue simmer of his gaze making her feel adored indeed.

Matters could not be better.

She sighed contentment and scarce even listened to Eurydice. Her sister had been over Nathaniel's scheme repeatedly, apparently fascinated with the doings of crime.

"Not that," Eurydice said with impatience. "I meant Haskell's eyes."

"His eyes?"

"They were blue today when he rode to your rescue. Indeed, they were like blue fire."

"Yes," Daphne agreed happily.

"But I am quite certain that at the tavern, they were brown."

Daphne blinked. "You might have been mistaken," she dared to say. "We barely glimpsed him at the tavern."

"I do not think so," Eurydice said with her usual conviction. "I noticed that they were quite nice eyes. I wouldn't forget them."

Daphne exhaled. "What a shame it is that you couldn't look again today, what with him riding immediately for the magistrate."

"It is a shame," her sister agreed. "I shall have to take a closer look once we arrive in London. Are we truly going to stay in the duke's house in Grosvenor Square?"

"Yes!" Daphne said, accepting the change of subject with relief. "He said it made more sense, since *Grandmaman* would have to let a house and his is simply sitting there, awaiting the pleasure of her arrival."

"She liked that turn of phrase," Eurydice said, which was true. "And we are casting him out?"

"Not exactly. She said he should stay somewhere else until we are married." Daphne realized that his impassioned response might have been what changed her grandmother's mind about the match. "He said he would get a special license instead."

"He does want to marry you!"

"And I cannot wait to marry him," Daphne said. All she wanted truly was an hour alone with Alexander, but she had a feeling that what they might do in that hour was better accomplished after their marriage vows had been exchanged.

She thought of the thrum in his voice when he had vowed to get that license and knew their match would be one of the happiest of all time.

She would ensure it was so.

IN HIS ROOM at the Mermaid's Kiss, Alexander savored a sip of brandy and considered the success of the day. He glanced out the window at the lights of Castle Keyvnor and felt unusual impatience to reach London. He had to push aside the vine to make space on the table to write his letter. It had recovered from its state earlier in the day and was on the cusp of blooming again.

The wretched story was true, after all.

He hoped the plant would fit in his coach, though he might have to ride with the driver for that to be so.

There was no question of leaving it behind or letting it perish. Daphne adored it and he was rather fond of its role in ensuring her safety on this day.

He picked up his quill, summoned the familiar tone, and began to write.

My dear Aunt Penelope—

Such news I have to share with you on this merry Christmastide! You will be heartened to learn that Dr. MacEwan's prescription worked admirably—I am fully restored to my former vigor, but it is not due to the sea air. I arrived in Cornwall to witness such excitement that it has driven all illness from me. Haskell chose the destination of Bocka Morrow when I told him to find accommodation in Cornwall, and for a reason of his own. It has been revealed that Haskell is a spy—yes, Haskell!—and he succeeded in unveiling a notorious jewel thief at Castle Keyvnor. The fiend stole a gift from one of the brides, but Haskell saw him apprehended. Even now, he journeys to London with the magistrate to see the villain brought to justice.

Of course, this put me in mind of Anthea's perfectly dreadful experience. You will be delighted to know that this same man was responsible for that offense, so justice has been served. He used the most enchanting young lady here to aid in his scheme. Once all was revealed, I could only express my heartfelt sympathy to her for enduring even a short-lived shadow upon her good name. In the end, she proved to be such a delight that she and I are to wed. You might know her grandmother, the dowager Viscountess North Barrows? I remember my grandfather talking of the Lord North Barrows' nuptials to that very lady...

And we shall soon have the pleasure of each other's company! I have sent word with Haskell to open the house in Grosvenor Square and will escort my betrothed, Miss Goodenham there, along with her sister, Eurydice, and Lady North Barrows herself. I had thought to leave the house to the ladies until Daphne and I celebrate our nuptials, but with each passing day, I see greater appeal in a special license. I will invite you to dinner to meet my intended once we have arrived in Town. I do indeed hope that Anthea can be coaxed to join us shortly. Daphne has a great deal of shopping to be done before the season and we both know what excellent taste Anthea has...

EPILOGUE

Anthea Armstrong was not surprised to receive a letter from her brother shortly after Christmas. She had been hoping to hear from him since his departure, and while Christmas had been festive, it had also been lonely. She missed Alexander's laughter.

It was snowing lightly and she sat before the fire in the library to read his missive, daring to hope it held tidings of his return. It was a nice fat letter, and she looked forward to a goodly amount of news.

To her surprise, Alexander's letter was folded around a plumper missive. His message was surprisingly short.

My dear Anthea—
The seed sprouted.
You lost the wager.
I look forward to seeing you at the London house so that you can meet my
betrothed, Miss Daphne Goodenham.
I shall let Daphne recount the tale of our whirlwind courtship, in all the
fulsome detail that ladies so adore.
Suffice it to say that I am well content and hope that you will ensure that
Daphne's first season is a triumphant one. I mean to stay in London long
enough for Daphne to tire of its charms, then retreat to Airdfinnan. Please join
us with all speed.

With greatest affection,
Your brother—
Alexander

It was marked with his seal.

Anthea was pleased by the news, though a little troubled by the notion of going to London.

Although she had made Alexander a wager.

She had to stand by her own terms.

She wondered, too, that Alexander had found a bride so quickly and feared the lady in question might not love him sufficiently well. The last thing he needed was a repeat of Miranda Delaney's betrayal.

Anthea opened the other letter with curiosity. Daphne's writing was graceful, the letters elegant and regular but not overly ornate. Even without reading a word, Anthea was half-convinced that Alexander had found an honest and beautiful girl to make his bride.

Dear Lady Anthea—
I am writing to introduce myself to you at Alexander's suggestion, though I would much prefer to do so in person. He seems to think that you will be skeptical of my existence without a letter from me, though why you might doubt his word is a complete mystery. He is the most honorable and constant man I have ever known, and already I trust in his word implicitly.
He told me that the seed of the vine was a gift from you, and I must thank you for giving it to him. Not only did it grow into the most beautiful plant, but its vigor seemed to encourage Alexander to trust in me. I have a curious sense that our courtship might not have come to so happy or so quick a resolution without those red flowers in his buttonhole. They truly are splendid and their scent is enchanting beyond all else. Even now, Alexander seeks a way to take the vine with us to London that it might be planted at the house in Grosvenor Square. I greatly look forward to seeing the original vine, with its fearsome thorns, on the walls of Airdfinnan.
Perhaps you will tell me the tale of Bayard of Villonne who first brought the vine to Airdfinnan. Alexander's version of the story seems to be short and lacking in romantic detail.
I do hope that you will come to London for our nuptials, and also to offer me

your advice. Alexander means to stay for the season, which is very exciting, but it will be my first and I would not wish to make a misstep. I should welcome your assistance.

I confess that I have always yearned to have an older sister, instead of always being the older sister, and so your existence is yet another wish of mine come true thanks to Alexander. I hope that we will also be friends, but truly, if you have any traits in common with Alexander, I know that I will love you dearly. There will be those, I am sure, who think our match a hasty one, but the truth is simple and I share it willingly—the Duke of Inverfyre, were he known by any other name, would be just as beloved by me as he is in this moment. I would adore Alexander if he were penniless. I never thought to meet such a man, and I am awed that I shall be his bride.

If you doubt the truth, you are welcome to ask my sister, Eurydice, who is always glad to surrender my deepest secrets to others. She has not a shred of artifice and is terribly clever—Alexander has told her of his library and she has already ensured her invitation to Airdfinnan. She may well set foot in his library and never be seen again.

I eagerly await the opportunity to meet you, my new sister.

With affection—

Miss Daphne Goodenham

Anthea read the letter twice. It was impossible to overlook the delight in Daphne's letter or to fail to note both her affection for her sister and her adoration of Alexander. Even Alexander's short message held a distinct note of satisfaction, and Anthea could well imagine his contented smile.

She wanted to *see* his smile and meet both Daphne and Eurydice.

Anthea took a fortifying breath and made her decision. She rang for Findlay before she could change her mind and watched the falling snow with her heart hammering as she waited for him. She felt a curious mix of satisfaction, trepidation and excitement, one that she had always associated with journeys to London.

"Yes, my lady?" Findlay said and she turned to him with a smile.

"Good news, Findlay. My brother is betrothed and will marry in London in the new year."

"Fine news indeed, my lady."

"And I will journey there to join them."

If Findlay was surprised that she meant to leave Airdfinnan, he hid it well. "Very good, my lady."

"I shall stay through the season. My brother wishes his bride to have her fair measure of London society and I hope I can enhance her enjoyment."

"Of course, my lady."

"I would like to leave in the morning, Findlay, and would appreciate you accompanying me to take charge of the London house. I believe there will be parties, as Alexander seems in a celebratory mood. Could you send Connaught to help me pack?"

"Of course, my lady." Findlay bowed, then hesitated before departing.

"Yes, Findlay? Is there something else?"

"Only that it is good to see you with a sparkle in your eye again, my lady," the older man said. He had been in the service of the family for so long that Anthea did not think his comment impertinent. "I do not doubt that this foray to London will be far merrier than your last."

Anthea's heart warmed. "Thank you, Findlay," she said, her voice a little husky. He gave her a nod and a glance that was encouraging, if not paternal, then departed to do her bidding. Anthea opened Daphne's letter and read it again, feeling her anticipation rise.

Two more sisters.

She dared to hope that Airdfinnan's butler was right.

～

A BARON FOR ALL SEASONS

THE BRIDES OF NORTH BARROWS #3

Rupert Haskell has always thought that Anthea, his friend Alexander's younger sister, would make an excellent choice of bride, but the loss of his inheritance made it impossible for him to court her. Caught between his honor and his heart, the only way he can show his esteem for Anthea is remove the stain from her name—even if that means having to watch her marry another man.

Anthea Armstrong left London in her debut season when she was falsely accused of theft. Now that the real villain has been apprehended, she's returned to town to arrange her brother's wedding. She hopes to once again encounter the mysterious suitor who stole her heart with a kiss at a masquerade ball…when she realizes the mysterious man is none other than Rupert Haskell, can she convince this proud man of honor to take a chance on love?

PROLOGUE

London—January 1812

The first of us to fall prey to the parson's mousetrap!" Sebastian Montgomery crowed, saluting Alexander Armstrong as he dropped into the leather chair in the library of his Mayfair townhouse. As was customary, the earl did not spill a drop of his brandy, although it wasn't his first of the night—or morning, as it were. The liquid sloshed in the snifter but didn't slip over the edge.

"Impressive," Rupert Haskell murmured and the Earl of Rockmorton grinned.

"Practice makes perfect, my good friend," Montgomery replied.

"I would wager you had drunk London dry with your practice," Alexander, the Duke of Inverfyre, noted with a smile.

Montgomery laughed. "No, no, the feat is to feign a large consumption while imbibing comparatively little. Far better for the budget." He patted his flat belly, encased in one of his lavishly embroidered silk waistcoats. "And the fit of my wardrobe."

"Not to mention the liver," Rupert added. He chose, as had become his habit, the chair furthest from the fire and only perched on the lip of the seat, while his two friends lounged at ease in their chairs. It changed a man to have his legacy snatched away. Rupert would never take any situation for granted again.

The three had become immediate friends upon their arrival at Eton years before, and had been consistently involved in adventures together while at school. The son of an earl, the son of a duke and the son of a baron, they had oft jested of how they would change society once they were of age.

Though they were of similar height and age, each as trim and athletic as the other, their coloring and situations were different: Montgomery, a much-favored only child, always took the lead; Alexander was more considering of other views, as befit a man with a younger sister to defend; Rupert, who had been an only child but one who faced greater criticism than Montgomery, was possessed of quick wits and a quicker smile.

They remained fast friends and confidantes, though only Alexander and Montgomery had come into their inheritances. Rupert, in contrast, never would though he strove to avoid any bitterness. The financial disparity among the trio could have driven them apart: instead, they had become closer in recent years. Alexander had hired Rupert as his valet and brought him into his secret task of spying for the crown. Montgomery could be relied upon for a loan or even an outright gift, although Rupert was more likely to ask for a favor, if he had need of assistance. The trio would still do any deed for each other and Rupert was beyond glad of the friendship and support of his oldest friends.

Montgomery toasted Alexander before sipping. He winced, baring his teeth. "Liquid fire. It is good for what ails me."

"And so much ails you," Alexander teased, rolling his eyes. They laughed together.

Montgomery's library was lined with books that he did not read and always had a roaring fire as well as a full decanter of brandy. It was a comfortable haven after their night savoring the pleasures of town. On this night, they had dined and they had danced; they had visited the theater and ultimately Alexander and Montgomery had gambled, all in the name of celebrating Alexander's pending nuptials. The clock in the hall chimed two and Rupert thought of his early start the next morning. He would have laundry to do before he slept this night.

Alexander had surrendered his townhouse to his betrothed, her sister and her grandmother, while he stayed with Montgomery. Rupert had a room in the servant's quarters and knew that Montgomery's staff would notice any anomalies in his conduct of his duties. He would be up at dawn to prepare Alexander's clothes for the day, polish his boots and press his cravat.

Watson, Montgomery's butler, gave a slight tap at the door and Rupert bounded to his feet, taking a place behind Alexander's chair. Watson, an older man and a severe custodian of decency, gave Rupert a look that could have curdled a man's blood. His gaze dropped pointedly to the glass Rupert had abandoned alongside the chair he had been occupying and he inhaled sharply in disapproval. "Will there be anything else, sir?" he asked in a frosty tone, bowing to Montgomery.

Montgomery, of course, had not missed the older man's reaction. "No, Watson, unless you would care to join us." He lifted his glass again even as the butler's horror showed for the barest moment. "We are saluting the cleverness of His Grace's valet."

"Indeed." Watson surveyed Alexander's attire, as flamboyant as was customary when the duke was in town, and if anything, his disapproval grew.

There were rhinestones on the duke's cuffs and glittering down the front of his waistcoat. His breeches were striped cerise and forest green, his coat was crimson, his waistcoat was chartreuse and there was a sprig of holly in his lapel. There were even three little bells replacing the tassels on his boots that jingled as he walked. Rupert thought Alexander looked like a demented elf, but it had been his friend's scheme to act as a dandy, the better that his wits be underestimated and his presence overlooked. The guise had served him well as a spy, but Alexander meant to retire now that he was to wed. Rupert was glad his garb would change. The silks and taffetas were a fearsome amount of work to maintain.

Watson clearly was not enchanted by the duke's appearance. Judging by the tight-lipped glance he granted Rupert, he might even have laid the blame for Alexander's sartorial flair at his valet's feet.

Montgomery, in contrast, favored the severe simplicity of Beau Brummel's suggestion, with dark chausses and coat, white shirt and cravat. His only ornamentation was his collection of embroidered silk waistcoats, one in every possible hue. Alexander dressed similarly when he was not in town, and Rupert looked forward to the return of his more austere wardrobe.

"Indeed," Montgomery said again. "I see you noted the extra glass, Watson, but Haskell here has revealed and captured the jewel thief that has plagued London society for years. Is that not fiendishly clever? Does it not deserve a small reward?"

Even Watson had to acknowledge this, though he did so with only a minute nod.

Montgomery enthused. "He caught Nathaniel Cushing in the act of absconding with the Eye of India at Castle Keyvnor. And saved the damsel in distress who the duke will wed." He saluted Rupert and apparently drank, but this time Rupert noted that the level of liquid in the glass did not diminish. "How frightfully enterprising of him, don't you think, Watson?"

The older man inclined his head slightly. "Most commendable, my lord."

"All while ensuring I looked sufficiently splendid to win myself a bride," Alexander added jovially. "Our journey to Cornwall was not without incident, to be sure." Earl and duke clinked glasses and drank in tribute to their own good fortune.

"Do not neglect to mention, my lord, that your health is infinitely improved by the sea air, perhaps even sufficiently so that Dr. MacEwan will permit you the season in London," Rupert added.

"The entire season?" Montgomery echoed in delight. "We shall find trouble to be certain!"

"I shall introduce my betrothed to society," Alexander corrected with a firmness that revealed his true nature. "She has not yet enjoyed a season."

"My felicitations to you on your pending nuptials, Your Grace," Watson said with a bow.

"I thank you, Watson. I am most pleased." Alexander gestured to the bottle of brandy, his eyes filled with mischief. "Will you join us, then?"

Watson took a step back, so affronted by this breach of protocol that he nearly fled the room. "I should not be so familiar, sir, but thank you for the offer." He bowed deeply and Rupert watched Alexander and Montgomery exchange amused glances.

"Then there will be nothing else, Watson," Montgomery said. "Alexander knows his way to his chamber. I say, could there be kippers for breakfast? I like them after a night of indulgence."

"Is that not every night?" Alexander murmured, his eyes sparkling.

"As many as I can contrive," Montgomery ceded easily.

"I will ensure that there are kippers, my lord." Watson bowed again. "Good night then, my lord and Your Grace." He bowed again then took his leave, quietly closing the door behind himself. Alexander waved Rupert back to his seat as Montgomery topped up his brandy.

"Hazard pay," Montgomery teased with a wink, then settled back in his own chair. "He will be watching you like the proverbial hawk."

"He already is," Rupert agreed. "But you need not feel sorry for me. I am most comfortable." The servant's chambers in Montgomery's house did not compare with his room at either of Alexander's houses, but they were more than adequate. Rupert was glad he did not have to share the small chamber with another servant.

The fire blazed merrily and snow fell outside the windows. The three men sat companionably, legs stretched out and ankles crossed.

"A bride," Montgomery said again, shaking his head at Alexander. "I suppose it is love?"

"Of course!" Alexander said. "She has stolen my heart away forever."

Montgomery rolled his eyes at this. "But then you always believed in love and romance, a legacy from your parents." They were silent for a moment in acknowledgement of the passing of that happy pair some years before. "Haskell and I remain the skeptical ones."

"What nonsense is this?" Alexander jested. "You fall in love daily."

"Hourly," Montgomery agreed with a wise nod. "It is best. I suppose you will be tedious and wed with haste?"

"I have the special license, but Anthea wrote that she is on her way," Alexander said. Rupert couldn't keep himself from glancing up in surprise, for he was unaware of these tidings. He felt the back of his neck heat in fear that his secret admiration of the duke's sister might have been noted but no one glanced his way. "We will await her arrival."

"Miss Armstrong has such excellent taste," Montgomery said with approval. "She will put the perfect touch upon the nuptials, to be sure. It is a shame that she abandoned London so quickly in her debut season. The prospect of encountering her made any jaunt so much more interesting."

Rupert felt himself bristle at this hint of Montgomery having an interest in Miss Armstrong. She deserved far better! Montgomery was a good friend, but he treated women abominably.

"She could not do otherwise, to her thinking, not with such a pall hanging over her name," Alexander said, clearly still annoyed that his sister had been accused without cause.

"Mr. Nathaniel Cushing has much to answer for," Rupert said with conviction.

Alexander regarded him. "And I suspect he paid some of that debt when he was caught for this most recent crime."

"It was only right," Rupert agreed. "It was cowardly to allow innocent young women to take the blame for his thefts."

"Or one particular innocent young woman?" Montgomery mused, as perceptive as ever.

"It was wrong. He was wrong." Rupert could not subdue the heat in his tone. "And I for one am glad that he is now facing the consequences of his actions."

They drank again, united in their agreement.

"But what of the gems?" Montgomery asked. "Were all his spoils recovered and returned to their original owners?"

"No, and that is the rub," Alexander said. "He had nothing in his possession. I wager they were all sold promptly and have now been scattered."

Rupert could not keep silent. "They must be found, though. Is there no scheme to do as much?"

Alexander considered him. "I have not been requested to do as much."

"Of course, there would have been insurance paid," Montgomery noted.

Alexander nodded agreement.

Rupert could not leave the matter alone. "But your sister..."

Both friends watched him silently. Rupert fell silent, thinking he had said too much.

"My sister," Alexander invited finally.

Rupert frowned. "Surely she will be suspected of having the gem until it is revealed to be elsewhere, or until it is returned. The stain upon her reputation will linger and she may find that many will spurn her company."

Alexander scowled at this prospect.

"He is right," Montgomery concurred. "They will whisper when she enters any room. You know how they are. Veritable vultures when it comes to reputation and gossip."

"I realize as much, but what is to be done?" Alexander said. "It has been ten years. The gem could be anywhere!"

"I would find it," Rupert said. "Or try to do as much, for Miss Armstrong's sake."

His old friends exchanged a glance and Rupert feared neither of them were in doubt as to his feelings. Not that he could act upon them, not when he was a mere valet. He could not regret his words to his father but he could regret their result.

"What a wretched moment for a man to be without a legacy," Montgomery drawled, his eyes glinting as he watched Rupert. "You could reconcile with the old man, you know."

Rupert shook his head. "So long as he disgraces my mother by flaunting his affair with Mrs. Blythe, I cannot speak to him with civility."

"How many brats has she borne him?"

"One boy."

"Is that not a foul situation?" Montgomery said, clearly not caring a whit. "I would contrive for all my friends to be rich, no matter the cost to others."

"There is nothing to be done for it." Rupert drained his glass. He was more fortunate than he might have been and he knew it. That was also thanks to Alexander, and he would not dishonor that man's name or sister at any price.

He would clear her reputation, even if he could do no more than that.

"Indeed," Alexander noted. "I am glad to have been able to share some advantage with you."

"And I am grateful, Your Grace. As you well know."

Alexander winced. "You need not address me thus when we are alone."

"But one can never be certain that we *are* alone."

"Truly, if Watson were not so principled, he might be listening at the door," Montgomery said. "He was so disappointed when my father died and the title fell into my undeserving grasp. Although I confess it is good fun to startle him."

"You should wed and redeem yourself in the eyes of your staff," Alexander suggested.

Montgomery laughed. "Not I!" He gestured with his glass. "It will have to be Rupert who succumbs next."

"There is little chance of that," Rupert replied evenly. "Even though my wages are generous for my station, my purse is not sufficiently fat to tempt a lady."

"And you will not wed beneath your station," Alexander said with approval.

"Take a mistress," Montgomery suggested. "Or two."

"He cannot afford two," Alexander noted.

"Just one will improve your mood, Haskell," Montgomery insisted. "I can suggest several candidates."

"I will guess that you will decline to suggest one in particular," Rupert teased, for he had heard the gossip.

Montgomery laughed. "I will not share Miss Ballantyne any more than is necessary, to be sure. Keep your maiden, Alexander, and enjoy her. I favor a woman who knows what she is about in the bedroom." He swirled the brandy in his glass and sighed with satisfaction. "Ah, Esmeralda."

Alexander ignored this. He regarded Rupert over the lip of his own snifter. "Have you a plan for finding the gem? I will do whatever necessary to assist."

Of course, he was as concerned with Miss Armstrong's happiness as Rupert. "You should not be directly involved, for if it is found, it will simply be assumed that you surrendered what was in your possession all along." Alexander nodded at the wisdom of this, though it was clear he did not like it. "I had thought that Mr. Timothy Cushing might have a notion or two. After all, he is a collector of gems. He might know how they might be illicitly sold or where such a feat could be done."

"And he did aid us with the capture of his nephew," Alexander said. "It might be possible to contrive matters so that it looks as if he has seen the gems found and even your role could be disguised."

"Indeed."

"Shall I write to him and request that he meet with you in private?"

"That would be most helpful, Your Grace."

"Then consider it done. I should have known that you would plan for the details and ensure that all is set to rights. You are the perfect man of principle, Rupert." Before Rupert could reply, Alexander drained his glass and rose to his feet. "And now I am for bed, Montgomery. I thank you again for your hospitality."

"Do not eat all of the kippers, I beg of you," Montgomery said with a smile. "I may linger abed in the morning."

"And miss my tangerine trousers? For shame, Montgomery. They are a sight to behold, but will leave my wardrobe soon," Alexander said.

"Mercifully," Rupert murmured and the three of them laughed together again.

Montgomery waved a hand. "Be sure to discard this particular ensemble, too. It is distinctive, to be sure, but utterly hideous."

Alexander bowed as if accepting a compliment and they laughed again before parting for the night.

At least he had convinced Alexander of the importance of finding that gem. Rupert would resolve the matter in Miss Armstrong's favor and be content with rendering that service to the lady who held his heart.

It was not enough to satisfy, but he would have to be content.

No doubt it would become easier in time.

CHAPTER 1

$\mathcal{A}$nthea Armstrong was never fond of travelling, but this journey had been a plague upon her patience from start to finish. The roads were often challenging in the winter, but the heavy rains in the north of England this year had turned many of them to mire. They had poor luck with inns and had seldom been able to book the better rooms—one fateful night in York, they had not found a room at all. This had occurred even though Findlay had abandoned Airdfinnan to guarantee her safe passage to London, and Anthea was convinced her brother's butler was better than most at seeing matters resolved with satisfaction. The weather had been miserable, her maid Connaught had come down with a cold, and the combination had left Anthea exhausted.

On the one hand, she had never been so glad to arrive in London in her life. She might fall at her brother Alexander's feet and weep with gratitude when they reached his townhouse in Mayfair. Perhaps the Fates recognized her reluctance to even go to town and contrived to make her appreciate the opportunity.

On the other hand, Anthea had plenty of time to question the wisdom of her decision to leave Airdfinnan during their arduous journey. Her brother's Scottish house had become her refuge and sanctuary these past years, and it only made sense that abandoning it left her with doubts.

Never mind that she would see again many of those who had witnessed her mortification in her debut season. To be accused of theft was a horror she would never forget, even though her innocence had finally been proven and the true culprit apprehended. She would be able to hold up her head in society again and that was one reason she had chosen to come south.

The greater reason was the chance that her elusive suitor of her debut season might take up his courtship again. Did she dare to hope that he was yet unwed? That he might remember her? The very notion made her shiver with anticipation.

To wed for love would be perfect bliss, in Anthea's opinion, and she was glad her older brother had found such joy. Of course, she wanted to meet Miss Daphne Goodenham, the lady in question, and her younger sister, Eurydice, and even their opinionated grandmother, Lady North Barrows. Anthea already had received a number of letters from Miss Goodenham and was convinced they would like each other. She seemed to be both cheerful and sensible, a very happy combination.

Not to mention the vine. A seed of the legendary vine of Airdfinnan had sprouted during Alexander's courtship of Daphne, just as the tale had insisted it would for the heir of their family hold-ing. Anthea—who had insisted Alexander take a seed with him— wanted to see the plant. Surely, it could not be as vigorous as all insisted.

But the greater concern was the fate of her most alluring partner. Anthea stared out the window, not really seeing the crowded road, and remembered an evening as dark and mysterious as this winter morning was bright.

The masquerade ball.

Maman loved a masquerade ball and invariably hosted one to launch the season when she was in town. That this one would also mark the beginning of her only daughter's debut season meant that it had to be more spectacular than usual. Papa had granted permission to do whatsoever was desired, and Anthea had been thrilled.

On the night in question, the townhouse might have been turned into a fairy palace. The rooms glittered with decorations, tiny candles and sparkling arrangements of flowers. Great sweeps of white embroidered cloth hung from the walls, making the ballroom look like a massive tent, filled with shadows and innuendo. The night was uncommonly warm for the time of year, so the doors to the courtyard were open and a breeze wafted through the ballroom, carrying the sound of laughter over the music. The combination was magical.

Anthea felt particularly splendid herself, in a new silk dress of emerald green, embroidered with gold on the hems. She had been loaned a parure from her mother's collection for the night, an elegant concoction of faceted citrines set in gold. She had gold slippers and a gossamer ivory shawl—and butterflies in her stomach when she descended the stairs. Guests were already arriving and Findlay announced them at the door in his most sonorous voice. The street was crowded with carriages, guests lined the steps to the street, and the hall already filled with women in their glittering splendor.

The orchestra played and the champagne flowed, Papa laughed with pride as he escorted her and Maman into the ballroom, one on each arm—and Alexander could not be discerned from the bevy of masked men awaiting the opportunity to dance with her. Anthea couldn't have been more excited. Papa and Maman led the first dance, then Papa escorted Anthea to the dance floor. She could only conclude that the masked man who danced with her mother was Alexander, and indeed, she recognized his signature grace.

She was breathless from dancing with Alexander when she felt someone behind her. Alexander smiled and bowed, and Anthea pivoted as the man bowed low. He was taller than her with dark brown wavy hair and his eyes seemed to sparkle behind his black domino mask. His lips were firm, and he smiled slightly as she met his gaze. There was an intensity about his manner that made Anthea catch her breath. He was a little more slender than her brother and Anthea's heart skipped a beat at the weight of his survey. She had no notion of his identity, which made his interest all the more exciting. Alexander had vanished into the throng, leaving no one to make introductions.

"Will you dance with a mysterious stranger?" the stranger asked, his voice a low rumble. He raised a brow. "Even without the benefit of an introduction?

"Do you not mean to confess your name, sir?"

"Then I would be neither mysterious nor a stranger, and it is my understanding that both have an allure for lovely young ladies like yourself."

Anthea felt her cheeks heat. "I thank you, sir, for the compliment."

"It is only the truth, Miss Armstrong. You are the most beauteous woman in the room, and the veritable queen of the ball. It is that and only that which prompts me to boldly present myself, without any soul to vouch for my character."

"I hope your character is above repute, sir. I would hesitate to dance with any man whose companionship might sully my reputation."

"I grant you my solemn word, Miss Armstrong, that I have no desire to put a shadow upon your name, and indeed, I would defend it and you with my dying breath."

"You seem most devoted for a stranger, sir."

"Perhaps your beauty strikes me to the heart." He smiled. "Or perhaps we are not so unknown to each other as you might assume." His gaze was warm and Anthea's mouth went dry. He bowed and offered his gloved hand.

Though she knew she should wait for Maman, Anthea placed her hand upon his. His fingers closed over hers, both strong and gentle, and she allowed herself to be led to the dance floor, heart racing. She caught a glimpse of her mother's smile of approval and knew his identity was not hidden from all. They must have been introduced.

He was an exquisite dancer, elegant and decisive, and he ensured that she always was turned to advantage. Soon they had a small appreciative audience, and Anthea could not resist his invitation to dance the next—and the next. By the end of the fourth dance, she was well aware that her aunt Penelope was watching them avidly.

"There are ices in the courtyard, I am given to understand," he said and Anthea would have followed him anywhere. He escorted her to the courtyard and the cool air was a sweet relief. She fanned herself as he got an ice for her and the allamande began. People moved inside to join the dance: suddenly and unexpectedly, they were quite alone in the courtyard. The night was clear and the stars shone overhead; the music and laugher carried to Anthea's ears but she felt that she enjoyed a forbidden moment with her mysterious stranger.

"I should go," she whispered.

"Will you not stay?"

Anthea could not resist. "I might if you confessed your name, sir."

"By the sparkle of your eyes, Miss Armstrong, the enigma is in my favor, and I would not lose an increment of your attention at any price." He smiled, and she thought that what she could see of his face was most handsome.

She laughed. "You tease me, sir."

He sobered. "Not in the least. Not for a moment." He leaned closer, his words low and his breath soft against her cheek. "I came this night solely in the hope of dancing with you and now I shall depart, content."

"You cannot leave, not so early as this."

"And yet I must, lest I be tempted to hope for more." His gaze swept down, she could see as much even through his mask, and she found herself unable to take a breath. "You are exquisite, Miss Armstrong, and a beauty to your very marrow. I wish you a most enjoyable evening."

"Will I not see you again, sir?"

"You might, at one event or another, if I can contrive it."

"Do you wish to contrive it?" she asked boldly and his smile flashed.

"More than life itself, my lady." His gaze was hot then and she felt warm all over again, but shivery as well.

"I would have a kiss to keep the memory alive," she said on impulse, startled by her own audacity.

"Miss Armstrong, you astonish me." He moved closer, though, and looked down at her, the heat of his proximity making her tingle. "But I cannot resist such temptation," he whispered, then bent to brush his lips across her cheek. In the last moment, Anthea turned her head and their lips touched with a most tantalizing heat.

It was a gentle kiss yet as different from those kisses she had known with family as might be possible. The very touch of his mouth against hers set her skin afire and made her yearn for so much more. Anthea heard the rumble of his laugh before he backed away. He surveyed her for a moment from the doorway, then bowed, spinning on his heel to stride into the ballroom. He vanished in the crowd more quickly than she might have believed possible. Though she might have pursued him in the hope of seeing his carriage or having a glimpse of some detail that would cast light upon his identity, Anthea could not.

For her aunt caught her elbow in one hand, her grip so sure that Anthea knew her absence had been noted. She was turned to meet another gentleman, and curtsied as her aunt introduced him. The son of a marquess, but not a man she knew. "My niece and god-daughter," Aunt Penelope said to the man in question, as if to warn him, and he nodded before asking Anthea to dance.

She did not know how many partners she had or how many dances she enjoyed. Anthea could think only of one. Her lips tingled still when she finally retired and she knew she would never forget her earlier partner—or her first kiss.

When would she see him again?

THERE HAD BEEN cards left for Anthea in the ensuing weeks, their timing almost always coinciding with her being away from the house. They had only a domino mask drawn upon them in black ink and no name, but it thrilled her each time she knew he had called. It was a tease and a reminder, a seductive game that she wanted to play to its finish. Findlay had refused to surrender any details about her caller and Anthea had looked for him at every event.

If she had encountered him again that season, she did not know of it.

Had the accusation that she was a thief eliminated his regard for her? Had he wed another since her departure? Was she a fool to hope to encounter him again?

If only she knew his name...

THE CARRIAGE REACHED the house just before noon and the horses stamped with impatience when bidden to halt. Anthea and her party had stayed just north of London the night before and the four bays would have been content to run yet further on this day, the first sunny one of their journey. Connaught sneezed mightily as the door was swept open, revealing Alexander's London house, so white as to be radiant in the sunshine.

"Thank goodness we are finally arrived, Findlay," Anthea said, offering her hand to the butler of Airdfinnan. "Though little could have been contrived better, thanks to your efforts—" She fell silent when her gloved hand was taken by a man other than Findlay.

It was Haskell, her brother's valet.

Well, he had once been Alexander's comrade, but some misfortune had befallen him and Alexander had offered him a post. It had been most thoughtful of her brother, but Anthea had avoided Haskell. They had met years before, when she had been only ten years of age and he had come to visit Airdfinnan. She remembered those happy weeks well, and recalled her infatuation with her brother's friend with some embarrassment. He had been kind then but surely it had only been good manners at root.

Not an unbridled affection as her own had been. For years, she had told herself that it was of no import, but each time their paths crossed, her heart thundered.

As it did now. Anthea could not resist the opportunity to take a closer look. Haskell was infinitely more handsome than she had noticed previously, and his slow smile of appreciation launched a flutter in her belly. Was his mouth the same shape as that of her mysterious suitor? She could almost believe it, but reminded herself of the years that had passed.

She was being a sentimental fool.

Anthea smiled politely, even as she found herself keenly aware of the strength of the hand that braced her own.

Why had Haskell met her coach? She would find meaning even in that, so foolish was her heart. For all she knew, he loved another. Why would he not?

Once she stood on the gravel, Anthea realized she had to look up to meet Haskell's gaze. He was dangerously attractive, to be sure, and a woman could forget herself when confronted with that knowing smile and the appreciative gleam in those eyes—but he was merely a valet. Anthea was not a snob, but even this scrutiny was unsuitable.

An attraction would be more so.

That, alas, did not keep her from feeling one. She had been without male companionship too long, to be sure.

Meanwhile, Haskell bowed before her. His jacket, she could not fail to notice, fit his broad shoulders admirably, and his gaze was steady. His eyes were brown and twinkled in a most beguiling way. And his hair. Dark brown and wavy, so thick she might have been tempted to push her fingers through it.

She recalled another man with such hair then caught herself. It must be a common hue.

She was losing her wits, to be sure.

"Welcome to London, Miss Armstrong." His voice was deep. "I trust your journey was satisfactory."

"If slightly too long, Haskell," she acknowledged then averted her gaze, seeking a reason for his presence. She immediately spotted Alexander's larger coach.

"The duke is just arriving for luncheon and bade me hasten to open your door," Haskell provided.

"And I thank you for your kindness," Anthea said, shivering slightly as she spoke. The wind was cold, the sky a crisp blue overhead and a bit of frost crunching underfoot. Although the coach had seemed chilly, she now missed the warm brick that had been under her feet.

Her brother's team of six black horses nickered and shook their manes as they stood before the larger coach, such a splendid team that more than one passerby paused to admire them. It was the black coach with his emblem on the doors in gold, and every inch of it gleamed in the sunlight.

Rodney was calling from his perch atop the smaller coach to the other driver about the welfare of the horses, Findlay was directing the removal of the trunks, and Pierce, the butler now in charge of the London house, had already opened the front door. The servants were on the steps to welcome her and Anthea looked between the two butlers, wondering whether they could survive together beneath a single roof. She steeled herself to negotiate the complications of staff.

She would do it early, before matters could escalate beyond redemption.

"Cheerio, Anthea," Alexander called, raising a hand as he emerged from the larger coach and strolled toward her. His voice was higher than usual and his tone so affected that she thought for a moment it could not be her older brother at all. "How was your journey, my dear?"

Anthea blinked and stared. Her brother, rather than attired in his customary black and white, was resplendent in mauve and yellow. Every inch of his waistcoat was embroidered and his cuffs were even jeweled. She had never seen striped breeches of such vivid hues upon him before, nor so many sparkling buttons upon his garb. He carried a walking stick that flashed in the light and she was certain there had to be rouge on his cheeks. He even had developed a round belly, which she knew would have taken considerable effort to gain since they last had seen each other a month before.

But Alexander was not a glutton. He was athletic and moderate in his appetites, as well as conservative in his dress. What on earth was amiss?

He halted beside her, eyes sparkling with mischief and bowed, then surveyed her through a quizzing glass which she had never seen him use before. "Has the journey been so traumatic that you are lost for words, dear sister?"

It was a jest of some kind. It had to be. She risked a sidelong glance to discover that Haskell was utterly serious. His eyes, though, twinkled merrily. Anthea could not imagine how he could fail to be privy to Alexander's scheme, whatever it might be, and assumed he was part of it.

"Alexander," she said, unable to curb her affection even given his odd appearance, and kissed his cheek. "Whatever is wrong with you?" she whispered for his ears alone.

Alexander winked. "Naught at all, my dear sister. You see before you a happy man indeed."

Was this the influence of his intended? If so, Anthea would have words for that young woman and her horrific taste. She was more than prepared to wage war on her brother's behalf, and saw Haskell quickly swallow a smile, as if he read her thoughts. A look like quicksilver darted between the two men and she knew then that they *were* co-conspirators.

"Tell me," she insisted, but Alexander simply took her arm, guiding her toward the house.

"It is so utterly perfect that you have encountered Haskell this morning, for I know you will wish to thank him yourself," he said, his words mystifying Anthea.

She looked toward Haskell, who walked on her other side but slightly behind her. She had the sense that the pair of them were protecting her, but that was nonsense.

"I do not understand," she confessed.

"Did I not tell you that it was Haskell who so boldly revealed and captured the fiend who had besmirched your name?"

Anthea looked at Haskell, who bowed. That hair invited her touch. When he straightened, his eyes glowed so warmly that she felt herself flush as she looked away.

He was a *valet*.

"He did?"

"Indeed. Little did I know that Haskell was a spy in the service of the crown, committed to capturing the jewel thief who has plagued society these past years." Alexander tapped on Anthea's hand. "He outed the scoundrel in Bocka Morrow, no less, tackled him in the maze of Castle Keyvnor and brought him to justice. It was most impressive, even if I did have to tie my own cravat for dinner."

Haskell was a spy and the man responsible for clearing her name? A wave of gratitude swept through Anthea, one that only grew warmer when she found that man watching her.

"I grant you my solemn word, Miss Armstrong, that I have no desire to put a shadow upon your name, and indeed, I would defend it and you with my dying breath."

She remembered those whispered words with sudden clarity and the vigor with which they had been uttered.

It could not be.

Could it?

Haskell had been Alexander's friend at Eton and later at Oxford. He had come to Airdfinnan one summer. He had spent time with her instead of hunting with the others and she had thought him kind.

Perhaps there had been more to it than that.

Anthea kept her gaze locked upon Alexander. "You wrote that the thief was Nathaniel Cushing." She dared not look at Haskell again lest her thoughts be guessed.

"Indeed, he had a routine of stealing the gems he delivered as gifts for his uncle, Mr. Timothy Cushing, the famed collector." Alexander said. "He then hid the stolen gems in the luggage of innocent young ladies and robbed them after they had left the party. Haskell deduced it all!"

Anthea took a deep breath and risked another sidelong glance. Of course, Haskell's gaze was locked upon her with no small measure of admiration. She felt her cheeks heat. "He always did have a talent for seeing a quandary resolved," she said, noting his smile. "I seem to remember a clock you repaired at Airdfinnan one summer."

"Indeed, and still it keeps perfect time," Alexander said.

"I thank you for your efforts, Haskell," she said. "It is a great relief to have my name cleared and the truth known."

"But the credit is not entirely mine," Haskell said, that smile curving his mouth again so that she longed to stretch out a fingertip... "It was your tale of meeting Nathaniel Cushing after your departure from town that fixed my suspicions upon him, my lady." He bowed again. "I must thank *you* for your aid."

Anthea felt uncommonly flustered. She could not form an attachment with her brother's valet, no matter what his past fortunes had been. "So long as justice is served and all ends well."

Haskell inclined his head slightly. "Indeed. You were always possessed of good sense, Miss Armstrong."

"I cannot wait for you to meet Miss Goodenham," Alexander said, leading Anthea up the stairs. Maids curtseyed on one side and liveried footmen bowed on the other. She smiled at each one, halfway thinking that Alexander had too much staff.

"I yearn to meet her myself," she said.

"I would also ask you, Anthea, if you would not mind managing the house with your customary efficiency for the moment," he continued in a lower voice. "It would be most useful for Miss Goodenham to have a tutor in this matter and you will be the best. She has a facility with accounts, from my understanding, but there is always more to learn. You know this household, its traditions and its staff better than anyone, after all."

"Not better than you?"

He grinned. "Perhaps not."

How curious that his betrothed, who Anthea knew to be young, would have such a talent with figures. Perhaps the grandmother exaggerated her skills, though why she would choose that one to share was an enigma. Most matrons would brag of dancing skills, drawing ability or a facility with languages. Anthea wished even more to meet the ladies in question.

"It would be my pleasure," she said, aware that her brother awaited her reply. Anthea noted Pierce looking daggers at Findlay and knew precisely how she would begin.

"Ah, look, Haskell!" Alexander pounced upon a letter on the silver tray held by the first footman. "Here, no doubt, is the introduction you requested." He opened the envelope and read the missive, then handed it to Haskell, to Anthea's surprise. "Mr. Cushing will see you tomorrow at three."

"Mr. Cushing?" Anthea echoed in confusion. "I thought he had been apprehended."

Haskell cleared his throat. "Mr. *Timothy* Cushing is the gentleman I would meet and His Grace has been kind enough to arrange the matter."

"But why?"

"Not all of the stolen gems have been retrieved, my lady, and I would request an inventory from him, with descriptions, in the hope that can be achieved."

"The crown should pay your wages, Haskell," Alexander said cheerfully. "When you are always about state business instead of mine own." He smiled at Anthea. "Although I suppose there is merit in seeing a task thoroughly done."

"I should think so," Anthea agreed, curious to know more. She remembered that much-younger Haskell being teased by her brother for being good to his word, and thorough.

The man in question bowed. "With your leave, Your Grace, I will collect your new waistcoat and trousers from the tailor on the same journey."

"An excellent scheme, Haskell. I shall wear them at dinner tomorrow evening, simply to please Miss Goodenham."

Anthea dreaded the sight of them, at that endorsement. Would they be more garish than this ensemble?

"Of course, Your Grace." Haskell bowed and pivoted to leave, striding away with purpose. Anthea could not entirely curb her desire to watch.

Haskell, a spy. That did make him intriguing.

Alexander tapped a finger on her arm, drawing her attention. "I have arranged a small dinner party tomorrow night, for fear you might be too tired tonight. Aunt Penelope, of course, desires to see you, and you know Montgomery."

"It will be a delight to see Aunt Penelope and the Earl of Thornedyke." She smiled then, noticing the pair of young women who awaited them with obvious nervousness.

One woman stood in the doorway to the library, her dark gold hair, solemn manner and slightly stocky figure revealing her identity to Anthea as readily as the book clutched in her hand. This had to be the younger sister, Eurydice, and clearly she had discovered the wonders of Alexander's library. Before her and at the bottom of the stairs stood a blond maiden so lovely that Anthea blinked in awe. It did not hurt her first impression of her brother's betrothed that Miss Daphne Goodenham gazed at Alexander with adoration.

"Your Grace!" she said, her eyes shining with pleasure as she curtsied and kissed his hand. "I have missed you, sir." She was a rare beauty, to be sure. Her hair was as golden as sunlight and her eyes clear green, her lashes thick and her lips ruddy. She was slender yet feminine and so clearly besotted with Alexander that Anthea would have forgiven her anything. Indeed, she gave an impression of being very sweet and entirely genuine, which Anthea guessed would appeal mightily to her brother. He had been the target of many an ambitious mama's scheme and disliked any contrivance.

Which did nothing to explain his current mode of dress.

How she itched to know the fullness of this tale!

"And I have missed you," Alexander rumbled in his usual deep tones, bending to kiss the hand of his betrothed. "But I had an errand at the tailor, one of which you will approve, my dear, I am certain.

She smiled. "I know I shall, sir." She bestowed a warm smile upon Anthea. "And this surely is your sister, sir."

"It most certainly is." Alexander introduced them.

"I am so glad you have arrived, Miss Armstrong," Miss Goodenham said. "Everything must be perfect for His Grace and I would request your assistance in ensuring that I make every detail as it should be."

"I understand you already influence his wardrobe."

Miss Goodenham smiled at Alexander. "The fashion is becoming so much simpler for men, and I think it would favor him well to be in black and white." She laughed a little and gestured toward his stomach with her fingertips. "And a little less pudding."

"Whatever you desire, my dear." Alexander kissed her hand again and she flushed prettily.

Anthea found herself warming to his fiancé, since she would return Alexander to the appearance Anthea knew best.

Alexander introduced the younger sister who gave a low curtsey. Her manners were exemplary but Anthea guessed that she wished to return to her book.

"What are you reading?"

"It is a novel recommended by the duke," Miss Eurydice said. "For it is about two sisters who are utterly different from each other." She turned the book, revealing it to be *Sense & Sensibility*.

"And do you like it?"

"Very much." She obviously wanted to open it and begin reading again.

"Alexander has rather good instincts when it comes to books. I cherish the ones he has given me."

"Oh, this one is from His Grace's library," Miss Eurydice confessed solemnly. "It is not my book. I am simply fortunate enough to be able to read it."

"I believe you might have time enough to finish a chapter before we dine," Alexander said to her and the younger girl's eyes lit. She excused herself, curtseyed again and retreated to the library with haste. "She has a fondness for the same window seat you always favored," he said to Anthea and she smiled, feeling that she had found a kindred spirit.

"We will have to talk about books. Perhaps I will read that one when she has finished it." Anthea smiled at Miss Goodenham. "Even though I have no sister, I have always wanted one."

She laughed with pleasure. "And now you are to have two. Better yet, Eurydice and I will have an older sister to rely upon for advice. I understand that your taste is exquisite, Miss Armstrong. I should most appreciate your assistance in every matter. His Grace's home is much larger than any I have lived in before, and I fear to make an error."

"You will not," Alexander said gallantly and she beamed at him.

"You should be a stricter critic, sir!"

"But I see nothing to criticize."

"Of course, I will be glad to be of assistance," Anthea said. "Alexander indicates that you wish to learn how to run his household."

"Of course!" The younger woman flushed slightly. "I would have you call me Daphne, if it pleases you."

Anthea smiled. "And you will call me Anthea, please."

"Thank you."

"Once I see Connaught settled, we will begin." Anthea glanced back at the two butlers and lowered her voice. "We must avert disaster first."

"Oh!" Daphne said, her eyes wide. "I had not thought of that," she murmured, her worried gaze following Anthea's glance.

"It will be readily resolved and best done quickly," Anthea assured her.

"I should like to watch," the younger woman said solemnly. "If it would not trouble you."

Anthea was only too glad to have such an enthusiastic pupil. With Daphne confident in her abilities, there would be nothing binding Anthea to her brother's household.

Did she dare to hope for one of her own?

*H*askell was checking the duke's linen when the staff belowstairs abruptly fell silent and rose to their feet. He turned to find Miss Armstrong entering the kitchen. The sight of her filled his heart with joy, just as it had the first time he had met her. If anything, she was more lovely than he recalled, tall and slender with a crown of red-gold curly hair. He had seen her only weeks before, but hourly could not be sufficient for Haskell. The young girl he had first admired had grown into a woman, still practical but infinitely more lovely.

She moved with grace and purpose into the kitchen. "Good day, everyone," she said. "Please do be seated again." Her smile put the staff immediately at ease. Not all were as quick to sit as she suggested, though: Pierce and Findlay remained standing as did the plump—and excellent—cook, Mrs. Stewart.

Even though Miss Armstrong had not been in residence at the London house for years, it was clear that she was remembered and with fondness. Once, Findlay had been the sole butler, but he had retreated to Airdfinnan to ensure her comfort and Pierce had been hired for the London house since Alexander had been spending more time in London.

Miss Goodenham followed Miss Armstrong, clearly intent upon

learning her task. Haskell admired the determination of Alexander's betrothed to be the best wife possible, but he particularly savored the opportunity to openly look upon Miss Armstrong.

"Pierce and Findlay," she began and they both bowed. "I should like to immediately address the question of authority in this house while you are both in residence."

Pierce frowned slightly and Haskell guessed that he feared he would have to answer to Findlay, who had served the family much longer.

"If I may be so bold, Miss Armstrong," Findlay said with a slight bow of his head. "I should like to request a short break from service while in London. I will be glad to return to Airdfinnan whenever it suits your convenience, of course."

Miss Armstrong smiled and it seemed to Haskell that the room basked in the sight. He certainly did. "Would you tour the sights, Findlay?"

"No, I would seek some tidings of a cousin of mine."

"Is she in town?"

"I do not know. She entered the service of a family more than twenty years ago and travelled to the West Indies with them as a governess. I have heard nothing from her in years—of course, she was inclined to correspond with my wife, gone these eight years—so I would like to see if I can learn any tidings of her while in town." Some of the newer servants gaped at Findlay for this long-winded confession, but Haskell knew the older man was given more leave to be familiar with the family.

To Rupert's surprise, Miss Goodenham's eyes widened in surprise. He knew that Miss Armstrong could not see the younger lady's reaction and wondered at its cause.

Miss Armstrong smiled at the butler. "I have no objection to such a quest, Findlay. Indeed, she may be most glad to hear from you. I hope you find her well."

The older butler inclined his head to Pierce. "Of course, I should be honored to be of any assistance in this household while I am here."

"I have all in hand..." Pierce began with his customary confidence.

"But there may be additional errands with the arrangements for the wedding," Miss Armstrong noted. "Your assistance would be invaluable in that matter, Findlay, and I shall rely upon you, rather than interrupting Mr. Pierce's routine. The house is full and there are many details to manage as it is. Of course, you must seek out your cousin, as well, but perhaps you might check with me each morning that we can best plan our forays."

"That would be ideal, Miss Armstrong," Findlay said with a bow. "I thank you kindly for the suggestion."

Haskell could not help but admire how neatly she had divided the managerial task between the two men.

"And then there will be no doubt of your wage," Miss Armstrong said.

"I thank you for your consideration, Miss Armstrong." Findlay bowed to her again.

"I think this arrangement is most admirable, Miss Armstrong," Pierce agreed. "As sensible as your reputation."

"Then we are agreed," Miss Armstrong said, bestowing a smile upon the other servants. Rupert did not know whether her gaze truly lingered upon him or whether he simply wished it to be so. "I shall not interrupt your labor any further. If we could review the menus for the week after luncheon, Pierce, I should be most grateful. I understand we are to have guests tomorrow evening and my aunt is particularly fond of Mrs. Stewart's white fish in cream sauce."

Mrs. Stewart beamed at this praise.

"Of course, Miss Armstrong," Pierce said.

"Perhaps it is not too early for fresh asparagus?" Miss Armstrong asked the cook.

"I shall be sure to seek some out, Miss Armstrong," Mrs. Stewart said then recalled herself. "But only if it is fresh and the price is right."

"You are always so accommodating, Mrs. Stewart. I cannot imagine what my brother would do without you."

"Thank you, my lady." Mrs. Stewart curtseyed deeply.

"Miss Goodenham has professed an interest in learning all I know of managing a household, and I wonder if we might refer to some of your records, Mrs. Stewart. The volume for my debut season would be particularly helpful in planning for the season ahead. We will have dinners and breakfasts to plan."

"Of course, my lady, but prices have increased something fearful."

"Naturally, Mrs. Stewart, but it will give us a place to begin."

The cook bowed again and went to a cupboard. Within it were bound volumes of different colors, some quite worn. She handed one to Miss Armstrong, her reluctance to surrender it clearly at war with her desire to help.

"I shall ensure it is returned with haste, just as it is now," Miss Armstrong said with a reassuring smile. "Miss Goodenham can copy what she finds necessary to study."

"Very good, my lady."

Miss Armstrong turned briskly to leave but halted when Miss Goodenham, still behind her, did not more. "Excuse me, Findlay," the younger lady said and all gazes rose to her. "What was the name of your cousin?"

The butler raised a brow. "I should not trouble you with it, Miss Goodenham."

"But I believe a friend of mine had a governess named Miss Findlay."

Rupert wondered at this, for it seemed from her manner that the lady told a small falsehood. To what purpose?

"Miss Amelia Findlay was her name," Findlay supplied with pride.

Color suffused the cheeks of the duke's betrothed. "Oh, then I am mistaken. My friend's governess had the given name, Harriet. I apologize for even mentioning as much."

"I am most obliged by your desire to assist, Miss Goodenham," the butler said with a bow.

The two women left then, the younger glancing back with some trepidation. Rupert saw Miss Armstrong's hand fall to Daphne's elbow, urging her back upstairs, and knew he had not been the only one to notice her reaction.

The kitchen erupted in chatter then, the two butlers shaking hands with each other over their new division of duties. The housekeeper commanded one of the footmen to show Findlay to his room and Mrs. Stewart ordered a girl to make haste in peeling vegetables for dinner.

Rupert bent his attention upon that cravat again and tried to compile a list of questions for his appointment with Mr. Timothy Cushing.

It was a wiser use of his time than recalling the beauty of Miss Armstrong's smile.

Though indeed, the curve of those lips made him recall his first glimpse of her...

~

RUPERT HAD ALWAYS KNOWN that Alexander Armstrong had a sister, of course, and that the siblings were fond of each other. That had not prepared him for his first glimpse of her—or his reaction to meeting her. He had never believed in love, let alone love at first sight, not until Anthea Armstrong.

Rupert's father had even left his mistress in London in order to accept an invitation from the Duke of Airdfinnan to hunt at his Scottish holding. A duke could not be denied, to the baron's thinking, and all the long ride north, Rupert and his mother were regaled by that man's ambitions for this new connection. He seemed to have forgotten that they had only been invited because Rupert and the duke's only son were friends from school. By the time they left York, his father had convinced himself that the duke had singled him out for particular favor.

Rupert had feared their two weeks in the north would be a disaster, but did want to see Alexander again. He hoped that their comrade Montgomery had been able to accept the invitation as well. The three of them would be able to run almost wild over the duke's many acres of woods and meadows. They would hunt and fish, ride and go hawking, a sport Rupert had yet to try. Perhaps there would be a country dance or two, and the food, he was convinced, would be splendid.

The house dated from medieval times and just as Alexander had oft told them, it was on an island. The road followed the river and Rupert caught glimpses of the towers rising high above the canopy of the forest ahead. There was even a pennant snapping from the tallest one, flying the duke's insignia against the sky. The walls rose sheer from the water on all sides, the keep as impregnable as Alexander had said.

There was a bridge over the river to the gates, which stood open. The horses shied a little and Alexander himself walked across the bridge to grasp the bridle of the lead horse. He spoke to the beast, soothing it, and the other three followed meekly into the courtyard of the castle opposite.

"Welcome!" Alexander said with a winning smile when their footman opened the door. He bowed low over Rupert's mother's hand, enquiring after her journey. There was a bustle of activity at the doorway as a couple who could only be Alexander's parents emerged to greet their guests.

They were followed by a slender maiden with red-gold hair whose beauty struck Rupert to stone. She was younger than he and Alexander and not just lovely—there was mischief in her smile to match Alexander's own.

This had to be his sister, Miss Armstrong.

By the time she stood before him and welcomed him to Airdfinnan, Rupert was lost. Cupid's arrow found its mark in that first glimpse and throughout their visit, his feelings only grew stronger. She possessed every trait he admired. She was clever and practical, she could ride and was a better shot than he was. Her laughter filled him with delight and there was no greater triumph than prompting it. He found her on rainy afternoons in the library, curled in a great chair before the fire, and they talked about books and travel, their conversation flitting between topics as if they had known each other all their lives.

Rupert intended to wait. He planned to court her. When her family came to London for her debut season, he had made all his preparations. He would attend the masquerade and gain her attention: he did not expect to steal her heart so readily as that. A campaign had to be waged and, knowing her taste in books, a mystery might stimulate her curiosity.

But his father saw fit to bring his mistress to the duchess' masquerade ball, instead of the baroness, his wife. When Rupert arrived with his mother just as his father was being announced, the duke's frosty glance at the baron was sufficient to chill all the champagne in London, and much of it on the Continent besides. The duke had barely acknowledged the baron and did not speak to Mrs. Blythe.

Instead, he bowed low over the baroness' hand and requested a dance. He had swept Rupert's delighted mother toward the dance floor as if she was the belle of the ball. The duchess had turned her back upon Rupert's father, then the entire company had ignored both him and Mrs. Blythe. Rupert had been glad to be disguised behind his mask.

His father had never forgotten what he saw as an undeserved insult.

His mother had remained a devoted friend of the duchess all her life.

And Rupert had been fool enough to argue with his father over the situation the next day, convinced as he was that he was in the right and justice must win. Oh, he had been young and in love! But as a result of that argument, Rupert was now a penniless valet, with no right to even profess his admiration for the lady who still held his heart.

Could the situation not be saved? He was the man who solved all the riddles: Haskell had to find a solution to this conundrum.

The obvious one, that he should reconcile with his father, was utterly out of the question.

~

LADY NORTH BARROWS was a formidable older lady with silver hair, attired entirely in black. She was stern with her granddaughters, but Anthea spied a gleam of fondness in her eyes more than once over their late luncheon. It said much for the older woman's character that she had brought the two orphaned girls into her home after the sudden deaths of their parents. To undertake the task of raising and educating them at her age spoke volumes about her commitment to them.

The sisters were polite and made good conversation over the meal, neither interrupting nor leaving an awkward silence. As was right and proper, Daphne was more actively engaged, while Miss Eurydice remained silent unless addressed directly.

The meal was marvelous as ever, but Anthea noted that her brother ate very little. She wondered at his ruse and was determined to learn the truth from him when they could converse in private. She had that opportunity sooner than expected, for the dowager requested that the girls assist her in returning to her room.

"I do apologize, Miss Armstrong, but our last journey to Cornwall has left me quite fatigued." Lady North Barrows tapped her umbrella on the floor. "It was all this hastening about in pursuit of jewel thieves, never mind a wedding and a betrothal besides. So much excitement!" She smiled at Daphne. "No doubt you wish to tell Miss Armstrong the entire tale and I can only beg you to show some restraint with the details when you do."

"Of course, *Grandmaman.*"

The older lady indicated Eurydice. "And you should confirm with His Grace that it is permissable for you to read his morning newspaper in his absence." The maiden in question flushed and opened her mouth to protest, but her grandmother carried on uninterrupted. "I have no doubt he has noticed that *someone* has been reading it before him and, gentlemen, as you will learn, Eurydice, can be most particular about their newspapers. I insist you ask permission this very day and I hope the duke will not be overly indulgent."

"I should never dream of it," Alexander said gallantly, rising to his feet to escort the older woman to the door.

"Do not spoil them, sir, I beg of you, lest you undo my years of labor."

"I should not dream of that either."

The dowager laughed with unexpected lightness. "I would wager that you do, sir," she charged, then continued into the hall, her grand-daughters close behind. Alexander watched them go with an indulgent smile.

"She must be relieved," Anthea said when the door was closed and they were alone together. "To have the one so well-betrothed must ease her concerns for their future."

"Indeed," he said, speaking in his usual tones and taking a seat beside hers. He leaned closer, dropping his voice in confidence. "I have promised her that Miss Eurydice need never wed, if that is her choice. She can remain in my house, as if she, too, were my sister, and if she elects to wed an impoverished man for love, I will aid them."

"You are good to them."

"I intend to be even better."

Anthea smiled. "So it *is* love."

"Can you doubt it?" He smiled. "You gave me the seed. Did you see the vine?" He rose to his feet and escorted her to the window, which looked over the small formal garden behind the house. A fountain sat in the very center of the space, silenced for the winter. Four paths divided the square space into quadrants with a precision that had always pleased Anthea.

When she might have recalled a certain evening with a masked man fetching her an ice, her attention was diverted by the enormous vine that threatened to fill the courtyard. It had been planted in the sunniest quadrant, and it engulfed both that space and half of the adjacent two. It seemed all the more vigorous since the courtyard was devoid of greenery, the planters that spilled with blooms in summer having been moved inside for the winter. Anthea stared at the large flowers of red as rich as velvet and marveled that they were real.

"I have never seen our vine in bloom. The blossoms are magnificent."

"And impossible to ignore." Alexander opened the window and Anthea caught her breath at the intoxicating scent.

There was something beguiling about that scent, something that turned one's thoughts to love and romance, to the memory of a forbidden kiss and the promise of a more romantic future. Anthea sighed and Alexander closed the window, as if to protect her from the vine's wiles. "The cold nights have not killed it?"

He shook his head. "It grows several yards a day. It will engulf that wall by Easter, I am certain."

"I wonder when its thorns will sprout."

"Perhaps when our vows are exchanged," he mused.

"It cannot know such a thing! It is a *plant!*"

Alexander shook his head. "It knew Miss Goodenham was in danger and warned me of it," he confessed with complete solemnity. "I would not be so fool as to assume I know all it can and cannot do."

Anthea frowned. "Now you are the believer while I am the skeptic."

He laughed aloud and led her back toward the settee. "It suits us well to trade roles once in a while."

"And what of this role?" She touched the lace at his cuff.

He sobered. "Haskell was not the sole one in service to the crown," he confessed in an undertone. "Though I disguised myself, the better to be underestimated. We made an effective team."

"How effective?"

"It would be vulgar to boast, but I believe we made a difference."

"And what will you do now?" Anthea feared in that moment that her brother would continue his noble duty but that doing so might imperil his new bride.

"I will shed this disguise in steady increments and return to my usual self." He winked. "Our tale is that my betrothed insists upon it and I am so besotted that I can deny her nothing."

"I thought you *were* besotted."

Alexander chuckled at the truth of it, looking untroubled. Nay, he looked smug and satisfied, like a lion after a robust meal.

"She knows?"

The pride in his smile was unmistakable. "A most perceptive young woman. She saw my truth immediately."

"How could you so hide your merit? It is no wonder it took you so long to find a bride!"

"But you will see that all ended for the best." He gave her a piercing glance. "And who better to wed than the one who sees through artifice to the hidden truth?"

"Why do I sense that you are telling me something of import?"

"Perhaps I am."

But Anthea could not imagine what he meant. She left him then to savor his own satisfaction and went to her own room, her thoughts spinning. Was there any way she might announce her presence to her mysterious stranger? She would leave her cards tomorrow at the homes of those people of her acquaintance, but she did not know who he was.

She was on the threshold of her room when the thought came to her. Of course! She would insist that Alexander host a masquerade for Daphne's debut, just as *Maman* had given one for her own debut. Her suitor would certainly hear of it, and Anthea could only hope he would attend.

Perhaps Alexander might ensure that he was invited.

"WE HAVE TO TELL THEM," Daphne whispered to Eurydice in the room they shared. Their grandmother had retired for an afternoon nap, as was increasingly her habit.

Eurydice secured the door, then returned to her sister's side. "The confession is not ours to make." They whispered together. They had been allies together since their parents' demise, no matter how they might disagree on some matters, and always would be so.

"But Findlay means to seek his cousin, Amelia, and we know…"

Eurydice touched her fingertip to her sister's lips to silence her. She was deadly serious. "We could suggest to Miss Armstrong that we visit Mme. de Roye, as she might wish to meet our former governess."

"Then we can ask her advice in private."

Eurydice nodded. "The tale is hers to share or not. Recall that she was in peril from her former suitor and that was why she took the disguise in the first place. We must be discreet for we dare not reveal her." She winced. "I would not answer to M. de Roye for any price."

Daphne chewed her lip. "Then we cannot rush the encounter, lest it is thought urgent."

"Precisely," Eurydice agreed. "And perhaps Findlay will find his truth before we can become involved."

"But I should tell His Grace. I could not bear to have a secret between us."

Eurydice frowned, considering this. "Perhaps you might tell him in confidence. He might then suggest that Miss Armstrong call."

Daphne smiled. "Yes! He will know what is best to be done."

RUPERT WAS SUMMONED, to his surprise, to the library by Alexander after the family had dinner. He knew that Lady North Barrows had retired, for her maid, Nelson, had been summoned, and Jenny had gone to aid the Misses Goodenham. He assumed that Miss Armstrong had also gone to her room, though Connaught had been sent to bed with her cold. Jenny or Nelson would aid the lady, no doubt.

He was astonished to find Miss Armstrong seated by the fire opposite Alexander. She wore a dress of pale gold silk which showed her coloring to advantage, and the same parure of citrine that he recalled from a long-ago evening. His throat was tight as he poured Alexander's brandy and he felt the lady's gaze upon him as he served it.

Had she guessed? Rupert could not decide whether it would be better or worse for her to have divined the truth.

He wanted to declare himself, but without any right to court her, he knew it best to remain hidden. How he hated having his heart and head at odds!

"Is Pierce ill?" she asked Alexander, which indicated to Rupert that she had no notion that they had danced together once.

Was she as haunted by that kiss as he was? There was something about the scent of that plant which drove Rupert's thoughts back to that encounter. Alexander always had a blossom in his buttonhole, for he credited the vine with his own happiness, but it seemed to taunt Rupert with possibilities that could not be pursued.

"He was instructed to leave us." Alexander shed his jacket with visible relief. Haskell moved quickly to take it, then folded it over his arm, intending to depart. The jacket had a small stain on the cuff, which was perhaps why Alexander had summoned him. He had learned that speed was best when removing a bit of oil.

"Stay, Rupert," Alexander said to his surprise.

Miss Armstrong was visibly startled that her brother used his valet's given name.

Alexander leaned back and sipped of his brandy. "As I told you earlier, Anthea, we have charted a steady progress back to my customary choices, the tale being that Miss Goodenham is influencing my taste, and it will be completed by the time we return to Airdfinnan."

"It should be completed by the time you wed." The lady spoke with conviction.

Her brother's gaze sharpened. "I have a special license, Anthea."

"And you are a peer of the realm, so a measure of ceremony is anticipated, plus I could not bear to see you make your vows like *this*." It was clear that Miss Armstrong could not hide her distaste and Haskell bit back a smile. "Papa would roll in his grave."

"You have been considering the matter."

"Ever since I heard the news, I have thought of how the wedding should be conducted," the lady confessed. She spoke decisively and Rupert knew she would suggest a scheme of good sense. "I had thought you might host a masquerade to launch the season. *Maman* always had one when she was in town, so it would be a tribute to family tradition as well."

A masquerade. Rupert's heart stopped, then skipped.

Could he contrive to attend?

To his astonishment, he found Miss Armstrong watching him, as if she sought his reaction.

Did she know?

Was that a blessing or a curse? The conflict within Rupert grew by leaps and bounds.

"A masquerade," Alexander mused. "How irresistible. Do you not agree, Haskell?"

"A masquerade is always a most welcome diversion," he restricted himself to saying.

The lady smiled in a mysterious way, her eyes glowing as she studied him for a long moment before turning back to her brother. "Indeed, there is always something alluring about dancing with a mysterious stranger," she said, her words and her attention making Rupert's heart stop.

She did know.

What was he to do about it? Honorably he should do nothing, but....*Anthea.*

"Such a ball would introduce Miss Goodenham to society with style." She cleared her throat. "It could be held to celebrate your wedding, in a month or so."

"A month?" Alexander sounded strained.

"If not two." She spoke firmly.

Alexander rolled his eyes. "You *do* have it all planned."

"There must be time for dressmakers, Alexander. A bride must have her trousseau."

He sighed. "I suppose you are right."

"I know I am right. Am I not right, Haskell?"

"You are absolutely correct, Miss Armstrong."

"And I am outnumbered," Alexander said with a sigh. "You have free reign with expenses in that matter."

Miss Armstrong nodded, clearly having expected no less. "And there must be a measure of ceremony. There should be at least three dinners and a breakfast, to ensure she meets those she should. I have begun a list, though I will consult with Aunt Penelope and Lady North Barrows...."

"I tremble at the schemes to be wrought by the three of you."

The lady laughed. "After that, you could remain in town for the rest of the season or take Daphne abroad..."

"Airdfinnan," Alexander said with resolve. "When we leave this house, it will be for Airdfinnan. My heir will be born there, also by tradition."

Rupert knew that Alexander was unlikely to leave Scotland soon after his return. He wondered then about his own future. Could he bear to be merely a valet, at Airdfinnan, with Anthea in residence, too? He was not certain he could bear the temptation, for even now his conviction wavered and she had only been in the house a day. He certainly did not want to dishonor her at all.

Perhaps he should leave Alexander's service. The notion made the pit of his stomach drop, but Rupert recognized its merit all the same.

"I hope Miss Goodenham loves it as much as you and I do," Miss Armstrong said. "No doubt her younger sister will adore the library and be content, but..."

"But?" Alexander invited.

"Your betrothed is young," she said bluntly. "I fear she may be bored."

"I intend to keep her occupied and entertained."

"Then you should stay the season and let her enjoy it all. By the fall, she might be with child."

"It is my plan that she will be."

The lady looked exasperated by his confidence. "Not *all* details are up to you, Alexander."

The duke grinned. "But I shall do my best to influence the outcome."

"I have no doubt of that."

"How long are you delaying my nuptials, then, Anthea? Two months? Three? Perish the thought that it should be longer than that."

"You had a hasty courtship," she countered. "The wedding night will be all the sweeter for the wait."

"Will it? What say you, Rupert?"

If he was to leave Alexander's service, a longer delay in London was more to his taste. "I think three months to be certain that the lady holds your heart securely is not too much to wait when you hope to spend a lifetime together."

Alexander turned to his friend. "Do you doubt her regard?"

"I have no reason to do as much, but Miss Armstrong speaks truly: yours was a short courtship and if your intended had any guile, it would be comparatively simple to disguise true intentions for a period of weeks."

"Do you think she does?"

"No, Your Grace."

Alexander smiled approval of that.

"Exactly," Miss Armstrong agreed. "We are allies in good sense, Haskell." He felt warm at her smile of approval.

Alexander sighed. "Who can one rely upon for good advice if not one's sister and good friend?" he said. "A wedding in April it will be then, and a masquerade to celebrate it, in my customary garb." He shook a stern finger at Miss Armstrong. "Do not compel me to wait longer."

"I shall not." The lady's eyes sparkled in triumph.

"I only hope that Montgomery does not lead me to ruin in that time."

Miss Armstrong gave his padded belly a poke. "Tell me it is false."

"It is merely padding," the duke ceded.

"Ha! It would take at least two months for you to plausibly lose that weight at any rate."

"Rupert has ordered plain broth for me and dry bread. I am ravenous by noon each day!"

She laughed, a most merry sound. "It is a situation of your own making. I shall not feel sorry for you."

"You should not. It showed me the measure of my intended." Alexander glanced at Rupert. "Does the timing meet your favor?"

"Indeed, it does. I had been concerned that a more rapid weight loss might induce others to fear for your welfare." He raised his brows. "Dr. MacEwan might see fit to send you to the coast and I know Miss Goodenham would be disappointed by such tidings."

"Dr. MacEwan," Miss Armstrong said with disgust. "Does he still plague your days?"

"You do not think much of his counsel?"

"Not if he was fooled by a padded belly."

"He does not exist, my dear sister, but was merely a fiction to aid my movements around the country."

"How devious you are, Alexander," she said, pretending to be affronted. Her sparkling eyes revealed the truth of her admiration. "I hope he has not led you astray, Haskell."

"Haskell is as steady as ever he was," Alexander said before Rupert could reply. "And a hero, as well."

"So you have told me." She regarded Rupert with a smile. "But I should never have guessed before this day that you had such a talent for artifice, Haskell."

"And is that troubling, my lady?"

"Oh no, I find it most…illuminating." Their gazes locked and held for a heady moment, one in which the world stopped for Rupert.

"And I cede to both of you," Alexander drained his glass and rose to his feet, breaking the spell. "And now, Anthea, in the name of respectability, I return to savor Montgomery's hospitality. No doubt he will be pleased to learn that I am to be his guest even longer."

"I doubt he will take offense. The earl is at ease with most matters."

"And you will see him on the morrow." Alexander let Rupert hold his coat. "Have you missed him as much as he says he misses you?"

Rupert froze at that query, especially as the lady laughed. "Oh, it is simplicity itself to miss the earl. He is such a rogue. One cannot help but be charmed."

"You could do worse, Anthea," Alexander advised. She glanced toward him, startled. "I would not stand in your way."

She was astonished to silence, which Rupert could only see as a good sign.

He could not however guarantee Montgomery's intentions, which did little to aid his sleep that night. Miss Armstrong could never be happy with such a careless scoundrel.

Never.

But in his own heart, he feared that she might. What could he do?

CHAPTER 3

To Anthea's dismay, Haskell's suspicions proved correct.

On her first morning in London, she took her brother's footman, Clarke, with her to deliver her cards at all of her acquaintances. Although she had remained in Scotland for years, she did correspond with a number of women who had debuted in the same year as she had. Elizabeth Somerset had married a French comte, Margaret Etheridge still lived with her mother and Teresa Newson had three sons by her husband, a viscount. Anthea's mother had been friends with Lady Feathering and the Duchess of Essington, and she felt obliged to call upon them as well.

Elizabeth's butler sent Clarke back with the card. Margaret's butler sent a message that the duke was welcome, implying that Anthea was not. Teresa's butler had taken the card but Clarke's expression had been grim upon his return. Lady Feathering had told Clarke that she would call, while the duchess' butler had not even opened the door. The curtains had moved on the window above, so Anthea knew she was deliberately being refused.

It was most disappointing that all of these individuals of her acquaintance still believed her guilty—or at least that there was sufficient doubt that they did not want to associate with her. It also meant that Haskell was right: the only thing that would clear her reputation was the discovery of the stolen gem.

As much as she wished to help, Anthea could see the good sense in her remaining uninvolved. How fortunate that she had a champion in Haskell.

And that made her wonder anew whether he had been her mysterious dance partner, the one who had vowed to defend her at any price.

Was there any chance of asking him outright? Did she dare?

She wondered whether Haskell's mother might be in town. She had every justification for calling since the baroness and her own mother had been friends, and there was a chance of learning some detail about Haskell's situation. She called, only to learn from the butler that the lady remained at the country house with the baron staying at his club.

Anthea suspected that the baron actually was with his mistress, and wondered whether he still consorted with Mrs. Blythe.

She returned to the house at virtually the same moment of Alexander's arrival, once again, and her heart leapt at the sight of Haskell. He merely bowed to her then Alexander insisted he take the smaller carriage for his appointment to Mr. Cushing.

"How can you be so crestfallen on such a fine day?" her brother demanded of her when they approached the house together.

To Anthea's relief, his garb was more sedate on this day. His coat was deep blue with flourishes of pink embroidery on the cuffs; his waistcoat boasted a veritable garden of pink blooms on bright pink silk, but at least his trousers were navy and plain.

"It is as predicted," she said with a smile. "My cards were not well received."

Alexander waved this off. "Who cares for the opinions of those who are so fickle?" He didn't wait for an answer but continued with a smile. "I have a quest for you, should you choose to accept. Miss Goodenham would like to visit her former governess, who is now married. She has wished to go since our arrival here, but her grandmother insists that visiting would be too much for her at the moment."

Anthea guessed that the older lady was not very interested in visiting a former servant. "I would be delighted to escort her there. I expect Miss Eurydice would also come along."

"I expect so," Alexander agreed easily.

"I will suggest as much to Daphne at luncheon."

"That will please her. No doubt a date can be agreed upon," Alexander mused. "I would think that the governess would be glad to see her two former pupils as well."

"What is her name?"

"It was Miss Brisbane, but now it is Mme. de Roye."

"He is French?"

"Yes." Alexander gave her a surprisingly sharp glance. "M. de Roye has a house in Cavendish Square."

Anthea blinked. "She did marry well, then."

"I understand his family were in trade, as were Miss Brisbane's. Her father owned Brisbane's Emporium. I have no idea how his family earned their wealth."

"Brisbane's Emporium! There was a place of marvels."

"There were those who say it has become less than it had been. I believe Mr. Brisbane had passed and it had a new owner. The de Royes retrieved it and Miss Goodenham believes they intend to rebuild the trade."

"They have corresponded then?"

"Yes." Alexander's eyes twinkled. "I fear Miss Goodenham may have a scheme for you to be of aid in this, Anthea."

She laughed lightly, glad of the request. "I would be delighted to offer any assistance."

"Excellent. Then we are resolved. And are all the arrangements as you would desire for dinner tonight?"

"They are. I reviewed the menu with Daphne yesterday afternoon, and she was quite intrigued by Mrs. Stewart's detailed budgets. I have asked her to compile one for the masquerade and she seemed most delighted by the challenge."

"I wagered she would be." There was no mistaking the pride and satisfaction in her brother's expression.

"You truly have found a most suitable bride, Alexander."

"And in the most unlikely of situations." He tapped a finger on her arm, those eyes sparkling. "You might take a lesson, dear sister."

"And what is that to mean?"

"Merely that love does not heed any summons. It appears when least expected and perhaps even when least convenient." He smiled at her. "But that does not mean it can be avoided."

Anthea could not have agreed more.

~

Mr. Timothy Cushing proved to be most helpful. Indeed, he welcomed the question of the fate of the gems with as much enthusiasm as Rupert could have hoped.

"It is a question I have pondered all these years, and a matter of some delicacy," he said when they were seated in his library. The older man was slender and spry, and he wore a large star sapphire in his cravat. "If they had been found in Nathaniel's possession, they could have been returned to their rightful owners."

"But they were not," Rupert supplied. "Not a single one of them."

The older man grimaced. "He was shrewd enough to sell them quickly, and if they were sold abroad, there is little that can be done to recover them. The crown's authority does not extend so far, regrettably."

"But there must have been some compensation to the victims."

"Of course, many had insurance and it will have been paid."

"I would wager that many would prefer to have the gems instead."

The older man's eyes twinkled. "You might be surprised. I had a visit from the son of the marchioness who had a remarkable emerald brooch stolen." Rupert strove to give no sign of his keen interest in that piece. Mr. Cushing pulled out a ledger as he spoke. "The son sold all of her jewelry after her death and I bought much of it. Some very fine pieces." He nodded in recollection. "But my point is merely that this son confessed in passing that the thief had done him a favor, in a way, as he believed the insurance was more than the gem would have fetched if he had endeavored to sell it himself. It was so strongly associated with his mother that no one else might have desired it."

The older man turned the pages of his ledger, his brow furrowed in thought. Rupert could see that the entries listed the missing gems, along with the date of their theft, a description and even a drawing, along with some additional notes.

Mr. Cushing looked up suddenly. "It is remarkable that sons are so often either the mirror of their fathers or their opposite. The marchioness and her husband, the marquess, were very fond of high society and lavish living. They were more concerned with their parties than their tenants. Their son, however, is the very opposite. He could have been a rake and a wastrel, but instead, he is determined to repair the estate and be an excellent landlord." Mr. Cushing considered Rupert. "What of you, Mr. Haskell? I have met your father, I am certain."

Rupert felt his lips thin. "My father and I do not agree on many matters."

"That is a shame. The world could do with more men prepared to risk their own welfare for a good cause, especially those who hold a large barony." He did not wait for a reply, but gestured to the book. "Here is a list of the gems I know were stolen, and my notion of where they ended up."

"Notion?"

"One hears rumors," the older man said primly. "I sketch each one, lest I forget the details."

The drawings were very detailed. Rupert read the notes on the first listing. "Paris?"

"Many of them were resold again there, I suspect," Mr. Cushing said. "As mentioned, there are fewer potential repercussions after the gem leaves England."

"Do you think Mr. Cushing journeyed there or that he had an accomplice?"

"He was disinclined to trust, as well as fond of Paris. I know he went there at least once a year, often more frequently than that."

"Despite the war?"

"There are always ways for the determined. To be sure, I thought he had a mistress there whose favors lured him back, which only shows the depth of my undeserved trust."

Rupert did not comment upon that.

"These pearls I even saw again," Mr. Cushing said, indicating one item. "There was no mistaking them, for they had a faint pink tinge and were so perfectly matched. They could never have been duplicated. The clasp had been augmented, but it was inescapably the same. The lady, who I suspect had no notion of their history, confessed that her husband had acquired them for her on the Continent. I enquired after the name of the jeweler." His lips pinched. "His reputation is not sufficient for me to use him, but others do. That was when I first suspected where some of the gems went."

"Did you make an accusation against the purchaser?"

"To what purpose? They had been modified to disguise their origins and they were never mine. It would have been my word against that of another and I am not a peer of the realm. When they have passed through many hands, it is difficult, if not impossible, to prove their trajectory. No, I made a note, in the hope that such a day as this might come."

"But you say they were never yours? I thought Mr. Cushing stole from you, when he made deliveries for you."

"Oh, his thefts were more extensive than that. He had a charm that ensured his invitation to house parties and events, and he used those opportunities to advantage, to be sure. I am ashamed that I ever employed him." Mr. Cushing winced. "Family persistence had its influence upon me, I am afraid. I admired those pearls and knew they had been stolen, no more than that." His finger moved to the next item. "This was an parure of rubies set in gold. Quite remarkable. They had almost perfect clarity and such a rich color." He sighed. "Some of my nephew's thefts, like this one, might have been commissioned."

Rupert was shocked. "Someone hired him to steal that specific set? As if they ordered a tankard of ale?"

"It is done, Mr. Haskell. Some collectors yearn to desire a piece so much that they do not care what must be done to claim it. They enjoy it in solitude." He stared down at the ledger, as if deciding how much to share, and Rupert was glad of his trust when he continued. "I saw a portrait in a library several years ago, a chamber kept most private. I was only invited there to view a necklace that the gentleman wished to sell. The painting was of an actress, quite famous at the time, wearing very little save some gems. It is impossible, of course, to be certain from a painting with its brush strokes, but I thought it might have been this parure. The gentleman noticed my scrutiny and quickly concluded our business, insisting that he had to protect the lady's modesty. Indeed, I was hastened from the premises without ever seeing the jewelry which was purportedly to be sold."

Rupert was amazed. "He must have forgotten about the portrait's details."

"I wager he appreciated other elements of that lady's charm," Mr. Cushing acknowledged then gave a delicate cough.

"What of the emerald brooch of that marchioness?"

Mr. Cushing nodded and turned the page. "I thought perhaps the duke had suggested our meeting because of that. The accusation against his sister made no sense. Their father could have bought her the crown jewels if she had desired them and the son, like his father, is known for his generosity to his family."

"And the lady's honesty is exemplary."

"Indeed." Mr. Cushing frowned at the entry. "I never saw or heard of it again." He indicated a drawing of the brooch in his ledger. "It was a large square-cut emerald, surrounded by sprays set with diamonds. Quite a distinctive piece and perhaps a bad choice for a theft as a result."

"How so?"

"It would have been readily recognized, for the marchioness to whom it belonged always wore it and she attended many parties." He frowned and sighed. "She passed so quickly after it was stolen, as if she could not bear to be seen without it. It would have been difficult to sell." He looked up. "She was already widowed, so her son came into his inheritance within the year."

Rupert could only admire that the son was so determined to do well by his father's tenants. "It might have been another commission."

"Possibly."

"May I make copies of your drawings of the missing pieces? I should like to locate as many as possible."

"Of course. I would like to have them found as well, and you may receive different replies to your inquiries than I have." The older man smiled modestly. "I have somewhat of a reputation when it comes to gems and their provenance."

"I would expect no less."

"While you are drawing, I will compile a list of jewelers and pawnbrokers who often trade in such items." Mr. Cushing nodded. "I welcome your aid in this, Mr. Haskell. It is even possible that some individuals will wish to reclaim their lost treasures."

"I am glad to be of aid, sir." Rupert set to copying the drawings, not troubling to hide that his greatest interest was in the emerald brooch formerly owned by the marchioness.

AUNT PENELOPE ARRIVED for dinner in a flurry of shawls and silk, her eyes sparkling with delight. An active woman of some sixty summers and Anthea's mother's older sister, she was a widow who adored parties, gossip and society. Her very presence made any room sparkle and enlivened the most dull conversations. Anthea greeted her in the foyer, delighted to see her again, and found herself smiling at her aunt's enthusiastic greeting.

"Oh, you do look well, my dear, even more pretty than I recall. Clearly the country suits you well." She looped her arm through Anthea's and they walked together toward the dining room. "Which is why we must see you wed before you vanish from town again."

"I have few expectations, aunt," Anthea confessed. "For I am not so young as others."

"Yet there are men who appreciate a woman of good sense over a giggling girl, to be sure." Penelope rapped her fan on Anthea's shoulder and dropped her voice to whisper. "And I intend to find one for you. Indeed, my dear, I take it as a challenge. Why should Alexander be the sole one to celebrate nuptials this year?"

Anthea had no reply for that, but her aunt did not wait for one. She greeted Lady North Barrows warmly, complimenting her on her own choice of shawl, then enquired after Miss Eurydice's book.

"It is very good," that girl admitted and once again it was clear she would have preferred to retire to read. It was a different volume than she had been reading the day before. Anthea saw that the author was Walter Scott. Perhaps it was *The Lady of the Lake*. She had enjoyed that book herself.

"Then we will not linger over dessert," Aunt Penelope said, her tone conspiratorial. "The better that you might read the end."

"I have only two chapters left," Eurydice admitted and Aunt Penelope laughed.

"Perhaps we should forgo dessert," she teased, pivoting to survey Alexander as he entered the foyer. "My nephew would do well to omit that course from his meal."

Alexander, who was just arriving, gave his aunt such a look that Anthea was certain she also knew of the ruse. His garb had moved another increment toward his customary simplicity that she was cheered by the sight. Haskell was behind Alexander and she caught his eye, then nodded approval. He smiled and inclined his head slightly, and even that much of his attention left her flushing with pleasure. It was too easy to recall those lazy August days on his first visit to Airdfinnan and their many amiable conversations. The way he looked at her now made her hope that his attention had been more than good manners.

How could she contrive a moment to speak with him in private? It would be scandalous if she was caught, but Anthea did not intend to be caught—and a reputation tarnished by choice had to be preferable to the condemnation she'd endured.

"And how did this fair flower bloom in London without my awareness?" demanded a familiar male voice.

Anthea spun to find Alexander's friend, Sebastian Montgomery, standing behind her, as bemused and impeccably dressed as ever. He had arrived when she had been talking to her aunt and she had barely noticed.

"My lord!" she exclaimed, truly glad to see him. Montgomery invariably prompted her smile. His hair was a little longer than she recalled and thus more curly, but he was just as handsome as ever. He enjoyed his own mischief so much that it was hard to hold any disregard for convention against him. "I was told you were to attend tonight but feared you might find more amusing company elsewhere and leave us disappointed."

The earl feigned horror. "Am I such a cur as this?"

"You have been on former occasions. An actress oft provides sufficient temptation, as I have been given to understand."

"True enough," he agreed ruefully, then took her elbow. He lowered his voice to a confidential whisper. "Beware, my lady, for you have entered a hive of deception and illusion."

"Not here." Anthea pretended to be shocked.

"Precisely here." He looked furtively from side to side. *"Within these very walls."*

"Should I wager that there is yet another spy in the house this night?"

"Then you know the secret tale." Montgomery looked so disappointed that Anthea smiled. He snorted. "You would be a fool to take such a wager, for I have no time for such folly."

"Even for the good of the crown?"

"Even so. I am wretchedly consumed with my own pleasure to the exclusion of all else."

Anthea laughed as she knew she was supposed to.

He shook a warning finger at her. "And there is another reason to avoid the parson's mousetrap."

"I did not imagine you had need of a list."

"One reason suffices for me: I do not wish to wed. But there are all these ambitious mamas who would argue that is not sufficient cause. I like to have a list at the ready."

"You should have it engraved and framed."

"I might!" He indicated Alexander and Rupert with a smile. "I do believe they had rather a good time of it, though."

"Any notable successes?"

Montgomery raised his brows. "Three spies for Old Boney, a counterfeiter and a jewel thief was the tally shared with me. And countless adventures." He winked at her. "Ravishing maidens, secrets, innuendo, adventure, swordplay at night." He sighed. "I cannot imagine why anyone would surrender such a life for matrimony. Next His Grace will take up matchmaking." He rolled his eyes at the very prospect.

"And what is so amiss with matchmaking?"

"It is an old woman's amusement, to be sure."

"But is it so wrong to wish others to find happiness?"

Montgomery laughed. "If that were the goal, it would be honorable indeed. I suspect, though, that it is simply a taste for meddling, or even a compulsion to ensure unhappiness in one's fellows."

"That is unkind!" Anthea charged with a smile.

"Is it?" Montgomery led her to the dining room. "Though I would not risk the comment before your aunt, it is an affront to imagine that you should have need of a matchmaker to find a spouse."

"I am not so young as that anymore."

"Pshaw! Nor are you so plain or so witless as to be without prospects."

"Is that a proposal, sir?" She teased, knowing the reply.

Montgomery laughed so heartily that a woman who knew him less well might have been insulted. Anthea had expected no else of him and smiled at his amusement. Then he surveyed her and winked anew. "Perhaps it should be."

"My lord!" Anthea did not have to pretend to be shocked.

"I would make any woman a wretched husband and I like you too well to be so unkind." He considered her, eyes twinkling. "But you might fare better with me than most, Miss Armstrong."

"I thank you for that, sir." They smiled at each other for a moment. "And it might be a better fate than whatever my aunt has planned."

"Indeed."

Anthea took a chance and leaned closer to whisper. "And what of Haskell?"

Montgomery blinked. "You would court a valet, even if he is a hero? Miss Armstrong, I had not thought you so burdened with a romantic disposition."

"I seek the truth of it," she confessed. "*Why* is he a valet? You were all companions at school," Anthea kept her voice to a whisper, well aware that the object of her curiosity was still watching her.

"Did you not know? He has not a *sou* to his name." Montgomery raised his brows at the very notion.

Anthea frowned. "How can this be?"

Montgomery waved away this detail. "It is not my concern to tally the fortunes of my comrades, and truly, I can think of no task more tedious." Montgomery grimaced as he removed his snuffbox from his pocket. He flicked open the box with enviable style and treated himself to a pinch of snuff. "The tale, if there is one, is his to share and his alone, Miss Armstrong," he said in a surprisingly stern tone.

He clearly was not expecting any reply, which was fortunate, for Anthea did not know what to say. She had always believed Mr. Haskell to be a man of principle—indeed, she had admired him for his noble inclinations.

But if he had been her mysterious suitor that night, a lack of any future prospects could explain both his disguise and his disappearance. In a strange way, Anthea was relieved, for he might not have been deterred by the shadow cast on her reputation at all. Indeed, he had undertaken a quest to restore her good name which made him a member of the small company who believed in her innocence.

She spared a backward glance and found Mr. Haskell yet watching her, his eyes unfathomably dark. Her very flesh heated at the weight of his perusal and she yearned for something she feared she would never possess.

Abruptly, he turned away and strode down the hall toward the library. Anthea recalled herself to her responsibilities with an effort: she had guests to attend. She could dream of Haskell and her masked courtier later, when she was alone.

Alexander stood with their aunt Penelope. His waistcoat was a brilliant hue of turquoise embroidered with yellow butterflies. His shoes had been dyed to match, but still, it was an improvement upon his previous choices. She noticed that Montgomery was biting back a smile, though he was not without a fondness for elaborate waistcoats himself.

The flower in Alexander's buttonhole was from the vine and the perfume it emitted was remarkably strong. It turned Anthea's thoughts in the direction of sweet kisses, romance and happy endings.

Montgomery looked Anthea in the eye. "You see what love does to a man's wits."

She had to ask. "Do you like her?"

"I do, actually," the earl admitted, as if surprised. "There is not a shred of artifice in her, and she adores him. He will indulge her, you will see, and they will become fat and complacent together once they have a few sons."

Anthea laughed despite herself at the prospect of her brother ever becoming complacent. She gestured toward Montgomery's embroidered waistcoat, which encased his tautly muscled form. "And this is another reason to avoid marriage vows? To keep your sleek figure?"

"As good a reason as any," he agreed easily, then they turned as one at the sound of a step on the stairs. Daphne descended to the foyer, her attention as yet upon the hem of her skirt. She was a vision of loveliness, dressed in a silk dress of silvery mauve, with elaborate beading along the hem and neckline. Her fair hair was twisted up, revealing her slender neck. She was clearly excited by the dress, which had to be new and a gift from Alexander. She fairly glowed with happiness as she curtseyed before Alexander. Anthea felt that a fairy princess had descended to their company and indeed, everyone fell silent in admiration.

"She is wearing *Maman's* amethysts," Anthea whispered, admiring how well the stones favored Daphne's coloring. It was a full parure, with necklace, drop earrings, bracelet and a hair ornament that gleamed against Daphne's blond tresses.

"Is that troubling?" Montgomery murmured, his concern unexpected.

Anthea shook her head. "No, they should be worn, and she looks well in them." She smiled at her brother's friend. "I would expect Alexander to lavish gifts upon his bride, and truly, this shows his affection most clearly. I hope their match will be a happy one."

"And you?"

"I can remain in Alexander's home and make myself of use to him and his bride."

"Do you not wish to wed?" Montgomery whispered.

"Only for love. At this point, I see no allure in compromise."

"And I salute your wisdom." Montgomery bowed slightly. "If you have need of an accomplice to evade your aunt's matchmaking schemes, I put myself at your service, Miss Armstrong."

Anthea was touched and flattered. "I thank you."

Montgomery bowed again, then offered his hand. "And now we are summoned to dinner. Shall I have the misfortune to be seated beside the bride's ferocious grandmother, do you think? She may devour me instead of the soup."

"I shall defend you, if need be, sir."

"And so already we come to rely upon each other. This season may be a most interesting one, to be sure."

"How marvelous to have such an ally," she said lightly, taking him at his word. "I cannot help but look forward to the months ahead."

Montgomery laughed, Anthea smiled, and they entered the dining room together.

She was more than aware of her aunt's considering glance but ignored it.

$\sim$

OF COURSE, Montgomery made Miss Armstrong smile—and she made him laugh. Seeing the two of them together convinced Rupert that their match might be inevitable. They obviously were at ease in each other's company. They found pleasure in matching wits, to be sure, were of suitable ages for a match, and there could be no objections from their families. Indeed, they made a striking couple.

And what could Rupert do to halt the progress of that happy affair? Not a thing, not when he was consigned to remain outside of the circle of events as a servant. He could do as much service to Alexander's sister as he liked—if her reputation was restored, he still would not be able to honorably court her. His life in service was not suitable for a lady of her rank, and he would accept no charity from Alexander.

It would be wrong to interfere, and yet he did not wish to see the affair progress.

He did not wish to stay in Alexander's service and see Anthea all the time, yet he could not bear to leave and be denied even a glimpse of her. He would not reconcile with his father, who continued to flaunt Mrs. Blythe and leave his mother weeping at their country house. The situation was damnable, no matter how he looked upon it.

Rupert had scorched more than one cravat in recent weeks, just ruminating upon it.

On this night, he had a notion, though. As quixotic as it might be, he wished to give Anthea a message. He wanted her to know of his affections, but also the restraints upon him. He could not write her a note lest it be found and was uncertain he might find the opportunity to speak with her unobserved—which would be inappropriate at any rate.

Fortunately, he had a much better notion of how his aim might be achieved.

"WHAT WILL your sister do when we are married?" Daphne asked when she was alone in the library with Alexander that evening. He had set aside his jacket and stoked up the fire, which she knew he did for her comfort. The rest of the family had retired, his aunt and the earl had left, the house was quiet, and they were truly alone.

It was Daphne's favorite part of her day. There was no pretense between them when they sat thus, and she had learned that she could speak to her intended about anything at all. Alexander was not a man to jump to conclusions or take offense over a comment: he was thoughtful, considerate and clever, and she realized each day how fortunate she was to be his betrothed.

She could not wait to become his wife.

He beckoned to her with a smile and she sat beside him on the settee before the fire, taking off her slippers and tucking her feet beneath her skirt. He wrapped one arm around her shoulders, pulling her against his warmth and strength, and she knew there was no finer place in the world to be.

"She will live with us, unless you would prefer otherwise. Do you not like her?"

"I adore Anthea! But she is so good and kind that I want her to be happy as well." She spared him a smile, liking how his eyes twinkled. "I want everyone to be as happy as I am."

He chuckled and pressed a kiss to her temple. "That is a wish I cannot fulfill."

"But I believe you could make a difference in this matter."

"Indeed?"

She saw that he did not understand. "You haven't noticed?"

"What haven't I noticed?"

"The way that Haskell looks at Anthea." She watched surprise light his expression, then continued. "And the way Anthea does *not* look at Haskell."

"Then you mean the affection, if there is any, is all on his side?"

"Then I mean they are quite taken with each other. She flushes when he enters the room, then is very careful to avoid glancing his way."

The duke considered this while he sipped his brandy.

"How do they know each other?" Daphne asked.

"Years ago, Haskell came to Airdfinnan to hunt. Anthea was ten that summer and I recall that they spent considerable time together. I thought it charming that he so indulged her. She was not that interested in the hunt in those days."

Daphne sighed contentment. "And so they have known each other all this time."

"One would not have known it. When I am at Airdfinnan, they scarcely speak."

"How could they when their hearts are so full?"

He turned to look at her. "You are certain?"

Daphne nodded. "As sure as I was of your truth."

"And you think I should facilitate matters?"

"I think that if Anthea loves Haskell the way that I love you, then no other man will suit her. I think that only he can make her happy."

Alexander frowned. "But Haskell has no inheritance and no expectation of one anymore."

"Yet you are as rich as Croesus."

Alexander looked down at her. "And you know I would do anything for Anthea."

"I do, but I suspect you have not thought of this yet."

He laughed again. "No, I confess I had not." His gaze sharpened. "Rupert is proud. He will decline any financial assistance I offer him."

"Then you must think of another solution. Anthea's happiness is at stake."

"What of Eurydice? Have you a future planned for her?"

Daphne had thought about this. "She might not wed and truly, you have ensured with your promise that she does not have to. Her desire might change, though. Could we give her a season in a few years?"

"Of course, if you wish it."

"I do."

"The better to ensure that everyone might be as happy as you," Alexander concluded, his tone teasing.

"Would the world not be a better place if everybody was happy?"

"It would indeed." They smiled at each other, the air aglow with their mutual admiration, and the fire crackled merrily in the grate. It seemed to Daphne that there was no air left in the room, that there was nothing of import in all the world save the duke. "I love you, Alexander," she whispered, as awed by that fact as when she had first realized as much.

"And I love you, my Daphne," he murmured ardently. "I shall do my best to ensure your happiness, to be sure."

"You already have, sir."

Then just as she had hoped, Alexander lowered his head and kissed her soundly.

CHAPTER 4

There was a book on her nightstand.

Anthea was quite certain it had not been there before. She had not chosen it and Connaught was still abed with that wretched cold.

Romeo and Juliet.

It was hardly a favorite play of hers. Star-crossed lovers who died tragically, feuding families who had likely forgotten the origin of their dispute, and a sad ending. Anthea much preferred people and characters to use their wits.

She picked up the book and realized there was a card in it, left to mark the place. Curious, she opened the volume then caught her breath. There was a domino mask drawn on the card and on the other side. The book was from the duke's library. She moved toward the light to read the marked passage.

> My bounty is as boundless as the sea,
> My love as deep. The more I give to thee,
> The more I have, for both are infinite.

IT WAS a sentiment to warm her heart, save for the fate of the couple in question. She wrote the passage on the back of the card and hid the card within her papers, knowing what she had to do.

She would send a message back.

And she would not be caught doing as much.

She went to the window. Alexander's carriage was before the house, so he had lingered to speak with Daphne. Jenny would not come to Anthea until Daphne was settled for the night, at Anthea's own insistence. Eurydice was almost certainly reading in bed.

Anthea opened her door to listen. Nelson's voice carried from the dowager's room, interspersed with comments from Lady North Barrows herself. Anthea had already learned that the maid often remained late with her mistress, tending to her various demands. Pierce would be belowstairs, for the sake of discretion, and Alexander would ring when he meant to leave.

She could only hope that Haskell awaited her brother in the foyer.

She moved silently in the quiet house, smiling when she heard the great clock being wound. Trust Haskell to realize that the clock needed attention. She recalled him repairing a clock at Airdfinnan once, and her fascination at his skill with the tiny pieces. He was patient and thorough, as well as unafraid to step up when a task had to be done.

She paused on the bottom step with the book, taking a moment to watch him. He moved deftly as he finished winding the clock, adjusted the time by a minute or two, replaced the key in the case, then closed the case carefully. The clock seemed to tick more loudly as if it appreciated his efforts. She watched him take a step back and watch the clock.

She took the last step, ensuring it was audible.

He started, then pivoted and bowed. "Miss Armstrong."

"How fortunate a meeting, Mr. Haskell."

"Is it, my lady?"

"I thought you might have left already."

"His Grace wished a moment with his betrothed first."

"Are they in the library?"

"They are indeed."

"How regrettable." She lifted the book and saw his eyes light in recognition. "I fear I have the wrong book, but I would not interrupt them."

"The wrong book, my lady?"

"This one is filled with admirable sentiment but it ends badly."

"Many love affairs do end badly, my lady."

"That may be so, I prefer to believe that love conquers all obstacles. Surely the divine will must be on the side of love?"

"Oftimes, it seems otherwise."

"All the more reason to believe, then."

"And what book would you read, my lady?"

"The volume of Shakespeare's sonnets," Anthea said. "As lovely in language yet with sentiment more aligned with my own views."

"Truly?"

"Truly. I have a great affection for Sonnet 116." Anthea held his gaze and quoted.

> "Let me not to the marriage of true minds
> Admit impediments. Love is not love
> Which alters when it alteration finds,
> Or bends with the remover to remove.
> O no! it is an ever-fixed mark
> That looks on tempests and is never shaken..."

HASKELL FROWNED. "But poetry is merely sentiment, my lady, and does not always acknowledge the constraints of life."

"Perhaps not, but I will speak bluntly, Mr. Haskell. I would thank you again, for endeavoring to clear my name, and also for taking on the quest of finding the missing gem." She smiled. "You guessed aright that my acquaintances are not welcoming my return to town, and I fear that it may influence Miss Goodenham's reception. I could not bear for her to pay any price on my behalf."

He immediately was concerned and she admired that he tried to reassure her. "Nor should I, but Mr. Cushing was most helpful today.

He had sketches of all the missing gems, a complete inventory, I believe, and generously shared all he knew with me."

"That was most kind."

"He, too, would like to see the gems found." Haskell frowned slightly. "I wonder, my lady, if you might recount to me the details of that unfortunate incidence. It is suspected that the thief used unwitting guests to carry the stolen gems away from the site of the theft, then waylaid them, but I would like to be certain of the details."

"I am convinced that is precisely what occurred," Anthea said. "My maid Connaught had fallen ill, so we were the first to leave the house party. She has a weakness for colds and I cannot bear to see her work when she should retire to bed."

"That is most kind of you."

"It is the only decent way to treat a maid."

He smiled and her heart fluttered at the warmth in his gaze. "Yet not all do as much. Yours is a kindly nature."

Anthea found herself both pleased and agitated. "Our departure was untimely, though, for the theft of the gem was discovered immediately after we left. A party was sent after us, for a housemaid insisted she had seen the gem in Connaught's hand and I had admired it rather fulsomely. It was an emerald brooch, set with many diamonds. Quite a spectacular piece."

"But you cannot have been the only one to admire it."

She smiled and shook her head ruefully. "But I was the sole one to depart early."

"And the housemaid's tale?"

Anthea frowned. "I remember that she was one who liked to have the attention of all upon her. It could very well have been a tale told for attention. Connaught swore she never touched it, and she has served our family twenty years. She was my mother's maid before mine. In my debut year, my mother insisted that I have a fully trained lady's maid and she hired a younger girl."

"You believe Connaught."

"Of course! I told them as much when we were pursued by authorities."

"Where did they reach you?"

"We had stopped at a tavern near London for a hot meal." Anthea named the tavern and he nodded, as if he knew it. "I wished to ensure that Connaught grew no more ill and I was famished myself. Imagine my surprise when Mr. Nathaniel Cushing appeared and insisted that he buy us luncheon."

"He must have followed you."

"Indeed. And he left first, citing an appointment, but Connaught noticed that he lingered in the yard instead of hastening away. I saw later that my cases had been opened, but I suspected the boys in the yard at the tavern. I could not see that any item was missing and thought it mischief at root, then the authorities arrived with their accusations." She flushed in memory. "It was most awkward, but I granted them leave to search all of our belongings."

"And your persons?"

"No," Anthea said. "I would not endure it, though Connaught was obliged to do as much. In the end they found nothing at all and released us, but another coach from the party had arrived and their whispered speculation was pure venom." Her old anger at the injustice of it all straightened her spine. "I have never had strangers doubt the veracity of my word and cast aspersions upon my nature with no evidence whatsoever, and I decided I would not tolerate such behavior a moment longer. We rode to Airdfinnan instead of this house, and I have been there ever since."

"I cannot blame you for such a decision," Haskell said. "Indeed, it seems most prudent given the prejudice against you. No lady of merit should have had to suffer such treatment."

She smiled at him. "And so I should have continued to suffer, without your happy efforts. I owe you more thanks than can be readily granted, Mr. Haskell."

"My lady, I merely..."

Anthea took a breath and stepped closer. Feeling most daring, she laid a hand upon his arm. Haskell froze, his gaze locked upon her. "There was a time when I dreamed we might once come to an understanding," she said quietly.

He inhaled sharply but did not move away. "I shared that hope, my lady, but now I know it to be impossible." He touched her hand fleetingly. "You should choose a suitor and wed, Miss Armstrong."

"I am not obliged to do as much…"

To her delight, his fingertip landed across her lips. She stared at him, lost in the darkness of his eyes. He was so earnest. "But you must. You must live a full life and be happy, instead of yearning for what cannot be."

Anthea's chest was tight. "I am told your fortunes have changed."

He sighed and looked across the foyer. "By my own deed, but I would not recall it. I could not, even to please you."

"Will you confide in me?"

His smile was sad. "My situation changed after your masquerade ball." His gaze clung to hers. "You must remember my father's error."

"How could I forget it?" It was too easy to recall the unexpected arrival of Baron Thornedyke with his mistress instead of his wife—as well as Mr. Haskell's subsequent arrival with his mother. She also remembered her father's insistence upon dancing with the baroness and snubbing Mrs. Blythe. She could still see the red suffusing the baron's features and his son's impassive expression. Rupert's eyes had flashed, though, and she had admired that he was indignant on his mother's behalf.

But not truly surprised, to be sure.

"I argued with him the next day, for he was wrong to treat my mother thus." He spoke with admirable resolve. "I told him to cease his public affections with that woman, and he told me I had no right to chastise him. We argued most heatedly and in the end, he cast me out and vowed to change his will, bestowing all his possessions upon the young son he had by that woman."

Anthea was shocked. "But surely you could challenge the will."

"Perhaps I could. The stain upon our name is such that I want nothing of his. And so—" he bent and touched his lips to the back of her hand "—my own aspirations must be put aside. I will content myself with being of service to you."

"And what if I am not content with that?"

"Then you must learn to be, my lady." He bowed then, obviously intending to step away from her.

"Do you think so little of my character that you assume I will only be happy in a wealthy situation? Truly, you think love has little merit, if that is so."

He surveyed her. "I think it is easy for anyone to discount the power of money when one has it. It takes the loss of it to show the full extent of its influence."

"But..."

His grip tightened on her fingers. "I have no doubt that your heart is true, my lady, but I have watched my mother's love fade as the future she desired and expected was taken from her, one increment at a time. I would hope to never watch a woman be so disappointed again, and I certainly will not be responsible for such a situation."

Anthea did not loosen her grip upon his arm. "Will you come to the masquerade and dance with me, one last time?"

His gaze searched hers before he shook his head. "It would be unkind to both of us."

Anthea tried to tease him, just a little, hoping to prompt his smile. "Your principles, sir, begin to vex me."

"My principles, my lady, are all that I have left." His voice caught on the confession, making Anthea realize that this choice was not easy for him. "You should know that I mean to seek the gems and locate as many as possible, my lady." His gaze clung to hers even as she realized the import of his words. "We are unlikely to see each other after this night." He bent to kiss her hand again, but Anthea wanted more than that.

If this was to be their parting forever, she would have another kiss.

She reached for him and touched Haskell's jaw with her fingertips. He froze and stared at her, startled by her breach of propriety. Anthea did not care.

This time, she would choose to be scandalous, for the sake of love.

She touched her lips to his, a sweet caress that left her trembling, and hoped that he would accept her invitation. He whispered her given name, hesitated only a moment, then slanted his mouth over hers. Anthea rose to her toes, twining her fingers into his hair and demanding more.

If this was to be their last kiss, she would make it one to remember.

Anthea kissed him.

She was the most tempting woman alive and the queen of his heart, the one person most determined to undermine his principles—and the one most likely to succeed. Rupert clung to the certainty that he made the right choice, even as he reveled in her sweet kiss.

He would do anything for her, but he would not disappoint her. He would not condemn her to a life that was less than she deserved, even to have her by his side. He would protect her from anything and anyone.

Even himself.

Her kiss was a glorious temptation to forget all he knew to be true, and Rupert savored every second of it. His arm was around her waist and she pressed against him, filling his senses with her touch and the faint scent of her perfume. Her fingers were in his hair, her light caress making him burn for more than just one kiss...

A subtle cough from the direction of the library made him straighten abruptly and turn away from the alluring lady. The back of his neck heated and he could not meet Alexander's gaze. He was well aware that Miss Goodenham stood at his friend's side, though her expression was less formidable. She kissed the duke's cheek, then retreated upstairs, looking curiously satisfied.

"Alexander, I must explain..." Miss Armstrong began, but the duke pointed imperiously to the second floor.

"There is nothing to be said, Anthea."

Miss Armstrong hesitated, then retreated, her slippers tapping on the stairs until there was no sound at all.

Rupert fully expected to be chastised by his old friend and braced himself for it.

Instead, Alexander did not speak. The silence between them was oppressive to Rupert's ears and he wished Alexander would say something so that he could apologize. They left the house and got into the carriage, the air crisp and cold. They had ridden a block, alone in the carriage together, before the duke spoke. His gaze was fixed upon the window. "I would grant her an allowance," he said softly.

Rupert shook his head, even as he was awed by his friend's offer. "You have already been more than generous."

Alexander impaled him with a glance. "I would see her happy."

"I could not bear to dishonor her."

The duke sighed. "You were always the principled one."

"I am sorry. My admiration for the lady overwhelmed my duty..."

Alexander interrupted him. "You could reconcile with *him*."

"Impossible. I vowed I would do as much only if he put Mrs. Blythe aside."

The duke nodded. "I see your reasoning in that. To betray your pledge to one woman would be no guarantee that you would be reliable to another."

Rupert nodded, glad to be understood.

Alexander studied him. "You could take orders. I would find you a living."

Rupert shook his head again. "Such a life would not suit your sister well and you know it." When Alexander did not speak, he continued. "She deserves more than such a life. I would not see her raising chickens and pinching pennies, would you?"

Alexander almost smiled. "I could buy you a commission."

Rupert was surprised by his friend's generosity. "And how would I repay you?"

"By making my sister happy."

"And would she be happy, following an army?" Rupert shook his head, haunted by the memory of his own mother's disappointment. "She is a lady. She was raised to be a lady and to have such aspirations. She needs a house to manage, a garden to plan, children to teach and to spoil. She needs the security of a country house, and perhaps a townhouse in town. She needs to dance at balls and welcome guests for tea."

Alexander smiled. "You have planned quite the future for her."

"It is no jest. She is the finest of women and she should have the best that can be offered to her. I had always doubted that Thornedyke Manor would be sufficient, but less than that? The wife of a valet? It is absolutely out of the question."

Alexander looked out the window again, his expression thoughtful. "And she agrees?"

"She is romantic."

His friend nodded. "That kiss leaves me wondering whether she shares your reservations."

"She may not share them now, but it is inevitable that she will," Rupert insisted. "I will not watch affection die for lack of coin, Alexander. I have witnessed my mother's disappointment and it has torn my heart. I will not do as much to the lady I hold in highest regard."

To his relief, his friend nodded once, though his expression was solemn. "You will tell me if there is any way I can be of assistance."

"You have already been kind." Rupert sighed. "I ask your leave to seek the gems tomorrow. Some may be in France."

Alexander met his gaze, his concern clear. "It will be a dangerous quest."

"It must be done. I have no reservations."

Alexander frowned but he did not argue the matter. Which meant that in his own heart, he knew that Rupert was right. "Then Godspeed to you."

Rupert would see Miss Armstrong's name cleared, then leave the duke's household as soon as possible. The prospect of never seeing Anthea again did not fill him with joy. The possibility of her marrying Montgomery brought him even less pleasure.

The wretched truth of it was that he had no choice: he could not discard honor in the name of love and that meant Rupert would have honor alone.

He did not have to like the truth of it.

It was a fortnight after Anthea's arrival in town that a visit was arranged to the house of the de Royes in Cavendish Square. Both Daphne and Eurydice were thrilled to restore the acquaintance with their former governess, but the dowager insisted that she would forgo the visit if Anthea accompanied them. She sent her greetings and goodwill, and Anthea was happy of the outing.

"M. de Roye is most wickedly handsome," Eurydice informed her when they were in the carriage. "Theirs is a most romantic tale."

"Indeed?"

Daphne continued the tale. "He worked for her father at Brisbane's Emporium, and Miss Brisbane was utterly in love with him years ago." She sighed contentment at this detail.

Eurydice sat forward, eyes shining. "Her brother, though, gambled heavily and was in debt to a villain."

"Truly?"

"Truly," Eurydice confirmed. Anthea already saw that the younger woman loved to recount stories. "It was all the villain's scheme, for Miss Brisbane had spurned him out of her love for M. de Roye and he vowed vengeance. He seized the Emporium after her father's death, for the brother lost it in the gaming hells..." Her voice faltered and Anthea wondered whether she knew the details of the tale. It was perhaps more fitting that she did not.

"But M. de Roye vowed to retrieve it all for her and he did," Daphne concluded brightly. A quick glance was exchanged by the sisters, and Anthea wondered at it. "And then they wed."

"And now they intend to rebuild the reputation of Brisbane's Emporium," Eurydice concluded.

"You could be of assistance, Anthea," the older sister said earnestly.

Anthea smiled. "I suspect, Daphne, that you might be more so."

"I do not understand."

"You will be the toast of the *ton* this year, if my brother has anything to say of the matter. If you let it be known that you only shop at Brisbane's, then that might make a great difference in their fortunes."

The younger woman's eyes lit with excitement and then resolve. "I shall ask Mme. de Roye about it. She is a most sensible woman and will undoubtedly have a plan."

Mme. de Roye proved to be of an age with Anthea, with hair that was a little more reddish. Her eyes sparkled with good humor and she looked to be pregnant. Her affection for the Goodenham sisters could not have been feigned. Their warm exchange of greetings made Anthea smile.

The house was large and welcoming, though the fact that it was in need of some refurbishing could not be disguised.

"My husband's grandmother owned it," Mme. de Roye confessed, glancing over the sweeping staircase. "And he spent many happy hours here both in his youth and after inheriting it. I fear he did not keep up with the repairs. We intend to refurbish it completely, but have been much involved at the emporium this winter. There is so much to be done!"

"And you must tell us every detail," Daphne urged.

The drawing room was large and comfortably furnished, filled with golden morning sunlight. They were served tea and little cakes, and Anthea simply listened as the sisters caught up on their governess' news. She was surprised that the butler was black, a most unusual situation in London. Many houses had one black servant, but they were seldom in positions of authority.

He came to the drawing room and bowed, a most handsome man with an elegant manner. "M. de Roye asked me to inform you that he will be home for dinner after all, madame," he said softly.

"How wonderful, Larousse," Mme. de Roye acknowledged. "I am glad that he was able to arrange as much. Thank you." She smiled when she apparently noted Anthea's glance. "Larousse has served my husband as valet and friend for many years," she said. "He came with him from Saint Domingue."

Larousse pivoted at the doors, inclined his head, then retreated, closing the doors behind him.

"Is that in the West Indies?" Anthea asked.

"Yes, Lucien's family grew sugar cane, which was the source of their wealth. I spent my childhood on St. Maurice, another island, so we share a love of that part of the world."

Anthea frowned, for it was curious that she had recently heard another mention of the West Indies. "I don't suppose you ever knew of a governess named Amelia Findlay?" she asked, then was startled when Mme. de Roye spilled her tea. "I ask only because our butler is seeking his cousin. He last heard of her when she took a post with a family departing for the West Indies and was hoping to find some news of her while in town. It was a number of years ago, however."

Mme. de Roye had paled. A glance passed between the other three women like quicksilver and Anthea knew there was something she did not understand.

"I apologize if my question was inappropriate," she said. "I simply hoped to be of assistance..."

Mme. de Roye set aside her tea cup and fixed Daphne with a look. "You are certain that your confidence is not misplaced?"

"I would trust Miss Armstrong with my heart and soul," Daphne replied with welcome resolve. Miss Eurydice nodded agreement.

Mme. de Roye moved to the seat beside Anthea. "I tell you this in confidence, Miss Armstrong, and hope that you do not think the less of me for it. I refused a man who then vowed to destroy all I loved. Miss Findlay was my governess and my friend, my sole ally after the death of my father and brother. And when she died, she insisted that I take her name instead, the better to hide from the villain, and lay her to rest under my name. She was quite resolute." The other woman took a shaking breath. "And so I became a governess and found a post in Cumbria with two delightful young ladies." She smiled at the Goodenham sisters. "Until we were summoned to Cornwall and Lucien—M. de Roye—unveiled my ruse and brought the fiend to justice."

This could not be all of the tale, but the details were not of Anthea's concern. "It seems that many disguises have been pierced in Cornwall of late," she contented herself with saying.

Daphne blushed crimson, but her eyes danced. "Perhaps it is the sea air," she suggested with a welcome note of mischief.

"Might I send Findlay to see you?" Anthea asked. "I am certain he would be glad to hear of his cousin's fate from you directly. His discretion is absolutely assured."

"Of course," Mme. de Roye said. "I still have her spectacles and several of her cherished books. I would be delighted to return them to her family."

That mystery solved and their course of action resolved upon, the women's conversation turned them to the season ahead and the new arrivals of fabric at Brisbane's Emporium. Daphne immediately suggested they make an appointment to view the inventory and Anthea saw the realization dawn in Mme. de Roye that the patronage of this particular duchess could remake their reputation with haste.

She sat back and sipped her tea, glad to have contributed to two most suitable resolutions.

Haskell's crossing to France was perilous and his journey to Paris more so. His French, fortunately, was excellent, and his progress proved that he could pass as a Frenchman when necessary. He found rooms in Paris in a quarter that was not entirely disreputable and began to seek out the jewelers on the list from Mr. Cushing. It promised to be a delicate business to try to find tidings of the gems without buying them outright himself and the delays chafed at him.

As the weeks passed and spring dawned upon the city, he began to wonder whether he would return to London in time for the birth of Anthea and Montgomery's first child.

The one gem of which he could discover nothing, though, was the marchioness' emerald, and he would not halt until he had located it.

For Anthea's sake.

Anthea's days in town settled into a rhythm that was not unpleasant, but certainly did not meet her aunt's expectations. She had no obligations to call on anyone and received few visitors herself. The one house where she was always received was in Cavendish Square and she became friends with Sophia de Roye. She accompanied Daphne on her expeditions to dressmakers and glovemakers, which invariably included a visit to a bookseller for Eurydice. She discussed the finances of the household and arrangements for parties with the older sister, then books and authors with the younger. They ate *en famille* and conversation flowed as they came to know each other better. Alexander's garb made steady progress to his usual choices, even in Haskell's absence, and the date of the wedding drew ever closer. The vine continued to flourish, virtually encasing the house with its vigorous growth, and the blooms began to fade.

That did not keep Anthea's thoughts from Haskell or romance. Her aunt strove to cast eligible men into Anthea's path, making introductions at every opportunity, but not a one of them caught her interest—and truly, it was difficult to admire any man who was so swayed by rumor and innuendo. It was all too easy to recall that the men who believed in her innocence were her brother and his two friends, and that did not help her to forget Haskell. She had to believe that he would return for the wedding, and surely then, if he had fulfilled his pledge to find the gems, she might manage to change his thinking.

Montgomery was as good as his word. Whenever Anthea found herself snubbed or that people quietly turned their backs upon her, Montgomery invariably appeared. He made her smile; he flattered her shamelessly and he must have danced with her more times than he desired. Her aunt also came frequently to Anthea when they were out, to introduce one young man or another, but these potential beaux invariably melted into the crowd as soon as Aunt Penelope looked away. Alexander was also gallant in ensuring that she was not alone, but he was much engaged in escorting Daphne and introducing her.

Anthea supposed it was only natural that she began to think about retreating to Airdfinnan. The gossips had her and Montgomery making a match, which was ridiculous but a result of his gallantry. That was an unexpected side of his nature and one that explained why he, Alexander and Haskell were such good friends. She had known that Alexander and Haskell were honest and principled, and to be sure, it was a relief to realize that Montgomery, despite his talk, was similar in character.

Several weeks after their initial meeting, Anthea accompanied Daphne and Eurydice to Brisbane's Emporium. They had been invited by Mme. de Roye to view a new shipment of silks that had just arrived from Venice.

"I have asked His Grace for permission to acquire two dress lengths," Daphne confided in the carriage, then smiled. "Although I have warned him that I must choose lavish ones to ensure they attract attention. No doubt they will be expensive."

"But he knows you do as much to assist your former governess," Anthea said.

The younger woman smiled. "He insisted that I choose two more, one for you and one for Eurydice." She beamed with pride. "He is most generous."

"He is indeed," Anthea agreed.

Daphne frowned a little. "I fear he might be too generous," she dared to say, her gaze flicking to Anthea. "I have no experience of living in a duke's home, but it seems there are many maids and footmen."

"Many," Eurydice agreed without looking up from her book.

Anthea smiled that her own view was shared. "You must have had several in Lady North Barrows' residence."

"There were the three of us, plus Nelson and Jenny, a housekeeper with a maid—it was Mrs. Jones and her daughter from the village—and always a cook with a scullery maid in the kitchens. We had neither a butler nor a footman. Seven of us lived in the house in total, and the dower house was not small."

"But there are some tasks that men do more readily," Anthea said.

"My cousin, Daniel, would send a man from the main house whenever we had need of one. Likewise, he was kind in lending us a coach and team, or inviting us to ride to hunt."

"Only Daphne liked that," Eurydice supplied.

"He let you borrow his books," Daphne countered and her sister smiled in memory.

"I cannot even think how many servants the duke employs," she said then, turning the page of her book. It was *The Castle of Otronto*.

"Fifteen footmen, nineteen maids, two butlers, a valet, a cook, a housekeeper, a coachman, an ostler and two stableboys," Daphne said with precision. "Doubtless there are more at Airdfinnan." She looked to Anthea for confirmation.

"Only two footmen and five maids, a cook, a housekeeper, and of course, the coachman and butler who are presently here. I think there are four boys in the stables and a huntsman, as well."

"And when we return there, will all this household accompany us?"

"I am not certain of the duke's plans in that regard."

"It makes little sense to take so many footmen and maids to Scotland," Daphne said. "And even less to leave them resident here with no one to serve." She looked out the window, clearly thinking. "If we are to stay in Scotland, I wonder if we should not close up the house here. I could write letters of recommendation for those servants we release, but I do not wish to cause offense with such a proposal."

"That is a most admirable suggestion," Anthea said, seeing that some of the responsibilities of Alexander's household were leaving her grasp. "Perhaps you should discuss the possibilities with the duke."

"I think I shall, so long as you do not feel that I am intruding."

"How can you intrude? You will be duchess, and the choices are yours to make." Anthea spoke with a smile, wanting to reassure Daphne, but she realized that her own role would be much diminished. In truth, she liked to be busy and the notion of having time on her hands was not a welcome one.

But she would not wed simply to avoid boredom, not at this point in her life. Love and love alone would suffice.

When would Haskell return?

CHAPTER 5

The silks were so exquisite that it was difficult to choose. In the end, Daphne chose a length of shimmering white, lavishly embroidered with gold and silver thread and embellished with beads. It would be made into a dress for her wedding. She also chose a deep crimson with gold embroidery that suited her very well. Eurydice chose an amber silk that seemed simple but caught the light in a most attractive way. Anthea chose a silvery green at the insistence of all the others.

Then M. de Roye asked if he could have a word with her. She left the others as they chose satin slippers to match their silks, and followed him to a back room. "I would seek your advice, Miss Armstrong, if you do not mind."

"Of course not."

"I intended to give Sophia a piece of jewelry, as she desired only a simple gold band for a wedding ring. I would like to have some token to commemorate that day."

Anthea smiled. "An admirable notion."

He closed the office door behind her and an older man stood up from the chair where he had obviously been waiting. He was dressed conservatively and had a satchel in his grip along with his hat. He was a bit plump and his hair was thinning on top and turning silver at his temples. He wore gold spectacles and Anthea guessed that he was a tradesman.

"This is Mr. Forsythe," M. de Roye said. "He is a jeweler who specializes in estate pieces. I want to choose an older piece for Sophia."

"The older pieces have more character, sir," Mr. Forsythe said. At M. de Roye's gesture, he opened his bag and unfolded a small portfolio. It was lined with black velvet, and a number of pieces were fixed on the lining. They glittered and sparkled in the light, all polished to perfection.

And there it was, the gem at the root of all her troubles. Anthea stared at the emerald and diamond brooch, though she tried to hide her reaction. That brooch was from no estate. Even if its owner had died in the years since it had been stolen at that house party, surely such an item would have been included in the inventory of any will.

Was this one counterfeit?

As much as she itched to touch the gem or ask after it, Anthea did not wish to reveal herself. Mr. Forsythe clearly did not realize the connection between the gem and herself, and she had not been introduced by name.

"I like this piece," M. de Roye said, indicating a brooch shaped like a bow. The ribbons were gold and studded with small rubies. Dangling from the knot was a large freshwater pearl. The pearl had an irregular shape, not unlike a large teardrop, and a spectacular gleam. "My grandmother had a similar one, though the bow was covered with diamonds."

"A very admirable piece, sir." Mr. Forsythe removed it and handed it to M. de Roye that he could examine it more closely.

"What do you think of it?" that man asked Anthea. His gaze was fixed on the pin in his hand.

"I think it elegant and distinctive, and also that it is something she could wear often." Anthea smiled. "It seems a waste to have a truly remarkable piece and be compelled to store it away."

"Indeed, indeed," Mr. Forsythe agreed. "Such treasures are to be enjoyed." His gaze flicked to her own necklace, a small aquamarine set in gold which matched her earrings. The set was sufficiently modest that she could wear it often and she wagered that Mr. Forsythe had valued it within a shilling.

"With your approval, then, I shall choose this one," M. de Roye said, then bowed to Anthea. "I thank you kindly for your assistance."

Anthea excused herself, leaving him to complete the transaction, her heart racing. She had to tell Haskell of this, and wished she knew when he might return. At the very least, he should be back for Alexander's wedding, and she could only hope the gem was not sold by then.

"Secrets and schemes?" Daphne teased her upon her return.

Anthea played along, touching her fingertip to her lips. "I dare not say. Have you found slippers that match the fabric?"

"Paris?"

Alexander watched his sister brace her hands on her hips and glare at him. She was as astonished and irked as he had ever seen her.

"What possible reason has Haskell to go to Paris?"

"I told you that he meant to find the lost gems. Evidently, many of them were sold in Paris..."

"Has it eluded your attention that we are at war with France? Paris is in France, Alexander."

"I am aware of that..."

She flung out a hand. "And this is how you treat a man who is both your servant and your friend? You send him alone into a hostile area..."

"Haskell means to leave my employ."

Her eyes flashed. "Is he no longer your friend?"

"He is one of my best friends, to be sure."

"Then..."

Alexander held up a hand. "And he was determined to finish what we had started. No man could have kept him from the task he had chosen for himself, and he would accept no assistance. You should know that Haskell is proud and principled."

Anthea cast him one last furious glance, then flung herself into a chair. "Irksome man!" she said under her breath. Then she flicked a nigh lethal glance his way. "I saw it today."

Alexander could have no doubt of her meaning. He moved to sit beside her. "Truly? I could acquire it..."

She silenced him with a touch. "No, you cannot. Haskell is right. People will think that we simply surrendered it after all this time." Her voice dropped. "You must summon him home with all haste."

"But I cannot," Alexander admitted. "I cannot draw any attention to him when he is in disguise and in truth I do not know his precise location."

"But that is so perilous!"

"He insisted upon it." He sighed. "We must simply wait, Anthea."

"Surely he will return for your wedding."

"I hope as much." He kissed her hand. "Have faith, Anthea, that all will end well."

She frowned then summoned a smile. "I will try," she vowed before leaving him, but he could tell by her tone that she had doubts.

Alexander sat long in his library that night, wishing he could contrive an argument that Haskell would find persuasive.

Perhaps if his friend could not be convinced, he would visit the baron himself.

~

THE BRIDE WAS RADIANT.

The Saturday in April chosen for the duke's wedding could not have been a finer day. The skies were clear and there was a light breeze as the ladies disembarked from the open carriage at the church. Daphne wore a white silk dress of a simple style, the fabric and the embroidery making it extraordinary. Her triple string of pearls had belonged to her mother, and had been given to her on the occasion of her wedding by Lady North Barrows. There were fresh lily-of-the-valley flowers twined into her golden hair and blue ribbons in her bouquet.

Her eyes danced with anticipation as her cousin, Daniel Goodenham, Baron North Barrows, led her up the steps to the church. Daniel and his wife had arrived in London in time for the wedding, a happy situation that would not have been possible if Alexander had insisted upon his plan for a quick wedding. His wife wore a lovely dress of pale pink that flattered her darker coloring very well.

At the insistence of her nephew's wife, Lady North Barrows had exchanged her usual black for a deep blue that made her look a decade younger. She had not surrendered her black umbrella, though, much less her inclination to give orders. All the same, her pride and pleasure in the happy event could not be disguised.

Eurydice wore a light yellow dress and bonnet, and had left her book at the house. Anthea had chosen her favored blue dress, though she had indulged in a new bonnet. The horses had white plumes in their bridles and ribbons in their harnesses. The entire party looked quite festive and many people waved as the coach went by.

Anthea was convinced she would see Haskell at the church and wondered how she might consult with him privately. She was fairly bursting to tell him, not only of the gem's location but of his folly in believing that she could only wed a wealthy man.

She would convince him of the merit of love somehow.

Anthea went into the church with the dowager, followed by Eurydice and Daniel's wife. Alexander stood at the altar with Montgomery, both of them dressed elegantly and looking most handsome. A number of friends and acquaintances had come to witness the exchange of vows, but Haskell was not there.

Anthea looked twice, to no avail.

Then Daphne and Daniel stepped into the church. Alexander's eyes lit with pleasure and Daphne smiled with delight, their expressions leaving no doubt of the fullness of their hearts. Anthea felt a little ache of yearning and dared to hope that one day, she might also have such a joyous day.

What if Haskell had not returned because he could not?

What if some dire fate had befallen him, when he had no one to come to his aid? The man was too noble, to be sure, though Anthea could not have admired him so otherwise.

And that admiration, she guessed, meant that she would never wed at all.

~

RUPERT HAD FAILED.

There was no evading the truth of it. During his sojourn in Paris, he had located all of the missing pieces from Mr. Cushing's inventory, save one. That marchioness' emerald brooch had vanished as surely as if it had never been. He had checked every possible avenue. He had exhausted his funds, and he had no reason to linger.

He had hoped to return home in triumph, but instead he had to tell Alexander—and Anthea—that he had failed.

He would leave Alexander's service and find another post, the better that he and Anthea might forget each other.

As he packed his few belongings, Rupert found that even the promise of a glimpse of his beloved was bitter.

Indeed, she was probably betrothed to Montgomery by this time.

PREPARATIONS for the masquerade ball had filled Alexander's house with excitement, even more than the wedding and Anthea could not escape the frisson of anticipation. It had been years since her mother's last ball but the collective memory was excellent of those events. With Alexander's approval of the expense, Anthea had ensured for every possible delight. The orchestra was one of the best available, the champagne was first-rate and ordered in quantity. The silver had been polished and the house cleaned thoroughly.

There were splendid flower arrangements, though none could compare with the vine. It had filled the courtyard with its tendrils and since the wedding, the flowers had fallen and seed pods had grown. They were remarkable, like large deep red beans with a high gloss. The vines had scaled the walls to the roof and it was clear that when the greenery died back, it would armor this house similarly to its sister vine at Airdfinnan.

Rumor of the plant had traveled through the *ton*, and Anthea wondered how many would attend purely to see it. There were many ladies amongst their acquaintances who were enthusiastic about their gardens, and Anthea hired four additional footmen purely to watch over the vine and ensure no one took a cutting.

It was impossible not to consider that the vine was a mirror of Alexander's affection for his wife. Anthea was glad to see how their love grew and deepened, how her brother made Daphne laugh and how she became bolder in her teasing of him. They were besotted with each other, as they should be in Anthea's view, and her joy for her brother's happiness was occasionally tinged with disappointment that she might never know such joy.

She had high hopes for this night of nights. She felt like a queen in a new silk dress of deepest blue, embroidered with silver on the hems. Her slippers were silver and she liked how the beads in the embroidery on the dress caught the light. The dress had been an indulgence, but she was glad to have such armor when she faced society in Alexander's home.

"It is perfect," Eurydice enthused from behind her. That girl had actually emerged from both library and book-of-choice to assist Anthea with the final arrangements. She was a willing helper in ensuring her sister's debut, though she had informed Anthea that she had no care for such frippery. The season was important to Daphne, thus it was important to Eurydice: the bond between the sisters was strong, indeed.

"I thank you for your help this day," Anthea said to her with a smile. "There are always so many details to attend in the last moment."

"I believe you have thought of everything, though my experience of such events is limited." Eurydice smiled with pride. "I referred to a volume providing guidelines for conduct of young ladies, and though it is an older work, there was a chapter about balls."

"And so you know what to do?"

Eurydice solemnly counted off the lessons on her gloved fingers. "Dance, only once with each gentleman who asks. No forays into gardens or dark corners. No imbibing of champagne. I should remain near *Grandmaman* to ensure that she has no needs, and if I can be of aid to you, the duke or Daphne, I should hasten to do as much. And finally, I should retire at eleven to my chamber, for it is only with the duke's special permission that I attend at all." She wrinkled her nose at this inventory and sighed. "Worst of all, I am to avoid all known scoundrels, rogues, or men of low repute, although I should *so* like to meet a rake."

"Why is that?"

"Because I have a notion that I should wed one, and I would like to discuss the merit of the idea with someone who knows more of the pertinent details." She shook her head. "I know precious little of rakes, scoundrels and rogues. It is a real impediment to understanding society."

Anthea opened her mouth, then closed it again, uncertain what she might say to that.

"But you know Montgomery," Alexander noted, and the two women spun to find him behind them. His eyes were twinkling as if he made mischief.

"Is the earl truly a rake, or does he simply pose as one?" Eurydice demanded, which prompted Alexander's laughter. "I can't be sure when he is telling me the truth."

"Oh, you need not doubt the darkness of his reputation. Though I should warn you that his taste runs more to actresses and courtesans than maidens."

Eurydice nodded. "I should like to meet a courtesan."

"I beg your pardon?" Anthea said.

"To know what it is like. It might be quite a wondrous life."

"How so?" asked Anthea, who had always thought just the opposite.

"She might have a house, paid for by a lover, as well as clothes and jewels, a carriage or a seat at the theatre. She might go to many parties and gambling hells and never pay for any of it."

"I would not have thought you intrigued by such entertainments."

"I should like to see it all, just the once. And I should like to have enough money for all the books I can read, maybe even more than that, and time enough to compose all the tales I would like to tell."

"And how does this dovetail with wedding a rake?" Alexander asked.

"I would have no time to entertain a true husband, much less to bear children or run a household for his friends and relatives to visit. I see from this event just how much trouble it is to organize one such a party." Eurydice smiled with conviction. "But a rake does not entertain at home. He attends his mistress in her abode, so his wife might do as she would with her time. I think that would suit me well."

"It might suit you less well than you imagine, Miss Eurydice," Anthea warned. "You might be shunned in society or worse, pitied by your peers, and I would never see you endure such a plight."

"People whose friendships are swayed by reputation are not true friends," Eurydice smiled at Anthea. "I will visit you, and we shall drink tea and read books in the duke's library and be as content as may be. I think it a sensible plan, though I see that you do not agree."

Anthea was convinced that the younger woman would forget this notion by this time she was of an age to wed, so changed the subject. "Are we not a handsome party tonight?"

Eurydice wore a new white muslin with blue flowers embroidered on the hem and a wide sash of deepest blue. Her slippers were silver satin and the ribbons in her hair were both silver and blue. She was only attending with Alexander's permission, for she wished to witness the festivities. Anthea did not doubt that her brother had also ensured that her attention had somehow been drawn to the book of manners she had mentioned. Doubtless, he had left it somewhere in the library where she was likely to discover it herself, or he might have given it to Daphne, who could be relied upon to surrender all books to Eurydice.

Alexander's garb was simple and elegant, which showed him to best advantage in Anthea's view. He looked dashing indeed. On this night, he wore a yellow rose in his buttonhole and its scent did not muddle Anthea's thoughts as the red blossoms had. "I have always admired you in blue, Anthea," he said, bowing over her hand. "The shade suits you most well."

"Thank you, Alexander."

"Is that not a new dress?"

"I thought I might indulge in one. My other ball gown is a little less fashionable."

"You should have ordered more than one."

"Perhaps later in the season. I want Miss Goodenham to steal every gaze."

He smiled. "And that she will," he said, donning his black velvet mask.

A cane could be heard rapping on the stairs and Lady North Barrows, resplendent in black taffeta and jet jewelry, descended with the assistance of her granddaughter. She had mustered for this evening. There were spots of rouge upon her cheeks and her eyes were bright with excitement for her granddaughter.

Daphne herself was gloriously lovely. Anthea caught her breath at the sight of her dress: she had known at first glimpse of the fabric that it would suit her admirably. She shimmered like sunlight or a goddess stepped down to earth. The silk was of the palest hue of gold and lavishly embroidered on the hem with beads and silken flowers. It caught the light, sparkling like sunlight on water. Her hair was dressed with pearls and golden leaves and it was clear from her contented smile that marriage suited her well. Her slippers were gold and when she curtseyed before Alexander, Anthea was certain his voice had been stolen away.

His heart, she knew, had long been in this maiden's possession.

He kissed Daphne's hand as the clock chimed nine and the doors were thrown open. The carriages had begun to arrive and their guests thronged through the doors, resplendent in their best, as Pierce announced each arrival. The orchestra began to play, the candles flickered and footmen appeared with sparkling glasses of champagne. Anthea took a breath, sensing early that the party would be a success, knowing better than to look for Haskell but unable to help herself.

At Alexander's touch on her elbow, she greeted the first of their guests. She strove to ignore the space that widened around her, though truly she wearied of those who trusted in rumor. After she had danced with Alexander and with Montgomery, she had no other partners.

She watched Daphne, who stepped more confidently into her place as duchess with each passing day. Anthea had done all that had been requested or expected of her, and was glad of her brother's happiness.

Perhaps it was time to return to Airdfinnan.

RUPERT ARRIVED LATE at Alexander's house and stood for a moment, astonished by the flurry of activity. He had not forgotten the masquerade ball, but he had not realized the date. If nothing else, it offered him the opportunity to leave Anthea a parting message. He slipped through the busy servant's quarters and made his way to the library. His dark coat was unremarkable, though he was glad his shirt was clean. He left a note for Alexander, not wanting to trouble him on this night, then readily found the volume he sought. He made his way up the servant's stairs undetected to leave it for Anthea.

He would leave this house for good, but could not resist the chance to look upon the merriment. He stood in the shadows of one door, admiring the decor and the music. The ballroom was filled with dancing couples, all elegantly attired and masked. Gems sparkled and ladies laughed. He spotted Alexander with his new bride, both of them apparently oblivious to any other soul in the room. Montgomery could not be missed as he laughed with a lovely woman Rupert did not know. The dowager sat with her cronies, beaming approval as she rapped her umbrella upon the floor. Miss Eurydice surveyed the dancers so intently that she might have been taking notes for some future work.

And Anthea stood alone, regal and lovely, shunned by the stain yet lingering on her name. She looked to be resigned to her fate, not seeking pity from anyone, but Rupert could not bear it.

He seized a mask from the tray of a passing servant and marched across the floor with purpose. He did not care whose path he interrupted in the dance, for his attention was fixed solely on Anthea. She seemed to sense his proximity, for she turned as he drew close and even though she was masked, her joy could not be disguised.

"Will you dance with a mysterious stranger?" he murmured and he bowed before her, just as he had asked her years before. He wanted to ensure that she had no doubt of his identity.

"Do you not mean to confess your name, sir?" she asked, proving that she also recalled that magical night.

"Then I would be neither mysterious nor a stranger, and it is my understanding that both have an allure for lovely young ladies like yourself," he said, as he had once before.

The lady's smile broadened. "I thank you, sir, for the compliment."

"Will you honor me with the next?"

The lady placed her hand with his and let him lead her to the floor.

Rupert savored the surge of pleasure that she was by his side, knowing it would be the last time, then Anthea shocked him with her next words.

"I saw it," she whispered and he looked at her with astonishment.

"I could not find it. I failed..."

"Because it is *here* in London."

He turned her into the dance, his resolve complete. "Tell me," he urged, and the lady did. Indeed, he could not fault her information for being so complete in its details.

"I wager you have a plan," she confided in a whisper. "For I know you can be relied upon to defend my honor."

His heart warmed at her trust. "I do, my lady. I most assuredly do."

ANTHEA FLOATED to her room after the ball was over, thrilled that Haskell had appeared, had danced with her and ensured he would resolve the question of the gem.

There was a book upon her nightstand, one she had not left there and she picked it up. It was from Alexander's library and like the last volume, it had a card inserted in the pages. Anthea smiled to see the mask drawn upon it, then looked at the book. It was the volume of *Sense & Sensibility* that Eurydice had been reading, and the card was near the end. It was placed alongside Edward's confession to Elinor.

> "I come here with no expectations,
> only to profess, now that I am at liberty to do so,
> that my heart is and always will be...yours."

No EXPECTATIONS.

Anthea felt a shiver of dread. She left her room and went back downstairs, pleased to see that there were candles lit in the library. She found Alexander there, frowning at a letter. He glanced up at her appearance, but his frown did not fade. "From Haskell," he said, waving the missive. "I thought I saw him tonight."

"What does it say?"

"That he has found all the gems but one. He intends to share the details with Mr. Cushing in the hope that they can be restored to their original owners." Alexander's voice dropped low. "And as grateful as he has been for the opportunity to serve as my valet, he resigns his post." He cast the note on his desk. "He says we will not see him again, but he wishes us well."

"No!" Anthea cried.

"He is gone, Anthea," Alexander said quietly and she paced the room, fighting her tears. Her brother cleared his throat. "I am certain he believes this to be for the best."

"And he is mistaken."

Alexander moved to stand beside her and she saw the concern in his gaze "You should know that I told him I would give you an allowance," he said softly. "I promised to find him a living if he took orders." Anthea met his gaze, her own wary. "I said I would buy him a commission if he wished to join the military."

"And he declined?" Anthea exhaled. "Perhaps his regard for me is not what I imagined." Could Haskell have misled her? Anthea would never have believed it but she could think of no other explanation.

"He believes you will be unhappy without wealth." Alexander smiled when she spun to face him. "It is not bad for a man to hold my sister in such esteem that he wishes to shower her with riches."

Anthea shook her head. "I do not want riches, Alexander. I desire only love. It will be sufficient..."

"I know. I believe as much and so do you, for we have the example of our parents. Rupert believes what he has been taught by his parents' example."

Anthea winced. "And their match is unhappy. I wish I could persuade him!" She closed her eyes against the ache in her heart, hating that there was so little she could do to gain her own happiness. "I would return to Airdfinnan," she said quietly, her decision made. "It is time for me to leave town again."

"But Aunt Penelope has such plans..."

"They will never come to fruition, Alexander, for the only man I desire will not ask for my hand. I fear I will be compelled to rely upon you instead."

He smiled down at her. "You know you are welcome, but I would see you happy."

"Then convince your friend to be less proud!"

"I would have done as much if I could—but would you care as much for him then? If he surrendered his defense of his mother to gain your hand, I doubt you would admire him much at all." Alexander did not wait for a reply. "I would ask that you linger another week, Anthea, then Findlay can return with you in the smaller carriage. I expect that Daphne and I will come to Airdfinnan in August. We can ask whether Eurydice or her grandmother wish to accompany you."

"Thank you, Alexander." Anthea turned to leave the library, utterly defeated, but her brother coughed slightly. She glanced back at him.

"Were you aware, Anthea, that Thornedyke Manor is in Northumberland? You will have to pass within forty miles of it, if you return home via York."

Anthea's heart lifted. Who better to change Rupert's thinking than his own mother? She must desire his happiness! "The baroness was a friend of *Maman's*," she said. "I tried to call on her but learned she was not in town."

"I believe she has not been in town these ten years," Alexander said. "She might welcome a visit from the daughter of a friend."

"I will write to her tomorrow." Anthea crossed the library again and kissed her brother's cheek. "I would compliment your cleverness but you might become vain."

He laughed at that. "I merely endeavor to ensure the happiness of all, as my lady wife commands."

CHAPTER 6

I suppose I can guess why you are here." Rupert's father smirked as he sank into his favorite chair at his club. "I have no coin to give you for I have just bought Richard a curricle and a pair of feisty bays. He will be the talk of the town in no time." When this reference to his son by Mrs. Blythe elicited no reaction, he accepted a glass of port, then surveyed his son in obvious anticipation.

"I did not come to ask you for money."

"What then? To beg forgiveness? You cannot imagine how I have looked forward to this apology." He saluted Rupert with the glass, then sipped, smacking his lips. "Do begin."

"I did not come to apologize, sir."

"Why else would you come?"

"I would request a favor."

Baron Thornedyke laughed so hard that he choked. He smacked down the glass with sufficient force that Rupert thought the stem might break, yet struggled to take a breath. The older man leaned forward and began to cough, finally wiping his eyes and resuming his original posture. He took a restorative sip of the port, his face red and his gaze filled with accusation. "Of course, you would not assist me. It would suit you well to see me dead."

"On the contrary, I do not wish for your demise, sir."

"You did not aid me."

"I did not believe you to be in genuine peril. Surely a laugh at my expense could not endanger you. It never has before."

The baron winced. "You have become more cutting, son." He sipped again and shook his head. "Why on earth would I do you a favor?"

"To be rid of me forever."

"Your timing is not all bad in this, Rupert. My solicitor has suggested all might proceed more smoothly in the event of my demise if you signed a codicil, refusing your inheritance. Do you want this favor enough to do as much?"

"I do." Rupert spoke without hesitation.

His father was visibly intrigued. "Why would you cast any chance or your inheritance away?"

"I have no desire of your legacy."

The baron snorted. "You would if you knew its size."

Rupert was skeptical. His father spent coin like water. "I thought you might prefer to have Mrs. Blythe's son take the title."

The baron considered this. His gaze filled with the knowledge that his wife favored Rupert's word above all others. "You will be back in a year with another demand."

Rupert shook his head. "Not I. I give you my solemn word. This one favor, and you need never see me again. And you will have my signature, if that is your desire, in exchange."

"What will you do?"

"I would change my name, journey to Canada, seek my fortune and create a new life for myself."

Rupert watched his father's eyes narrow in assessment. "What would you have me do?"

Rupert smiled, for this was the easy part. "Buy a specific token for Mrs. Blythe and have her wear it everywhere."

"Why?"

"Because its disappearance has cast a shadow upon the name of an innocent lady. I would see her reputation restored, which can only be done by the rediscovery of the gem."

"Can the theft be traced to me, if I do this?"

Rupert shook his head. "It has passed through too many hands."

"Swear it."

"I do."

"I shall see you pay if you are wrong." His father's suspicious nature was consistent, if nothing else.

"I am not wrong, and the gem will please Mrs. Blythe, I am sure."

"What matter to you if a lady's reputation is sullied?"

Rupert felt his color rise. "She deserves better."

His father laughed. "You love her! Ah, your mother's son to your marrow." He drained his glass, his decision made. "I will do this in exchange for your signature, but do not return to me when you learn your lesson. The lady will not have you if you have no inheritance, Rupert, whether you would take her to Canada or not. You merely clear her name so she can have another. That is what you should know of women."

Rupert said nothing, letting his father believe what he wished. The sole thing of import was that Anthea's name would be cleared.

THE FRIDAY before Anthea's planned departure, they were invited to the theatre by Aunt Penelope. Their aunt kept a box there and Anthea suspected that lady would make one last effort to introduce her to eligible young men.

It seemed that all of London came to Drury Lane that night, perhaps because many of them intended to leave for the country soon. There was a festive air, even though the night was warm and the roads were crowded with carriages. There was a veritable crush in the corridors and Anthea for one was glad to escape into the relative comfort of the private box. Eurydice claimed a chair with an excellent view of the stage, as might have been anticipated, while Daphne and Aunt Penelope embraced. More than one lady spared Alexander an appreciative glance. No doubt there was a great deal of discussion about the good fortune of Daphne Goodenham. Lady North Barrows had declined to join them, citing a desire to retire early.

They were chatting in advance of the curtain when the whisper began. It dawned at the back of the theatre and swept through the audience like a tidal wave. It was filled with urgency, setting heads to turning and plumes to dancing. Anthea wondered what the reason could be, then she saw a man usher a woman into a large central box.

"He flaunts that woman so," Aunt Penelope murmured, taking a good look despite her disapproval. "No wonder the baroness has retreated to the country for good."

"Who are they?" Daphne asked.

"Baron Thornedyke and his mistress, Mrs. Blythe. She was an actress and said to be a courtesan before he took a house for her. They have a son—oh! There he is! He must be quite fifteen now."

Haskell's father was trim and not unattractive, obviously the source of Haskell's own good looks. His hair was silver at the temples and he was elegantly dressed—but Anthea could not approve of him treating his mistress as his wife.

Mrs. Blythe was wearing a silver dress with a daring décolletage, as well as a veritable flock of ostrich plumes in her headdress. Her gloves were long and white, and diamond bracelets sparkled on her wrists. She had dark hair and dark eyes, and was a beauty even in her forties. She surveyed the patrons, as if they were her audience and the box she occupied was the stage, then removed her wrap, fairly challenging them to look upon the magnificent gem pinned to her bodice. Given that she wore all silver and white, and that her skin was so fair, the green of the stone was as unmistakable as its size.

It was the emerald brooch that Anthea had been accused of stealing. It caught the light, the diamonds of the setting sparkling like stars, and the whisper that had seized the company changed to a gasp of admiration.

"Goodness, that looks like the marchioness' favored emerald," Aunt Penelope said, lifting her opera glasses for a better look.

Mrs. Blythe preened, clearly enjoying the attention and perhaps misunderstanding the reason for it. Baron Thornedyke smiled and bowed, waving to friends in the audience, ensuring that he and his mistress were noticed by all.

"So that is where it went," Aunt Penelope murmured, slanting a glance at Anthea. "That changes all, does it not?"

"I cannot think what you mean," Anthea said, her heart leaping.

Haskell had contrived this. She could lay the credit at the feet of no other. She was smiling as the curtain rose, but the applause did not drown out the sound of speculation. It could not be that every soul gathered there had seen the gem and understood its import, but Anthea felt that everyone discussed it. She felt the weight of a hundred gazes and knew what the chatter was that almost obliterated the sound of the actors' words.

Just as her aunt had foretold, popular opinion pivoted in Anthea's favor as quickly as it had turned against her. There was a line of eligible bachelors outside the box at intermission, though the man she wanted most to see was not there.

The baroness had replied, graciously inviting Anthea to Thornedyke Manor. She had to use that opportunity to ensure that Haskell somehow learned of her gratitude.

She yearned for the opportunity to argue her case, but feared she would never have it.

Instead, she would take a book and leave it for him as a gift.

~

THORNEDYKE WAS LOVELY IN MAY, and the weather could not have been finer. The carriage made good time and they reached the house by mid-afternoon. Eurydice was nigh as curious as Anthea and they both surveyed the property with pleasure when they disembarked. The house was made of stone, not unlike Airdfinnan, but was surrounded by lush gardens. They could smell the flowers even from the drive and the baroness herself came to greet them.

She was tall and slender, and there was an echo of Haskell's smile in hers as she welcomed them warmly. She was a little tanned and laughed when she confessed that she spent every sunny day in the garden. "Smythe, we will have tea in the rose garden," she called and that butler bowed before disappearing. Then she urged the two younger women to look upon her flowers.

They were glorious, of such variety and vigor that Anthea could only exclaim over their perfection. She and the baroness chatted of acquaintances as they made their way to a delightful pavilion, open to the air and surrounded by roses.

They had only just sipped their tea when they heard the gallop of hoof beats. The baroness turned to look toward the house as the butler strode toward her with two letters on a salver. "An express post, my lady," he said with a regal bow.

The baroness recoiled from the document and Anthea glanced at it, noting that the sender had the surname Blythe. What audacity the mistress had in writing to the wife? She averted her gaze and sipped her tea, drawing Eurydice's attention to a particularly splendid pink rose.

"And still you have not opened the one that arrived from the solicitor this morning," the butler said, a slight bit of censure in his tone.

The baroness still did not take either.

"Good or bad news, it will not improve with the delay, *Maman*," a man teased lightly and Anthea glanced up to find Rupert himself entering the pavilion. They stared at each other for a potent moment, then the butler excused himself and the baroness performed introductions.

"Is it possible that you are already acquainted?" the baroness asked, looking between them. Anthea flushed. Rupert dropped his gaze.

"Of course," Eurydice said. "For Haskell was the duke's valet. I thought you had left for Canada," she said to him.

"My mother wished me to visit first," that man confessed.

The baroness considered Anthea and her son with a smile. "And I must admit, I delayed his departure in the hope that he might meet a lady whose company would convince him to remain."

"I gave my word, *Maman*."

Anthea looked into the depths of her tea, uncertain how to make the situation less awkward.

Rupert took the solicitor's letter and opened it while his mother poured him a cup of tea. Evidently, he expected it to be some matter of routine, even though it had come express, for his eyes widened in shock and he sat down hard. He frowned and handed the missive to his mother. She read it quickly, then gasped and paled, leaning closer to read it once again, as if she did not believe her own eyes.

Haskell, meanwhile, frowned and lifted the other letter. He opened it and read it. His expression was so impassive that Anthea knew it concerned an issue of importance.

"We shall leave you to your mail," she said, rising to her feet.

"But I have only just tasted my tea," Eurydice protested, winning a lethal glare from Anthea for that. The younger girl got to her feet. "Yes, of course, we will," she said.

"I would ask you to remain, Miss Armstrong," Haskell said, his voice husky. "These tidings bring great change."

Anthea met his gaze in confusion, noting how dark his eyes had become. Indeed, the intensity of his attention was such that she could scarce swallow, let alone make a sound. She sank back into her chair but could not lift her cup of tea—for Rupert perched on the chair beside her, his gaze unswerving.

"My father has died," he said. "He and his son, Robert, had an accident while racing a new carriage in Hyde Park." His gaze dropped and she could not read his thoughts. "Evidently, they died immediately."

"I am so very sorry," Anthea said, impulsively touching his hand. To her surprise, he gripped her fingers for a moment before releasing her hand.

"He was not without kindness," the baroness whispered, then let her tears flow.

"You should read this missive, *Maman*." Rupert offered the second letter.

"I will not!" his mother replied with indignation. "She should not write to me..."

"But Mrs. Blythe offers an olive branch," he said softly.

His mother looked up, then took the letter and read it, her eyes widening as she did so. There was a second document with it and she looked between them, apparently incredulous. "I would not have thought it possible," the baroness whispered.

"What did she write?" Eurydice asked with an impatience Anthea could only share.

It was Rupert who replied. "My father had me sign a document, forgoing my inheritance in favor of his son by Mrs. Blythe. Since

Richard is dead, Mrs. Blythe sent the document to my mother that it might be destroyed."

"She could have done that herself," Eurydice noted.

"But she likely feared she would not be believed," Anthea said.

"Precisely." Rupert smiled warmly at her. "Which means that out of tragedy comes new hope." He dropped to his knee beside her, claiming her hand within his, and Anthea's heart raced. "Will you, Anthea Armstrong, do me the honor of becoming my wife? Thornedyke is not Airdfinnan..."

"But I would wed you, sir, not your home or your title," Anthea said with conviction. "I would be happy in a hovel with you by my side. Though I know you do not believe it, I vow to spend my life teaching you that love truly can conquer all."

He smiled then, a sight that filled her with rapture. "I believe that lesson may be learned more easily than you fear." He lifted a brow. "Will you?"

"Of course, Rupert!"

The baroness dried her tears. Eurydice watched with open curiosity, but Anthea did not care. Rupert drew her to her feet and into his arms.

"She brought you a book, though," Eurydice interjected and Anthea watched Rupert smile.

"Did she?" His eyes glowed as he looked down at her. "Which one?"

Anthea smiled. "Virgil's *Eclogues*."

Rupert chuckled. "Because of the tenth poem, which ends: *Omnia vincit amor: et nos cedamus amori.*"

"What does that mean?" Eurydice asked. "It's something about love."

Anthea translated even as she stared into Rupert's eyes. "Love conquers all; let us, too, yield to love."

"Let us indeed," he murmured in agreement, then kissed her soundly in the rose pavilion at Thornedyke Manor.

It was the first time he kissed her there, but it certainly was not the last.

~

A MOST INCONVENIENT EARL

THE BRIDES OF NORTH BARROWS #4

Eurydice Goodenham is convinced that a marriage of convenience with the notorious Sebastian Montgomery, Earl of Rockmorton, would be ideal: in exchange for one child, she can retreat to the library of his country house to write, while he continues his scandalous life in London. But when she finds herself falling in love with her unpredictable, mischievous and secretly honorable husband, does she have any hope of claiming his heart?

Sebastian is bored with the world's amusements, until his friend's ward makes a startling proposal. He can't help but challenge Eurydice's expectations in return. A wild escape to Gretna Green convinces him that his unexpected bride is perfect for him—except that Eurydice doesn't believe in love. Can Sebastian win this bluestocking's reluctant heart in time to save a Christmas—and a marriage—going awry?

North Barrows, Cumbria—August 1815

$\mathcal{E}$urydice Goodenham stood with her hands folded before herself, watching as dirt struck the coffin.

Her grandmother, Octavia Hambley, Viscountess North Barrows, was dead. She had taken a chill in the spring and been unable to shake it. No matter which physician was summoned, the illness had persisted, lodging in her lungs with a tenacity that echoed the lady's own. Four months they had battled, illness and dowager, and in the end, the illness had won.

Eurydice could not help but feel she had overlooked some detail that might have ensured her grandmother's recovery. She had consulted every reference and made many suggestions, though none had helped. All said, she had done her best and more, but she was keenly aware that her best had been insufficient.

It was a hot day with a haze on the hills that promised at least a heavy dew that night, if not more. Eurydice was warm, even in her lightest summer muslin, but discomfort was irrelevant. She could not believe that her grandmother was dead, even though she had been granted custody of the dowager's beloved umbrella. She clutched it now, unwilling to relinquish it. It seemed fitting that the umbrella should attend the service, just as Nelson and the other servants did.

It was not the first time she had attended a funeral of someone she held close, but this time, Eurydice understood the ramifications of death better. Her parents had died when Eurydice had been only five, leaving her and her older sister alone. She remembered uncertainty but had never guessed at Daphne's terror of the future until told of it years later. She certainly remembered their grandmother arriving from Bath, austere and commanding, then sweeping them up on her way back to the North Barrows dower house. Lady Octavia had been stern but she had loved them fiercely and done her best for them.

Eurydice did recall her grandmother's relief when Daphne had wed the Duke of Inverfyre. He was a good man, kind to her sister and their children. Eurydice liked watching him with their two sons, Malcolm and Edmond. It was a revelation to her that a somber and sensible man could be so playful—even silly—with Malcolm the toddler, and the sight made her smile. She'd learned from his lullabies to the infant Edmond that he had a fine voice. He had been generous with their grandmother, as well, inviting her to stay whenever she chose, for as long as she chose. The duke had promised the viscountess that Eurydice was secure in his household for so long as she chose to remain, giving her the freedom to not wed at all. Eurydice knew he had brought Daphne from Airdfinnan near the end to repeat his vow to their grandmother one last time.

Lady Octavia had died convinced that her responsibilities were fulfilled.

The funeral for the viscountess was held at North Barrows, in the church where she had been married decades before, and she would be buried beside her beloved Alasdair, Viscount North Barrows. Upon the death of Eurydice and Daphne's father—Malcolm, the older son of Alasdair and Octavia—the estate had passed to his younger brother, Samuel, with the stipulation—made by Alasdair—that Octavia could reside in the dower house for her lifetime. The estate was currently held by Samuel's son and Eurydice's cousin, Daniel. He had permitted the party from Airdfinnan to stay at the dower house until the funeral and had even offered them whatever they desired of the furniture. Eurydice had no doubt that his wife had plans for the house, which was in need of renovation. She loved it as it was, but knew she was unlikely to ever cross its threshold again.

She gripped the umbrella, her throat tight as the dirt obscured the coffin. Daphne stood beside her, holding the duke's arm, their older son before them and the younger in the nursemaid's arms. Daniel and his wife and children stood on the opposite side of the grave. Nelson, the viscountess's lady's maid for years, sniffled loudly from the ranks of the servants. There were mourners gathered from the village, as well. The final blessing was pronounced and Eurydice let her tears fall.

Her life had been disrupted twice by death and left in uncertainty. It had been less of a shock this time, for her grandmother had faded visibly since Daphne's wedding, but still she was aware that her position was precarious.

The duke had given his word, but what if he died? What if he and Daphne were killed unexpectedly, as her own parents had been? All might go awry for Eurydice if her sister no longer drew breath. The children doubtless had a more secure future, the oldest being heir to the dukedom, but Eurydice felt that the ground was loose beneath her feet.

She had no desire to wed for romantic reasons, as Daphne had, but it made good sense to marry for practical ones. She would be able to guarantee her own future, then, if she chose wisely. Once she had made a jest that she would wed a rich rogue, but increasingly, she saw the merit of such a notion. The rake in question could continue to be a scoundrel in town, and she would retire to the country to read and write in peace.

It was a perfect scheme, for even if he died, she would inherit a measure of his wealth as his widow. In fact, she would ensure as much by making the provision in his will a stipulation of their match.

Fortunately, she knew a rogue who would suit her well.

All she needed was the audacity to propose to Sebastian Montgomery, Earl of Rockmorton—and the good fortune to have him accept.

CHAPTER 1

Sebastian Montgomery, Earl of Rockmorton, was enjoying a brandy in the library of his friend's Scottish house, Airdfinnan. It was a most suitable pastime for a day cursed with driving rain, though he consumed very little of the brandy. He swirled it in the glass and savored the scent of it, as was his custom.

He had received another letter from his mistress in London, the alluring Esmeralda Ballantyne, and truth be told, he did not wish to open it. He much preferred to watch the rain.

Doubtless the missive was filled with pledges of affection, requests for his return, paragraphs of yearning enough to make him yawn and ultimately, demands for some token of his supposed affections. Esmeralda had been different from other mistresses for years, but of late, she had become the same.

She had, despite her many charms, become predictable.

Sebastian despised this part of an affair. He had to break it off, but he also disliked being responsible for any woman's tears. Usually, he convinced himself that his mistresses' lamentations were contrived, and that all they truly loved was his generous spending.

He tired of flinging coin hither and yon. He tired of insincerity. He tired of fashionable society. And, to his own astonishment, he even tired of scandal.

Clearly, having his friends happily wed and merrily breeding was affecting his *bonhomie*.

He should have returned to London months before, but had lingered in Scotland all the same. He did not care to hunt particularly, though he did enjoy a bracing walk. What he liked was that his friend Alexander Armstrong's house was a home, for all its size and magnificence. He liked the open displays of affection between duke and duchess, the camaraderie between the servants and the unpredictability of two small boys, often bent on mischief. He had proven himself to be of assistance on such errands more than once.

Airdfinnan made him realize how solitary his own life had become.

Not that he had any plans to change his situation. Entanglements only led to disappointment, heartbreak and sorrow. No, Sebastian Montgomery had resolved twelve years before that his heart would never be shattered by loss again—and the sole way to achieve that objective, to his thinking, was to lead the life of a veritable hermit.

An occasional visit to Airdfinnan was simply a sample of the road not taken. It appealed precisely because it was so different from his own life, and he would not be seduced into making a terrible error.

Sebastian swirled the brandy and considered the wording of the missive he would send Esmeralda, terminating their arrangement. He would be polite but firm, as always he was. Resolute. If he did it by mail and immediately, by the time he returned to town, she would have found herself another lover. There would be no tedious scenes in public or awkward moments at the theater, and he would be able to seek a new recipient for his affections.

The other trouble was that he did not look forward to the search for a new nocturnal companion. He had always savored the hunt only when it came to women, but this particular chase had become so predictable.

What Sebastian desired most was a surprise. A challenge. A quest.

Even an adventure.

He was unlikely to find it in the duke's library in Scotland while the rain beat against the windows. Nor was he likely to discover it at the bottom of the brandy decanter. How tedious that at thirty-two, he suddenly had need of an occupation.

He was staring at the blank paper as if his letter would magically write itself when Miss Eurydice entered the library. She appeared to be unaware of his presence, but that did not surprise Sebastian. The younger sister of the duchess was often lost in her own thoughts or bent upon her own quests. She was definitely unlike other women of his acquaintance and, as a rare species of femininity, she interested him. It appeared that she sought a book in this particular moment, for she immediately began scanning the shelves.

It was a pity that she cared only for books. Since the marriage of the duke to her older sister, Daphne, several years before, Miss Eurydice had blossomed into a most enticing young woman. She had to be eighteen years of age by now and though Sebastian did not care in the least for maidens, he certainly admired the result. Her hair was still a darker blond than that of her sister, and she had grown taller, slimming through the waist and gaining more curves in a most attractive way. The view of her from behind was most charming. Sebastian could even glimpse her trim ankles when she stretched to reach a volume from a high shelf.

She had a general indifference about her appearance, which he liked. He disliked when women were concerned only with their hair or their faces—there was something more honest about Miss Eurydice's disregard for such details. This also meant that her hair was often in slight disarray despite her maid's herculean efforts. The curls that escaped their bonds fascinated Sebastian—there was nothing quite so feminine as a stray curl against a soft cheek, in his view, or anything more likely to tempt his touch. Such was the curse of unruly waves in her hair, he supposed, but the sight of her often reminded Sebastian of the look of a woman who had been thoroughly sampled. Had she been lounging abed with a satisfied smile, Miss Eurydice would have been a fine subject for a painting, one he could have looked upon for considerable time.

Perhaps that was why he noticed her, for Miss Eurydice had certainly not been sampled at all, much less thoroughly. Sebastian doubted her luscious lips, so faintly pink and full, had been kissed at all. The idea of changing that situation made him smile in the precise moment that she became aware that she was not alone.

His small sound of amusement—in imagining his friend Armstrong's outrage should he act upon his thoughts—might have been responsible for that change.

Miss Eurydice spun and glared at him, a becoming flush rising on her cheeks when she found him watching her. "You!" she said, with complete disregard for social convention. "Why do you always creep up on people?"

"I do not creep..."

"You most assuredly do, sir. This is not the first time I have found you watching me as if you meant to pounce." She marched toward him, apparently fearless, but hugged a book to her chest as if it might protect her. Her eyes narrowed, as if she wished to look dangerous. Sebastian thought she was delightful. "I would warn you not to have ideas, but I expect it is too late."

"Truly?"

"Truly. I believe you are the kind of man born with ideas."

Sebastian laughed. "Then you are a good judge of character, Miss Eurydice."

She looked back toward the door, then leaned closer, her expression intense. "Which is precisely why I would speak with you." Her voice was almost a whisper, so husky that Sebastian could not halt his sudden desire to touch her.

It was that cursed curl on her right cheek that was responsible.

Sebastian cleared his throat. "I beg your pardon?"

"I had hoped to find you alone."

Sebastian was surprised by this. It seemed to him that the last thing a respectable maiden should desire would be to find him alone.

"I would speak with you." She wrinkled her nose in a most delightful manner. "I would, in fact, request your assistance." As he watched, she perched on the desk, her manner confidential, and continued as if he had encouraged her. "I know you were of aid to Lady Anthea that winter in London and I find myself in need of similar...assistance." She met his gaze, her eyes bright with challenge.

They were hazel and thickly lashed, remarkably lovely, in fact.

Sebastian straightened, fascinated. "Am I to know what manner of aid you need?"

"It is not complicated. Even you should be able to guess as much." She was still gripping the book as if her life depended upon it. He glanced down to see her ankle and calf revealed and in close proximity and felt a familiar heat surge through him. "You must have heard that they intend to give me a season." She rolled her eyes at the very prospect.

Sebastian grinned. "And you do not want one?"

"Of course, I do not want one! Why should I have any desire to attend parties and balls, to dance and to shop and to chatter with strangers?" This recitation of urban pleasures would have cast most young ladies of Sebastian's acquaintance into rhapsodies, but it was clear Miss Eurydice was not convinced. She shook her head in disgust and Sebastian fought his urge to smile.

That curl. She was adorable.

"It sounds abominable," he managed to say solemnly.

"It would be!"

"And what do you suggest instead?"

"I want to be left alone to read." She lowered her voice yet more. "Even *write*." She held his gaze for a long moment as if to assure him of her sincerity. "Why would I desire to go to London?" She didn't pause for him to reply. "But you know how the duke can be. He is certain it is the proper thing to do, and my sister is thrilled, and before I know it, I will be packed into the coach and headed south, condemned to *dancing*." This last she said with such scorn that Sebastian felt compelled to protest.

"I like dancing."

Her eyes flashed. "You would."

Sebastian had no reply to that condemnation.

She wagged a finger at him. "But of greater import is the fact that I do not."

"You might like it with the right partner."

Her expression was pained. "Because I should fall in love and lose my heart forever and just touching the hand of my beloved at intervals would fulfill all the yearning in my soul." She shook her head. "I think not."

What a curious conversation.

"I think you read too much," he ventured to suggest.

"I think you read too little, but such opinions are irrelevant to the discussion at hand."

Sebastian was not accustomed to being chided—much less to having an attractive woman frown and avert her gaze in his presence, her attention clearly not upon him. "Well, my views might be of import as you are asking for my help."

"There is that." She put down the book with a frown and continued solemnly. "This is truly about Daphne. Now that they have two sons, she wishes to be entertained and the duke wishes to see her entertained. She desires to go to London and he wishes to make her happy."

"Is that not a husband's role?"

Miss Eurydice exhaled in exasperation but ignored that comment. "Giving me a season is simply an excuse." She glared at him, as fierce as a kitten. "I decline to be an excuse."

"Most young ladies would be delighted to be given a debut season," Sebastian felt compelled to note. "Especially one funded by a duke inclined to be generous."

Her expression was pained. "Surely you do not imagine that I am like most young ladies?"

"No. Certainly not. You are...most unique."

Instead of giving her pleasure, his comment made her sign in despair. "Truly, sir, I thought you had been given an education. I cannot be *most* unique, or *very* unique or *utterly* unique. It is not possible."

"Whyever not?"

"Because the word 'unique' is one of the few adjectives in the English language that cannot take a modifier. Something is unique or it is not. It is that simple."

"Ah. I shall consider myself to have learned something this day, then."

Miss Eurydice slipped off the desk and retrieved her book. "I had feared you might decline to be useful. How disappointing to be right."

She turned to leave the library and Sebastian felt he had to defend himself.

"What exactly would you have me do?"

"You do not want to know."

"I do! In fact, I burn with curiosity."

"You do not."

"Do not underestimate your ability to confound a man, Miss Eurydice."

She smiled then, facing him with consideration in her eyes. "But you will not do it."

"You might be surprised." He leaned forward, bracing his elbows upon his knees to watch her. He smiled. "And you will never know unless you ask me."

"There is that." She marched to the door and he thought she meant to leave. Instead, she closed it firmly, pivoted and impaled him with a glance. "Marry me."

Sebastian nearly fell off his chair. As it was, he considered the possibility that he had imbibed too much brandy and was imagining the conversation. He checked the glass and the bottle while Miss Eurydice watched, then met her gaze with a frown. "Marry you?" he repeated.

"You need not look so surprised. I thought all women wanted to marry you and you think all women are the same. You have a fortune of reasonable size, a title and are not so difficult to look upon."

Sebastian found himself mildly insulted. "I thank you for that."

She shook a finger at him. "But what should be different about this match is that it would not affect either of us in any material sense. It would solely be convenient."

"I cannot imagine there is anything convenient about having a wife." He certainly could not conceive that there would be anything convenient about having Miss Eurydice as a spouse. Doubtless, she would challenge his assumptions each and every day thereafter...

Which did promise to be interesting. Hmm.

"But I do not mean to be a wife, not in that sense." Her becoming blush made her meaning clear.

Sebastian was fascinated. "What other sense is there?"

"The legal one. We would wed and you would reside in your house in Mayfair. You would live as always you do, and people will be scandalized, as always they are by your deeds, and you would be content."

He blinked at this uncommon suggestion. "And you?"

"And I would retire to your country house." She straightened in sudden shock. "You do have one, don't you?" she asked with concern. "One with a library?"

Sebastian smiled. "I do have one, in Cornwall. It has a very nice library as I recall. Even some books. Maps, too, I believe, and the most enormous fireplace."

"Cornwall! Oh, that is even better."

"How so?"

"There are pirates in Cornwall, or tales of them, and, best of all, it is very far from London. You would not be able to visit often at all and I should not be obliged to go to town often, due to the expense and inconvenience."

"But..."

"When did you last visit your country house?" she demanded pertly.

"It has easily been three years. Perhaps four."

"Exactly. It will be perfect!" She smiled at him as if he had been responsible for all the marvels of the world. "We could be wedded before Christmas."

"I am not going to marry you..."

"Whyever not? It will make no difference to your life except to save you from uncomfortable situations. You will always have the excuse that you are married already."

There was something to that argument, but Sebastian feared he was being beguiled. "But people will expect that we have a child," he protested.

"Many couples do not have children." Miss Eurydice sighed. "If you so desire it, I suppose we could discuss that matter at some later date. The fact is that I simply do not have time to bear a child right now. I need to finish my first book and there is so much yet to learn."

Sebastian stood up and shook his head, frowning down at the hopeful maiden. "This is madness."

"But I thought you of all men would be prepared to abandon

convention." She shook her head and that curl danced, inviting his touch. "I must say that I am disappointed."

"Which particular convention should I have abandoned?"

"That you would ask me to wed you, not the other way around. But you would not have thought of it, you see, so I had to make the suggestion."

"I see." He looked at her, waiting with such obvious anticipation for his agreement. What did they say about opportunities that seemed too good to be true? "And all you wish from this arrangement is to live at my country house?"

"Well, I should need some funds settled upon me," she said.

"Aha!"

"But it could be arranged that any provision would only come to me upon your death."

"I do not intend to die soon."

She shook her head solemnly. "No one does. That is why I would need an inheritance that could not be taken away after your demise. While you live, I am certain you would allow me funds to survive."

Sebastian recalled then that the parents of Daphne and Eurydice had died suddenly when the sisters were young. Armstrong must have told him of it. And their grandmother, of course, had been laid to rest the previous summer. It was only reasonable that she thought of practicalities for she had witnessed the changes that occurred after a death firsthand.

He was unaccountably relieved. For a moment, he had thought her a mercenary and worse, he had never guessed she had that trait. She was not avaricious, simply practical.

"It might be wise for me to have a sensible wife," he mused aloud without meaning to do as much. He never could be bothered with accounts, but left it to his estate manager.

She smiled so brightly that he blinked again. "Then we are resolved?"

"No, we are not resolved," Sebastian said with exasperation. "Even if it might be sensible for me to have a practical wife, I have little interest in sense or practicality..."

"I do not believe as much," Miss Eurydice interjected, but he carried on as if she had not spoken.

"I have no intention of wedding at all, and if I did, it would not be..." He faltered then, not wanting to hurt her feelings.

"It would not be to me," she supplied readily. She leaned over and examined the address on the letter he had received that morning. "It would be an actress or a courtesan, an infamous beauty of copious charms." She tapped the return address on the letter. "Someone like Miss Esmeralda Ballantyne."

"Not a courtesan."

"No? Once again, your conventionality surprises me, sir." Her eyes were sparkling in a most unexpected manner. Was she teasing him? Sebastian wondered how he had failed to note her charm sooner. "I should think a courtesan would have suited you perfectly for a wife." She shrugged. "Until, of course, you tired of her charms. I suppose you mean to hasten back to town to Miss Ballantyne." Her expression was innocent but those sparkling eyes hinted that she had seen through him.

"I am just writing to her, to end our arrangement," he admitted without intending to do as much.

Miss Eurydice laughed. "Your page is blank, sir. When did you begin?"

"I do not know what to say," he admitted and pushed a hand through his hair. "I do not wish to provoke her tears..."

Miss Eurydice urged him aside. "I shall show you how useful our agreement will be," she said, to his utter mystification. She urged him aside, then sat down in his place and dipped the quill into the ink. "My dear Miss Ballantyne," she said as she wrote the same words on the page. Her handwriting was not as he might have expected, but neat and economical. It could not have passed for his own but it was not frilly, like Esmeralda's writing. "Thank you for your missive, which arrived this morning. I delighted in your tidings from town. I have happy news of my own to share with you, although admittedly you may not share my joy. I have become betrothed to Miss Eurydice Goodenham while enjoying the duke's hospitality at Airdfinnan, and we will be wed here in Scotland before the Yule. I will escort my bride to my country house —" she looked up, a question in her gaze.

Had he ever seen eyes of such remarkable color? There were flecks of gold and green and brown within them.

"Rockmorton Manor," Sebastian supplied.

She looked down at her work again and continued to write. "...Rockmorton Manor immediately after the nuptials. We will celebrate the Yule there together, and I will not return to London until March at the earliest. I do hope that you remain well, sincerely etc. etc."

She put down the quill and looked up at him, her expression triumphant. "You see how useful a bride can be?"

"It is in your handwriting."

"I daresay you can copy it. How complete *was* your education?"

"Minx!" Sebastian said and she laughed so merrily that he thought of kissing her to silence.

"Well?" she prompted.

"I shall ponder the suggestion," he said, knowing he would not be able to do otherwise. "I thank you for your consideration, Miss Eurydice."

"You need not be overly flattered," she said as she walked to the door. "I had need of a scoundrel who could be relied upon to keep his word, and you are the only one of my acquaintance."

Sebastian shook his head, unable to keep from smiling at that. "I suppose you will consider that kismet."

She laughed again. "I could only do as much if I believed in love conquering all. No, sir, I think it only a stroke of fortune, and I hope it is one we will act upon." She smiled at him, as fetching a sight as he could imagine, then swept out the door, leaving Sebastian Montgomery with much more to consider than he might have anticipated just an hour before.

Marriage.

To Miss Eurydice.

It was a notion that should have filled him with dread, but Sebastian had the sense it might provide precisely the adventure he sought.

She certainly was not predictable, and she would not expect him to be smitten with her.

It sounded perfect.

~

IT WAS A BEGINNING.

In fact, Eurydice thought the presentation of her suggestion had gone rather well. The earl had been surprised, of course, but she had not expected otherwise. He had not refused out of hand, but had seemed to be intrigued.

She would not consider her own reaction to his interest. That was simply nature at work. Of course, the warmth in his gaze as he surveyed her had made her pulse leap a little. Of course, she had found it difficult to catch her breath when he stood up and loomed over her a little. He was so much larger and stronger than she, so very muscled and trim. He was handsome—indeed, he could not have been so successful a rake and rogue otherwise. Her reaction was almost enough to make her regret her condition of a marriage in name only. What would it be like to meet a man abed? To be kissed? The very prospect prompted the most delicious shivers.

At least she had left the matter open to negotiation. At the time, she had done as much only to keep him from refusing outright, but she wondered what it would be like to have the earl's hands upon her. They were strong hands, long-fingered and tanned, graceful and yet able with a delicate sensibility. They matched his mouth, which could draw in a taut line of resolve or curve upward unexpectedly into a rakish grin.

She supposed that if they wed, there might be a kiss to seal their vows. That would satisfy some of her curiosity to be sure. And it would be sufficient, perhaps, to allow her to move beyond such seductive notions and complete her book.

She must ask him more about Rockmorton Manor and its library.

How curious that her heart was racing as she descended the great stairs for dinner that night. It was simply a meal, as dinner had been these past four months since the earl's arrival. But there was a tingle within her this night, for Eurydice's proposal had provoked a change.

It was only sensible to be curious as to how much of a change it made.

EURYDICE ENTERED THE DRAWING ROOM, only to discover that she was early. She could hear Daphne coming down the stairs, bringing the boys to say goodnight. She was carrying Edmond while Malcolm insisted on descending the long staircase himself. Alexander had to be in his library, for there was a light in there. She moved to the window to watch the ceaseless fall of rain.

"There is a quibble," the earl whispered, his voice so soft and low that the sound gave Eurydice shivers.

She spun to find him lounging in a wing chair immediately behind her. It faced the window, which was why she had not seen him. As ever, he was impeccably dressed in dark trousers and a dark jacket, a white shirt and perfectly tied cravat. His hair was so dark that it seemed to gleam blue, like a raven's wing, and his dark eyes were filled with mysteries. His waistcoat was a rich deep blue silk, embroidered with gold. He looked wicked and gloriously handsome, which had to be why her heart leapt for her throat.

"A quibble?" she managed to say, wondering all the while what had seized her wits earlier in the day. What had made her imagine this was a man who would keep his word?

"Perhaps more than that," he said with apparent regret. His eyes were sparkling, though, and she did not trust him at all. "You see, I must have an heir."

"That was not part of the proposal."

"But I think it must be."

"We agreed to review the question later..."

"We did not agree. You made the suggestion, no more than that." The earl shook his head and rose to his feet, towering over her once again. "But I believe it is a matter we must negotiate in advance, to ensure that we have a right understanding before it is too late." His gaze was warm and he was very close, his watchfulness and the topic at hand making Eurydice feel fluttery.

"An heir. Must it be a boy?"

His brows rose. "I should think so."

"But if we had a daughter first, that would mean the conception of *two* children."

"If not more," he agreed, a smile curving his lips. He leaned closer and whispered. "Do you not expect that I will ensure your enjoyment?"

Eurydice frowned at him and retreated a step, declining to be charmed. "I have no doubt you would ensure that the conception was a merry matter, but I have attended my sister at two deliveries. That part can scarce be worth a night's pleasure."

"It cannot be all bad."

"I assure you it is wretched."

He watched her closely. "Then why did the duchess bear a second child? The first was a son. They could have stopped."

Eurydice shook her head. "They are in love. There is no telling what madness they find reasonable."

The earl laughed, clearly surprised into it. His laughter prompted the duke to pause on the threshold and look. The earl forced himself to sober again just as Daphne arrived in the foyer and Malcolm shouted for his father. The earl's eyes, though, were filled with a beguiling merriment. "You do not believe in love, then?" he murmured.

"I believe that what many call love is truly lust, and fades with time." Eurydice frowned. "Or possibly with earthly satisfaction." She risked a glance at the earl, surprised to still find that she had his avid attention. "I would expect *you* to know better."

He grinned. "I am familiar with that situation, to be sure."

Eurydice considered her sister and husband in the foyer, averting her gaze from her companion with an effort. "But I suppose there are some who *do* find love in marriage. I would guess it to be rare. What do you think?"

"That it is fiercely uncommon." He spoke without doubt.

"And thus not a reasonable expectation for anyone."

"No," he said, exhaling the word. He sounded wistful, which surprised her into watching him. His expression changed immediately as if he would hide his thoughts from her and he looked dangerous again. "Although many maidens do hope for it, by my understanding."

Eurydice wanted him to be certain of her expectations. "Not I. I think one must be prepared to sacrifice a great deal for such a situation, and that in the end, it might not be so happy after all. Think of Lady Anthea and how she was prepared to wed the baron, even when he was not going to be a baron." She shook her head at the whimsy of the duke's sister.

"You do not think they would have been happy?"

"I believe that Mr. Haskell's concerns were valid. Even if one sacrifices much for love, one may not even achieve that happy state in the end. So much relies upon the other party." She shook her head again, more resolute now. "I would prefer to concentrate on my own efforts and what results I can make from them."

"Your writing."

She smiled, glad that he understood her. "Which may come to naught, to be sure, but I enjoy it so."

He smiled and her heart skipped again. "Then it is worth the endeavor."

Eurydice rushed on. "I would never expect that my husband, especially if our match was an agreement to suit convenience, would lose his heart to me. In fact, I should be disappointed if he so lost his wits."

The earl nodded. "What if we agree that we shall not attempt to conceive an heir for one year after our nuptials are celebrated?"

"One year." Eurydice considered this. She could write a good deal in a year of solitude and comfort. Perhaps she might even compose a second book in that time. "But there is another consideration, sir."

"Is there?"

She drew herself up primly, disliking that she had to make her objection aloud. "You have had many companions of a most intimate nature," she said, knowing she sounded prim. "An heir is one matter, sir, but you will not give me—" she lowered her voice "—the French disease."

He blinked, looked away, and seemed to be at a loss for words.

"I know that women are not to speak of such matters, but the duke has some very interesting medical treatises in his library, even with illustrations, and I have taken the opportunity to become informed."

That seemed to restore his good humor for some reason, for when he met her gaze again, his eyes were dancing. "Since you are so informed, I would welcome you to examine my person. Is there not a telling rash in such instances of infection?"

Eurydice glared at him even as her cheeks seemed to have taken fire. "You must see a physician, one who will certify that you are not so infected."

"That would be so much less interesting than submitting to your own examination. And I would be delighted to improve upon your education. There are those who would say that book-learning is a distant second to experience." He was enjoying himself overmuch, to Eurydice's thinking.

She found herself sounding stern as a result. "That will not be necessary, sir. I would put my trust in the word of a reputable physician."

He mused upon that. "But I could become so in that year, by your own reasoning."

"Then, sir, you will have to abstain from such pleasures before you come to my bed. After we have our heir, you can do as you will."

"Abstain?" The earl was visibly shocked. "For an entire year? That is madness..."

"Those are my terms, sir."

"I make you an offer, Miss Eurydice, that I should see the physician and if you find his word acceptable, we will wed and begin the challenge of creating an heir immediately."

"When should I write my book then?"

"After the bundle of joy arrives, of course. You will have years of leisure once your duty to my lineage is fulfilled."

"I think not," Eurydice said, thinking of the change in her sister after the birth of her first son. Daphne had always liked sums and had helped *Grandmaman* with the accounts. After the arrival of her first boy, though, she had abandoned that task for an entire year. It seemed her thoughts were consumed with the marvels of son and husband.

Eurydice dared not risk her book's future.

She noticed that the earl was watching her closely and knew he was tempted by her offer. She recalled the duke's conviction that his old friend liked both a challenge and a gamble and resolved to give him one.

"How disappointing. I thought we came to terms." She straightened as if overcoming a setback. "But do not fear for me, sir. London is awash in rogues. Perhaps I will find one during my season. Or perhaps I will be wedded to a man sufficiently rich to possess a library. I do not even care if he has a title."

"You would wed a tradesman? Or a solicitor?"

"If he had sufficient funds for a library, of course."

The earl's dark brow rose. "Just not the pox."

"Precisely." Eurydice smiled that he understood her priorities. "Perhaps the suggestion of a season is of merit, after all." And she left the earl then, staring after her, as she joined her sister and the duke. She bent down to address their oldest son, as if the earl did not exist. It was a bold play and one that made her heart clamor in fear that she had miscalculated.

Eurydice had chosen on impulse, hoping the dare would be sufficient.

Fortunately, it was not long before she was proven to be right.

Sebastian let Miss Eurydice worry about his decision.

At least that was his strategy. He sincerely hoped that she was worried about it, but she gave no indication at dinner that she was concerned in the least. In fact, she might have forgotten his existence completely.

It was not how Sebastian preferred women of interest to respond to his presence, much less his attempts to charm. He spoke to Miss Eurydice repeatedly at dinner, but she gave only the barest acknowledgement of his comments, as if she humored him. Armstrong was mightily amused, Sebastian could see as much, and the duchess appeared to be puzzled by his attentions to her sister.

There was no opportunity to speak with Miss Eurydice after the meal, for she professed herself to be bored with cards and chose to retire early, declaring her anticipation of finishing a most wonderful book.

It had to be the first time that Sebastian had lost a lady's attention to a work of fiction, and he did not welcome the change.

"I suppose you are anxious to return to town," Armstrong said when the two men were left sipping their brandies before the fire. "You have utterly exhausted the possibility of conquest at Airdfinnan."

"Do you think so?"

"Attempting to charm Eurydice is a true mark of desperation. She has not a romantic fiber in her being, and no interest in men at all, as far as I have noticed." Armstrong shrugged. "I thought that might change as she grew older, but I perceive no difference. Daphne believed that the prospect of a season would pique her interest."

"I will wager it has not."

Armstrong shook his head.

"She does not seem to be the kind of young lady who is tempted by a shopping expedition, unless it is for books," Sebastian suggested and Armstrong laughed.

"Precisely so. But it is of no matter."

"How can it be of no matter whether she marries or not?"

"She has no fortune, less than fifty pounds per year, but I gave my promise to her grandmother that I would always ensure her welfare, whether she chose to wed or not." Armstrong gestured to the full bookshelves. "She is more than content here and when she has read them all, I have no doubt she will present me with a list of suitable acquisitions. She charms the children and is no trouble to have in the house at all. She is not demanding, she does not have expensive taste, and indeed, it is easy to forget her presence entirely."

Sebastian frowned. He could not overlook Miss Eurydice's presence and never imagined he would again. "It seems a meager bargain on her side."

"Does it? Comfort, shelter, good food and all the books she desires? I would wager that Miss Eurydice thinks the matter most neatly resolved." Armstrong drained his glass and set it down. "Now I will say goodnight." He yawned but the gesture was so obviously contrived that Sebastian smiled.

"You need not feign exhaustion to me," he charged with a smile. "Even I have been in residence long enough to know that the duchess will have had time to retire to her chamber by now."

Armstrong's grin was quick and wicked. "I did not wish to make you aware of what you were missing. Why didn't you bring Miss Ballantyne?"

"And scandalize all of Scotland?"

"You enjoy scandalizing everyone."

"But Miss Ballantyne has no affection for hunting, country houses, Scotland or rain." Sebastian shrugged, realizing how very discontent Esmeralda tended to be when matters were not to her taste. She could be a gem, but was only one that sparkled in its favored setting. "Better she remained in comfort in London."

"Then you should have told me in advance and I would have found some other eligible ladies to invite. I daresay the Dempsters could arrive in a fortnight if invited now."

"Do not trouble yourself on my account," Sebastian said. "I will have departed by then." He stood up, setting down his own empty glass, and smiled at his old friend. "I would not wish to wear out my welcome."

"Never!" Armstrong declared and they left the library together, each to retire to his own rooms. Considering what awaited him there, Sebastian made a detour to the library to choose a book.

If he was going to wed Eurydice, he had best become familiar with her pleasures.

He was standing before the bookshelves before he wondered precisely what kind of book she was writing herself.

"A YEAR IS UTTERLY IMPOSSIBLE."

Eurydice jumped at the sound of the earl's low voice. She was in the dining room the following morning, content to be alone at breakfast, for she had the duke's London newspaper. It was three days old, but she expected to be able to devour every line before anyone else appeared. She alone was an early riser in the household, though she sometimes heard the children in the nursery when she emerged from her bedroom.

The dining room at Airdfinnan had a high ceiling and large windows on three sides. On a glorious autumn day like this one promised to be, it was bathed in golden sunlight. Eurydice had eaten her eggs and had a full pot of fresh tea, as well as that newspaper. This room, all to herself, combined with the other pleasures of the day was her notion of paradise.

Though she could not deny that the earl's appearance improved it yet more.

"You do not customarily come down for breakfast so early," she said, realizing too late that she sounded rude.

He was loading a plate from the sideboard and she took the opportunity to survey him while his attention was diverted. He truly had fine legs. He turned quickly, surprising her, and smiled when she averted her gaze. "Should I confess that I was awake all the night long, considering your challenge?"

"Only if that is true."

"It is not. I slept admirably." He took the place opposite her and she poured him a cup of tea. He nodded his thanks and began to eat, craning his neck to read the headlines on her newspaper.

As he seemed disinclined to continue, Eurydice had to ask. "Then why are you awake so early?"

"Because I slept so well. I retired in a timely manner, instead of spending much of the night—and morning—carousing, gambling and womanizing." He lowered his voice and gave her a devilish look. "There is a wretched lack of women at Airdfinnan."

"At least those of the easy virtue you so admire."

He did not seem insulted by the barb. "Exactly. Which is why I will return to town on the morrow." He wagged his knife at her. "The question is whether I shall be betrothed or not when I leave."

Eurydice's heart skipped a beat, then lodged in her throat. He was watching her with a knowing expression in his eyes and that cursed smile, the one that made her wonder if he could read her thoughts. "I understood you had declined."

"I understood that we negotiated." He put down his knife and fork and fixed her with a look. "The simple fact is that it would be impossible for me to be celibate for a year. That condition is out of the question."

"What do you suggest then?"

"A month."

Eurydice sputtered in the act of sipping her tea. "A month?! How much could I write in a month?"

"I have no idea, but if you have half the wits I think you do, you should be able to write a great deal that is considerably better than the book I read last night. It was, in fact, responsible for my sound sleep."

"What book?"

The Castle of Otronto." He yawned mightily even as Eurydice gasped in outrage.

"But that is the very foundation of the gothic novel as we know it today," she said. "You can't possibly have found it wanting..."

"It was dull. And absurd. Fathers marrying their son's betrothed, mysterious knights, enormous heads and far too much racing about in the dark with knives and swords." He shook his head and finished his breakfast, then impaled her with a look. "I have no doubt you can do better."

Eurydice did not know what to say. She was both offended that he had criticized a work she admired and flattered that he thought so highly of her talents. The earl had no basis for such an opinion, to be sure, and Eurydice realized belatedly that he was trying to charm her. That took the power from his words.

She glared at him. "You, sir, will use any tactic to win your way, even flattery. One year is my condition and it stands."

Instead of appearing to be dismayed, his eyes twinkled. "But a year is quite impossible, Miss Eurydice. You must see that. How long have I been at Airdfinnan on this visit?"

"Four months."

"You are counting the days!" he teased.

Eurydice felt herself flush. "My sister noted the length of your stay the other day. She wondered whether you were quite well to linger here so long."

He laughed. "In the first week, there was that amiable daughter of the innkeeper in the Finnan Falls..."

"I do not wish to know of your exploits!" Eurydice protested, both outraged and fascinated.

"But you must, in order to understand the severity of the challenge you place before me."

"It is most uncommon, sir, to recount your exploits..."

"But we have left convention well and truly behind, Miss Eurydice," the earl countered with a look. Eurydice was compelled to nod agreement and he continued. "And in the second week, the newest maid of the household saw fit to entertain me one morning." He smiled like a cat that has found the cream. "Now there is a fine way to begin the day..."

"Sir!"

In the morning?

Why had Eurydice never thought of that?

"Almost as good as a lazy afternoon abed, in my experience," he confided and she blinked. "I shall spare you the intervening details, and hasten to the most recent incident. Two weeks ago, Baron Thornedyke and his wife were here with their twin sons, along with that luscious lady's maid in her service..."

"Cease, sir!" Eurydice protested and he did.

She was not certain whether to be relieved or feel she had only half the tale. She poured more hot tea into her cup then sipped it so quickly that she burned her tongue.

And he knew of her discomfiture, the wretch. His eyes danced as he watched her.

"The point, then, is that it has been nine days, Miss Eurydice. *Nine.*" The earl scanned the room then met her gaze again, his eyes bright. "A month will be a walk through hellfire, but I would endure it to please my bride. A year is utterly out of the question."

Eurydice found herself swayed by his intense expression. "But it is not sufficient time. You must see a doctor and possibly take treatment..."

"I am not ill. I guarantee as much."

"But..."

"But I am not so cavalier as you would believe, Miss Eurydice. I share your concern about illness, to be sure."

Eurydice did not know what to say to that. It was so startling to imagine that they had any common concerns.

The earl leaned across the table to make his appeal, his voice dropping low. Eurydice found her reservations melting beneath his steady gaze. "One night a week, beginning after one month's delay," he suggested. "It is the barest minimum to ensure that I can be monogamous."

"I might conceive right away."

"You might, and then you would be rid of me. You could write all the day and all the night at Rockmorton Manor." There was a glint in his eyes that Eurydice did not entirely trust. "What kind of book are you writing, by the way."

"I can't speak of it. Not until it is done."

"Ah," he said wisely, those eyes glinting.

"You have a scheme," she accused.

"It would be fair to say that you had a scheme first."

She laughed, for that was true, and he watched her, a warmth in his dawning smile that fed an answering heat within herself.

Goodness, he was an alluring man.

"I would even let you read my newspapers first," he murmured in a low voice.

Eurydice was shocked by how readily she was tempted. "But if you are near the limit of your tolerance, sir, when should we be wed? And how shall you endure another month?"

His smile flashed. "Is it not reasonable for a man and his betrothed to kiss? It will be like small hors d'oeuvres to whet the appetite before the meal."

The notion of being nibbled by the earl was most distracting. "But, but…"

"But you have only read about such intimacy in books," he guessed, rising from his seat and moving around the table toward her with deliberate grace. Eurydice felt both stalked and thrilled.

"True," she managed to admit even as she stumbled to her own feet. Curiously, she had no urge to flee even though her heart was racing.

The earl halted immediately before her, then lifted a hand. He captured a curl upon her cheek, watching it wind around his fingertip with a smile. Then he touched that warm fingertip to her cheek, ever so gently, launching an army of shivers over her flesh. Eurydice swallowed, amazed at her reaction to that simple caress, and was amazed to find her knees weakening. He was close, so close that she could feel his breath upon her lips, so close that she could have drowned in those dark eyes. "Do we have an agreement, Miss Eurydice?" he murmured.

"But I proposed," she said, hearing that her own voice was breathless. "It is you who must be willing."

"Oh, I am willing, Miss Eurydice, if you accept my terms." He bent and touched his lips to her temple. Eurydice caught her breath and inhaled the clean masculine scent of him, feeling a frisson of pleasure. His lips were firm and warm and she closed her eyes, awash in a most delightful medley of sensation. "Do you?" he murmured and Eurydice feared she would agree to anything just to have his attention.

A month, she forced herself to recall. Then couplings every week thereafter. And otherwise to be left to her own devices. It was a surprisingly small price to pay for the security and freedom she desired and she was not so witless as to let opportunity slip away.

"Of course, sir," she whispered. "I chose you, after all."

The earl laughed then, no more than a surprised exhalation of breath, then his fingers were beneath her chin. She had a glimpse of the expression in his eyes, sparkling with merriment but also tinged with solemnity, before his lashes swept down, hiding his thoughts, and he claimed her mouth with a kiss.

It was a sweet kiss, surprisingly so, a gentle and cajoling kiss that had Eurydice rising to her toes in a quest for more. Her hands had just landed on his shoulders and his arm had wrapped around her waist when there was a footfall on the threshold.

"Upon my word!" the duke declared, outrage in his tone. "Is this what routinely occurs in my dining room each morning?"

"Of course not," the earl said easily, pivoting to confront his host so that Eurydice was behind him. She felt her cheeks burn and was glad the earl held fast to her hand. "This is the first such happy instance, Your Grace, for Miss Eurydice has accepted my proposal." He gave her fingers a minute squeeze, acknowledging that this was not quite true, but Eurydice knew as well as the earl that the duke would not accept any deviation from convention. She kept silent, fearing Alexander's reaction.

And rightly so.

"You shall not wed!" he declared, striding into the room with purpose. Alexander's customary good nature was utterly lacking and he looked prepared to fight. "Eurydice, would you leave us, please?" he asked tightly when she did not move.

"I would hear this," she protested.

"I think she should hear whatever you have to say," the earl said, holding his ground and her hand.

Alexander glared at them. "I forbid such a match."

"On what grounds?" the earl asked, a challenge in his tone.

The duke's eyes flashed brilliant blue. "It is utterly unsuitable, and if you do not know as much, Eurydice, Montgomery should." He glared at his friend. "A man of any merit would acknowledge that truth."

The earl was unmoved, even by the slight against his nature. Indeed, he smiled. "Perhaps the lady will reform me."

"Perhaps you take advantage where you should not," Alexander retorted. "You and I will discuss this in privacy, immediately." And he abandoned the dining room, marching toward his library with purpose.

"I suppose he must give his permission," Eurydice acknowledged with reluctance.

"Nonsense," her betrothed said with unexpected resolve. "We have an agreement and we will keep it. I advise you to quietly pack your belongings."

"Sir?"

The earl winked. "He will cast me out for such an affront. I will depart immediately thereafter and we shall wed this very day."

"But that is impossible..."

The earl dropped his voice to a dangerous whisper. "It is not. You will meet me at the stables and we will stop at Gretna Green on the route south."

Eurydice's mouth opened and closed again as she stared at him. "But that would be scandalous."

His eyes sparkled. "And what will you write about, Miss Eurydice, if you do not live with adventure?"

Eurydice had no reply to that.

Against every possible expectation, the earl was right.

"And since we are in league together, I believe you should call me Sebastian," he advised as if he had read her thoughts.

"Sebastian," she said softly and liked how he smiled in pleasure. "Eurydice, of course." She curtsied.

"Of course." He bowed, then his wicked gaze dropped to her lips again, he leaned an increment closer—then Alexander shouted a summons, curse him. The earl—Sebastian—retreated a step. He sighed with great forbearance, clearly enjoying that he would set the entire household at odds, and Eurydice could not help but smile. "Make haste," he whispered.

She nodded once and the earl kissed his fingertips, then winked before he bowed again and went to be chastised by the duke. Eurydice scarce could keep from laughing at his manner.

Wicked man. He would lead her astray unless she watched her step. Gretna Green!

She would not just wed, but would elope. This, indeed, would be an experience to inform her writing.

Eurydice halted on the stairs, struck by an errant thought. Sebastian was a rake and a scoundrel. What if this plan to ride to Gretna Green was a ploy to seduce her and leave her despoiled?

The notion stopped her cold. She did not think that Sebastian was that sort of rogue, but she had never been alone with him. She knew little of such men and could not be certain.

Which only meant that if she was going to put herself in his power by leaving Airdfinnan with him, then she had best be prepared to fend for herself.

She would pack appropriately.

HIS DRIVER and team had been ready, his valet packed and his portmanteau loaded on the carriage by the time Sebastian was hurled out of Airdfinnan by his old friend, Armstrong. Sebastian could not have planned it better himself.

He had a moment to fear that his intended was one of those women who could not pack with haste when Eurydice darted out of the shadows of the stables. She had her valise in one hand and a black umbrella in the other. She was wearing her boots, bonnet and a dark cloak. She also had a stack of books under her other arm. She looked both resolute and thrilled, errant curls all around her face. Sebastian could not recall when he had last seen such an alluring woman.

He saved the bundle of books before they tumbled to the ground, touching his finger to his lips. He then handed her into the carriage, using the door on the opposite side from the house. His coach was much smaller than either of Armstrong's, but then he usually rode by himself, his staff outside. Once they were settled, he rapped his knuckles on the roof, suspecting that they would make better time than Armstrong could. His team were well-rested, as well as young and vigorous, and the smaller coach was light.

He indicated that Eurydice should take the seat facing backward, and sat in the other himself. The guard on the bridge would think him alone. She evidently planned for the same illusion, for she laid down on the seat to be entirely out of view. He tucked her valise beneath the seat and she put the books on the seat beside her. They were bound together with a belt and he wondered which ones she had not been able to bear leaving behind. The umbrella she gripped like a weapon.

He did not speak until they were over the bridge and Fletcher had cracked the whip. The horses cantered at speed down the lane, making the coach rock.

"Did anyone see you?" he asked, helping her to sit up. Of course, the exercise had allowed half a dozen curls to escape her ribbons.

"No one. They were all trying to listen to the duke without seeming to do so."

"That would not have taken much effort."

She smiled. "He did shout quite loudly. I had no notion he had such a temper."

"Well, the thing with Armstrong is that when he becomes deadly serious, he cannot bear to be teased. It is the surest way to send him into a fury."

She eyed him, her gaze filled with understanding. "You did it on purpose."

"I knew he would not change his mind. The best plan was to provoke him, the better to grant you sufficient time to pack."

She waved a gloved hand. "It was the work of an instant."

"Even choosing which books to bring?"

At that, she winced. "I have a list of the ones I was compelled to leave behind." She reached into the small purse that dangled from her wrist and presented it to him. "Perhaps you might indulge me with their replacement."

Sebastian felt his eyes widen as he scanned the very extensive list. She might prove to be a more expensive wife than he had anticipated. "Perhaps we should check the library at Rockmorton first. We would not wish to have duplicates."

She stared at him. "Don't you know what books are in your library?"

"I haven't the faintest notion. I don't go to the country to *read*, Eurydice."

"You should," she said. "It would be idyllic." She retrieved her list and tucked it away. "It is my sole copy," she informed him.

"I shall consult with you whenever I feel inclined to visit a book-seller," Sebastian said. He meant it to be a jest, but as he said the words, he found the pledge to be utterly reasonable.

She eyed him for a moment, as if uncertain whether to trust his word.

"I will," he vowed.

"Good," she said. "I would not wish you to be waylaid by the books with pictures."

Sebastian might have taken umbrage, but could not do so when her lips twitched so. They watched each other across the bouncing coach for a long moment, then he eased to one side. "You should sit here."

"Is it safe?"

"You are to be my wife."

"But we are not wedded yet, and a month will be a long time for you, to my understanding. I should not wish to tempt you overmuch."

"Too late," he said on impulse, reaching to tuck back one of her curls. He leaned toward her and lowered his voice. "I am only here, Eurydice, because you *have* tempted me."

She flushed crimson but her gaze did not waver. In that moment, Sebastian suddenly understood the appeal of maidens. Indeed, he was looking forward to introducing Eurydice to the pleasures of the flesh. That notion made him smile, which did not pass unobserved.

"You are thinking something wicked," she charged.

"I routinely think wicked things."

"Something particularly wicked. Tell me."

"Or?"

"Or I will not share my realization with you."

"A realization?"

"One key to the success of our plan." She nodded wisely and he thought perhaps she was bluffing.

He patted the seat. "Come here and I will tell you."

She moved immediately, abandoning her books on the other seat. Her thigh was close to his, thick cloak not hiding that truth at all. Her shoulder bumped his as the coach took a turn and he glanced down to find her watching him. "Well? I am here, sir, as you may have noticed."

Sebastian smiled. "I did notice, to be sure."

"You were thinking something wicked," she prompted.

"I was thinking of how interesting it will be to teach you of the pleasures of the flesh."

She did not smile but eyed him solemnly. "You have never been with a maiden?"

He shook his head. "I have never found innocence alluring."

"Whyever not?" She was genuinely curious.

He averted his gaze, considering the question. "I like to be sure that all parties involved know the implications and ramifications of their choices. Surprises, I find, are unwelcome, particularly in the bedroom."

Her expression turned coy. "You might find me less innocent than you expect."

"Because you have read the medical treatises in Armstrong's library?" Sebastian shook his head and wagged a finger at her. "You may find that experience is vastly different from book knowledge."

"That sounds like we should make a wager," she said, much to his surprise.

"That you will not find the truth better than your anticipation?"

"Oh, it will likely be better, but I doubt it will be different otherwise."

"I would wager otherwise. In fact, I could take that as a challenge."

"You have a month to consider the matter."

Sebastian smiled, knowing already what his choice would be. The coach turned and lurched onto the post road. He checked his watch and thought they were making good time. "We might make Gretna Green tomorrow," he said with some satisfaction.

"But we should not go there," Eurydice said, to his astonishment.

Sebastian stared at her. "Have you changed your thinking? We have an arrangement, if you so recall..."

She touched his sleeve fleetingly, blushed and smiled. "Alexander will expect us to go to Gretna Green."

Sebastian could not argue with that. "Likely."

"He is my guardian and I am not yet twenty-one years of age, and we know that he disapproves of our match." She nodded. "He vigorously disapproves."

"Yes. I cannot imagine what made him so cursedly conservative. Do you think marriage itself is at root? He has always been responsible, but there was a time when he could be relied upon to support harmless mischief."

Eurydice surveyed him so sternly that Sebastian fell silent. "Despoiling his ward is hardly harmless mischief."

"I am not going to despoil you. I am going to marry you! I gave my word!"

"But you can do as much only if Alexander fails to intercede before we exchange our vows." She said this with a satisfaction that Sebastian hardly thought the situation merited. "Which is why we must *not* go to Gretna Green at all."

Sebastian was confused. "So, you would rather be despoiled than married."

"Don't be ridiculous," she chided. "Gretna Green is the obvious choice for a hasty marriage, but the fact of the matter is that our vows must simply be exchanged in *Scotland*. Hardwicke's Marriage Act of 1753 is not law in Scotland and it is that law which prohibits our match, at least for several years yet." She reached for her stack of books, and removed one with an effort. It was a thick tome bound in black leather, which she began to thumb through with haste. "Fortunately, I had been researching the law regarding marriage in England and had this book in my room when you and Alexander began to argue in the library. I brought it along in case it might prove useful."

Why would she be researching marriage law?

Sebastian had no time to ask before she opened it to a page which included the text of the marriage act in question. She presented it to him proudly. "You see?"

Sebastian stared at the dense page of text, then at her. "You mean we could have just been wed in Finnan village?"

Eurydice shook her head. "That would have been a foolish choice! The pastor in the living granted by the duke would never have wed us against his patron's will. No, that would never have done." She sighed. "Never mind that the duke, as my guardian, could demand that our marriage be annulled, even if we have exchanged our vows, if it had not been consummated. See, here?"

Instead of looking as indicated, Sebastian closed the book and sat back. "So, you *have* changed your mind."

"We have an agreement, sir, and that is to consummate our match in thirty days, after you have visited a physician."

"We cannot outrun Armstrong for a month, no matter where we wed."

"We do not have to," she said calmly. "We must simply evade him."

"It is not that big of an island," he protested and she smiled. "I surrender. What is your scheme now?"

She laughed at him, a most charming sight. "Scotland is a large territory, and one with many churches, sir. We might try the tollhouse at Coldwater or even Lambton. They are in the trade of offering hasty marriages as well as Gretna Green and Alexander will not expect us to journey so far out of our way." She bit her lip, frowning slightly. "And then we must encourage the assumption that our match is consummated. We could take rooms and by the time Alexander finds us, we will have been there some days and nights." She met his gaze steadily. "It will be assumed to be too late for an annulment then."

Sebastian could not think of a single objection to this scheme. "That is sound thinking, Eurydice," he said, not hiding his admiration a whit.

She blushed crimson, but he knew she was pleased. "And surely it is deserving of some celebration."

"Celebration?" she managed to say before Sebastian framed her face in one gloved hand, smiled into her eyes, then bent and kissed her soundly.

This time, he was not so cautious as before, but kissed her as he thought a woman should be kissed. To his delight, after Eurydice gasped in surprise, she kissed him back with no small measure of her own enthusiasm.

This unlikely union was showing definite promise.

CHAPTER 3

Sebastian was dangerous, to be sure.

And his kiss was even more so. This embrace left Eury-dice flustered, shaken and utterly thrilled. She had never imagined that a simple kiss—the meeting of two pairs of lips—could be such a marvelous experience. She nearly forgot herself and all her notions of good behavior, nearly flung her arms around his neck and surrendered to pleasure.

Fortunately, she recalled her senses in time and tore her lips from his. She would have been despoiled, for certain, and through no small effort of her own.

For good measure, she retreated to the other side of the carriage and put her books in her lap. When she looked up, Sebastian was smiling at her.

Surely he could not have a scheme of seduction?

"I thought you were a maiden in search of adventure," he said, a thread of humor in his voice. Was he teasing her or revealing his plan? Eurydice could not see his eyes for he occupied himself with his snuffbox.

"I thought your word had merit, but feared just then that I had been mistaken."

He looked up quickly, so quickly that she saw his surprise. "We will be wed," he said tightly, as if insulted. "I gave my word."

"Then you will not be troubled if I insist that all demonstrations of affection wait until that happy objective is achieved." Eurydice sounded pompous and she knew it, but she had feared that she had judged him mistakenly.

Sebastian wagged a finger at her. "I agreed upon thirty days, but you must allow some crumbs from the table."

"Must I?"

He frowned then. "It was merely a kiss," he said, as if it had been nothing at all.

Eurydice suddenly felt her innocence quite keenly. "Not to me," she said.

"Truly?" His eyes lit with familiar devilry. "Then perhaps there is hope for me yet."

Eurydice regarded him with suspicion. "What is that to mean?"

He smiled and leaned closer, removing her books from her lap and setting them on the seat beside her. "That you appear to be the sole woman of my acquaintance who is unswayed by my charm."

Eurydice found herself fighting a smile. "The sole one?"

He nodded solemnly but she did not believe him for a moment. "You must see that the situation is provocative."

"It is hardly provocative!"

"Oh, but it is. I am tempted to take the challenge of winning your approval." He took her hand and pressed a kiss to its back, looking up so suddenly that she was snared by his wicked expression. "Perhaps even endeavor to steal your heart."

Eurydice pulled her hand from his grasp. "Ours is a purely practical arrangement."

"That does not mean it must be entirely...bland."

"What manner of spice do you seek?"

He smiled then, leaving no doubt of his meaning.

"You cannot win my heart," Eurydice said firmly, even as she wondered whether it might be done. If only he had not been so very handsome, and confident, and charming...

"All the more reason to try," Sebastian replied. "I must occupy myself with some task for thirty days, to be sure."

"You might read some books," Eurydice countered. "I could offer some recommendations."

"I have no doubt that you could. I could read yours."

"No," she said flatly for it was not fit to be shown to anyone yet.

"Should I be insulted that you trust me so little?"

"It is not fit for anyone to read as yet."

"Ah." His eyes widened and she knew he would try to make her laugh. "Would that medical treatise you found in Armstrong's library be amongst your recommendations?"

"It might encourage your interest in monogamy," she replied. "There were *illustrations*."

Sebastian grimaced, dismissing this, then fixed her with a playful look. "But would you truly desire my undivided attention? I thought the premise of this arrangement was that we would each pursue our own lives, unencumbered by the expectations of the other."

"Of course, it is. But you cannot wish to visit a physician monthly."

"Not part of the wager, my dear Eurydice. I will go once, this very month, as agreed." He leaned forward again, that challenge in his eyes. "Perhaps I should try to steal your heart away, so we might be so consumed with each other that this marriage becomes a real one in every way."

"Do not tell me that you are a romantic, sir!"

"Can you not believe it?"

Eurydice shook her head. "Surely you of all men cannot believe in the merit of love?"

"Quite the opposite," he assured her solemnly. "Because I have seen true love and felt its power. When it is gone, the void cannot be filled." Before she could ask, his gaze brightened and his tone became less serious. "But what of you? Are not all maidens romantics, particularly those who wish to write books?"

Sebastian a romantic. Eurydice would never have expected as much. Had someone broken his heart? What kind of woman had she been? Why had she abandoned him? There was a tale Eurydice would like to hear.

"True love is nonsense," she said. "And love at first sight even more so." She was forced to make a concession beneath his bright gaze. "Although, both make for good stories."

He laughed. "Do you not think of life as a story? I consider myself to be living the tale of my life: whenever the telling of it might bore an attentive reader, I know that I must do something outrageous to enliven the tale."

Eurydice stared at him in surprise. "That is a most compelling perspective," she had to admit.

He bowed his head slightly. "I thank you. And what is your creed of life?"

"Only that there is insufficient time to read all the books, so I must make use of every moment."

"To read or to live?"

Eurydice hesitated. "I had thought to read."

"But reading of an experience is hardly the same as living it oneself," Sebastian argued. "I vote for living each day to its fullest. I will read in my dotage when I have not the strength to enliven my own tale."

"I doubt that day will come soon."

"I hope it never comes, but in the meantime, Miss Goodenham, do tell me why you don't believe in true love."

He watched her, smiling slightly, as the coach rocked. Eurydice heard the hoof beats of the horses and the calls of the driver, the creak of the leather seats and the jingle of the trap. She could not look away from the dark splendor of Sebastian's eyes, though, or evade the impression that he would wait forever for her confession.

She cleared her throat finally. "My parents' marriage was arranged, as was that of my grandparents. I daresay their affection grew over time, but the initial impulse was practical. They were good candidates, each for the other. I admire the practicality in that."

Sebastian nodded, his gaze straying to the window. "And what of your sister's match?"

Eurydice stifled the urge to wince. "The original impulse was inarguably a material one."

She had Sebastian's undivided attention then, his eyes as bright as those of a cat. "How so? I thought they were immediately smitten, each with the other."

"Daphne was always determined to wed a duke. I believe the matter was settled in her mind the moment she saw the crest upon his coach." She watched Sebastian's expression become inscrutable and wondered at his own views. "They may say it was love at first, but I am skeptical."

Sebastian nodded thoughtfully. No doubt he was troubled to find himself alone in his views. "The duke's sister and the baron?" he invited.

"They were companions one summer at Airdfinnan in their youth and came to like each other well when there was no mention of marriage at all. I would call them friends who became more affectionate in time."

He tilted his head to study her. "Then you do not believe in true love?"

"Not as it is presented in tales, a grand sweeping passion that compels its victims to forget all else." She meant to be mocking but the earl did not smile.

"But what if I could change your mind?" he asked softly.

Eurydice laughed. "By persuading me to fall in love with you? I am far too sensible for that, sir."

He leaned back, his eyes dark. "And there, you have offered the challenge to fill my every waking hour for the next month."

"It cannot be done."

"Even better. I so dislike an objective easily won." He smiled, his confidence so supreme that Eurydice could only shake her head in amusement at him.

"And what of your heart? Will you tell me your tale of lost love?"

"That is not the matter at hand," he said firmly, then patted the seat beside him, changing the subject. "If you are so impervious to my so-called charm, then there is naught to be risked by sitting beside me."

Eurydice looked at him. She saw that he was issuing a challenge of his own, and she impulsively chose to take it. She moved across the carriage with purpose, but her move coincided with the couch taking a turn. She lost her balance and tumbled into Sebastian's lap, only to find his arms around her waist and his knowing gaze all too close. "Now that is how a dare should be accepted," he murmured, his gaze dropping to her lips.

Eurydice twisted free and dropped to the seat beside him, sparing him a glare. "If you try to despoil me, I will ensure you regret it," she whispered with heat.

"Which is why I would never dream of doing as much," he said lightly. "You are precisely the kind of person who would never forget to avenge a wrong done against her."

Eurydice was intrigued. "How do you know that?"

"Because you are so serious of nature, Eurydice. In that, we are complete opposites."

She twisted to look at him, not wanting to miss any change in his expression. "Are we?"

"Do you doubt it?"

"I think you contrive an appearance, perhaps to keep curiosity at bay. I confess that I come to wonder what lies behind your mask."

His gaze flicked then he smiled again. "A pity, then, that we are to have a marriage of convenience and live at such great distance from each other." He winked. "By your own choice, as well, so you cannot complain of the bargain."

Eurydice frowned, sensing she had lost something of merit. "You are vexing, sir."

He laughed again, his usual mood restored. "It is, I regret, a habit of long standing." Then he turned his attention to the view, leaving her thoughts swirling with unanswered questions.

Would he try to convince her to fall in love with him?

It was only sensible that she wished to know who had stolen his heart—and why that person was no longer in his company. If anything, the confession made him more fascinating than before. She had been so certain that Sebastian had no secrets or hidden sides to his nature.

And now, she yearned to know them all.

She doubted he would relinquish them readily.

～

THERE WAS little Sebastian liked better than to challenge expectations. If Eurydice suspected that he meant to despoil and abandon her, he would undermine her assessment of his character by being a perfect gentleman.

When she fell asleep on his shoulder in the late afternoon, he did not steal a kiss or even as much as a caress. Indeed, he abandoned his favored seat, rolling his jacket into a pillow for her, and tucking her cloak around her so she could sleep beneath his watchful eye. Her suspicions made him into a nursemaid. When they finally halted for the night at an inn that was not nearly far enough from the main road for comfort, he secured the last available room for her before urging her awake.

"I told them you were my sister," he whispered when her eyes opened. "And en route to a convent. They agreed that you could go up the back stairs, the better to avoid being seen by the men in the tavern."

He pulled her hood over her face before ushering her into the inn and sheltered even the servants' view of her with his body. When she was in the small room with a single candle, he bade her lock the door while he fetched her a meal.

"Must you have a maid?" he asked with a wince. "It would leave a witness of your presence."

She frowned, looking disheveled and adorably sleepy. Her gaze darted to the dark window. "Do you think he will..."

He laid a finger across her lips to silence her, then bent to whisper in her ear. "We are not far from the main road. We may be caught up before dawn, but the horses had to stop."

"Then surely his will, as well."

"He might have taken a change of horses." Their gazes held for a long moment, and Sebastian knew she understood that the depth of Armstrong's concern for her welfare would govern that man's choices.

"And what of you?"

"I will sleep in the tavern, in my cloak. This is the last remaining room." He glanced around. "Indeed, it might be the only one."

"But..."

Again, Sebastian silenced her with a touch. "I keep my promises, upon that you can rely." He stared into her eyes until she nodded, glad to see a little smile of pleasure curve her lips. "Three raps on the door will be me with dinner," he whispered. "Unlock it to no others."

She nodded agreement and Sebastian left her in the dreary little chamber. He heard the key turn in the lock when he was on the stairs.

It was almost half an hour later when he returned, accompanied by a maid who would not be left behind. She carried a steaming bowl of stew, while Sebastian had the small jug of ale and a hot brick wrapped in flannel. He made a show of talking loudly to the maid on the stairs and to his relief, a hooded Eurydice met them at the door. She was clever, both to disguise her identity and to ensure that the maid did not hear his signal.

He would have liked to have lingered and spoken to her, perhaps reviewed their plan for the morning, but the maid was attentive, and in the end, he left with the girl. Again, he heard the key turn in the lock and dared to be reassured.

It was much later that he realized he should have known better.

SEBASTIAN SPENT a long night awkwardly sleeping in a chair with his cloak wrapped around himself. The locals drank ale in the tavern until the wee hours of the morning, singing heartily near the end, which made an early retirement impossible. He spent those hours thinking of Eurydice and the challenges she offered, endeavoring to itemize them all.

She did not find him alluring.

She was not charmed by him.

She did not believe in love.

He sincerely doubted she had any intention of loving him, ever.

Despite the practical nature of their arrangement, Sebastian found this prospect troubling. It was not just new and unwelcome. At issue was not just that he was unaccustomed to women being disinterested in him, but that he was increasingly interested in Eurydice Goodenham. He was already fond of her. He liked her very much and was sorely tempted to convince her to love him.

For his own side, Sebastian did not believe in the merit of a practical marriage. His parents had been besotted with each other, having fallen in love at first glance. They had defied the expectations of their families to elope together, then had made steady progress together in overcoming each and every objection to their match. Their love had been the bedrock of their lives, unshakeable from that first meeting. They had been fearsome when united in purpose, indomitable together as they could never be alone. Indeed, it was the lofty ideal of their partnership and the romance behind it that persuaded Sebastian to live alone for the duration. He would not compromise for a pale shadow of what he knew was possible, so he would do without.

But then there was Eurydice Goodenham.

In the shadows of the tavern, he acknowledged why he had accepted her challenge. For the novelty of it, to be sure, and the very audacity of her making such a suggestion—and because she intrigued him in every possible way. At the time, he had made the excuse to himself that it was a fine disguise for the life he meant to live, but the truth was he had recognized her as the only woman he could love. He was in peril of being the sole person in love in his marriage, thus by every passing hour, he wondered more what it would be like to capture Eurydice's heart.

How could the feat be done?

How could he claim her heart and keep her respect?

Was it even possible for Eurydice to fall madly in love? Sebastian could not be certain, which was troubling indeed.

Why love her? Sebastian had no doubt that she would fight savage beasts for any person she held in affection. She was fierce in her loyalty, to be sure, and absolute in her choices—yet she was not predictable. He could imagine awakening each day, wondering what she would say or do next to enchant him. She was clever and he liked how they solved issues together. Her quick wits had already proven an asset. Once an ally, she would never be shaken from one's side.

But would she ever trust him so much as that? Sebastian could not imagine that she would ever be so foolish. Would she come to love another man in time? That was a troubling possibility. He would have to ensure that no sober and responsible gentlemen ever crossed her path if he meant to have any hope of claiming her heart.

But how could he do as much if she was in Cornwall while he was in London? There was a puzzle he could not readily solve.

There was no doubt about it—Eurydice was more adept at challenging his expectations than any person Sebastian had ever met before.

And that was the heart of the matter, to be sure.

～

WHAT A VEXING MAN.

Sebastian's inconsistencies were wretchedly annoying and that made him distracting as well. Eurydice sat in her room, unable to engross herself in any of the books she had brought. That was a first, particularly since she had only just begun a new novel by Mrs. Radcliffe that promised to be most intriguing. Yet instead of concentrating upon the tale, she found herself thinking about her betrothed. Worse, her every thought was tinged with sentimentality.

She took out her pen and ink to work upon her own book, but the story evaded her completely. It seemed flat and disinteresting compared to her current situation. Instead, she sought to make sense of her intended on paper. In the bottom of her valise was a collection of calling cards she had appropriated when last at the duke's London house. They were useful as bookmarks and for scribbling notes. She chose one from Mme. de Roye, as the lady in question was a clear-thinking individual. It could not hurt to have a measure of her former governess' influence in this matter.

Eurydice drew a line to divide the back of the card into columns, then a plus sign above one and a minus above the other. The positive side was too easy to fill. Sebastian was handsome, charming, titled and rich enough for her. He had a mischievous sense of humor and could make her laugh. He was not witless, by any means. He possessed both a house in town and one in the country, both with libraries. She pursed her lips, tapped the pen, then added another trait.

He could kiss very well.

She underlined 'very'.

Eurydice added that item to the list of his shortcomings as well.

He could only kiss well because he had a great deal of experience with that particular feat, because he was a rogue, a rake and a scoundrel. He consorted with many women and had seduced most of them, she would imagine. He had recounted his exploits since arriving at Airdfinnan, and Eurydice had never suspected a man would have such earthy appetites—while he complained of his dearth of companions. In London, he must bed a different woman every night.

There was every likelihood he had the French disease already and their agreement might be moot in the end.

Eurydice looked out the window at the darkness, wondering why that prospect troubled her. They could annul the marriage for lack of consummation if no physician would assert his good health.

Could she believe any such assertion? Eurydice would not have put it past Sebastian to manufacture such a document to ensure that he had his way. She added 'untrustworthy' to the list on the negative side.

And that was the meat of the matter. She did not trust him—and worse, she did not trust herself in his presence, particularly when he touched her. It was all too easy to surrender to sensation—and Sebastian knew it. He tempted her on purpose.

He had no notion of what books were in his library. She underlined this fault, as well.

She added 'wicked' to Sebastian's list of faults, then amended it to 'mischievous'. She did not truly think there was any evil in him—he was simply 'selfish' with no regard for others.

He certainly would have expectations of a partner in bed, which compelled her to consider her own shortcomings. How on earth would she manage to keep his interest even for an interval every week? She knew virtually nothing about the pleasures of the flesh, even though she had studied the medical treatises in the duke's library.

Would he ruin her and abandon her? Or would he simply abandon her? Eurydice had no certainty of what Sebastian would do and that irked her. For example, just when she had braced herself to fend off his affections here at the inn, he had defended her with unexpected gallantry. He had ensured that she had a room of her own, a hot dinner, a firm bed and a key to lock the door herself. Evidently, it was not his scheme to ravish her before their vows were exchanged. Evidently, he could be relied upon to keep his word.

Or did he mean to lull her into complacency?

Eurydice could not say.

She wanted to trust Sebastian, but that trust would have to be earned more than it had been thus far.

Against every expectation, he believed in love and apparently had lost his heart once to no good end. That made her feel a bit sorry for him. How unexpected that he should be a romantic!

What if his beloved returned? If Eurydice was happily settled in the situation she desired, that prospect should not have mattered. To her horror, she discovered that it bothered her greatly.

He could not be succeeding in stealing her heart with such haste —could he?

Curse the man. She would be awake all the night thinking of him!

One of the books Eurydice had brought was a volume about the history of Britain and Scotland. She had chosen it in order to learn about Sebastian's own holding of Rockmorton, but now she opened it to refer to one of its excellent maps. She easily located Coldstream and could guess the location of this particular inn. It was a good day's ride eastward to the toll house, and could be done without entering Edinburgh.

Would she remain a maiden if she spent another day in the coach with Sebastian?

Eurydice could not be certain.

If she was not, and Sebastian did not wed her at Coldstream, then she would be a disgrace to her family. Eurydice was not so concerned about scandal for her own sake, but she didn't want to disappoint Daphne—especially as she would be reliant then upon the duke's support.

She went to bed, but remained awake, thoughts spinning with her uncertainty. No one had ever caused her a sleepless night and Eurydice had to wonder whether it was a good portent that she intended to wed the first individual to do so.

She was still awake when a gentle rain began to fall just before the dawn, and rose to wash and dress. She might have been the sole one out of bed when hoof beats clattered in the yard. Eurydice went to the window, curious as to who arrived so early in the day—and had therefore ridden all night—and her heart stopped cold.

It was the Duke of Inverfyre's coach that came to a halt in the yard. There was no mistaking either the vehicle or its familiar insignia. In the damp morning, the horses' breath turned to steam as they snorted and stamped. Alexander himself erupted from the carriage before it had halted completely, the storm on his countenance telling Eurydice more than she needed to know.

She hid herself instinctively, her breath coming quickly as she thought. Their scheme would be revealed and foiled, unless she made a quick choice. She summoned the maid to finish dressing, then flung her belongings into her valise. She wrote a note on the back of one of Sebastian's own calling cards before packing away her pen and swore the maid to secrecy with her last half-penny.

She could only hope that Sebastian understood and trusted her.

On the stairs to the kitchen, she encountered Jenkins, which surely was a sign that all would proceed in their favor. She gave him instructions and he hastened into the yard ahead of her. Eurydice's heart was hammering as she fled the inn, keeping to the shadows and out of view of the duke's driver.

Sebastian had been the one to advise her that she had to live an adventure in order to have a tale to tell. She was only taking the advice of her betrothed, after all.

Sebastian must have dozed for he was shaken awake with a jolt.

The light filtering into the tavern was pale silver, and he could hear a light rain falling on the roof. He felt chilled and his feet were downright cold. Someone had brought him a tankard of ale, leaving it upon the table before him.

More importantly, Armstrong leaned over him, shaking his shoulder as if he would wrench the bones loose. The duke looked tired, furious, and resolute. It was not an encouraging combination or Sebastian's favored way to greet the day.

"Where is she?" Armstrong demanded.

"Who?" Sebastian asked, though he knew exactly who his friend sought. Truly, the duke had shown more persistence than expected—or he had slept too long himself. How could he ensure that Eurydice was not discovered? He sat up, desperately trying to summon his wits.

"Eurydice, of course," Armstrong snapped, then glared at Sebastian. "Where *is* she?"

"How should I know such a thing?" It was Sebastian's favored ploy, to reply to a question with another one, particularly if that implied he did not know the answer. How intent was Armstrong upon locating her? The duke had ridden this far and at night, which indicated that he would not be readily swayed from the chase.

Sebastian pushed a hand through his hair when Armstrong relinquished his grip and felt the stubble on his chin. The chance of a good shave, let alone a hot bath, seemed remote in this moment.

The duke dropped into the chair opposite and studied him with narrowed eyes. Experience had proven that blue gaze could ferret out the most deeply buried secret, so Sebastian lifted his ale, the better to avoid that look, and took a sip.

What the deuce was he going to say?

Something fell from beneath the tankard and dropped in Sebastian's lap. Armstrong did not notice.

"She is gone," that man said. "Vanished from Airdfinnan the same time as you. Of course, I assumed she was with you, after what I witnessed just before your own departure."

Sebastian spared a glance down at the calling card, which was one of his own. How had it gotten beneath the tankard? To his surprise, there was writing on the other side.

Make haste!
—E

He blinked and read it again. The handwriting was almost, but not quite familiar. Eurydice had done a passing job of mimicking Esmeralda's hand. At another time, he might have admired the feat, but all he could think was that Eurydice was gone. She had left while he was sleeping, and as much as Sebastian wanted to pursue her immediately, he was keenly aware of Armstrong's watchful gaze.

To where should he make haste? Coldstream?

If she had left, had she taken his coach? His horse? Either could only put her in peril and he nearly leapt to his feet to ensure her safety.

"Do you know where she is?" Armstrong demanded.

Sebastian shook his head. Thanks to Eurydice's choice, he had no notion where she might be found and he did not have to deceive his friend. Strangely enough, he did not feel a surge of gratitude toward his betrothed for this. "I have no idea."

It was true.

A maid brought a tankard of ale for the duke and he ignored it, leaning forward instead. "What is that you have?"

"A missive," he admitted, glad that Eurydice had used her wits.

The duke read it upside down and shook his head. "Your mistress pines for you, it appears."

"It does," Sebastian was content to let Armstrong believe it was from Esmeralda. How clever of Eurydice to have anticipated that the other man might see it.

"Did Eurydice confide in you, perhaps at dinner the other night?" the duke demanded. "You two were having a merry discussion."

"She was chiding me for reading so few books, and telling me of the wonders that might be found within your library." All true.

Armstrong's brows rose.

"She mentioned a medical treatise." Sebastian shrugged as if mystified, then drank more of his ale. At his gesture—which he contrived to make as leisurely as possible—the maid nodded that she would bring them fresh bread and cheese.

Where was Eurydice? Sebastian felt he'd been given a puzzle to solve without enough clues—or sufficient sleep.

"Why are you on this road then?" It seemed that Armstrong would not be easily waylaid.

But then, he had ridden all this way.

Sebastian conjured an explanation. "If you must know, I met a lady from Edinburgh last summer who insisted that I should call when in the vicinity." This was unassailably true. He smiled. "I contrive to be in her vicinity."

Armstrong's smile was reluctant. He sat back, though, and sipped of his ale, glancing at the card, then studying Sebastian closely. "What of Miss Ballantyne?"

"She need never know." Sebastian realized he had never replied to Esmeralda's missive. He still had Eurydice's version in his pocket but no additional paper at the ready. What if he sent that to Esmeralda? Would she know the difference?

"Doubtless she will be thrilled."

"I have no such expectation," Sebastian said. "I have been away a long while."

Armstrong nodded at the card. "And you ignored her injunction."

"Indeed." Sebastian did not like misleading his friend, but he knew Eurydice had been right about the duke's power to end their match. That man had a concern for her welfare that was good if inconvenient.

Sebastian was concerned for her welfare himself, though he knew how and why she had left the duke's holding. Why had she left *him*? Where had she gone?

"I thought you two might have contrived an escape together." Armstrong punctuated this with a glare. "I was thinking you might ride to Gretna Green," he added, as watchful as one of his hunting hawks.

Sebastian snorted, trying to dismiss the suggestion. In point of fact, it was troubling to be so readily anticipated. "But then I would be wed! Can you truly imagine that I would willingly enter the parson's mouse-trap? Much less that I would do as much with an innocent maiden? You know me too well to believe such a possibility!"

It was not quite a lie, for Sebastian had not denied the idea outright —he had simply expressed skepticism that Armstrong might believe such a story.

Armstrong did not take as readily to the ploy as Sebastian might have hoped. He set aside his ale and spoke with grim resolve. "Know that I will go through every chamber in this place before I depart. If I find her and you are deceiving me, Montgomery, we shall duel."

Sebastian swallowed, though he contrived to hide his concern. The simple fact was that Alexander was a far better shot than he. A duel between them was not likely to end in his favor. As vexed as Armstrong was, he would not waste his shot.

Relief came from the most unlikely of corners, for Jenkins cleared his throat to reveal his presence. "All is ready, as you instructed, sir," he said after a bow. "We are prepared to leave at first light."

"Excellent," Sebastian said, leaving a coin for his ale. He gave no indication that he had not ordered the early departure and dared to hope that this was Eurydice's doing. He inclined his head to Armstrong. "You will excuse me, of course? I vowed to have luncheon in Edinburgh."

Armstrong frowned. "I will still search for her."

"And I wish you the best of luck."

Armstrong's eyes narrowed to blue slits, but Sebastian took his leave while he could. He was in the yard before he addressed Jenkins in an undertone, unable to quell his concern. "Is she...?"

Jenkins nodded. "I hope I was right to take instruction, my lord."

"Indeed, you were."

Sebastian's coach was waiting, his driver looking sleepy but prepared to depart all the same. Jenkins held the door and Sebastian swept into the coach, hiding his relief that Eurydice was tucked into a corner, clutching that umbrella. The surge of relief that passed through him was almost overwhelming in its intensity. If anything had happened to her...

It was not just Armstrong's retaliation he feared, to be sure.

"Were you seen?" he asked quietly, smiling as he waved toward Armstrong, who stood watching from the doorway to the inn.

"I should never have gotten this far if I had been," she replied quite reasonably.

Sebastian rapped on the roof, then treated himself to a pinch of snuff, as if he had not a care in the world. The coach turned and left the yard, but he did not breathe a sigh of relief until the inn was far behind them.

That had been too close for comfort.

"You are quiet," Eurydice said when they had traveled a goodly distance in silence. She had never known Sebastian to be content with the company of his own thoughts, but he had not spoken since they left the inn. "Are you vexed with me?"

"I am considering the potential risk to my person resulting from this match," he said, then granted her a grim look. "Armstrong means to challenge me to a duel if I am found to have any involvement in your disappearance from Airdfinnan."

"I suppose we should have anticipated as much," she said, wondering at his concern.

"For one who is not yet wed, you are quick to embrace the prospect of widowhood."

Eurydice laughed, thinking he made a jest, but he did not even smile. She frowned then. "Surely you do not think he will catch us?"

"I cannot see how he will not."

"But surely you will not lose?"

"Surely I will. Armstrong is an infinitely better shot than I am. It comes from consistently shooting things."

"That cannot be. You came to Airdfinnan for the hunting..."

He interrupted her crisply. "And who fells more birds than I do, each and every time?"

Eurydice blinked. "I thought you were not trying."

"I assure you that my efforts make no difference." Sebastian shook a finger at her. "And he will not waste a shot. He is furious."

Eurydice was not certain of the import of this, so she asked. "Do you change your mind as a result?"

"No, but we must change the terms of our agreement," he said immediately and with such resolve that she knew there would be no negotiation. "He intends to search the inn for you, and he will not find you. He will conclude that you were in my coach, and he will follow us."

"He cannot keep us from wedding!"

"Of course, he can. But if we are committed to this course, then we must be equally committed to the match."

"What does that mean?"

Sebastian shot her an intense look that launched a shiver through her. "That it will be consummated immediately. This very night. It is our sole chance to eliminate his objections."

"But..." Eurydice felt hot and then she felt cold. "But the French disease..."

Sebastian shook his head. "You will have to accept my word with regards to my good health."

"But thirty days..."

"You will have to write your book *after* we have conceived. We will remain in London until that happy news, then you can retreat to Cornwall, write your book and deliver our son."

She had never seen Sebastian so resolute. His eyes glinted and his lips were set.

He leaned closer and dropped his voice low. The carriage suddenly seemed very small. "I do not mean to die just yet, Eurydice. So, you must choose. Either you agree to these new terms or I will surrender you to Armstrong myself with all haste."

Eurydice was horrified. "You cannot!"

"I will," he said, and she could not be certain whether it was merely a dare or not. "I doubt he is an hour behind us. We can see you en route to Airdfinnan before luncheon."

"You would not." Eurydice feared, though, that he would.

"To save my own hide, I most certainly would," Sebastian replied with surety. "If you know nothing of me, you must know that."

She sat back, thoughts churning. She did not want to return to Airdfinnan and she did want to marry Sebastian. She liked him more with each passing exchange and was even more convinced of the merit of their match.

Never mind that her curiosity was awakened about the intimacies exchanged between man and wife. If she agreed, this very night she would *know*. The prospect stole her breath away, but not her wits. If their match was consummated, then it could not be annulled. Her financial future would be secure.

And against every expectation, she trusted Sebastian in this. Was it the change in his manner, or the fact that his heart had once been wounded? Eurydice could not say, but she was utterly certain.

She trusted in that, as well.

"I agree," she said, offering her hand.

Sebastian's good mood was immediately restored. He smiled and his eyes twinkled as he folded his hand around hers. "I do so admire that you have good sense," he murmured, his words so low and silky that she shivered.

"You knew I would accept your terms," she charged.

"I gambled that you would, and it appears I was right." He grinned at her. "Could it be that you are not so immune to my charm, after all?"

"Perhaps my choices are limited."

"There is always choice, Eurydice," he said softly, then gave her hand a little tug, pulling her closer. "Fear not, Eurydice, I will ensure the first time is as good as it can be."

And before she could dispute that assertion, Sebastian kissed her again. The kiss was different than his earlier two, for it was more leisurely and cajoling. How could there be so many kinds of kisses? Eurydice knew she would have to begin a list.

Then, because he had contrived to win her agreement, she felt compelled to be less predictable. Eurydice kissed him back, suspecting that she had to meet him halfway to persuade him of her own conviction. She twined her fingers into his hair and met his ardor with a measure of her own.

Sebastian caught his breath as if surprised, then pulled her into his lap, slanting his mouth over hers and kissing her more deeply. The sensation was remarkably pleasurable, launching shivers over her flesh and awakening a heat in her belly. Eurydice found herself enjoying this kiss far more than she had ever thought possible. She opened her mouth to him, touching her tongue boldly to his, and Sebastian made an incoherent sound that thrilled her.

Was it possible that she had some power in this transaction?

Was it possible that Sebastian found her alluring?

Or had he simply been too long without an intimate union?

Eurydice cared less than she knew she should. She wrapped her arms around his neck, savoring the hard strength of him against her. His hands slid down her back in a smooth caress that made her heart skip and he twined one of her curls around his finger before stroking her cheek.

He was gentle as well as passionate and Eurydice was reassured.

All too soon Sebastian broke his kiss and settled her on the seat beside him. He cleared his throat and looked out the window, as if they were perfect strangers. But Eurydice saw the flick of pulse at his throat and the way he clenched his hand. They were both equally affected by that embrace and she could think of no better sign for their scheme of conception.

Surely a practical match could have its pleasures?

All the same, she had no notion what to say, a rare and awkward situation. The carriage bounced onward, the horses galloped and the whip snapped. The rain drummed on the roof and the windows were steamed so that the view was obscured. Eurydice's pulse gradually slowed and her breath steadied. Her lips continued to burn, though, and that delicious tingle did not subside. Sebastian's thigh was so close to her own that she could feel the heat emanating from him.

And most curious of all, she had no care for her books.

If this was but a kiss, she clearly had need of further information to prepare herself for the night ahead. She untied her bundle of books and selected the medical treatise from the duke's library. She took a fortifying breath, then opened it to a chapter she had never yet dared to read.

But before she had turned the third page, her sleepless night and the rhythm of the coach caught up with her. Eurydice's eyelids drooped and the book slid from her grasp as she fell asleep, her head on Sebastian's shoulder.

～

SEBASTIAN CAUGHT the book as it slipped from Eurydice's lap but had to read the title of the selected chapter twice.

Coitus.

Then he read the first paragraph to verify that the subject was as expected.

He closed the book and smiled. She actually had brought the medical treatise and was consulting it with regards to their wedding night ahead. Sebastian chuckled and tucked the book into the bundle with the others. He tucked his cloak around his betrothed and drew her against his side, watching her sleep. She had been awake early enough to witness the duke's arrival. She slept so deeply now that he wondered whether she had slept at all the night before.

What did she know of intimacies between man and wife? Likely very little. Her mother had died when she was a small child and Sebastian could not imagine Lady Octavia enlightening her grand-daughters. Did Eurydice talk about private matters with her sister, the duchess? Possibly, but if that were the case, whatever she had learned had been insufficient to satisfy her curiosity.

Hence the book.

He would have to take great care this night to ensure that she had her pleasure. She learned quickly, that was for certain, for already she showed an alacrity with kissing that tempted him to forget her innocence. He sighed, knowing that restraint was not one of his better traits.

But there had been a chance to end their arrangement, and Eurydice had not taken it. Not only had she ensured their escape, but she had accepted the change of terms. The notion that she truly did wish to wed him gave Sebastian a warm glow about his heart. Perhaps she too felt something dawning between them. Could it be that people found a love match like that of his parents in other ways? He knew his father had been smitten at first glance, and perhaps, if he met Eurydice now for the first time, Sebastian's reaction might be the same. It was not all bad that they had known each other for years, for that fostered a trust between them that could not be quickly gained. He looked down at her and touched one of those errant curls, knowing that he would miss her pert commentary when she departed for his country house.

In fact, he came to suspect that London might have less appeal without the prospect of Eurydice's company. He thought about introducing her to the pleasures of the city and knew he would spoil her dreadfully at the dressmakers and other shops. He knew she had been to the theatre, but he would take her to all manner of exhibitions and shows. He would teach her to drive his carriage, just to see her eyes light with triumph, and he would indulge her in bookstores, just to make her smile. He fully expected that she would not allow him to evade his responsibilities and he did not mind that in the least.

Would their son favor her or him? He hoped the boy was fair with Eurydice's eyes. He hoped the boy had her wits. He hoped, rather wickedly, that they might have a girl—or several—first.

What of her book? What kind of story was she writing? Would she let him read it? He found himself cursedly curious as to its subject, and a little jealous that it had such a hold over her imagination. She would even wed him to guarantee her writing time. Perhaps she would trust him with an excerpt in time.

Sebastian was so snared by his musings that it seemed they reached the tollhouse quickly. In truth, it was after luncheon, but he did not find himself hungry at all. He was too concerned about bringing their plan to fruition. He awakened Eurydice and escorted her from the carriage.

The service itself was short and unembellished, a bit disappointing, to be sure. There were no flowers, no music, no friends and family gathered to witness the event. The tollhouse was built of stone and illuminated by a single lantern, which was not nearly sufficient to make it merry on such a dreary day. The rain pounded down unceasingly. The officiant droned through the words as if he read a list for the market, but Eurydice smiled up at Sebastian, her eyes alight in the most alluring way. She repeated her vows without hesitation, her hands clasped within his, and when he said his part, the deed was done.

He paid the fee and took Eurydice's hand, knowing that half of London would be astonished to find him married. "And now to Edinburgh," he said to Eurydice with a smile that she returned. When they reached the carriage, Jenkins held the door, then offered his congratulations. Sebastian thanked him then dropped his voice low. "Bamburgh will be our destination, if you please. There is a large inn there, if I remember correctly."

"Of course, my lord."

"You think His Grace will follow us here and thence onward," Eurydice said softly when they were underway again.

"Why should he not?"

She nodded thoughtfully. "How far is Bamburgh?"

"We will arrive before dinner, eat in our rooms, then see the deed done. It is possible we will be found this very evening."

Eurydice bit her lip. "I will write to Daphne in the morning, before we depart," she said. "I cannot leave her to worry."

"And by then, our match will be fixed." He took her hand. "You remain certain?"

"I do."

"I found the service uninspired. You?"

"It was efficient," she acknowledged with a quick sidelong smile and he laughed.

"I would have liked there to have been flowers."

"Then let us fill your house with them once in London."

"Our house, Eurydice," he said, kissing her fingertips. "It will be your home, as well."

Her eyes sparkled. "My library, perhaps, in your house," she teased. "I cannot wait to inventory your books." She reached for her own but he stopped her with a touch.

"Leave that wretched volume alone. I will show you all you need to know of coitus."

She flushed crimson. "But I like to be prepared..."

"I assure you, all will be well." He brushed his lips across hers once again, hearing her catch her breath and knew it would be so.

He would ensure as much.

"Now, tell me of your book."

"I..."

"Some shred of detail, Eurydice, as a token of your trust." He thought she might not take the dare but he should have known better.

She settled against him and began to talk softly, and Sebastian knew a curious satisfaction that was all new.

It seemed that Eurydice was not the sole one encountering new experiences.

THE INN WAS LOVELY, well-appointed and comfortable, and their rooms were large and gracious. There was both a sitting room and the bedroom, with its great carved oaken bed. The maid bustled around, lighting fires in both rooms, turning down the bed, setting a table for supper in the sitting room. Lamps cast a welcome golden light in both rooms. Eurydice suspected that the sitting room had a fine view of the sea, but on this night, the rain obscured it—and then the maid drew the drapes over the window, as well, to preserve the heat. Even the sound of the rain was muffled.

The meal was hearty fare, plentiful and blessedly hot. By the time they had eaten their fill, she felt nearly herself again. She had been a little shy about telling Sebastian anything of her book, but he was an attentive listener and asked sensible questions. He had taken her endeavor seriously, which was unexpected—and very nice. Indeed, she had a short list of considerations about the direction of her story, thanks to his inquiries.

How curious that she was not in the least bit interested in them on this night.

Sebastian stood after the meal, and said he would retire to the common room for a cup of ale. She understood that he meant to watch for the duke. In the meantime, two maids brought a bath for Eurydice and filled it in the sitting room. She was relieved to remove her mired clothes and to sink into the wondrous warmth of the water. One maid vowed to launder her undergarments by the morning, seeing as Eurydice had packed so lightly.

On another night, she might have savored her bath and the prospect of reading in the cozy rooms, but she knew what was ahead. She did not dread their inevitable intimacy, not precisely, but she never liked being unprepared. Eurydice did not linger, but rose from the tub while the water was still warm, not waiting for the maid's return. She donned her chemise and combed out her hair, noting that her hand shook slightly. She retreated into the bedroom as Sebastian and Jenkins returned, closing the door almost completely.

She could not resist the allure of that medical treatise, though she was unable to concentrate on the words as she heard Sebastian disrobe. She opened the book to the same page and tried to read, sitting on the one chair in the room. Sebastian shared a jest or two with Jenkins, then she heard the water splash as he bathed, as well. He was not shy about taking his bath and truly, she was reminded of the enthusiasm of birds for puddles in the garden. She yearned to peek, but kept her gaze fixed on the book, well aware that Jenkins was yet in the sitting room. The water splashed finally and Sebastian thanked the servants who came to take the tub away. He bade Jenkins a goodnight, then the door to the corridor was shut.

Eurydice heard a key turn in the lock and then there was silence.

Her mouth went dry and she ran a fingertip down the page, not comprehending the words at all. It was so quiet that she could not be certain of Sebastian's location, if he had moved at all. The hair pricked on the back of her neck, as if she was being watched, and her heart skipped a beat.

"Are there illustrations in that chapter?" he murmured from startling proximity.

Eurydice jumped and dared to look. He was standing in the doorway in a silk robe, arms folded across his chest, dark gaze fixed upon her. He looked larger and more dangerous than he had earlier, as well as quite unpredictable. His hair was wet, but those dark eyes seemed to pierce all her secrets. He did not even appear to blink.

Had she ever seen a more handsome man?

Eurydice swallowed. "Very few." His silk robe was loosely belted but hung open to his waist. It was gold with a rich sheen, but almost the same hue as the tanned skin of his forearms. She could see his bare chest, graced with dark curly hair, and a great many intriguing shadows. She did not dare to let her gaze drop lower.

Sebastian nodded solemnly, even as a twinkle lit in those eyes. "How vexing to have so little information on a matter of such great concern."

"Indeed," she agreed, feeling that the room was unnaturally warm.

He took a step into the room and dominated the space, filling it with his presence and his warmth. Eurydice was not certain she could take a full breath.

"Perhaps this is a circumstance in which experience is better than the knowledge gained from books," he suggested.

"Perhaps," she managed to agree.

He looked pointedly at the book. Eurydice set it aside, heart hammering. He beckoned to her with one strong hand and she rose to her feet, hating that her knees trembled. Sebastian moved closer, his ease with the situation completely at odds with her uncertainty. His hands fell to the belt of his robe and Eurydice looked down, noting that his feet were bare on the carpet. "What do you most want to know?" he asked softly and again, she was aware of the patter of the rain, the crackle of the fire.

She took a steadying breath. "I would like to see," she confessed. "I cannot envision how..."

"You must have your examination of my person," he teased. He laughed when she blushed, unfastened the belt, then shrugged out of the robe. It fell to the carpet in a puddle of golden silk as he lifted his hands.

Eurydice stared. His body was more different from her own than she could have imagined it might be. He was all hard planes and smooth surfaces, taut with muscled strength, spare and lean. He was beautiful, elegantly proportioned and powerful. He was also vigorously healthy and unblemished. He turned, his hands raised, letting her survey him completely. When he faced her again, she realized he was smiling at her.

He was also clearly aroused.

"It is not always thus," she said. "It could not be."

"It is not," he agreed. "Anticipation changes its state as does arousal, of course."

"How very curious." She leaned closer for a better look and he laughed again.

"It is no different from your own body, in some ways."

"Your body is very different from mine."

"But not in showing the effects of arousal."

"I do not understand."

He gestured to her chemise with a playful fingertip. "Your turn."

A lump rose in Eurydice's throat. She did not think she was particularly lovely and feared suddenly that he would find her charms inadequate. "You cannot look upon me."

"Of course, I can and I will. We are wed, Eurydice." His tone left no room for negotiation.

"But you might not like me."

He looked down at his erection, then lifted his gaze to hers. That twinkle was back. "I assure you that I do."

She laughed then, surprised into it, and his own smile spread wider.

Eurydice reached for the tie of her chemise, but her fingers fumbled with the simple bow. Sebastian closed the distance between them and lifted her hands away. He planted a kiss on each palm, his gaze flicking to hers, before he untied the bow slowly himself.

"There is nothing to fear," he murmured softly, opening the neck of her chemise with his fingertips, sliding them across her shoulders.

His touch left a warm trail across her skin. She stood, holding his gaze, and waited.

"Your body also shows its arousal," he whispered, easing the garment from one shoulder. Her breast was exposed and she glanced down to find the nipple taut.

"See?" Sebastian slid his hand lower, cupping the weight of her breast, then eased his thumb over that tight peak.

Eurydice caught her breath at the jolt that raced through her body.

"And look again," he advised.

She saw that it was even tighter and more ruddy. Her throat tightened and she felt warm beyond all.

He winked at her, the very image of mischief, then bent his head and kissed her nipple.

No, he suckled it and the sensation was a marvel.

Eurydice caught her breath, then found herself clutching his shoulder as the pleasure rolled through her body. His skin was smooth and warm, and she felt his muscled power. When he released the nipple, it was even more turgid and red.

"I did not know," she confessed in a whisper, but Sebastian gave his attention to the other.

She reached out, feeling bold, and touched one of his nipples. It was flatter than hers, but the peak rose to her touch in the same way. She bent on impulse and kissed it, then suckled it as he had done with hers, and heard him catch his breath.

"Minx," he whispered and she laughed.

"It *is* similar," she said.

"And here," he said, guiding her hand to his erection. She touched him, timidly at first but then with increasing confidence as he guided her. There was a bead of moisture on the tip. He reached between her thighs and Eurydice gasped when she felt his caress. His fingertip, too, glistened with moisture when he showed it to her.

"Why?" she whispered.

"That is different. Your moisture facilitates our union, and mine is the precursor of the result of our union."

"The semen is released..."

He touched her lips with his other hand. "If you recite from that book, we will never proceed," he warned and she smiled a little.

"It seems incredible," she said, eying the size of him.

"It feels incredible."

She flicked a look at him, thinking he might be jesting with her but he was deadly serious. "I thought it would hurt."

"Maybe not as much as you anticipate. I will do my best," he vowed, and then, before Eurydice could ask, Sebastian lifted her in his arms, kissing her to silence in the same smooth gesture. She felt that she was floating, then he placed her on the bed, still kissing her as his fingertips feathered over her body.

She kept her eyes closed, concentrating on his touch and how her body awakened to his caress. His hand moved between her thighs and she gasped when he touched her, astonished by the pleasure he conjured with his touch.

It was not long before she felt a tumult building within her, something she had never experienced before but which felt exactly right just the same—though not as right as the release that left her trembling in its wake.

That truly shook every last one of her assumptions about matrimony and the merit of having a spouse.

~

Eurydice was a marvel and Sebastian knew himself to be lost.

She was both shy and bold, willing to experience a new sensation but uncertain how to proceed. She learned quickly, though, mimicking Sebastian's movements with such alacrity that his resolve to take it slow was almost overwhelmed. She gained her release with astonishing speed, for she was remarkably responsive, and he found himself beguiled by her delighted smile and the rosy flush that tinted her skin. It was clearly her first and he felt a sense of triumph that she was so delighted.

How unexpected that he, who was no stranger to amorous liaisons, should feel on the brink of a new discovery just as Eurydice was. Her sense of wonder made him appreciate the marvel of a happy union— and ensured that he wished to make all of this wondrous for her.

He had to be leisurely.

Sebastian stretched out beside her and kissed her then, coaxing her ardor again with his caresses. He felt as if they were sheltered in a haven of warmth and golden light, safe from the world and its woes— even as he was aware that Armstrong had to be coming ever closer. He caressed her again, watching her arch to his touch, then she stroked him with newfound confidence.

"That cannot be all," she whispered in a husky voice, her eyes dancing. "You have not had such release."

Sebastian rolled to his back, encouraging her to straddle him. It would be easier for her atop him. Eurydice surveyed him with a satisfaction that made him smile, and he could not resist the golden splendor of the curls tumbling to her waist. Her hair was a marvel, tumbles of golden curls that belonged in a Renaissance painting.

"I have you at my mercy," she teased.

"You do, indeed," he confessed, for it was true. He was in thrall to her and he was not surprised that she guessed as much.

Her gaze fell upon his erection again, then she sobered and met his gaze once more. "I do not know what to do." She wrinkled her nose in that most adorable fashion but did not retreat. "Show me," she invited in a whisper that resonated in his veins.

His daring bride. Sebastian guided her to rise above him, then eased himself against her. She was so soft and welcoming that he caught his breath, then moved against her slowly.

"Oh!" Eurydice whispered, exhaling the sound, then she eased herself lower. He whispered to her, advising her to be slow and gentle, knowing that she might kill him before she had explored him to her satisfaction. She ran her hands across his chest and closed her eyes as she took all of him, then laid her cheek against his chest.

"Oh," she said again, a strain in her voice, and he felt her tremble. His arms were full of her soft sweetness, and her hair tangled around his fingers, spilling onto his chest. He kissed her temple, then moved within her, hearing her gasp again. She sat up and braced her hands against him, her eyes shining and her cheeks flushed. She moved then of her own volition, and it was Sebastian who was overwhelmed with pleasure.

"Temptress," he managed to whisper. "I intended to teach you!"

Eurydice laughed and moved again, watching him closely as she learned what he liked best. Her pride in her ability to please him might have been the most seductive thing he had ever seen. Sebastian was lost in a haze of pleasure, captive to his new wife's determination to satisfy him. She moved and she halted, she caressed him and she kissed him, she rode him with increasing confidence until he thought he might not live to see the morn.

Eurydice rocked atop him with increasing confidence and Sebastian could not decide whether he wanted her to take him to the summit or continue her sweet torment all the night long. Time stopped and the candlelight flickered, the room filled with a glow that was theirs alone. She moved with increasing vigor and his pulse thundered with rising need. His heart was pounding and his chest was tight, his very skin seemed to be stretched taut yet he hoped to last until she found her pleasure again.

Then she reached back and caressed him on the underside of his scrotum.

Sebastian roared with the fullness of his release, gripping her hips and driving deep until he could conjure no more.

When he was trembling in the wake of his release, Eurydice tumbled to the bed beside him. He did not have to look to know that her eyes were dancing with satisfaction. He was too busy catching his breath.

And this had been only the first time.

"Wherever did you learn that?" he demanded when he could speak.

"It is in the book," she confessed, and he turned in time to see her smile at his obvious surprise. She was glorious, her hair a-tangle, gilded from the candlelight, her eyes shining and he could only stare in wonder. It was how he had envisioned her, aglow in the wake of pleasure, gorgeous and alluring.

How had she made this feat entirely new?

It was love that changed all and Sebastian knew it well.

"Many men have an area of sensitivity beneath the scrotum, which, if pressed or caressed before ejaculation vastly increases the pleasure of that deed." Eurydice explained, obviously quoting the relevant passage.

"Forget what I said about not needing the book," Sebastian growled and she laughed with a delight that prompted his own smile.

He had already reached for the cloth to wash up when he saw the blood on the linens. The sight made him realize that all had changed. Eurydice was his wife and always would be. There could be no annulment.

The match with Eurydice had been like a jest, and Sebastian had agreed with the surety that he risked nothing at all. Now his heart clenched, for he had stepped directly into the one situation he had sworn to avoid forever.

He was falling in love with his wife, and she did not believe in love.

He flicked a glance her way to find her frowning slightly as she checked the book for more suggestions. She had experienced pleasure, to be sure, but sensation had not awakened emotion.

He would be a stud and a source of financial security to her and no more.

How would he bear it?

Sebastian had to leave this chamber and consider his path, before he was seduced by his bride again.

~

WHAT WAS AMISS?

Eurydice had been certain that all was well, then Sebastian's manner had abruptly changed. He had become still and his expression had turned inscrutable. It had been the blood on the linens that had prompted the change, though she could not say why. He had known she was a maiden. Did he regret that they were thoroughly wed, and that it was too late for an annulment? He had dressed quickly and left her, ignoring her questions and calls, even though it was the middle of the night.

As the moments passed and he did not return, Eurydice feared that he found her company disappointing.

She had seen Esmeralda Ballantyne once, at the theater, and readily recalled that woman's beauty and poise in his moment of doubt. Miss Ballantyne was elegant and assured, perfectly attired, and as different from Eurydice as it was possible to be. Eurydice knew she would not benefit from a comparison.

Sebastian had regrets.

Eurydice washed and donned her chemise, then sat on the edge of the bed, trying to identify precisely what had gone awry. She must have failed to satisfy him. Was there some art to ensuring a man's pleasure that she did not know? Eurydice expected that there was and that she had failed some secret test, but even a vigorous study of the medical volume did not reveal any helpful detail.

Indeed, after this interval, she could have written a more compelling description of coitus than the book contained.

Previously, she had admired how Sebastian did not hold back in expressing his views or revealing his thoughts. She had found him easy company, but evidently those who met him abed saw another side of his nature. Would he be moody like this each week when they met abed? The book offered no suggestions that a person's manner might change after intimate knowledge of another.

Eurydice could only conclude that their mating had fallen short of his expectations.

But if he did not confide in her or explain the trouble, how could she do better?

Why would he not confide in her?

Eurydice was mystified and no amount of pondering her husband's actions that night proved to be illuminating at all.

When he returned, it was almost dawn. Eurydice feigned sleep, for she did not know what to say. He undressed in darkness and laid down with his back toward her. While she tried to choose the best words to utter first, she heard his breathing slow.

In moments, she knew he was soundly asleep, and her questions would have to wait. She would have neither answers nor sleep this night.

What an inconvenient man he was.

CHAPTER 5

On the morning after her wedding, Eurydice awakened early. On this day, though, instead of writing or reading, she remained in bed and watched Sebastian sleep. He looked younger in slumber, his hair tousled and his breathing slow. She felt the most curious sensation in the region of her heart, gratitude mixed with yet more, for he had been a gentle yet passionate lover. He had ensured her pleasure first and been patient with her ignorance, and it had seemed to her that something marvelous had dawned between them. It felt tentative and precious, as fragile as a butterfly—and in truth, it had been dismissed all too quickly.

She had to repair the matter, somehow.

Eurydice studied Sebastian and wished she could read his thoughts and divine his secrets. She was not sufficiently bold to awaken him with a touch, so convinced was she that she had erred the night before.

She had to make matters right somehow.

The sky had turned pearly when she heard the hoof beats. She guessed who arrived outside the inn, by the speed of the horses. She went to the bedroom window and looked all the same. The duke appeared to be more tired, but the glance he fired up at the inn was so fiercely blue that Eurydice took a step back.

Her heart stopped cold.

She could not let him challenge Sebastian to a duel.

She had to resolve the situation favorably, for she was not prepared to surrender her new husband yet—no matter how incomprehensible he might be. Eurydice did not doubt that the two friends might argue if they confronted each other and she had to hope that she had more skill with diplomacy than she was rumored to possess.

When the maid came to say that a gentleman called for the earl, Eurydice was half-dressed. She dressed quickly with the girl's assistance, then left Sebastian sleeping when she went down to meet the duke.

He was pacing in the common room, and spun to confront her. "I knew it," he said through his teeth, then took a step closer, those eyes flashing. "Is Montgomery too cowardly to show his face?"

"Of course not," Eurydice said, speaking crisply. She had noted before that the duke responded to such shows of confidence. "He is sound asleep."

"I will not speculate upon the reason for that," the duke muttered darkly.

"Will you break your fast with me?" Eurydice smiled. "I suppose it is too much to hope that you have a London newspaper? I do so enjoy it in the morning."

The duke exhaled in frustration, then surveyed her. "It is done, then?"

"It is done and I am content." She gestured to a table, well aware that the maid listened avidly.

"You should not have done it."

She kept her tone reasonable. "But you would never have allowed it if I had asked you."

"He will not make you happy, Eurydice," the duke warned in a low growl. "The heart is no good guide in these matters when it comes to some men..."

"I did not wed for love, Your Grace," Eurydice said, boldly interrupting him. He fell silent and stared at her. "I said once that I would wed a rogue, that he might do as he desired in town and I might retreat to his country house to write."

"But that was just a girlish whimsy."

"On the contrary, I still believe it to be a sensible course. I do not mean to change Sebastian's ways, and I have no expectations of doing so." Even as she spoke, Eurydice realized that her expectations had changed. She did not want to retreat to Cornwall, not if it meant leaving Sebastian behind in London. "Our agreement is that I will give him a son and he will grant me the freedom I desire. It is blessedly simple."

The duke sat down heavily. "I cannot imagine this will prove sufficient for you."

"It must, for I have chosen it, and you have saved the expense of giving me a season..."

"Which I would have spent gladly."

"And my sole regret is that you have pursued us so diligently and so far." Eurydice smiled again. "I appreciate, Your Grace, that you take great care of your responsibilities. I would have simply told you of my desire, but I did not believe you would agree."

"I would not have done so, for certain. Montgomery is not a suitable spouse for you."

"How can you speak thus of an old friend?"

The duke frowned. "He has changed since our younger days. He has come to care only for himself and the implications of that for you is my concern."

Eurydice was not convinced. Sebastian had been kind and considerate of her, even if he had been changeable the night before. She was confident that they would surmount whatever error she had made—if he deigned to speak to her again.

"Then we must contrive to dismiss your concerns," she said to the duke, knowing that neither he nor her sister would rest easy until they had seen her content with their own eyes. She had an idea about that. "We continue to London today and will remain there through the holiday season. Perhaps you might come for dinner on Christmas Day? I am certain that Daphne would enjoy a visit to town."

The duke fought a smile and lost. "Christmas?" he said, then chuckled. "You must know that Montgomery despises the festive season."

Eurydice had no such idea. "Who can do as much?"

"I think you will learn much of your new husband in the coming weeks, Eurydice, and I shall be glad to witness the results." The duke nodded, accepting a tankard of ale and raising it to Eurydice. "I accept your invitation gladly, though I would give a shilling to see Montgomery's face when you share that news."

"But you are friends and he has just spent several months at Airdfinnan." Eurydice was dismissive of this concern, convinced as she was that the duke was unkind in his assessment of Sebastian.

"I look forward to the day. We will let you know when we arrive in town." The duke toasted her and drank deeply, more amused than Eurydice knew he should have been.

Sebastian did not truly despise Christmas, did he?

~

"You did *what*?" Sebastian demanded of his new wife when he awakened just before midday. He had slept hard after fighting his doubts, but her confession brought him immediately to full consciousness.

Surely she made a jest!

But Eurydice was utterly serious. "I had to keep him from challenging you," she said, as if her invitation to the duke was an entirely reasonable solution. "You said yourself that you would lose, and I am not yet prepared to be without a spouse."

"I thank you for that," he said, more than a little annoyed by her tone. She could have made a sweet confession and reassured him completely, but Eurydice was maddeningly reasonable.

"We have a wager, sir." She lifted her hands. "You have not yet visited a solicitor to secure my future and who can say whether we have conceived your heir as yet? The book indicates..."

"Curse the book!" Sebastian roared, vexed beyond all.

At Christmas. Why had she been compelled to issue an invitation for Christmas? It was as if she would shred his heart before his very eyes. It was bad enough that he felt this magical sense of a dawning love, but she would make him confront what he had lost before he knew what he had gained. Sebastian felt in turmoil. He had planned to undertake the journey of conquering her reluctant heart in easy stages, but she leapt ahead without regard for his concerns.

A silent Eurydice watched him as warily as she might consider a rabid dog. "You are irked," she suggested cautiously.

"I am annoyed indeed!" Sebastian retorted. "You have stepped far beyond your station, madame. I would never have invited the duke to my home during the season, and had you troubled to ask me, you would have known as much!" His voice rose over the course of this lecture but Eurydice was not daunted.

"You are not thinking clearly," she chided him gently. Sebastian bestowed his most chilling glare upon her, to no discernible effect. Indeed, she came closer. "You have just spent several happy months as the duke's guest at Airdfinnan. It is fitting to reciprocate. I asked them only for dinner!"

"Not at Christmas!"

She frowned and shook her head. "When else? My sister will not rest easy until she has witnessed our happy situation," she said, using a tone appropriate for soothing a wild beast. "The duke will not rest easy with my sister so unsettled and one meal..."

"I do not serve Christmas dinner in my home!" he repeated, biting off the words.

"Whyever not?"

"Because I do not celebrate Christmas."

"Of course, you do." Eurydice was dismissive. "You simply do not want to face him, but the sooner this is resolved, the better."

"I am no coward."

She lifted a brow. "Everyone has a festive dinner on Christmas, at the very least..."

"I do not. Not anymore."

"Then what do you eat on December 25th?"

"I usually drink." That was not entirely true. Sebastian had stopped drinking at any volume twelve years before. He cultivated a reputation of imbibing great quantities of wine and brandy, but in truth, he consumed very little.

He had been drunk when he had received the news. Never again.

Sebastian dropped into a chair, pushed a hand through his hair and tried to echo Eurydice's calm tone. He knew he failed. "This scheme is quite impossible and I would have told you as much if you had troubled to consult me. My servants know they have the day off, because they do each and every year. You must cancel this invitation and you must do so immediately."

Eurydice perched on the lip of a chair opposite. "And if I decline to do so?"

Her audacity confounded him. "Then you will have guests to dinner who find an empty table and no host."

She surveyed the room, obviously thinking. "And if I could contrive a meal without denying your servants their day of leisure?"

"You will not." Sebastian leaned forward so that they were almost nose to nose and held her gaze. "In fact, with this choice of yours, our plan must change again. You will depart immediately from London to Rockmorton Manor and remain there."

She looked startled, then inclined to argue with him. The gleam in her eyes was so remarkably stubborn that he dared to hope she did not wish to be parted from him, but her words dismissed that possibility. "But we have an agreement. How shall we conceive an heir then? How will I keep my side of our bargain?"

"Is this not what you desired initially?" Sebastian countered. "You will have the run of the house, and I will stay in town, and you may feed Christmas dinner in Cornwall to whoever you like! Perhaps you will even discover that you are with child and can send me the happy news."

She fixed him with a look. "You are afraid."

"I assure you I am not." It was a lie and Sebastian hoped she did not know it.

"Liar," she said flatly, proving his worst fear true. She could see the secrets of his very heart. They had to part ways. "Why do you refuse to celebrate Christmas?"

"I will not speak of it."

A familiar glint lit Eurydice's eyes and he knew before she spoke that she would not follow his instruction. "Tell me why and I will consider cancelling my invitation."

"You will cancel it either way. You will *not* be in town."

She folded her arms across her chest. "This is about last night, is it not? I disappointed you in my...actions."

Sebastian was astonished that she could think he would find fault with their glorious union. It had been transformative, magical, a prospect of future joy...but she had not seen it that way. There could be no more compelling evidence that he alone was emotionally entangled in this match.

Eurydice shook her head, not waiting for him to continue. "No one performs any act perfectly on the first occasion for it. I would ask you for instruction that I might improve for the next time..."

She would wear him down. She would steal his heart, and then she would lock herself in his library, ignoring him forevermore once she had her security, and he would be bereft again.

Not again.

Sebastian could not bear the possibility.

"There will be no next time!" he insisted.

She regarded him as if he had lost his wits. "You have great confidence in the power of a single union to produce a child. The book..."

"—is of no merit whatsoever," he said, interrupting her crisply. "You will leave London for Cornwall and there will be no second incident and we will speak of this no more." He took a breath, uncertain why precisely he did not feel in command of this situation, even though he was making plenty of commands. "And you will cancel your invitation." He turned to the washstand, resisting the urge to dunk his head into the cold water. That might clear his thoughts.

"No, I will not cancel it," she repeated. "You will not deny me the pleasure of Christmas with my sister and her children, whether you choose to celebrate the season or not."

"Go to Cornwall then!"

"And how shall we conceive your heir at such distance?"

"Perhaps I will visit, in the spring."

She lifted a brow. "And how many mistresses will you have bedded during the delterval? No, sir, we must conceive that son first, before you resume your ways, which means I must remain in town."

He pivoted to face her, hoping his expression was daunting. "Did you not pledge to obey me just yesterday afternoon?" he demanded.

Eurydice smiled but her eyes narrowed and her posture was taut.

"You could not have expected that concession to be so readily won, particularly when you are irrational, sir."

"Irrational?" The charge stung because Sebastian knew it was true.

If she had pledged a dawning affection then his resistance would have been overwhelmed, if she had wept a single tear, he would have been undone, but Eurydice, being Eurydice, argued with a cold logic that only fed his dread of the future.

"You need a son. We are wed. I will remain in town until I conceive, which certainly will not be by Christmas, and even if it is, no physician will be certain in so few weeks." She took a breath. "And in the meantime, my invitation will ensure that you are not shot in a duel."

Sebastian had to respect that she did not back down readily.

He heartily disliked that she was not ceding to his will. "Eurydice..." he began, his voice a low growl.

She stood and brushed her skirts with purpose. "What do you drink Christmas day?"

"Brandy." It was a lie but one she would believe.

"Then I will ensure you have sufficient when I provision for our guests." She turned to leave their chamber, her manner so satisfied that Sebastian wanted to shout after her, give her a shake—or seduce her all over again.

And there was the rub of it. In mere days, his new wife was provoking him to forget all the rules he had adopted to ensure that his heart and his happiness were never at risk again.

She had to go to Cornwall before he lost the last of his wits.

Indeed, it might be too late for that.

THEY JOURNEYED in silence the rest of the way to London, stopping only for one night. Sebastian did not come to Eurydice, despite her hopes that he might. He sent Jenkins to summon her in the morning and met her at the carriage. He made the necessary polite motions, but his attention was elsewhere, his expression impassive and his gaze distant.

Sadly, his ill humor was not fading.

Nor was Eurydice's resolve.

How could he fail to explain to her what she had done wrong? Truly, it must be a matter of some intimacy, but they were man and wife. There should be no secrets about their lovemaking. It was only common courtesy to explain to her, but he denied her that.

The argument could not be undone, but worse, Eurydice had no notion how to repair the damage. Each hour they passed in silence together made her more sharply aware of what she had lost. She missed his charm and their conversations. She missed his smile and the mischievous glint that lit his eyes. She missed having his attention and to be sure, she missed his kisses. If this was to be her future, it was a grim prospect.

She liked Sebastian.

No, Eurydice realized in the vicinity of Norwich, she was falling in love with him. She wanted a marriage in every way, a partnership and a union, and in that, she suspected she was a fool. What if the duke was right about his friend's nature? She no longer desired to retreat to Cornwall, for there she would be without Sebastian. The prospect of hours alone, a large library and time to write lost its appeal without regular interactions with her husband.

At the same time, she could not rescind her invitation to the duke, lest Alexander conclude that she was unhappy and challenge Sebastian to a duel. She could not change the invitation, inviting Daphne to visit her alone in Cornwall, for that would scarce convince anyone of her marital bliss. She could not bear to leave Sebastian, yet she could not live with his cold indifference.

If she told him of her growing regard, she did not doubt that he would laugh at her—or claim that he had succeeded in winning her heart after all.

What a wretch he was, challenging her every notion and leaving her feelings in a muddle—when his apparently were not engaged in the least. He had said he had no interest in maidens, and he had lost all interest in her when she had failed abed.

Surely, there had to be books she could consult...

They arrived at his London house without having exchanged more than two words all day. The staff were outside the door to greet her, so

Sebastian must have written to announce their arrival and her presence. Sebastian introduced them all to her, with no sign of pleasure, though she thought she detected a gleam of approval in the eye of the butler, Watson. He was an older gentleman and Eurydice hoped he had served the family long enough to know some of her husband's secrets.

It would take some delicacy to encourage his confidence, but Eurydice was determined that it should be done.

She had to make this marriage work.

She had to ensure she gave every appearance of happiness in less than one month's time. Her sister would not be fooled.

And she wanted to regain Sebastian's attention. Somehow, she would seduce him this very night. Perhaps enthusiasm, or the surprise of an invitation to her chamber before the passing of a week, would suffice. Eurydice was desperate.

Sebastian clearly did not share her view. He turned to the driver. "My wife will have need of the coach tomorrow morning, if you please, for she will journey to Rockmorton Manor."

The driver blinked. "In Cornwall, sir?"

"The very same," Sebastian said with a tight smile. "I doubt the house has moved." The driver flushed but Sebastian had already turned to Eurydice. She hated that she was to be dismissed, like a naughty child. "I wish you a good journey," he said to her, his tone formal. "I will absent myself, anticipating that you will leave in the morning."

Eurydice gasped. He could not do this! "But I..."

He fixed her with a steely look. "It was our initial arrangement, my lady. Perhaps I will see you in the spring."

Eurydice could not argue with him, much less correct him, in front of his entire staff—and he knew it.

Sebastian bowed to her, then pivoted and strode into the street, calling for a cab as his own carriage was unpacked before his house. Eurydice watched him go, well aware of the surprise of the household. She did not have to wonder at his destination. He would visit a mistress or courtesan to ensure his satisfaction, and gain the pleasure she had not granted to him.

Miss Esmeralda Ballantyne, no doubt.

Even if he had sent that letter from Airdfinnan, the lady in question would have only just received it and would certainly welcome him back into her affections.

It turned out that Eurydice's original plan was highly unsatisfactory, after all.

Sebastian clearly did not share her doubts, for he did not spare her a backward glance.

Eurydice squared her shoulders, fixing a confident smile on her lips before she turned to face the staff. "He has so missed his club," she said. Leaving no interval for speculation, she confessed to Watson that she had no ladies' maid. "At Airdfinnan, I shared my sister's maid and of course, I could not persuade her to leave with me."

"I shall seek a suitable lady's maid for you at once, my lady," Watson vowed. With a flick of his wrist, the other servants returned to their tasks. A word from the older man and the footmen were bringing in the luggage, Jenkins was directing those who carried Sebastian's portmanteau and arrangements were being made for the horses to return to the stables.

And Eurydice was entering her new home, alone.

THE HOUSE WAS GRACIOUSLY PROPORTIONED, though not as grand as the duke's London residence, which had been designed for entertaining. Eurydice had not expected Sebastian's house to be as large, and truly, she found its size both cozy and charming. The duke's homes could be somewhat daunting in their splendor: this one reminded her of the dower house at North Barrows where she had passed much of her childhood. It was a home for a family.

The decor was elegant and it was scrupulously clean. The dining room was flooded with sunlight, which she liked, and the library had a considerable stock of books, as well as two promising chairs by the fireplace. There was another pair of doors that seemed to be secured. The house had an air of welcome that Eurydice admired and one that made her wonder about Sebastian's family. She knew vaguely that his parents had passed away, but would have assumed as much since he had come into his inheritance. She also knew that he had no siblings.

Her curiosity grew with every step she progressed into the house. There were miniatures in one cabinet, but she did not ask Watson about them as yet.

The butler led her up the stairs to the next floor where there seemed to be four rooms, two facing the street and two facing the back of the house. He led her to one at the back, which was bright with morning sunlight and comfortably furnished. "How lovely. Thank you, Watson."

"I trust it will suit, my lady." The older man turned to leave.

There were beautiful watercolors framed on the wall and Eurydice moved to study them. She was hungry for details about Sebastian's life and family, for he had surrendered little. "Did someone in the family paint these, Watson? They are admirably well done."

"The mother of the current earl, my lady. She often painted *en plein air* at Rockmorton Manor."

Sebastian's parents. He had never spoken of them. Was there a reason? "She was talented."

"Indeed, my lady. A most gracious and talented lady."

Eurydice realized then what she hadn't seen yet in the house. "Is there a portrait of her?"

The butler seemed startled. "In the drawing room, my lady, there is a fine portrait done of the earl and his lady just after the arrival of their son, the current earl."

"I should like very much to see it."

"The drawing room, my lady, has been closed up these twelve years," he began, warning her.

Eurydice smiled. "I would like to see the portrait," she said crisply. "And then I will have a cup of tea in the library." With any luck, she would find a reference to her current conundrum there.

Watson, like the servants in the duke's household, responded well to firm instruction. "Excellent, my lady."

Eurydice removed her hat, coat and gloves, then followed Watson to that pair of doors. They were locked and when he opened them, she saw that he had told no tale. A cloud of dust rose from the floor inside. The furniture looked ghostly, draped in cloths, and the shades were drawn against the daylight. He moved ahead of her, obviously familiar with the room and its contents, and opened a pair of drapes. Dust motes danced in the sunbeam that slanted into the room, and Eurydice saw that it was a graceful room, decorated in apricot and gold. There was a harpsichord in one corner and a large beautifully carved fireplace dominating the opposite wall. An ornate gold clock sat on the mantle, protected by a glass dome.

And over the mantle was hung a very large portrait in a gilt frame.

"Why was this room closed up, Watson? It is lovely."

"It was done after the earl and his wife died, my lady. The current earl wished it so."

She turned to look at him. "When did they pass?"

"Twelve years ago, my lady, on the same day."

She assumed there had been an accident, which was how her parents had come to their end. "The same day?" she echoed, inviting more of the tale.

The butler cleared his throat. "It was most unfortunate, my lady. The earl took ill and when he developed pneumonia, his wife insisted upon nursing him herself. She took the illness after him, and they died within hours of each other."

Eurydice felt her throat tighten at this sad news. "And the present earl?"

"Was here, my lady. His mother had sent him to town lest he take the illness as well. She always feared for his welfare, given that he was their only child." He coughed gently and Eurydice understood he had more to say, if she invited it.

"Did he realize his father was so ill?" she asked, making a guess.

"He did not, my lady, at his mother's insistence. She wanted him to enjoy Christmas as always they had together, and she believed the former earl would recover." He shook his head. "Alas, she was mistaken." His voice broke just a little and Eurydice understood that this couple had been held in high affection by their staff.

They must have been good people.

Eurydice stopped before the portrait and studied the depicted couple. They were handsome, to be sure, young and clearly happy. The man was tall like Sebastian and there was something in his smile that reminded her of her husband at his most mischievous. He looked down at the lady, who was seated in a chair, one slippered foot extended. She was a glorious beauty, with ebony hair and rosy cheeks, dark eyes glinting with pleasure. The object of her delight was the toddler in her lap, a laughing young boy who had to be Sebastian. The image was so filled with love and joy that Eurydice's throat tightened.

This was what Sebastian had known. He had grown up, surrounded and bolstered by such love, and its loss could only have rent his heart in two. She would have been more devastated if she had been older when her parents died, old enough to have known them well and loved them truly. How fortunate he had been—she could almost envy him— but she recognized that the loss of his parents, both at once, would have been devastating.

That was why he had insisted that the room be closed up.

"Christmas," she said, realizing only now the import of the butler's words.

"Yes, my lady. They passed on December 25."

No wonder Sebastian despised the festive season. Did he blame himself for his parents' death? He certainly might blame himself for not being with them at the end, even though it had been no fault of his own.

He would have the world believe that he did not care, but Eurydice began to understand that, perhaps, he cared too much.

What if she could restore his joy of the festive season? What if she could give him that sense of a secure home that he had to miss? Eurydice had only vague memories of her parents and their love, but she knew very well the rooting that Lady Octavia had given her. She had felt safe at the dower house of North Barrows and secure in the promise of the future.

She had to at least suggest as much to Sebastian before she went to Cornwall.

"Thank you, Watson," she said, hearing the unevenness of her own voice. "It is a glorious portrait."

"Indeed, it is, my lady," he said with a bow. "If you will take your repose in the library, I will bring you tea there."

"Thank you, Watson." She knew she did not imagine that the butler beamed at her before he bowed and departed. She had need of one ally, and it seemed she had found one already.

Perhaps Watson could help.

~

To Watson's delight, the earl had not just married on whim but had taken a sensible woman to wife. The butler had heard of Miss Eurydice Goodenham, of course, for there had been much chatter about her older sister marrying the Duke of Inverfyre, but he had known very little about the younger sister's nature. Just moments in her presence reassured him enormously as to her character.

And truly, the earl's abrupt departure and his command—one which his wife had no intention of following—proved that this lady had shaken his assumptions. Watson had known the earl from infancy and had thought for some years that a challenge would do him good.

That challenge had arrived in the person of his new wife.

By the time Watson had sent out a call for a lady's maid and carried the tea to the library, the lady was there with a stack of books by her side. To his relief, a fire had been lit in that room and she was seated before it, engrossed in one of them.

She looked up with a smile as he set down the tray. "Thank you, Watson."

He poured her tea, noting that she drank it strong and clear, and to his surprise, she cleared her throat.

"If I might have a word, Watson," she said and he nodded agreement.

"Of course, my lady." At her quick glance, he shut the door to the library and returned to stand before her, waiting.

"It appears I have made a *faux-pas*, but it cannot be undone and I would request your assistance in salvaging the situation."

Watson was intrigued. The lady did not strike him as impulsive or flighty and he could not imagine what error she might have made. "Of course, my lady."

She looked down at her tea, choosing her words. "The earl and I chose to wed hastily, as you must have guessed, and exchanged our vows at Coldstream the day before yesterday. My sister is married to the Duke of Inverfyre and it was from his Scottish home, Airdfinnan, that we departed with the intent to marry." She took a sip of tea. "The duke—" she added with care as she set the cup and saucer aside "—was not pleased." She met Watson's gaze, inviting his understanding.

"I see, my lady."

"He pursued us, with the objective of ensuring my return to Airdfinnan and that of challenging the earl to a duel."

Watson struggled to keep his brows from rising.

"And so, when the duke located us on the morning after our nuptials, I knew that his concern was an echo of my sister's fears for my welfare. I insisted that ours was a match destined for success, but the duke remained skeptical. To see such concerns set at rest, I invited the duke, the duchess, and their two young sons here for Christmas dinner."

"Ah," Watson could only manage to say.

"I had no notion that the earl did not celebrate Christmas or that he routinely granted a day's leave to his staff. He was and is vexed with me for issuing this invitation, but I will not rescind it. The earl must not be compelled to duel with the duke." She spoke firmly. "His honor will insist that he accept the challenge, but he has told me that the duke is a much better shot. They have known each other for a long time."

"Indeed, my lady. We have welcomed the Duke of Inverfyre here on occasion."

She inhaled. "And even my husband insists that the duke will not waste his shot, not when he believes he defends the honor of his wife's family. The rift must be repaired, and I see this invitation as the simplest way of managing that." She appealed to him with a look.

Watson could only agree with her conclusion.

"I understand, my lady." He straightened. "Will the duke and his family be staying here, my lady?"

"I expect they will prefer to stay at the duke's own townhouse in Grosvenor Square. Doubtless my sister will write to accept the invitation and confirm their plans with me. She is very organized." She smiled with obvious affection. "Their boys are darling but quite active. They may leave us turned upside-down in just those few hours."

Watson could not help but smile. "It has been a long time since there were children at Rockmorton House, my lady."

"The earl and I will endeavor to see that changed, Watson," she replied, the implication clear that such a goal could only be pursued if her rift with the earl was also repaired. "I should so appreciate your help with this event. I do not wish to add to my blunder, and in fact, I must find a way to restore my husband's confidence in me."

Watson bowed. "You may leave the preparations to me, my lady. We have had the honor of the Duke of Inverfyre's presence here before, as mentioned, and I will ensure that every preparation is made for his...reassurance."

This time, the lady's smile lit her eyes. She was a very pretty lady. "Thank you, Watson." She paused for a moment, revealing that she knew the import of her next words. "Perhaps the drawing room could be cleaned, the better that we can entertain our guests."

"Of course, my lady." Watson bowed again. "There will be three candidates in the morning for the post of your lady's maid, with the hope that one meets with your satisfaction. On this day, Millicent, the head housemaid, can be of service to you. You need not be concerned about the servants on Christmas Day—most of them miss the bustle of the festivities in a big house."

She nodded, then settled a little deeper into her chair. "I feel very fortunate to have arrived at a house so well in hand. Thank you again, Watson."

Watson bowed and left, feeling rather fortunate in his new mistress himself.

CHAPTER 6

Sebastian had no notion what to do.

That was a new situation for him and an utterly unwelcome one. He was falling in love with a practical woman who did not believe in love—not only was she his wife, but she wished for a financial settlement. There was a jest in that if he had the will to unearth it, but Sebastian did not.

He did not want to be home.

He did not want to be elsewhere.

He wanted to be with Eurydice, but that would not do, not until he had decided upon a course of action. Had his wife been any other woman, he could have cast himself at her feet, begged forgiveness and charmed her into accepting his love in the blink of an eye. The strategy would scarcely be a success with Eurydice—which was, of course, the heart of her appeal. She defied his every expectation and he adored her.

Sebastian Montgomery was smitten.

Yet if he confessed as much, Eurydice would be disappointed in him for such a show of emotion. Had she not said she could not respect a man driven by his emotions?

He walked along the Serpentine and then Pall Mall, seeking a solution to his woes. How did one persuade a woman like Eurydice to fall in love? He had no notion. She was not seduced by his charm, she was immune to his commands, she challenged his expectations, broke the rules of his household, made him laugh, brightened his days—and could not have cared less about him or his fate, so long as he consulted a solicitor before he died. Never had a woman so confounded him.

Never had he been so enchanted by an amorous union. Not only did the responsibility of introducing Eurydice to pleasure change all for him, but her reactions and her joy had made it a marvelous night. He wanted more. He wanted her every day and every night, he never wanted to be parted from her—she would conceive with haste and laugh at his weakness for her.

Then she would read a book, abandoning him to agony.

He had been a fool to accept her proposal.

Eurydice had not known about the agonizing loss of his parents and could not have known that he blamed himself for accepting his mother's instruction at her word. He had been merrily enjoying himself in town while his father and then his mother fought for their survival—and drunk in the bed of a courtesan when they both died. He had thought he was celebrating the season, as bidden to do.

Instead, he had been so selfish that he had not even realized the two people of greatest importance to him in the world were dying.

For twelve years, he had lived with his guilt, insisting upon solitude so he could never fail anyone else. He had lived supposedly for pleasure alone, but really, he had been evading the responsibility of caring about anything or anyone.

Then came Eurydice into his life. Within days, if not hours, her practical wager had begun to change into something greater. The minx was destroying his barriers and melting the ice in his heart with fearsome speed—and he had realized as much when she had not just invited Armstrong to visit at Christmas, but did so to save Sebastian's hide.

It was no jest that Armstrong would triumph in a duel, but Eurydice's concern had not been indicative of any tender emotion. He had not yet amended his will to include her and ensure her future security.

Practical Eurydice would laugh at him if she knew his emotional state, and then she would tease him for it.

If she did not pity him.

It was a situation beyond his ability to repair. If nothing else, Sebastian could see one detail resolved. He went to his solicitor and made the modification to his will, leaving his entire estate to Eurydice and any children of their union. He then went to his club and drank a large brandy quickly. It was only late afternoon, he had not eaten and he had not downed a brandy in a long while. The liquor set a fire within him that warmed him in a way that was not unpleasant.

Sebastian called for another and soon lost track of the time.

THE MORNING after their arrival in town, Watson informed Eurydice that the carriage was waiting for her, just as the earl had instructed. Eurydice had enjoyed an excellent breakfast, though she had not slept well.

She had perused the books in the library, working her way through every single shelf, and had found no reference to assist her. There were law tomes and histories, many volumes concerning the natural flora of England, and a considerable collection of books on animal husbandry and farming. She explored every volume of promise but did not find a word of advice on intimate matters between man and wife. There were no less than three books of manners and four on conduct at court, and it was probably a good thing that none of them had chapters about the amorous arts. There was precious little literature to Eurydice's thinking, though she thought it a sad measure of her desperation that she would seek illumination about such a subject from novels.

Sebastian had not returned for dinner so she had eaten alone, then descended to the kitchen to thank the staff. She talked of her plans for Christmas Day with them and knew they did not feign their enthusiasm. Watson vowed that he would recall every detail of how the former lady had seen the festive season celebrated and Eurydice left with a list and a lighter heart.

It would have been better yet if she had encountered her husband.

She had no notion when Sebastian had returned during the night, or even if he had, but no one in the household appeared to be concerned so she did not ask. It seemed that a wife should know if her husband was in residence.

At breakfast, the newspapers from that very day had been delivered —at Airdfinnan, they were typically two or even three days old—but Eurydice found no pleasure in them. As she pulled on her gloves, she suggested to Watson that Millicent would suit her well enough and that he should perhaps hire another house maid. She left the house to meet the carriage.

"Have you no luggage, my lady?" the driver asked.

"Not to visit Brisbane's Emporium," she said with a smile. "If you would be so good as to take me there and wait. I doubt I will be long."

Driver and footman exchanged a significant glance, but Eurydice did not concern herself with that. "Yes, my lady."

There was one soul in all of London whom Eurydice could ask for advice of a most intimate nature. By wondrous coincidence, Sophie de Roye was also the owner of Brisbane's Emporium, the establishment Eurydice was determined to patronize in the decorating of Rockmorton House for the holidays. There was nothing in the way of decorations, Watson had informed her, and she could only imagine that assistance in the preparation of festive treats would be welcome. She had a list of staff and intended to procure small gifts for each of them, just as Daphne did each year at Airdfinnan. Eurydice was glad of her older sister's example in this, for before Daphne had wed the duke, their lives had been much simpler. With any luck, she would not err and embarrass Sebastian.

The halls of Brisbane's Emporium were decked in Christmas splendor. There were holly and ivy garlands draped behind the counters and mistletoe arrangements dangling overhead, ready to be taken home and installed in one's foyer. A group of men and women with angelic voices were singing carols in the lobby, collecting donations for the poor. A baker had set up a seasonal shop just inside the main entrance, offering sausage rolls, shortbread, plum puddings and mince pies for those who declined to make their own. There was eggnog and mulled wine to take home, and gingerbread that could be enjoyed in the store. An entire counter was laden with brightly colored candy, making it the object of fascination for many children. The counters were filled with glorious gifts—shawls and pins and fans and purses, snuffboxes, pins and tempting trinkets—to acquire for one's loved ones. The aisles were bustling and Eurydice could fairly hear the coins adding up. Just the sight of the festive displays raised her spirits.

They would have a Yule log at Airdfinnan and the boys would be excited by the prospect of gifts. The duke would put his ledgers away early each night to read them tales before the fire, and during the day, there would be long walks or rides. The fires would crackle and Eurydice sighed that she was missing such familiar joys.

But she would make her own joys in her own home.

She wound her way through the shoppers and found Sophia in the very thick of it all, looking both happy and busy. Eurydice knew that her former governess had a daughter and a son now, but Sophia's eyes danced just as merrily as ever and her freckles seemed to have multiplied.

"Eurydice Goodenham!" that woman cried with pleasure and seized her hands, then kissed her cheeks. "How did I not know that you were coming to town? Are you staying at the duke's house? Where is your sister?"

"They are yet in Scotland," Eurydice confessed and Sophia fell silent, her gaze becoming guarded. "I am here alone." She flushed under Sophia's stern eye and continued before she could be chided. "With my new husband," she confessed in a whisper.

Sophia's eyes widened, then she ushered Eurydice into the back room, securing the door against listening ears. "And how did I not know that you were married?" she demanded.

Eurydice surrendered her shopping list first and Sophia dispatched a clerk to see it fulfilled and packed in the carriage. She then ordered tea. Eurydice explained about her elopement and Alexander's fury with the situation, watching her former governess' disapproval grow steadily.

Sophia frowned, then took Eurydice's hands in hers again. Her expression was solemn. "I could write to the duke and the marriage could be annulled..."

"It cannot be annulled."

"Then you are..."

"Yes, and so I must remain here. Sebastian cannot resume his affairs with courtesans and actresses, not until I conceive his child. That is the only way to keep our wager." She bit her lip and Sophia squeezed her hands.

"Do you love him, Eurydice?"

Eurydice shook her head. "I thought not. I thought it impossible, but...now I wonder."

"And does he love you?"

"I fear he was disappointed by another."

Sophia was dismissive. "Yet she is gone and you are his wife. You must work with the opportunity presented, Eurydice."

"But I fear that the true issue is not my invitation to the duke, but Sebastian's own disappointment in the match."

Sophia was outraged. "Why should he be disappointed in you? You are clever and..."

"Decidedly inexperienced abed."

"That is an asset in a lady, Eurydice. Never forget as much. He cannot have expected otherwise."

"But he may have wished for more. In fact, I am certain he must have done. And now he dreads the ordeal of a regular seduction. Worse, I cannot find a reference to assist me."

"A reference?"

"A book. All knowledge is in books."

Sophia laughed as if she knew she should not. "Oh, Eurydice, all knowledge is not in books, especially that of the most intimate kind."

"Then how will I learn?"

"You must learn to seduce your husband yourself," her former governess said in a tone that brooked no opposition. "Give him your undivided attention. Ask him about his interests. Truly, Eurydice, you are good at conversation and better at winning approval than you appreciate. Talk to the man..."

But Eurydice could not do as much if Sebastian did not return home.

Had he gone to a lover?

Or had some dire fate befallen him?

And how could she possibly learn to seduce him without guidance.

She put down her tea when she realized that one person in London might possess the answers to all those questions, and more. But did she dare to call on Esmeralda Ballantyne?

~

Esmeralda Ballantyne had seen a great deal of the world and its marvels, not to mention a hearty measure of human foible, but she had never seen Sebastian Montgomery in his cups. She fairly tripped over him in a gaming hell, astonished because she had not realized he had returned to town.

Her first thought was that he was pretending to be more drunk than he was, then she saw how badly he was losing. She had never seen him lose, either. What was wrong with him? In a rare protective urge, she interrupted the game, scooped Sebastian up with the assistance of several servants, and took him home.

He slept all that night and would not leave his chamber the next day.

"You are brooding," she charged when he would not unlock the door. She rattled the knob, to no avail, even though this was her house.

"I am thinking," he muttered, his voice low and gravely.

It was on the tip of her tongue to advise him not to injure himself with the uncustomary activity, but she knew it was a waspish comment —and one borne of her own awareness of his disinterest in her. "Am I not to be thanked for my intervention?" she asked. "You might have lost a fortune last night." There was no reply but she heard a rustle of paper. She saw a note being slipped beneath the door and frowned with impatience even as she picked it up.

It was addressed to her.

It was dated some days ago and advised her of Sebastian's marriage.

"Who on earth is Miss Eurydice Goodenham?" she asked, not truly expecting a reply. The door had been somewhat taciturn thus far.

"My wife," he growled. "Leave me be, please, Esmeralda."

Esmeralda frowned. "Do you love her?"

"I promised my fidelity to her until she bears our son and my heir."

Esmeralda read the note again. "Then you do love her," she said softly, knowing full well that the Earl of Rockmorton would not have made such a concession otherwise. "What are you doing here?" she demanded, less softly than she had spoken before. "Should you not be with your wife?" She bit off the last word just as Sebastian opened the door. He looked rumpled, dangerous and utterly seductive.

"She does not believe in love," he said.

"Then you should change her mind," Esmeralda replied.

"I cannot..."

"You changed mine," she admitted, the edge of disappointment in her voice.

He looked so astounded that she knew he had never guessed. "But..."

Esmeralda turned away. "Go home, Sebastian."

"She is not romantic. She is practical," he said as Esmeralda walked to the summit of the stairs. "I do not know how to proceed and I fear..." He frowned and shook his head, falling silent.

"You fear?" she prompted by this hint that he cared about anything at all.

"To lose her, of course. To go through that pain again."

She had never guessed that he had endured a loss. In all their time together and supposed intimacy, he had never shared that. He had shared his body but no more, while she had been prepared to surrender everything. All for nothing. What manner of bargain was that? Worse yet, he had not known. He had thought their transaction fair.

Impatience rose hot within Esmeralda and made her speak when she should have remained silent. "Then you are a witless fool and you will lose her. That will do your heart more injury, for the situation will be entirely your own fault."

Esmeralda descended the stairs and had just poured herself a small glass of wine when her butler cleared his throat. "A lady to see you."

She glanced toward him and he inclined his head, offering the card.

Miss Eurydice Goodenham.

She stared at the card as if it was written in Sanskrit. Respectable women did not come to Esmeralda's house—in fact, many respectable men avoided it. The wives of men Esmeralda entertained most certainly did not call upon her.

Did Sebastian's new wife know that he was in her guest bedroom?

How could she know?

What else could she possibly want?

There were those who would have found it amusing that Esmeralda was to play matchmaker for the first time in all her days, but she was not one of them. Her heart was breaking even as she indicated that the lady should be shown in.

～

Miss Ballantyne's house had not been difficult to find. It was small and a bit tawdry in Eurydice's view, but she expected the choice of colors would look their best at night. There was a lot of gold and a substantial amount of purple, as well as feathers and velvet beyond expectation. She had no doubt that she was not amongst the lady's typical callers.

She was received, which was a relief, and shown into a drawing room of unusually lush reds and pinks. In the midst was Esmeralda herself, her dark sleek hair perfectly done, her pale silk dress revealing as much of her figure as it covered, and the emeralds in her lavish necklace matching her eyes perfectly. She seemed to be faintly amused, and her gaze flicked over Eurydice in a way that made Eurydice keenly aware of the differences between them.

"I understand that you have some acquaintance with my husband, Sebastian Montgomery, the Earl of Rockmorton," she began when her hostess did not speak.

"I am and I do," the lady acknowledged. "Will you take tea?"

"Thank you." Eurydice accepted the cup of tea she did not want and tried to summon her audacity. "I know this is unconventional, but I hope that you will grant me a favor."

Esmeralda smiled. "You may have heard that I have little interest in convention," she said, pouring herself a cup of tea. She remained standing, as did Eurydice, but sipped her tea as she waited.

"I know little of men and their satisfaction," Eurydice admitted, her cheeks burning. "But I would like to ensure that my husband finds

377

pleasure in our union. Could you teach me something of the arts of seduction?"

Her hostess choked on her tea in that very moment. She put it down, the cup clattering in the saucer. "You wish to learn the arts of seduction?" she echoed.

Eurydice nodded. "Solely to be a good wife and partner to my husband, of course," she added, feeling her face become yet more red. "I know that he has expectations and I fear that I have not fulfilled them adequately as yet. All skills can be learned, with diligence and practice, however I have been unable to find a suitable reference. That is why I am asking you. You know more of him in such matters of intimacy, after all." Her speech completed, she took a breath and fixed her hopeful gaze upon Esmeralda.

Her hostess stared down at her cup. "Forgive my surprise. I have never been asked such a question," she admitted.

At her gesture, Eurydice sat down, perching on the lip of a settee best intended for lounging. She surveyed her surroundings again, feeling the worst was behind her. She had asked: the reply was out of her hands. "This is quite a remarkable room."

"Do you think so?"

"I do. It is more feminine than any drawing room I have visited before, more like a lady's bedchamber." She smiled at her hostess. "I like all the roses, and the pink hues suit you well. You look like another flower in their midst."

The lady again seemed to be without words. She sipped her tea as did her guest.

"I profess myself surprised that you have never been asked such a question," she said. "For one consults experts in all other matters. How does one learn these skills then?"

Her hostess's eyes widened slightly. "I believe husbands often tutor their wives."

"Is that how you learned the amorous arts?"

"I have never wed," the lady confessed. "I have never felt the compulsion."

"I can well understand that impulse. I would not have done as much myself if it had not been a question of financial security. And now, I must keep my side of the bargain."

"I see." Her hostess frowned. "Perhaps you should ask your husband."

"Well, that is the trouble," Eurydice confessed. Miss Ballantyne was remarkably easy to talk to. "He is not speaking to me and I am not entirely certain of his whereabouts." She sipped her tea. "I have vexed him mightily, I fear."

Miss Ballantyne's eyes began to sparkle. "Perhaps that is good for him," she whispered.

"I do not understand."

"It is not healthy for anyone to have all matters proceed their way." Miss Ballantyne seemed to have made a decision for she set her cup aside and rose smoothly to her feet. "I predict that he will return shortly and suggest that you ask him for this advice."

"About the amorous arts?"

Miss Ballantyne nodded and smiled. "He might quite enjoy the tutelage." She crossed the room and lifted a small book from a shelf, eying it for a moment before pivoting and presenting it to Eurydice. "And in the meantime, this might give you some of the answers you seek."

"Thank you!" Eurydice did not even have time to read the title before she heard a footfall on the stairs.

"Eurydice?" Sebastian demanded from the doorway. "I thought I heard your voice." He looked as far from his usual composed self as was possible. Indeed, he looked tired and more than a little haggard. His cravat was undone and he was not wearing a jacket at all.

He looked like a man who had just risen from bed. At this hour of the afternoon, Eurydice could guess what he had been doing there. Had he not been the one to recommend lovemaking at this very time of day? She straightened, knowing her color was high.

"What are you doing here?" he asked.

"I could ask you the same, sir."

"But you were going to Cornwall."

"No, you instructed me to go to Cornwall, but I did not obey, sir. I had no intention of going, not with my sister coming for Christmas." Eurydice glared at him, so disappointed that she wanted to weep. "I had thought to secure the future of our marriage instead, but I see the fullness of my error now. You need not fear for my obedience: I will now leave you to your leisure of choice." With that, she curtsied to her hostess—who looked decidedly amused—then pivoted and left the house, her chin held high. Sebastian called after her, he even swore mightily, but Eurydice was not swayed.

How *dare* he?

And how could she have been so wrong about him?

He was precisely the rogue she had believed him to be at first, and she had been fool enough to fall in love with him.

Alexander had been right.

IN HIS ABSENCE, Sebastian's house had been transformed. He stood in the foyer for a long moment, fighting the colossal headache that was the reward for his sins, and wondered if he had entered the wrong house. Although it was not completed, the foyer was adorned with greenery and red ribbons on one side, a festive display that his mother might have contrived. Greenery and more ribbons were being woven around the bannister and he could smell beeswax candles burning. The doors to the drawing room were open instead of securely locked, and four maids were busily cleaning it. He could smell fresh baking from the kitchen and heard the laughter of busy maids. The house was warm and fairly glowing, so welcoming that he might have been transported thirteen years into the past.

Watson, however, glowered at him with a new level of disapproval from the base of the stairs. This was unassailably his house.

Sebastian approached the drawing room doors warily, as if the illusion might be shattered by proximity, then looked upon the room that he had not seen in years. It was an attractive room, but his gaze rose immediately to the large portrait over the mantle and his throat tightened. "Why is this room opened?" he asked, knowing that Watson had followed him.

"Because your lady wife instructed that it should be, sir."

"But I have instructed otherwise."

"It had to be prepared when we understood that the Duke of Inverfyre and his family would be arriving for Christmas dinner." Watson's lips tightened. "While the duke has been at ease in the library on previous occasions, his family cannot be accommodated in such a confined space." The older man sniffed. "If you would prefer that it be closed up again, my lord, now that there is no prospect of guests, I will ensure that is done."

Sebastian gave his butler a wary look. "My wife has rescinded her invitation then?"

"Lady Rockmorton has declared she will not be in residence for Christmas." This clearly was the root of the older man's sour mood. Sebastian supposed that he had liked Eurydice, which was only reasonable.

He liked Eurydice himself.

Would he have a chance to tell her of his love? His ears still burned from Esmeralda's challenge and her amusement at his predicament. He had not been able to get a cab and feared he had arrived too late.

"She cannot have left," he argued, keeping his tone reasonable with an effort.

The butler straightened, his expression formidable. "I believe she was bidden to do so," he said, his tone frosty with disapproval.

Sebastian charged up the stairs and knocked upon the door of the chamber Eurydice must have used. It was the larger of the two guest chambers. A woman's voice acknowledged his knock and his heart leapt—but when he opened the door, he found only a maid cleaning the fireplace.

Eurydice's belongings were gone. Indeed, the room was so tidy that she might never have been there. He spun and opened the other guest room door, his own chamber, his mother's chamber, and found no sign of his confounding bride.

Of course not. She would be in the library. He leapt down the stairs and flung open that door, only to find Eurydice seated by the fire. She was reading a small book bound in crimson leather. Her bags were packed and set beside her, with her books and umbrella, too. She was wearing her hat and her cloak, though it was unfastened. She looked as if she had been compelled to halt her departure by the siren's call of a particularly compelling volume.

He had been saved by the book.

She eyed him, as fierce as a wet kitten, then glanced down at the volume in question and continued to read.

"I must apologize," Sebastian said, closing the door behind himself, both to ensure that she did not flee and to keep the servants from hearing him beg her forgiveness.

"With what expectation?" she demanded, dropping the book into her lap. "That I will forgive you for returning to the bed of your mistress, after one—" she held up a finger and shook it at him. He saw only that she had already donned her gloves "—*one* night of coupling that did not meet your expectations?"

She thought him disappointed in their wedding night?

Eurydice did not grant him a chance to reply but swept to her feet, her eyes flashing with fury. "To think that I was fool enough to imagine you a romantic, to hope that we might make a true union in time, that you could even come to love me as I was fool enough to begin to love you. You are a wretch and a cur, a rogue and a scoundrel of the full magnitude of my original expectation, and you are unchivalrous, sir, to grant me what I first requested of you, if only to show how much it is lacking." To his astonishment, tears shone in her eyes and threatened to spill. "You could have left me in my ignorance, sir. You could have never tempted me to care for you, if this had been your intention all along. I knew you to care only for your own whim, but I did not think you *cruel*."

She seized the ties of her cloak but Sebastian heard only one part of her lecture. He touched her arm and she froze, her gaze fixed stubbornly on the floor. He saw the flash of a falling tear and it shattered him utterly, ensuring that he spoke the truth in his heart. "I left, Eurydice, because I could not believe you would ever come to love me as I already love you," he admitted and she looked up, her expression one of wonder. He smiled at her. "I feared not only your mockery but that you would leave me in disappointment."

"Do not tease me, Sebastian," she threatened huskily. "I could not bear it, not after this day."

"It is the truth, my lady." He took her hand in his, vastly encouraged by her reaction. "If you will consent to be my lady, in every possible way."

"Sebastian!" she whispered, then flung herself at him, dampening his shirt with her tears. They were tears of joy but Sebastian still did not care for them. He kissed her gently and wiped them away, then kissed her with all the passion dawning in his heart. She kissed him back, so sweet and giving that he knew himself to be the most fortunate man in the world.

"The book is right," she whispered when she could speak again. Sebastian did not wish to let her go and kept his arms locked around her as he stared down into her shining eyes.

"What book?"

"The one Miss Ballantyne gave me." She indicated the red volume she had been reading. "*A letter of Genteel and Moral Advice to a Young Lady* by Wetenhall Wilkes. It says 'Never fix your liking on any man that has not those qualities which you have labored after yourself, and who is not likely to be a friend to virtue.'"

"This does not sound like an endorsement of my own nature," Sebastian ventured.

Eurydice laughed. "What you would have people believe of you is not your truth, sir. You are a romantic and you are honorable. You are gallant and kind." Her lashes swept down as her smile turned mysterious in a most delightful way. "And I have no complaint of any of that."

"And here I thought you had found the guide you sought," he said.

She smiled up at him. "Sophia bade me ask you to teach me," she confessed, blushing deeply. "As did Miss Ballantyne."

"But do you intend to tutor me in what you like best, my bold wife?" he teased, delighted to hear her laugh.

"Perhaps we should tutor each other," she suggested, eyes dancing.

"And achieve our goals together: first an heir, then a book."

"If not more of each," she agreed, her happiness more than clear.

Sebastian stole a satisfying kiss. "Then let us lock the door, lady mine, and commence our lessons immediately."

"A fine suggestion, sir," she agreed, then reached to capture his lips with her own. He carried her to the settee before the fire and no one said much of anything for a goodly time.

The cook remarked that night on the vigor of the new couple's appetite for dinner, but Watson only smiled, more satisfied with the situation at Rockmorton House than he had been in years.

The weather in December was beastly, to Daphne's thinking. A frigid wind chased the pair of carriages on their southward path from Airdfinnan, stealing every crumb of heat and rocking the vehicles on their path. Sleet fell on the roof and turned the roads to ice, then snow tumbled from the leaden skies in earnest. Worse, Daphne felt dreadful, her innards in such turmoil that she was in peril of being sick in the coach.

Alexander was solicitous and watchful, but she dared not confide her suspicions to him just yet. They stopped at York, then at Thornedyke Manor where his sister, Anthea, and her husband, the baron and Alexander's friend, offered every possible comfort. It was revealed that the couple had decided to journey to London with them, equally curious to witness Eurydice's happiness, and Daphne was glad of Anthea's company.

Malcolm, of course, found it all a grand adventure, no less that he would have additional playmates in Anthea and Rupert's twins. Truth be told, Daphne felt a bit of sympathy for the servants compelled to share the smaller carriage with her sons. On the other hand, it was delightful to have Alexander pull her into his lap and to slumber against his shoulder as the carriage rocked on its seemingly endless journey south.

It took them six more days to reach London, the most trying journey of Daphne's experience. There was snow on the ground when they reached the house in Grosvenor Square, but Findlay was on the steps to greet them and Daphne smiled, certain that all in the house was in readiness.

Alexander scooped her into his arms when she almost slipped and chided her as he carried her to the house. "We should not have made this journey," he said sternly. "You are not well and I will blame myself forever if you take a cold..."

"I do not have a cold, sir, nor am I like to get one with you to warm me."

His blue eyes narrowed as he looked down at her, as fierce as a guardian angel, and she knew she would never cease to be thrilled in his company. "You are not well and do not insist otherwise."

"The carriage rocks so," she confessed. "It was the rhythm that troubled me."

"The carriage is in perfectly good repair," he retorted. "It does not rock any more than customary, even in that ferocious wind. And it never bothers you, at least it has not since—" He stopped on the stairs and looked down at her in shock.

Daphne smiled. "Precisely," she said, smoothing his cravat.

"Again?"

"Again."

Alexander looked so adorably astonished, as if he could not fathom how she might have conceived another child. In truth, the astonishing fact was that they did not yet have a dozen children.

"But you did not tell me," he whispered.

"I did not know for certain. I still do not."

"But..."

"I am no physician, sir."

"But you should have called for one, and then we would have known."

"And then you would have forbidden me to come to London."

His eyes narrowed, though he could not fully hide his pleasure. "You *knew* and you risked your own health."

"I suspected," Daphne corrected. "And I said nothing because I had no choice but to come."

"There is every choice," Alexander began as he carried her up the stairs to her chamber. "We could have come in the summer…"

Daphne silenced him with a fingertip and his gaze dropped to meet hers. "Almost twenty years ago, my sister became my responsibility, Alexander. Though our grandmother subsequently took us in, I had vowed to Eurydice that I would do whatever was necessary to ensure both her welfare and her happiness. Time has not eroded that duty, and indeed, my grandmother reminded me of it when last we spoke." She wriggled and he set her on her feet, still holding fast to her elbow as she wavered. Her tone was fierce, though. "I must be certain that Eurydice is well and that Sebastian will make her a good husband. I do not believe it to be possible, Alexander, and I must be *certain.*"

"You should have told me," he said, urging her to a chaise.

She sank into it with gratitude, for it did not rock. "I will tell you whatever tidings I have, when I know them to be true." She leaned back. "But this way, we are here, I can witness the situation myself, and there is a chance that Lady Octavia will not be haunting me over my failed duties."

"There are no ghosts," he chided.

"And you call yourself a Scotsman," she chided in return and he smiled. "Perhaps there might be a cup of beef broth," she said, giving the duke a task so he did not berate her further.

"I shall see to it," he said, brisk and efficient, turning to stride across the chamber. Daphne watched him go, the admiration she felt of both his figure and his nature making her heart glow. It was no mystery why she could not resist him.

"Perhaps a girl this time," she called after him and he glanced back from the doorway.

His gaze warmed at the possibility. "A girl," he whispered then shook his head, marveling. "Girl or boy will be most welcome, so long as my wife is hale." His voice turned husky. "How can you bring me more joy than already you have, Daphne?"

"I would not wish you to become bored, sir," she teased, drawing off her gloves.

"Never that!" he vowed with a laugh then returned to give her a most satisfying kiss.

One more day and Daphne would know for certain. She could not imagine her sister with that charming rogue, Sebastian Montgomery. As much as she enjoyed his wit and company, he had often vowed he would never wed and she feared for Eurydice's future. She only hoped that all was well.

On the morrow, she would know.

THE DUKE'S party arrived at Rockmorton House just after noon, as bidden, while the church bells pealed merrily to herald Christmas Day. Anthea and Rupert were descending from their carriage, and they exchanged joyous greetings in the street. Mme. and M. de Roye rose to greet them in the drawing room, as did Eurydice and Montgomery. The de Roye's daughter, Louisa, was the oldest of the children and immediately began to issue instructions to the younger boys, to noisy result. The children were spirited away to the old nursery by the three nursemaids who had accompanied their charges to London. Alexander smiled that Watson vowed to ensure that the three maids would have a proper tea and he doubted it would take long for the children to fall asleep after the excitements of the day thus far.

Alexander himself was struck by the change in Montgomery's home. He had visited many times over the years and had even stayed in the house, but he had never seen it so filled with life and laughter. It wasn't just decorated for the festive season, something he was certain he had never witnessed, but the drawing room doors that were always closed had been thrown open. The house fairly glowed. The magnificent portrait of Montgomery's happy parents seemed to beam down on the noisy gathering of friends with approval.

The change was remarkable and Alexander could not find fault with it.

He also could not mistake the sparkle in Eurydice's eyes. His wife's younger sister was abundantly happy, it was clear, and Montgomery himself could not seem to keep himself from grinning. Greetings and small gifts were exchanged all around. They had tea and sherry and quite good shortbread, and the children raced through the room at intervals. Lucien, M. de Roye, was encouraged to play the harpsichord, which Alexander suspected had been tuned and pampered precisely for that happy office.

Daphne took her sister aside for a short chat and he was glad to see the sisters laughing together. When his wife returned to his side, she granted him a glance that told him she was satisfied and he was glad of it. The conversation flowed readily, as if all of them had been friends for years, and dinner was a most merry affair.

The clock in the foyer was striking midnight when they rose to return home. There were carolers in the street, their angelic voices carrying through the crisp night air. The guests donned their cloaks and gloves, exchanging farewells and good wishes, then Alexander saw Daphne stare into the shadows beneath the staircase and frown slightly. He followed her gaze and felt this own eyes narrow.

He thought a shadowy figure lingered there, a woman dressed completely in black, her clothing a little old-fashioned and her white hair drawn tightly back. He was startled to realize that he knew only one woman of such appearance but Lady Octavia, once Viscountess of North Barrows, was dead. All the same, the apparition nodded at Daphne and seemed to smile. Alexander heard the faintest of whispers, which might have been the words 'well done,' then he blinked and the vision was gone.

There was just an umbrella stand there, holding one black umbrella with a carved handle. It was an umbrella Alexander remembered well, the one he had heard rapped upon the floor countless times, the one that Eurydice had inherited from her grandmother. He offered his hand to his wife who flushed and smiled, her relief so evident that he did not have to ask after it. He kissed her hand and placed it on his arm to escort her to the carriage, well content with the match he himself had made.

Another child. Could he bear such happiness?

As they crossed the threshold, Alexander heard the decisive rap of an umbrella on the tile floor behind him, but surely that was only his imagination at work.

Read the story behind the red-flowered vine in **A Duke by Any Other Name** in Claire's medieval romance,
The Beauty.

Turn the page to learn more!

THAT VINE IN THE BEAUTY

In **A Duke by Any Other Name**, Alexander is Duke of Inverfyre and heir to castle Airdfinnan. A vine grows there and family tradition insists that the vine blossoms when the laird loses his heart. The vine first appears in Claire's books in **The Beauty**, as does Airdfinnan castle. Meet Alexander and Anthea's forebears in this sweeping medieval romance of a wounded knight, a stolen legacy and the captive bride who dares to believe that wrongs can be made right.

Certain she will never wed for love, sworn to let no man possess her for her beauty alone, Jacqueline de Crevy has vowed to become a bride of God. But en route to the convent of Inveresbeinn, her party is ambushed by a knight, who snatches Jacqueline from her saddle and spirits her away with him.

He is Angus MacGillivray—not the black-hearted ravisher she fears but a valiant man of honor who has returned to Scotland seeking justice…and revenge. Angus has come home from the Crusades to find his family murdered and his birthright seized. Sworn to reclaim his rightful lands, he has kidnapped the stepdaughter of Duncan, chieftain of Clan MacQuarrie—Angus's avowed enemy.

But his lovely captive refuses to be the chattel—or ransom—of any man…until Jacqueline senses the yearning heart beneath Angus's embittered facade. In spite of himself, Angus has let this defiant beauty touch his very soul. And as desire flames between them, a lady fair and her battle-scarred knight will fight for a love that could banish all the sorrows of the past…

~

The Beauty
Available now!

~

ABOUT THE AUTHOR

Deborah Cooke sold her first book in 1992, a medieval romance called **Romance of the Rose** published under her pseudonym Claire Delacroix. Since then, she has published over fifty novels in a wide variety of sub-genres, including historical romance, contemporary romance, paranormal romance, fantasy romance, time-travel romance, women's fiction, paranormal young adult and fantasy with romantic elements. She has published under the names Claire Delacroix, Claire Cross and Deborah Cooke. **The Beauty**, part of her successful Bride Quest series of historical romances, was her first title to land on the *New York Times* List of Bestselling Books. Her books routinely appear on other bestseller lists and have won numerous awards. In 2009, she was the writer-in-residence at the Toronto Public Library, the first time the library has hosted a residency focused on the romance genre. In 2012, she was honored to receive the Romance Writers of America's Mentor of the Year Award.

Currently, she writes paranormal romances featuring dragon shape shifter heroes under the name Deborah Cooke. She also writes medieval romances as Claire Delacroix. Deborah lives in Canada with her husband and family, as well as far too many unfinished knitting projects.

Visit Claire's website
http://Delacroix.net

THE ROSE RED BRIDE

THE SNOW WHITE BRIDE

The Ballad of Rosamunde

The True Love Brides

THE RENEGADE'S HEART

THE HIGHLANDER'S CURSE

THE FROST MAIDEN'S KISS

THE WARRIOR'S PRIZE

The Brides of Inverfyre

THE MERCENARY'S BRIDE

THE RUNAWAY BRIDE

The Champions of St. Euphemia

THE CRUSADER'S BRIDE

THE CRUSADER'S HEART

THE CRUSADER'S KISS

THE CRUSADER'S VOW

THE CRUSADER'S HANDFAST

The Brides of North Barrows

Something Wicked This Way Comes

A Duke By Any Other Name

A Baron for All Seasons

A Most Inconvenient Earl

Blood Brothers

THE WOLF & THE WITCH

THE HUNTER & THE HEIRESS

Short Stories and Novellas

BEGUILED

An Elegy for Melusine

To learn more about Deborah's contemporary and paranormal romances,

please visit

DeborahCooke.com